Stormswept COLORADO

STORMSWEPT COLORADO (Hart County Series Book 3)

Ebook Cover Photography: Wander Aguiar

Cover Design (Ebook and Print): Angela Haddon

Produced by Diana Road Books

HART COUNTY BOOK 3

HANNAH SHIELD

Before you read...

For detailed content warnings, which include potential spoilers, please see my website at:

https://www.hannahshield.com/stormswept

Prologue

Ayla
September, Last Year

"Fifteen minutes," my tour manager warned, popping her head through the doorway to my dressing room. "Then you need to be in place."

I didn't take my eyes off my phone screen. "Got it."

"Don't make me drag you out of here."

"I *know*. We've had this conversation before."

I'd told my team how important this nightly ritual was to me. I wasn't going onstage without it. Might as well have been a rider in my contract, along with the sparkling water, kettle-cooked potato chips, and extra-dark chocolate that awaited me at every venue. Some things a girl couldn't live without.

The call rang twice. Three times. And then a window popped open with an adorable face. My lips split into a grin as I heard my two favorite words in the entire world.

"Aunt Ayla!"

"Hey, you."

"Want to see the picture I drew today?"

"Of course I do. But wait a minute. Let me see that smile again. I think something's missing."

Maisie giggled. "It's my tooth."

"Your *toof*?"

She tipped her head back and laughed. Prettiest melody in the world, if you asked me. And I did have some strong opinions on music.

Ashford, Maisie's dad, appeared on the screen behind her. "Hi, Ayla. Where are you tonight?"

"Toronto."

"Dad, I'm talking to her." She playfully pushed her father away. "Where's Toronto? Is that California, like where Emma's from?"

I smiled. "Nope, way off. It's in Ontario, Canada."

"Are you going to buy me a present from there?"

"*Maisie,*" Ashford said.

"Don't I always? I'm going to need another suitcase for all your presents the next time I visit. Now, what should we sing for your bedtime song? I only have a few more minutes."

I loved how they didn't comment on my over-the-top makeup and beaded costume. Probably because my relatives in Silver Ridge, Colorado, had seen me in this same getup plenty of times on video calls just like this one. Maisie and I had a standing date before her bedtime, and we rarely missed it, even when I was on tour. Well, especially then.

I'd missed so much of Maisie's life. When Ashford and I had first worked out our differences, I'd gotten choked up every time I was around Maisie because she looked exactly like Lori, my older sister. And like me too. Except my hair was pale blond, while Maisie had Ashford's chestnut color. We had the same emerald irises though, with a ring of darker green around the outside.

Remembering Lori was always bittersweet. Yet Maisie recharged my batteries. Made me feel like Ayla Hopkins, Lori's little sister, instead of *Ayla Maxwell*, pop star. I had mixed feelings about the Hopkins name given its other associations. But I would always be proud that Lori had been my sister.

Maisie wanted to sing along with me to her current favorite song, a hit from another artist. "Isn't this song the best ever, Aunt Ayla?" she gushed.

Ashford was still in the frame, smirking. "Ayla might not agree. That's her competition."

"It's a great choice, Maisie." I was determined not to be jealous. Gotta love the honesty of a seven-year-old.

A lump gathered in my throat as her sweet, high voice rang out. Full of innocent confidence. She reminded me of myself at that age. I'd always loved to sing.

You're too loud, my dad would say. *Don't put yourself on display. Good girls don't do that.*

I shoved that voice away. My music had made a difference in people's lives. My songs brought a little extra beauty into the world, and that was something to be proud of.

After we finished singing, I said, "I'd better get going. Almost showtime. Say hi to Emma for me. And say woof to Stella."

"Nooooo, don't go yet! I miss you!"

Oh, I loved that. "I miss you too. Talk to you soon. Promise. I love you."

"Love you too, Aunt Ayla!"

After I ended the call, my tour manager hadn't reappeared. My back-up singers and dancers would be in the greenroom right now, psyching themselves up for showtime. I should be there with them. But I needed another minute or two to myself.

Whenever I thought of my dad, it left an icky feeling inside me. A stain I needed to wash away.

I turned toward the flowers, cards, and small gifts that lined a counter. Things sent by local businesses and fans. My team vetted everything to make sure it was all safe and uplifting. Maybe that made me sound too sensitive, like I couldn't handle criticism or negativity, but if I gave oxygen to every hater I'd never have a moment of peace again.

I ran my fingers over the petals of a red daisy. There were other more exotic blooms too, and they'd filled the air with a subtle, lovely perfume.

Plenty of people appreciated what I did. I had people who loved me. Maisie and Ashford and legions of fans.

Sometimes it was overwhelming how much the fans wanted to know about me, how they got caught up in the tiniest details about my schedule, my clothes, my lyrics.

But where would I be without them? Irrelevant. Then another up-and-coming singer, maybe the one Maisie liked, would take my place.

I'd worked so hard for this. Sacrificed.

Plucking the small card from the flower arrangement, I opened the envelope to read the message inside. There was no name. Just a handwritten message.

You have no idea how beautiful you really are. I've always been your biggest fan.

A little over the top, but okay. Not unusual. I was surprised there wasn't a name and a phone number. Messages like that usually came with the wild hope that I would contact them.

Then I noticed another folded piece of paper inside the envelope. I unfolded it, finding an image. A printout of a photo.

It was *me*.

I didn't understand.

Nausea rose in my stomach. Trembling overtook my body. Memories too.

When the door to the dressing room opened, I was struggling to breathe. The tour manager had reappeared, along with Cheryl Traynor, my artist manager and the woman in charge of my entire career trajectory. She didn't come to every show, but she was here tonight.

Cheryl took one look at me and rushed over. "Ayla? You okay?"

"These flowers." I cleared my throat, trying to stuff down the emotion. "Where'd these come from? Who sent them?"

Cheryl glanced at the tour manager, who just shook her head and shrugged.

"Is something wrong?" Cheryl asked me.

Reluctantly, I showed her the photo. "This was with the card. I want to know why someone has it. This is... It's personal."

Cheryl studied the image. It was an old picture from when I was a teenager, on the porch of the last house where we lived when I was sixteen. I was pretty sure Lori had snapped this with her digital camera. Just before I left for good.

Just before...*that night*.

"There are a lot of photos posted of you online. You know how people are. Someone you went to high school with wants to get some likes because they knew you once upon a time."

As if I didn't know that. My heart knocked against my chest.

"But we'll look into it," she promised. "Are you well enough to go on?" She pressed a hand to my face. "You're clammy."

"We can't have her passing out onstage," the tour manager said.

Their clipped tones had bolstered me. My team didn't coddle me, and I didn't need them to.

I'd been taking care of myself since I was sixteen. I'd tried to build walls around me, and sometimes the cracks showed. But I couldn't afford to fall apart now.

"No, I'm going on. Someone get Ricky?" My makeup artist. "I just need a touchup."

Cover it up, I thought. *Paint it over so no one sees*.

That photo meant nothing. My past was gone. Dead and buried. I wouldn't let anyone see how much it really affected me.

ONE

Teller

FEBRUARY, THIS YEAR

MY HOMETOWN WAS my favorite place on earth. Especially mornings when the sun lit the sky in gentle shades of orange and peach, when the birds were chattering in the pine trees beyond my porch, and the mountain air was that perfect balance of crisp and sweet. When everything was calm and easy.

This was not one of those mornings.

I shifted my weight, hands resting casually on my duty belt. "Jimmy, I still don't see why you found it necessary to call 911."

He pointed a finger at Rosie, the owner of Main Street Market. "Because that shrew won't let me buy my toilet paper."

Rosie crossed her arms. "And I told this old fool that the limit is two."

"Last time I checked, this was a damned free country!"

"I've had a two-pack limit on toilet paper for years now, and you know it."

I sighed. If this was a sign of my day to come, it was going to be a long one.

Rosie Alvarez ran a tight ship here at the market. But for some reason, she had an on-again, off-again romance with Jimmy Perkins, the man currently creating a disturbance in her store.

From the sounds of it, I guessed the two of them were currently in the *off* position.

I glanced at Jimmy's cart. "Is there a reason you're stocking up on toilet paper, batteries, and...geez, how much orange soda does one man need?"

Jimmy looked at me like I was dumber than something he'd scraped off his mud-crusted boot. "Storm of the century's coming this weekend, Chief Landry. You'd best be getting the town ready. Not obstructing a man in his right to stock up on the essentials."

"But that's still no reason to call 911 claiming false imprisonment," I pointed out.

"I can't leave until I have my desired purchases." Jimmy's head waggled, making his gray ponytail shake. "Basically the same thing."

I didn't know if this dispute was a lovers' quarrel, some kind of foreplay, or both. But either way, I wanted no part of it.

I closed my eyes, calling on those yoga breathing techniques in the videos Piper liked to send me. What was it? Something about a victorious warrior?

"Let's just get this sorted out."

After a few minutes of mediation, Rosie decided to let him buy three packs of toilet paper instead of two. Which, to me, wasn't the best idea. Just encouraged him. But Jimmy had dropped the troublesome act and had a shine of affection in his eyes by the end of their negotiation.

Then Rosie swatted his behind as Jimmy left. "We'll talk more about this later, Jimmy Perkins," she said sternly. He winked.

Those two, I swear.

"Next time, could you work out your relationship issues without involving the police?" I asked.

"Haven't got a clue what you're talking about." Her cheeks stained as red as her dyed curly hair.

Sure she didn't.

Through the window, Rosie and I watched her boyfriend trot out to the parking lot. Regular business had resumed in the checkout line, the noise in the market returning to its usual chorus of small-talk and the beeps of the scanner. Through the windows facing Main, I saw locals in knit caps and down coats as they went about their day.

The sky was pure blue, and the sun was bright. One of those winter days that almost looks like summer until you step outside and feel the chill.

Rosie turned to me. "What do you think about this storm that's coming, Teller? *Chief*, I mean."

I smiled at her slip. Rosie had known me since I was a kid, back when I'd bagged groceries after school for extra cash. And for that employee discount. Those days felt like a long, long time ago.

"It's wise to prepare as usual," I said. "But no need to go overboard. It'll hardly be the storm of the century. In fact, we need the precipitation. It'll be good for the snowpack." If we didn't get enough snow in winter, that meant fire danger in the warm months.

But weather patterns worked on their own schedule, especially in the mountains. It could be dumping snow in one part of the county and bone dry a few miles away. The old timers liked to get their farmer's almanacs out and make predictions, but they were wrong just as often as they got it right.

"But will it interfere with the wedding?" Rosie asked, and several more heads over in the checkout line nodded. Because of course they were listening. "That's what I'm worried about."

Ah, *The Wedding*. The event that needed no modifiers in Hart County.

Ashford O'Neal and Emma Jennings would be getting married this coming weekend in Hartley, the county seat. It was going to be a big celebration, and it seemed like most of our town of Silver Ridge was invited. People in these parts had been looking forward to Emma and Ashford's nuptials since before the two were even engaged. He was the single dad with a tragic history, and she was the optimistic young music teacher who'd changed his life. Everybody adored Ashford's daughter, Maisie. They wanted to see that happily ever after in person.

I'd known Ashford since our families lived across the street from each other growing up, and I was happy for him. The ceremony would take place Saturday afternoon. I'd gotten the obligatory invite, so I was driving out tomorrow night, on Friday.

Did I appreciate all this fuss about the wedding, though? Not so much.

A mountain pass stood between us and Hartley, and it was difficult driving in blizzard conditions. But this wouldn't be a blizzard. My police department would coordinate with the Hart County Sheriff's Office as usual. Just another day at work for us. I was more worried about folks driving back to Silver Ridge after too many cocktails.

At social events, my typical M.O. was to make sure things didn't get out of hand. According to my sister Piper, I was chief of the fun police.

I leaned my elbow on the customer-service counter. "Storm is set to hit Saturday evening, but everyone will already be in Hartley by then. We'll be nice and cozy at the inn by the time that storm arrives. It'll snow a couple feet, but the plows will have it handled by Sunday morning as usual."

Rosie nodded. "Suppose you're right."

Our audience moved along, returning their focus to their shopping. "Thanks, Chief," one woman said as she passed me.

"Y'all have a good day, now." I adjusted my belt, nodding, then checked my watch. I had a lot of tasks ahead of me and only so many hours to do them.

But Rosie touched my arm before I could break for the exit. She leaned forward to drop her voice into a mock whisper that was nowhere near quiet.

"I heard from Dixie Haines that Ayla Maxwell has already arrived in town. Just this morning Dixie spotted Ayla at the coffee shop. I've been playing her music on rotation for days, just in case she comes in to the market." Rosie pointed a finger at the ceiling.

"Didn't notice," I deadpanned. I'd been trying to ignore the dance beats coming from the overhead speaker system.

"Do you think she'll sing at the wedding reception?"

"I highly doubt it."

"Wouldn't it be romantic, though?" She fluttered her lashes.

"I wouldn't know."

Rosie nudged my arm teasingly. "Ah, yes. You're the town's most eligible bachelor, and you're committed to staying that way. Don't frown like that. I'm not judging."

"Just so long as you're not trying to fix me up." Which was a favorite pastime of every other woman of a certain age in town.

I couldn't even tell you how many granddaughters and nieces had been foisted on me.

Rosie held up her hands. "I can't help it if I'm in the mood for love with the wedding almost here, and now my favorite singer in our midst. Even you can't be immune to that excitement, right?"

I shrugged. For some reason, my heart rate kicked up as I imagined seeing Ayla Maxwell again.

Ayla was Ashford's sister-in-law, and she'd visited Silver Ridge a few times in the last couple years or so. For a while, our local population had kept its calm about her celebrity status.

But with *The Wedding* just on the horizon, excitement had streaked back up into high gear. And the popularity of our local ski resort had drawn more and more tourists.

My department had been planning for Ayla's presence in town. Her arrival in Silver Ridge could mean traffic jams on our two-lane highways. Gawkers forming crowds on Main, pushing and shoving to get a glimpse of her. Even paparazzi and reporters from out-of-state. A bunch of disruptions that would take department resources to sort out.

A much bigger problem than a few feet of snow.

"There's that sexy love song of hers. Listen to that sultry

beat." Rosie lifted her arms and shimmied her hips. "It always gets Jimmy in the mood. Know what I mean?"

I coughed. Oh, please no. "I'd better be going." I rapped my knuckles against the customer-service desk. "I'll see you at the wedding, if not before."

As I left, the song playing from the speakers wedged into my brain, refusing to let go. Ayla's smoky voice and the suggestive lyrics.

Fine, it was sexy. Rosie had that right.

Ayla Maxwell was a beautiful woman. Nobody could deny that.

But something about her just...raked across my nerves. Setting me on alert whenever she was near.

She was a diva who was used to getting her way. Probably explained why I'd gotten testy with her the first time we met. I was protective of my constituents, and her sudden presence had drawn all the wrong kinds of attention to our town.

But in the spirit of community peace, I could try to make a better impression during this visit. Could even be friendly. Everyone in town knew me as straight-laced and serious, but I wasn't an ogre. I would be professional and courteous next time I saw her. Nothing more and nothing less. Like she was any other visitor to Silver Ridge.

If I could just get that song out of my head.

TWO

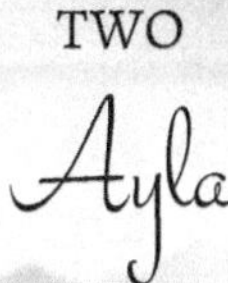

Ayla

I HAD JUST ARRIVED in Silver Ridge last night for the big wedding weekend, and things were a little...chaotic.

We were working on the wedding favors in Ashford and Emma's dining room. The space looked like a hurricane of craft supplies had blown through, leaving destruction in its wake.

Yet the familiar scents of the O'Neal residence filled the air, like always. Maisie's strawberry shampoo, Emma's herbal tea, Ashford's cologne. Things that, in the last year and a half, had come to feel like *home*.

I grabbed a cellophane bag to fill with Jordan almonds. "Is Ashford okay? He looked pretty stressed when I saw him earlier."

At least Maisie was occupied with her toys in her room instead of bouncing off the walls.

Emma groaned. "I love my fiancé, but he has been getting on my last nerve. He thinks this storm will interfere with the wedding."

"I checked the forecast before I left LA. I thought it wasn't that bad."

"It's not," Grace said soothingly, reaching for the spool of ribbon. "The storm will bring just enough snow to make all the trees around the Last Refuge Inn look beautiful. The wedding will be perfect. Ashford is just a worry wart."

That was definitely true.

"How about you go relax for a while," I said to Emma. "Let Grace and me take care of the rest of the favors. And later, I can take Maisie outside to burn off some energy."

"I don't want to leave you with all the work." Emma glanced at the messy table. "This is a step down from your usual scene, Ayla. You were at a movie premiere two days ago."

"I promise, that was *way* more boring than anything this weekend will be. Treat me like a normal person. I'm just Aunt Ayla. Did you forget I grew up on Army bases?"

"Right." Emma nodded. She was from a military family too. "Good point."

I aimed my thumb at Grace. "She's the one who's living with a billionaire. If we want to compare who's out of touch."

Grace pushed her glasses up her nose. "Hey! I'm the same nerdy girl I've always been."

I laughed, my skin warming with how happy I was to be here.

Chaos or not, I loved every second.

I'd been looking forward to this trip for ages. I may have begged, just a little, for Ashford and Emma to take my hectic schedule into account when setting their big date. I wasn't above bribery. But that hadn't been necessary. Emma was a sweetheart, and even though Ashford and I had our differences in the past, I'd never met anyone more loyal than him.

He'd told me I was part of the O'Neal family now. And he'd been true to his word.

Grace, Ashford's younger sister, would be the maid of honor. Her boyfriend Dane Knightly, the billionaire investor, was best man. The weekend promised to be full of simple pleasures. Time with the O'Neals, winter weather, and vicarious romance.

That was the only kind of romance in my life these days. Not that I was complaining.

The only thing I *wasn't* looking forward to? Seeing the Silver

Ridge Police Chief again. But maybe I'd get lucky, and I could avoid Chief Teller Landry altogether.

Fingers crossed.

Emma's phone rang, and she scrambled to check the screen. "Crap, that's my mom. I better take this."

After she disappeared down the hall, Grace blew out a breath. "A little intense around here."

We shared a glance and both cracked up.

"A bit. But now that I've arrived, I can help with anything you all need. Just wish I could stay longer than Sunday."

"You're in high demand." Her grin turned mischievous. "A couple weeks ago, some pictures of you popped up on my feed. You and that handsome record label guy."

"You can't believe everything you see in the tabloids. You should know better than that."

"But that's why I'm asking instead of assuming it's true."

"I'm too busy to date right now. I'll be back in the studio soon." Plus endorsements, endless promotion, interviews, photo shoots. None of it as glamorous as it sounded.

Especially after my last album didn't do as well as expected. I was supposed to be hustling right now. Striving to get back to the top of the charts.

Grace nodded thoughtfully. "You must love it, though. Getting to be creative all the time. To make your voice heard. Literally."

"I do love it. It's not always easy. But I can't imagine living any other way, you know? I'm so lucky. I've got to take the good with the bad."

A wrinkle appeared between Grace's eyebrows. "Hey, when we were in New York last fall, you mentioned something about an overzealous fan bothering you. Is that still going on?"

I forced down the dismay that suddenly rose up in my stomach. Ignored the bitter taste in my mouth. *Breathe.*

But I was a performer. I'd had plenty of practice hiding what I really felt inside.

"There was one small incident last September. Nothing since."

"Just using the word *incident* makes it sound bad."

"Then pretend I used a different word. It's no big deal."

Didn't matter that we'd never found out who really sent those flowers to me in Toronto, despite my team's efforts. Never figured out how the person got access to that old photo of me, either. A photo that had never appeared online anywhere.

Months had passed since then. Everything was fine.

And I didn't want to think any more about the dark sides to my career or my past. Not this weekend. My slump in the charts, my uncertainties about the future… That could all wait until when I was back in LA.

"Now tell me more about you and Dane," I said.

Maybe there was a storm headed to Hart County, but I needed to keep my mind on happy thoughts and clear skies.

Luckily, today the Colorado weather gods were pulling out all the stops.

About an hour later, I found myself strolling down Main Street with Maisie. Grace and I had finished the wedding favors and cleaned up the craft supplies. Then Grace had taken Ashford to run some errands, and I was in charge of entertaining my niece, which left Emma free to take a bath or a nap.

Such a hard job, I know. Taking my favorite little girl in the world out for an afternoon adventure. But I was up for the task.

Maisie and I skipped along the sidewalk together, holding hands. The air was that perfect kind of chill that was invigorating instead of uncomfortable. Not a cloud in sight, with yellow sunlight promising a hefty dose of vitamin D.

"Where should we go first?" I asked. "The park?"

I glanced back and saw an SUV with dark-tinted windows following about a block away, keeping pace with us. But the sight reassured me instead of raising concern.

That was Bryan, my driver and sometimes-bodyguard.

I'd also worn a baseball cap and sunglasses, though I still got some curious looks. The locals were used to me by now. Tourists could be another story. The ski resort drew plenty of them, and the media attention on my Silver Ridge connections had inspired some of my fans to visit in the hopes of seeing me.

But it still wasn't as much of an issue as the paparazzi who liked to follow me on a daily basis in LA. Most of the time, I kept my cool when dealing with reporters. But every once in a while, my temper got the best of me.

Back home, my house was in Malibu, where I lived in a quiet, gated community. I rarely traveled with a big entourage unless I was on tour. The last thing I wanted was to roll in with a bunch of handlers and a massive security detail and take over the town. *So* not my style.

Bryan hung back at enough distance that I had some freedom, while staying close enough to swoop in if needed. It was a delicate balance.

Just another one of those realities of being me.

Maisie tapped her chin, a tiny replica of her dad. "How about we go to Silver Linings?"

"You goof. We went to the coffee shop this morning. I seem to remember you eating a cinnamon roll as big as your head."

"But I didn't get to have a muffin," she said reasonably.

"You're determined to get as many treats out of me as possible this weekend, aren't you?"

"Is it working?"

It kind of was. Maisie knew I was a soft touch.

After not being in her life for so many years, I tended to give Maisie anything and everything she wanted. But maybe it was just my deprived inner child coming out.

I wanted to give Maisie all the things my sister and I didn't have growing up.

Well, a loving father was number one on that list, and thankfully Ashford had that covered. I was determined to fill in any other possible gaps.

The fact that Lori was gone only made the empty spaces

inside of me ache more painfully. So, was I overcompensating? Possibly. But I didn't tend to do things halfway. I rarely took no for an answer.

Especially when it was a territorial man standing in my way.

That was why I hadn't given up on reconnecting with Ashford and Maisie, even though my brother-in-law tried to avoid me for years.

Ugh, speaking of territorial men.

"There's Uncle Teller!" Maisie said, waving at the police SUV as it rolled slowly by. Police Chief Landry sat in the driver's seat, arm draped casually over the steering wheel, sunglasses hiding his eyes. He smiled and waved back, but his mouth twisted a moment after.

That frown had to be aimed at me. Annoyance flared inside me like a sudden burst of lightning.

So much for avoiding my least favorite Silver Ridge resident.

From the moment we'd met last year, Teller Landry had made it clear he didn't like me.

"*So you're who all that fuss is about?*" he'd asked, his tone dripping with disdain. As if I'd wanted those reporters to mob Ashford and Emma's building. As if I hadn't been desperate for a break from the constant attention. The chief had wanted to make sure I knew he wasn't impressed with me.

I'd gotten pissed at him right back. "*I didn't ask for anyone to make a fuss over me. But isn't it your job to keep these reporters from harassing your citizens?*"

Since then, Landry had barely been civil whenever we crossed paths. He hated when I visited Silver Ridge.

But I wasn't so impressed with that man either. Even if he was a close friend of the O'Neal family and enough of a presence in Maisie's life to warrant an uncle title.

In truth, he made me nervous. It wasn't just the fact that he was a military man, like my father had been, because Ashford and Callum had been in the Army too. Same with Dane. It wasn't those intense-looking battle scars on the chief's face, either.

Nope, it was the constant scowl he wore around me.

My temper wanted to leap to the surface. I'd never done a thing to that man except exist. But if Bryan noticed I was upset, he might jump out of the SUV and charge to my rescue. A clash between my bodyguard and the local police was *not* high on my list for this weekend.

Maisie wasn't looking at me. So I lifted my hand. Extended my middle finger. And scratched my head with it, keeping that finger way up high so Chief Landry couldn't miss it.

There.

Now Teller knew exactly what I thought of him too.

THREE
Teller

"You okay, Chief?" Finn Mackie, one of our dispatchers, said as I walked into the station. "You look...well, even less happy than usual."

"I'm fine," I grunted, heading for my office. Then I stopped and turned. "I usually look unhappy?"

Finn's eyes darted to Officer Seth Duncan, who was on the front desk this shift. Seth shook his head lightly, lips pressed together like he was holding in a laugh.

"Is that a trick question, sir?" Finn asked.

"Never mind," I muttered. But I had to wonder if the very sight of me was that off-putting to everyone, or just to visiting celebrities.

Ayla Maxwell had just flipped me off. When all I'd been doing was driving down the street.

I'd smiled when I spotted Maisie. I had no clue what my face had been doing when I noticed Ayla. She was almost unrecognizable in the hat and sunglasses. But there was no hiding that platinum hair. Or her slender waist and curvy hips, which her coat didn't diminish at all.

There was something delicate about Ayla whenever I saw her in person. She was smaller, more fragile than I would've expected.

I'd actually been worried, seeing her and Maisie out there by themselves.

Until I'd seen the SUV with dark-tinted windows driving behind her. *Good.* She'd brought security.

But make no mistake, that woman was a spitfire. Pure diva. Ready to throw attitude my way at the slightest provocation, or none at all.

Damn.

In the past, my officers and I had bent over backwards to accommodate her. Like increasing patrols in the area around Ashford's home whenever she was in town. And this was the thanks I got?

So much for trying to fix that first impression. She hadn't even given me a chance.

Maybe Ayla was a lost cause where I was concerned.

I settled behind my desk and started on some paperwork. But I didn't make much progress before my younger sister Piper was barging into my office, her skin flushed and her eyes wide.

"Teller, I swear I am going to kill him."

I leaned back in my chair. "Not the kind of thing you should admit at a police station."

"And *that* is not funny."

I schooled my features as I stood up and came around the desk. "You don't mean Ollie, do you? Is he at school?"

Last time Ollie was unsupervised here at the station, the kid had managed to get into a box of handcuffs we'd just had delivered. We still hadn't found the keys.

"Of course I don't mean Ollie. And *yes*, he's at school."

"Then what's up?"

"*Danny.*" She spit out the name like a curse. And it might as well have been.

"What did your ex do now?"

Piper was ten years younger than me. Dad had worked on offshore oil rigs as a roughneck, which took him away from us for months at a time. Mom coped with the stress by leaving us on our own a lot.

There'd been rumors when Piper was born that she wasn't Dad's. I remembered the first time some kid on the playground teased me about it.

We both got sent home, me with bloody knuckles and that kid with two black eyes.

With our mom checked out from her parental duties, I'd picked up the slack. Looking out for Piper, making sure she did her homework and didn't run too wild. Which, with a baby sister like Piper, had not been easy.

Piper owned Silver Linings Coffee on Main Street, and that suited her outgoing personality perfectly. Piper was the head of our town's unofficial welcoming committee. Never met a stranger she didn't want to call a friend.

We couldn't have been more different.

And yet, whenever there was trouble, she came to her big brother. Sometimes Piper just needed me to tell her everything would be okay.

"It's what Danny isn't doing. Writing me back. I keep texting to ask when he's going to see his son, and he's ignoring me."

Piper's ex was a real piece of work. Danny had been a shitty husband and a worse father. They'd been divorced for several years. But last year, he'd left Silver Ridge and hadn't shown any interest in being in Ollie's life.

My hands rested on Piper's arms. "I'll try calling Danny. See if I can get through to him."

"He won't listen." She pressed the heels of her hands to her eyes. "Ollie was up crying last night. Missing his dad. He doesn't understand why this is happening. What if he blames me?"

Shit. "He won't. He loves his mom, and that will never change. I'll keep being around for Ollie too. Like I have been. Like I always will be."

I felt bad enough that I'd been gone so much myself during Piper's life. When I was a kid, I'd sworn never to repeat our father's mistakes. And then, what did I do? Joined the Army and then the Special Forces. A career that took me away from my sister when she needed me most.

Piper had met her ex in college. Could I have stopped her from marrying him if I'd been around more? Probably not. Piper was too strong-willed to bend to my advice if she didn't want to. But I could've done more to support her.

Instead, an IED had almost killed me along with half my unit. And Piper had to help get *me* back on my feet after I returned to civilian life. Just another thing for Danny to complain about in the days before their divorce.

Serving in the Special Forces was the honor of my life. I didn't exactly have regrets. But being Piper's brother and Ollie's uncle were pretty damn important to me too, and I still had a lot to make up for on that front.

I pulled her into a hug and rested my cheek on her hair. "It'll be okay."

Piper sniffled and wiped her eyes. It took a lot for her to reveal her insecurity, much less shed tears. "I was spiraling. Thanks for talking me through it. Sorry to barge in."

"Anytime." I grabbed a tissue from the box on my desk, one I kept there for witnesses and crime victims. She blew her nose.

I sat on the edge of my desk. "Hey, Piper? Do you think I seem...mean?"

Her bloodshot eyes scrutinized me. "Mean?"

I shifted my weight. "Grumpy. Like I'm always unhappy or something. Do I put people off?"

She was trying to keep a straight face, but I knew my sister. She was laughing. "Do you remember that time Grace and I were playing treasure hunters, and you got annoyed at us for digging holes in the backyard? And she climbed a tree and wouldn't come down because she was scared of you?"

My lips pressed into a flat line. "You and Grace were five."

"Yeah, but she didn't usually run away from scary things. *You*, though?"

"Grace and I get along great."

"Nowadays, sure. My point is, you can be intense. Intimidating. Even when you don't mean to be. This can't be a surprise to you."

I stuck my hands in my pockets, searching for the right words. "I'm known for being serious. Maybe even uptight. But I didn't think I was unlikable."

"Why do you even care?"

"So I *am* unlikable?"

"Good lord." She rubbed her face. "Where is this coming from? You never care what anyone thinks. Are you talking about someone specific? Did somebody hurt your macho, manly feelings?"

I grumbled, crossing my arms. "*No.* I'm speaking generally." And not about a gorgeous Grammy winner who couldn't stand me. This wasn't about her at all. "Just thinking about the qualities of a good police chief. I can't operate effectively if I'm going around terrifying people."

She held her pointer finger and thumb an inch apart. "You're only *slightly* terrifying."

"Slightly terrifying is still terrifying. My constituents have to be able to trust me."

My sister paused, trying and failing not to roll her eyes. "This town respects you more than almost anyone. You always tell the truth the way you see it, and if that rubs somebody the wrong way on occasion, so be it. Anybody who knows you thinks you're a great guy. Fair and loyal and reliable. Very trustworthy."

She hadn't mentioned *easygoing*. Because I wasn't. But I wasn't the type to doubt myself either. Not usually.

Piper smacked a kiss on my cheek. "Now I'd better skedaddle. I'll see you later, right? You're good with watching Ollie? If you want to go to Ashford's bachelor party after all, I can figure something else out. Since you're so concerned suddenly about being social."

"Ashford doesn't need me at his bachelor party. I'll be at your place to watch Ollie. No change of plans."

She studied me another moment. "Okay. Thanks, Teller. Love you."

"Love you too."

During my time serving my country, there'd never been a question about returning to Silver Ridge. I'd been the police chief of our small mountain town for a few years now. Most of the time, it was great. Maybe I had a tendency to be cynical and skeptical.

Especially of people who showed up here and expected the rest of us to pick up after their messes.

But I knew I was where I belonged. I was forty years old. Set in my ways. If that made me unlikable, too bad.

We had a good life here. *I* had a good life.

Once, I'd dreamed of having a wife and kids of my own. The whole white-picket-fence package. I'd even been engaged, but that was ancient history. I'd given up on that kind of thing a long time ago.

Maybe it was for the best it hadn't worked out. Too many people were already counting on me.

And I wouldn't have it any other way.

FOUR

Ayla

THE AFTERNOON with Maisie couldn't have gone better. First, we visited the hardware store. Silver Ridge Hardware & Supplies wasn't your typical home improvement center. It was more like a gift shop that happened to have some wrenches and chainsaws in the back.

Maisie and I never made it past the locally made preserves, handmade children's toys, and adorable tchotchkes they sold up front. My niece loved getting prizes from there, and I loved soaking in that small-town ambience.

After that, we spent time at the park with her brand new toys. A whole family of tiny horse figurines, a barn, and a corral. Maisie also got a book about horses, and she informed me in great detail about everything she learned as she read.

There'd been a bit of drama when Stella tried to run off with the black stallion, but we recovered the horse figurine before any real damage was done. *Phew.*

A few people at the park had seemed to recognize me, but I stayed focused on my niece, and they left us alone. My driver Bryan had been able to relax on a nearby park bench.

Now, we were back in Maisie's room. She was setting up her horse sanctuary on her dresser, while I sat on the floor, my back to her bed. "There you go," Maisie cooed at the dappled mare. "This is your new home. You'll love it here."

I rested my head against the mattress and smiled.

The afternoon had been exactly what I needed. Just a few hours of feeling normal, like I wasn't the starring attraction of the celebrity circus.

Some people thought that being famous meant my life was perfect. But I'd been stabbed in the back so many times. A few years ago, my former assistant had sold a story about me to the tabloids, violating her NDA for a quick buck. I wished she was the only one.

True friendships were even harder. Plenty of people wanted to be seen with Ayla Maxwell, but it wasn't so simple to find someone who saw me for *me*.

Yeah, I knew how that sounded. Champagne problems. All my dreams for my career had come true and then some. I had more money than I would ever want to spend.

But that didn't make me any less lonely when I was on the road or at some award ceremony, surrounded by people who saw me as a product instead of a human being. I was only as valuable as my last big hit.

Which made this time with Maisie and the O'Neals even more precious to me. I loved visiting Silver Ridge. Maybe it was a cliché, but the small-town pace of life was slower. I had time to stop and breathe here.

"What's all this?" Ashford stepped into Maisie's room, grinning fondly at her.

"Dad, look at my horse ranch! Isn't it pretty? Aunt Ayla bought it for me."

"Did you remember to say thanks?"

"Yes! Twice! Thank you, Aunt Ayla. See, Dad? That's three."

"I stand corrected."

I reached out to brush her dark hair from her eyes. "You're so welcome, cutie-pie."

Ashford's gaze slid over to me. "We're going to need a new house just to hold everything you and Dane buy for her."

"That's what aunts and uncles are for."

Maisie went back to playing, and I got up. Ashford and I stepped out into the hall. I followed him toward the living room. "So, are you thinking about getting a new place?" I asked.

He shrugged. "It's been on my mind. Need to get through this wedding first. But I've been scoping out some places."

I nudged him with my elbow. "If you need help with a down-payment, all you have to do is ask."

"Dane's offered the same. But there are some things a guy has to do for himself."

"You'll work it out. Just be sure your new house is zoned for horses. I see a pony in your future."

Ashford shot me a glare. "Don't even think about it."

I poked him in the side, loving that he and I could joke around like this after so many years of being estranged.

When I left home at sixteen, I broke ties with my family, including Lori. It was one of my biggest regrets. My sister and I had reconciled shortly before she died, but I'd lost years of being with her. Having a family. Knowing Maisie as a baby. Ashford had thought I was a terrible person, and honestly, I'd had my doubts about him.

Then a couple of years ago, the pressures of fame had nearly broken me. I hadn't been able to trust anyone. Not even the people closest to me. The label execs, my manager, my assistant... I'd had to be strong to make it in this business, but too often I'd been tricked or taken advantage of. It had felt like the walls were closing in.

I checked myself into a rehab facility for exhaustion and anxiety. But even there, paparazzi had climbed the fences to get photos of me. I left in secret one night, bought a car with cash, and drove all the way to Silver Ridge.

Ashford and Emma helped me find a safe place to stay over in Hartley, with Emma's aunt and uncle. I'd finally gotten the peace and quiet I so desperately needed. Ashford and I talked through all our misconceptions and mistakes.

After that, everything changed. I hired a completely new team, including Cheryl as my artist manager. I started making more decisions on my own and fighting for my freedom, even if I had to claw for it piece by piece. It hadn't been easy.

I would always be grateful that Ashford hadn't turned me away when I needed him.

"Where's Emma?" I asked.

"She had a couple piano lessons this afternoon. Last ones before we get to be on vacation." Ashford glanced at the clock on his phone screen. "Then we'll take Maisie to the babysitter, and we've got the bachelor/bachelorette thing at Hearthstone Brewing at seven."

"Perfect. Can't wait to start celebrating."

Maisie suddenly appeared. She had a way of sneaking up on us and listening when we had no idea she was there. "Daddy, can I go to the battler party too?"

"*Bachelor* party. And it's not for kids. We already talked about this, monkey."

"But Aunt Ayla gets to go. She's not that old."

Ashford smirked at me, and I hid a smile. "I *am* known for my youthful energy onstage," I pointed out. "But I'm twenty-seven. Older than Emma. I'm all the way grown up." Even if sometimes I didn't feel like it.

Maisie pouted.

"You always have fun with Dixie," her dad said. "Stella's going with you too. You can bring your new horse toys."

"It's a horse *ranch*." She pivoted on her heel and marched back down the hall to her room.

"You see what I'm dealing with?" Ashford muttered.

I patted his shoulder. "You're a lucky guy, O'Neal."

He laughed softly. "I really, really am. Do you want me to swing back here later, and we'll head to Hearthstone together?"

"No, I'll meet you there. Bryan will take me."

"Sounds good. Just want to make sure someone's looking out for you." Ashford pulled me into a one-armed hug. "You're my sister. Don't forget that."

I hugged him back. I would never get over losing Lori, not entirely. But having Ashford as my big brother meant the world to me.

Locking the door to Ashford and Emma's building, I stepped toward the curb and the waiting SUV.

Icy air swirled the skirt of my dress, leaving goosebumps up and down my bare legs.

"Ready for your evening?" Bryan opened the passenger door for me.

"So ready. The wedding festivities are about to officially begin."

I jumped into the passenger side, while Bryan went around to get in the driver's seat. Main Street was close enough to walk, but my driver preferred to keep the vehicle close in case I ever needed a quick exit.

I'd changed out of my jeans and T-shirt, opting for a floral-print dress, a long coat, and a pair of cowboy boots. It was freezing outside, but that wasn't going to stop me from dressing cute.

I'd also left my hat and sunglasses behind. But tonight was supposed to be fun. A celebration. I didn't want to spend the whole time hiding.

"Where to first?" Bryan asked with a lopsided grin. "We'll have to navigate around all this rush-hour traffic." He gestured at the road ahead, which had maybe two other cars puttering along and a handful of pedestrians.

"A change of pace from LA, right?"

He shrugged. "I'm not complaining."

"I saw the cutest baby store earlier when I was out with Maisie. I thought we could do a little shopping for Brody before we head to the brewery."

His grin widened. "You know I won't argue with *that*."

Bryan Krueger had been a mixed martial arts fighter before changing careers to something more stable and less likely to result in bodily injuries. Yes, he was my bodyguard, but mostly he drove me around and scowled at anyone who got too close.

Despite his usual suit and tie, he looked like a bruiser. But he had a heart of gold. Recently, he'd married his longtime girlfriend Mikaela, and baby Brody was their pride and joy.

Things were completely platonic between me and Bryan, but under different circumstances? He would've been my type. A little rough around the edges. Tall, with his dark hair buzzed close to his scalp.

Also, did I mention biceps as big as my thighs? *Yowza*.

Bryan's physique reminded me of a certain police chief. Another man I had no business considering attractive.

And why couldn't I stop thinking about him?

I resolved to put Teller Landry out of my mind.

Bryan parked, and we made our way toward the baby store I'd spotted earlier, hoping it would still be open. The sun had already disappeared behind the mountains, and rustic streetlights lit the pavement and the Main Street storefronts.

Then I heard the shouts. My head turned toward the sound before I could stop myself.

"Shit, that's Ayla Maxwell! *Baby*, you're even hotter in person!" A group of college-age men stood on the other side of the street, gawking at me. Their bright neon jackets pegged them as tourists from the ski resort.

One of them put his arms in the air and thrust his hips. I jerked my gaze away, disgust swirling in my stomach. Maybe I should've worn the hat and sunglasses after all.

Bryan made a low, growly sound in his throat. "Fucking assholes. Just ignore them."

"Already on it." I couldn't react. You never knew when someone was filming, and they might edit the video to make me look like the bad guy.

"Oh come on, Ayla, come take a picture with us! Baby, please!"

Did they seriously think I'd stop and talk to them after they behaved that way? What was wrong with people?

Bryan put a hand on my shoulder, and we kept walking. I didn't want their taunts to affect me, but tremors still ran along my arms, making my hands shake. A toxic mixture of anger and dismay.

Laughter and more shouts followed us as we continued down the block. But the men didn't cross over to approach me. Probably because Bryan was here looking all murderous. Doing his job.

Those guys were nothing compared to some of the trolls online. I had people on my team who managed my social media and tried to weed out the worst comments, but things always slipped through. Bullies were the same the world over. They wanted to steal someone else's joy. Turn it into something twisted and ugly.

Most of the time I just let the bad stuff flow past me. I had a thick skin. But when something truly awful caught me off guard, I couldn't stop my physical reaction. That urge to rage at the world for being so awful.

Like the flower arrangement I'd received in Toronto with the old photo of me. It had reminded me of my childhood. My father, the colonel. The biggest bully of all.

"You okay?" Bryan asked.

Forget about them, I told myself.

"Yeah. All good." A few deep breaths later, and I was back to my happy mood. I'd had such a wonderful day in Silver Ridge so far. I refused to let anything spoil it.

FIVE

Teller

THE AFTERNOON WORE ON. Work pulled me in, and I was in such a flow that I lost track of time. Until Seth Duncan, the officer on front-desk duty today, knocked on the frame of my open door. "Hey, Chief. What're you still doing here?"

I stretched my arms over my head, realizing it was after five. I'd arrived at the station at seven that morning, which wasn't unusual. But I was supposed to babysit Ollie tonight. Didn't want to be late.

Not that I was *ever* fully off duty, not a hundred percent.

"Got caught up in reading reports," I said. "Sheriff Douglas gave me a heads-up. There was another vandalism incident. Northeast corner of the county this time."

Seth adjusted his wire-rimmed glasses. "Similar to the ones we've seen around Silver Ridge?"

"Yep." I stood, joints creaking from sitting still for so long. Geez. "Coffee?"

"Sure." Seth followed me to the break room. A half-empty box of cinnamon donuts lay on the counter. Seth grabbed one, but I resisted the urge.

The coffee smelled burned, so I dumped it in the sink and started brewing a fresh pot.

"It was a ranch property," I said. "Isolated. The vandal or vandals broke into the barn in the middle of the night, made a mess, set loose some of the animals. Threw a rock through a window of the main house. Nearly scared the owner to death."

Seth propped his hip against the counter. "So are these teenagers, do you think?"

"What teenagers?" Finn, one of the dispatchers, strolled into the break room. He was going off shift. Officer Susan Nichols was close on his heels. She was just coming on.

"The string of vandalisms around the county," Seth explained. "It could be kids blowing off steam."

That had been my first hunch too. Some bored high school seniors, killing time during their final semester. But flipping through the photos of the scenes, it hadn't felt like just kids messing around. There was something darker to it. An edge. The broken window at the latest scene hadn't seemed like petty mischief.

Especially because the owner was a woman, and she'd been home alone. Same with every other property owner where these vandalisms had occurred. Some of them women who always lived alone, others whose partners or roommates were away.

No irreparable damage had been done. Not yet, anyway. But the culprit had left a signature at each scene: spray-painted graffiti in the shape of a flower.

This kind of thing got under people's skin. Made them feel unsafe. Whoever was responsible might escalate to something worse.

An extra complication was how the incidents were spread across the county. Some in my jurisdiction, some in the sheriff's. Some in other towns. It had become a joint effort between departments. In a large rural county like ours, we all had to band together on something like this.

But I had a good crew working for me. Susan was my senior officer, and she'd already been here when I became chief. She'd been married for thirty years. Had three grown sons and a biting sense of humor.

Seth was our newest addition to the team. Susan loved to poke fun at him. He was too easy to rile up. But he was a good guy, and smart. A whiz with computers, which was important in this day and age.

We were a rural police department, but we had body-worn cameras, reporting requirements, and databases to maintain like every other department in the state.

Finn had joined dispatch just out of college, and no junk food was safe around him. The dispatchers were shared between us and the fire department, but since the dispatch office ran out of my building, I saw them as part of my crew as well.

I looked out for all of them. This department was a family. The officers and admin staff took care of each other, laughed together.

But as much as I loved them, I had to keep myself apart.

That was what it meant to be the chief. I was in charge. The boss who set an example for the others and couldn't simply be their friend. Even if that might've been nice.

"We don't have any leads yet," I said. "Just keep your eyes and ears open. Never know who might've seen or heard something, and it'll lead us in the direction of the culprits."

Susan unwrapped a protein bar. She carried those things with her everywhere. "Seth will probably be too busy keeping his eyes out for a blond singer who just got to town."

Seth started to flush red. "My cousin wants Ayla Maxwell's autograph. That's all."

Susan laughed. "I think you're in loooove."

Finn stuffed a donut in his mouth and snickered. "Sorry, Seth. But you think Ayla Maxwell would give you the time of day?"

"It isn't like that!"

Susan hummed the melody to a familiar song. Same one Rosie had been playing at the market. The really sexy one. It had this particular line about "*Your fingers tracing a path to ecstasy.*" The words only got racier from there.

A pair of jewel-green irises appeared in my mind, narrowed like they hated the sight of me.

I swallowed roughly. "That's enough. Don't start singing those lyrics or we'll have a hostile work environment on our hands."

Susan's brown eyes glowed with mirth. "But how do you know what the lyrics are, Chief?"

I opened my mouth. Shit, she had me there.

Fine, I knew every word to that song. But only because of one night getting sucked into watching Ayla's music videos online. *One*. Wasn't my fault. It was some weird brain chemistry thing that made pop songs and viral video clips addictive. The music studios had probably studied it in a lab.

Ayla was something to watch, though. A natural performer with the kind of ethereal beauty that made people shut up and pay attention. And the way she put her whole body into singing was even more compelling than her features. Like she was projecting every lyric from somewhere deep inside.

"You a big Ayla Maxwell fan?" Susan asked.

A stern look from me had them all quieting down.

Geez. I really was the fun police, wasn't I?

But that had never bothered me before. Which begged the same exact question I'd been pondering earlier. Why did I suddenly care?

I poured coffee in a to-go cup. "I expect us all to behave like professionals with Ms. Maxwell. Same as always. That won't be an issue, will it?"

"No, Chief," they said in chorus.

"I'll make sure the rest of our department is on the same page, but you can help me by spreading the word. If anything related to Ms. Maxwell comes up, direct it to me. I'll handle it." It was one thing for her to be rude to me. But my officers shouldn't have to deal with that.

My sister Piper had put the nail on the head earlier. If I had to be the unlikable guy, so be it.

"Yes, Chief."

With my coffee in hand, I returned to my office. I was about to pack my things up and get myself home when Susan appeared in my doorway. "We just got a report of a disturbance on Main. Central business district."

"Then go ahead and handle it. I'm about to head home."

"I know, sir, but you said you wanted to be involved in anything related to Ms. Maxwell. Some kind of fight's broken out."

Oh, *damn it.*

SIX

Ayla

BRYAN and I made it to the baby store only minutes before it was supposed to close. But as soon as we stepped inside, the shop owner started gushing about my music and said we could stay for as long as we wanted.

"I'm just so excited to have Ayla Maxwell shopping at my store. I'm Natalie, by the way."

Fame had its drawbacks, but it did have some nice benefits too. I would be the first to admit it.

"Great to meet you, Natalie. This place is adorable. I had to stop by."

She glowed with pride. "Are you looking for anything in particular?" Her eyes darted toward my stomach, and I could just imagine the headlines now.

I touched Bryan's arm. "Something for his one-year-old son. And maybe for his wife." I emphasized that last word. "Bryan's my driver."

"No problem," Natalie said brightly. She showed us some options.

I lifted up a pale blue outfit that could've fit on a doll. "Look how tiny these are. So cute."

"But little man takes after his daddy. He's already wearing 2T and growing fast." Bryan held up a cute T-shirt with the Colorado flag. Beneath, it said *Future Mountain Man*. "What about this?"

"I *love* it. That's a must-have."

My phone buzzed, and I took a break from shopping to check my messages. Cheryl had written. Dramatic music played in my head. Dun dun *dun*.

My manager never wrote unless she had something important to say.

CHERYL

Video interview confirmed for tomorrow at two your time. Do NOT make me reschedule again. They were already threatening to cancel the cover feature. You definitely have access to a piano, correct?

Yes, there's a piano here I can use. But would it be the end of the world if they cancel? Do I really need another magazine cover?

Said NO ONE EVER who wants her next album to sell.

I rolled my eyes. But okay, fair point.

Bryan stepped over to me. "Everything alright?"

"Yeah, it's just Cheryl. Reminding me about an interview tomorrow."

The magazine wanted to record segments of this interview for social media, and they wanted me to perform a few songs. It was supposed to be authentic, stripped down, just me and a piano. And it had to be this Friday. They'd loved the idea of me visiting the small town where my sister once lived.

Scheduling this kind of stuff was beyond frustrating. A timeline was etched in stone, impossible to change, until suddenly an executive in some fancy office decided it wasn't.

But I wasn't going to complain. Because this video interview would be a good excuse for why I couldn't have dinner with Emma's parents on Friday night in Hartley. I'd met

Emma's uncle Aiden and aunt Jessi before, and they were wonderful people. But her whole extended family? That sounded overwhelming. Dinner with the parents was just...not my thing.

Bryan would drive me to Hartley once the interview was over, and I'd be there for the whole wedding day.

CHERYL

> Speaking of your next album. Paul Ruxton has been calling again, asking how songwriting is going. I told him you've got months and he should mind his own fucking business, but if you have anything to tide the execs over, it could help.

Ugh. Next topic, please?

Songwriting wasn't a straightforward process for me. Inspiration came in fits and starts. Sometimes a whole song appeared at once in my mind, the chords already itching to be set free from my fingertips. Other times, I got only glimpses. A feeling. Vibes that slowly took form into something more substantial. Yet those songs tended to be my favorites. Worth the wait.

But the executives at my record label, like Paul, wanted to see continuous results. I was their show monkey, and I was supposed to dance. Pose for pictures. Produce new albums on command. It was a constant battle.

At least I had Cheryl in my corner. She tried to stand as a barrier between me and the label execs. Eventually, the songs would come. Even with my past struggles, the music always showed up for me.

Putting my phone away, I went back to shopping. After a few more minutes, I had some outfits for Brody to add to Bryan's pile. The shop sold locally made body care for moms too, so he picked out a gift set for Mikaela.

When it was time to pay, I slid my credit card into Natalie's hand before Bryan could hand his over.

"Come on, you don't have to do that," Bryan said.

"No. But I want to. Buying gifts for other people's kids is one of my favorite hobbies. You wouldn't deny me, would you?"

He snickered. "Nah, you do you. Thanks, boss."

The owner swiped my credit card. But then Bryan muttered a curse. He nodded at the storefront windows. "Uh, Ayla? We may have a problem."

When I turned to look, my stomach fell.

There was a crowd of people waiting on the sidewalk right outside. Natalie, the boutique owner, had switched the sign to closed, so nobody had come in. But people had their phones up taking pictures.

I recognized some of them. Those guys who'd shouted and made raunchy gestures from across the street earlier.

"I'm so sorry," Natalie said. "I don't think they're from around here."

"No, I figured not. But it's okay. I'm used to it."

I was nervous though. The crowd blocked the door. A few people even had their faces pressed to the windows to see in.

Bryan strode over to the door, no doubt scowling at them. A couple of people moved back, but somehow Bryan's presence just seemed to agitate the others even more. The men hooted and hollered at us like we were animals in a zoo exhibit. Their voices were loud enough now that we could hear them through the glass.

"*Ayla*! *Come outside!*"

Crap, this wasn't good.

Usually, people who wanted my autograph were pretty low-key about it. But mob mentality was a very real thing.

"Is there a back exit?" Bryan asked.

Natalie wrung her hands. "No, but I could call for a police escort if you want."

I shook my head emphatically. Calling Silver Ridge PD was the last thing I needed. A lecture from Chief Landry about how much of a problem my presence caused in town? No, thanks.

"It'll be fine." I was reassuring myself just as much as the others. I had Bryan with me, and I'd dealt with countless crowds of fans before. We were just fine.

I finished paying and tucked both my bag and Bryan's under my arm. He looked worried. "I'll go out first," he said. "Clear the way, then I'll come back for you."

"I'd rather just get this done. I'll stop a moment, say hi and take a few selfies. Then we can move on."

Bryan glowered. "Hell, no. We can't give those assholes any oxygen. I am not liking the vibes out there."

Okay, he was right. But after my day out with Maisie, this was disappointing. And it scared me to think what might've happened if a crowd like this gathered when she was with me. What if she'd heard those guys cat-calling me earlier?

Even worse, I was supposed to head over to Hearthstone Brewing right after this. What if the crowd followed me there? What if they wouldn't leave Ashford and Emma's guests alone?

I should've worn the hat and sunglasses. Taken the side streets and alleys.

Don't put yourself on display. Good girls don't do that. You're more trouble than it's worth.

My father's voice. Every once in a while, it snuck into my mind like a dagger. A cheap shot from nowhere. But it just made me all the more defiant.

Lifting my chin, I banished my fears. "Lead the way," I said to Bryan. "Let's go."

Natalie unlocked the door. Bryan went out first. "Step back please. Let us through." He reached backward so he could place his hand at the small of my back in a protective gesture. He angled his body, half shielding me and half ready to shove a path through the crowd.

I stepped outside. The shouts started immediately, setting my teeth on edge. "Ayla, can I get an autograph?"

"Ayla, we're your biggest fans, can we get a selfie?"

I forced a smile. "Sorry, everyone. I can't stop right now. Have a nice night." *Keep going. It'll be fine.*

The crowd jostled. Someone shoved into me.

"Ayla, smile!"

"Show us your tits!" another guy taunted.

My stomach lurched. "Learn some manners!" I shouted back, even though I shouldn't have responded at all. Shouldn't let my temper out.

"*Move*," Bryan yelled. "Get the fuck out of the way!" The voices and laughter crescendoed, and a hard grip closed around my wrist. I didn't see who it was.

Suddenly, everything was happening so fast.

Bryan shoved someone. I cried out as the hand around my wrist pulled hard. A fist lashed out at Bryan's face, catching him in the nose. He threw a punch.

And then, all hell broke loose.

SEVEN
Teller

THERE WAS a damn *riot* in the middle of Main Street.

"We need backup," I said into my radio. Then lifted my chin at Susan. We'd just jumped out of my department SUV. "Focus on dispersing the crowd. It's a chaotic situation, and we need to get it under control."

"Copy that." But she looked nervous. Susan had been on the force for going on fifteen years, but she was a small-town cop through-and-through. We rarely dealt with anything like this. Not even that snarl of reporters that showed up the first time Ayla Maxwell was in Silver Ridge.

A shop owner had called this in. Mentioned Ayla was here. But where was she? Was she okay?

My throat went tight, my awareness sharpening as I scanned the crowd. Men were trading blows while others ducked out of the way.

Blood poured from the nose of a massive guy with a buzz cut. I saw him slam his meaty fist into another guy's stomach. *Shit*.

"Break it up!" I sprinted for the center of the fray, nudging gawkers out of my path when they wouldn't move.

Then I saw blond hair flying, so pale it was almost white.

Pretty pink lips open in a yell. Five and a half feet of pure attitude in the eye of the storm.

My heart did a strange flop in my chest as time seemed to slow.

A tall, skinny man in a ski jacket had his fingers around Ayla's wrist. She was trying to pull away. Heat and adrenaline flooded my bloodstream, and time lurched forward again.

"Hey, back off!" I roared.

The kid holding on to Ayla glanced over, saw me coming, and bolted through the crowd. I reached her, immediately putting myself physically between her and the mayhem.

"You need to come with me."

She turned in my direction, her expression doing a complicated dance when she recognized me. "But Bryan—"

"Ayla," I barked. "Let's *go*."

She wasn't listening. There was a law-enforcement rule of thumb when dealing with uncooperative members of the public. ATM. Ask, then tell, then *move*.

I had to get her out of here.

"Wait—" she started.

But I was done asking. Bending to wrap my arms around her hips, I hoisted her up.

Every part of me jolted at the sensation of having her pressed to me. Her silky hair brushed my cheek, and I caught a whiff of something darkly sweet, like caramel. The warm weight of her body settled against me like it belonged there.

But it also seemed to wake her back up, because she cried out in protest. "What the *hell*! Put me down!"

I was already weaving through the crowd. I heard Susan issuing orders and breaking up the worst of the fight. Our backup was only minutes away.

My main concern was Ayla. Removing her from this equation.

I had no idea what had sparked that brawl, but Ayla's presence was nothing but fuel to that fire. My job was to get her somewhere safe.

The first open doorway I saw led into Main Street Market. Rosie stood there staring in shock at the street fight. She stepped out of the way when I rushed toward her. "Chief?"

"We're fine," I said. "Anybody asks, we're not here."

"Put me down!" Ayla yelled again.

I knew how this looked. Like I'd just scooped up the most beautiful woman to ever set foot in this town and was carting her away for purposes of my own. But now wasn't the time for explanations.

Once I was through the main entrance, I turned right. Headed for the bathroom. It was empty. I barreled inside, switched on the light, twisted the lock.

I set Ayla down, and she tried to wiggle her way past me for the door.

"Oh, hell no. You're not going anywhere."

"You can't keep me in here." Her glare was enough to send a lesser man running with his tail between his legs. Or more likely, with his balls shriveling.

"Actually, I can." I backed her up against the wall, my palms pressing to either side of her to cage her in. "You're out of danger. Take a moment. Breathe."

"Don't tell me what to do." Her deep green eyes glinted with fury.

"Are you all right? Did one of those assholes out there hurt you?" My focus raked down her body, scanning for injuries. She had on a long coat and a soft-looking dress that flared out at her waist and ended above her knees, revealing plenty of tan, shapely leg. Her smooth skin disappeared into a pair of cowboy boots. The leather was broken-in like she wore them a lot.

"Could you give me a little space? Or is that too much to ask? Assuming you're done ogling me."

"I wasn't *ogling*." But I did drop my arms and stepped back, keeping myself in front of the door in case she tried to make a break for it again. Or maybe claw me with those pointy pink nails. "Just assessing if you're hurt. That's my job."

"Just your job. Not like you really care."

"Of course I care." I swallowed down my protest, regaining my calm. *You could try being grateful*, I thought, but managed to keep that comment to myself. "Do you need medical assistance?"

"I'm not hurt. But my driver Bryan is. He got punched in the face, and he's still out there. He was trying to protect me."

Did she mean that big guy with the bloody nose? My insides did a weird shimmy. "My officers are sorting things out. They'll call paramedics. It's better if you stay put. If I take you back out there right now, it'll cause more of a scene."

Her scowl deepened, but she didn't disagree.

There was something magnetic about Ayla Maxwell. Most of the world knew that already. I'd seen it in her music videos and photos of her online. Seen it the times that we'd crossed paths before.

Magnetic, and also frustrating. Because she took offense at every little thing I said or did.

But with her skin flushed and her chest heaving and her intense gaze locked on mine, I had never seen anything so breathtaking.

My radio squawked. "Chief, come in."

Lifting one arm, I tapped the button at my shoulder. "Chief here. I've got Ms. Maxwell secured in the market. Stand by." Then I brought my eyes back to Ayla's face. "What happened?" I asked. "How did this start?"

"You're blaming me, aren't you?"

"Did I say I was blaming you?"

"It's obvious. You hate me. Every time we've met, you've made it clear that you don't want me in Silver Ridge."

My eyebrows lifted. "I'm not the one flipping people the bird unprovoked on a public street."

Ayla flinched. "I guess that wasn't my finest moment." She sat on the closed toilet seat lid. "I can't believe this."

I leaned against the wall. "Not a typical afternoon for me either."

"You don't lock women in bathrooms with you on any given Thursday?"

"I prefer to lock women in bathrooms with me on Saturdays."

Ayla almost snickered before remembering herself.

I pressed my lips together to stifle my own urge to laugh. None of this was funny.

The setting was pretty absurd, though. A painted wooden sign across from the toilet said, *Go with the flow*. Frilly curtains hung over the high window, and a wallpaper border near the ceiling featured dancing gnomes. At least Rosie's employees kept the place scrupulously clean.

We were both quiet for several breaths. I crossed my arms, shifting from one boot to the other. "Can you tell me what happened?" I asked again.

She cleared her throat. "Um, Bryan and I were going to do some shopping. Some college guys were cat-calling me from across the street. Making rude gestures."

The muscle at my jaw pulsed. Those little shits. "Not locals, I'm guessing?"

She frowned. "Why is that important?"

"Because if they're Silver Ridge boys, I'll make sure their parents hand their asses to them. Or I'll do it myself."

Ayla paused, teeth tugging at her lower lip. "They looked more like tourists. Dressed like they'd been skiing. I guess they decided to continue their vacay with some light sexual harassment."

I shifted, crossing my arms. Cat-calling wasn't illegal, but it still made the anger in my blood reach a low simmer. "I wish you'd called the non-emergency line. I've told you in the past that my officers and I are here to help."

"Yes, you've been helpful, and you've made me feel bad about it every time."

"That was never my intention. This is my job, and I'll do it. If you'd called, I could've had a word with them, that's all. Before they caused a bigger issue."

"You assume every problem around here is caused by an outsider."

Not true. But I wasn't going to start arguing with her again either. "These upstanding citizens who harassed you were part of the street brawl, I imagine?"

She nodded. "Bryan and I went into a boutique. We were there for about half an hour, bought a few things. When we were ready to leave, we noticed there was a crowd gathered outside. The college guys in ski jackets were among them. Bryan tried to get me through the crowd, but things went downhill fast. Somebody grabbed my wrist. I didn't even see who. I think Bryan might've pushed the guy, trying to get him away from me, and then Bryan took a fist to the nose." She shivered. "I hope he's okay."

Sounded like she really cared about the guy. Was he more than her driver? Was he her lover?

There was that hot jab of discomfort again.

But I was glad he'd defended her. Suggested he might deserve her.

"Your friend was going strong a couple minutes ago when I saw him. Bryan might have a broken nose, but he'll be fine."

"Yeah. Um, thank you for getting me out of there. I'll have to thank your officers as well."

A thank you, I thought. *Was that so hard?*

"You're welcome. Nobody should be subjected to that kind of harassment or attack, and on behalf of Silver Ridge, I apologize that it happened."

Her eyes lifted, two spots of vivid green that pulled me in.

Then she blinked, squinting at the wall in front of her. "Does that sign actually say, *Go with the flow*?"

I didn't stop myself from laughing that time. "Yep. With a waterfall in the background. Rosie owns the market, and she has an odd sense of humor." Which had to explain what drew her to Jimmy Perkins.

"And a distinctive decorating style."

"Gnome wallpaper isn't popular in LA?"

"That trend must've missed the west coast." Suddenly Ayla was smiling tentatively. Like we were sharing a moment instead of clashing.

And *fuck me*, that smile of hers. So different from her videos. This one was almost shy, pink full lips with a hint of her front teeth.

It hit me like an unstoppable force, making it hard to breathe.

Then that brief moment was gone as quickly as it had started.

Her gaze broke from mine, her eyelashes fluttering. "Can you find out what's going on out there?"

On the radio, I asked Susan for an update. "Hey, Chief. We've got the brawlers separated and we're taking statements. Some suspects took off on foot, but we've got plenty of witnesses. Just doing our best out here to manage the scene."

"I'm sure you've got it well in hand. Do you have a Bryan..." I glanced at Ayla.

"Krueger," she supplied.

"A Bryan Krueger. He's in town with Ms. Maxwell."

"Yes, sir. He's here. I spoke to him. He's getting treated for minor injuries by one of the fire department EMTs. Bloody nose and split knuckles. But otherwise in good shape."

Ayla exhaled, her shoulders relaxing.

"Got it. I'm still inside the market with Ms. Maxwell. I'll need someone to clear the way for us so I can get her out of here without causing another scene."

"Copy that, Chief. Could also use your guidance on who to bring down to the station for booking."

I put a hand on my hip. "Everyone involved in the fight. We can't take this lightly." I didn't want to send the impression that people could show up in my town, start knocking heads together, and skate without any repercussions.

"Yes, Chief."

I signed off just as Ayla leaped up to standing. "Wait a minute, does that really mean you're arresting *everyone*? That doesn't include Bryan, right?"

"Everyone means everyone."

"But you can't arrest Bryan. *Please*. He was only trying to help me. And defend himself. The other guy punched him first."

"All I saw was Bryan's fist landing in someone else's stomach. I'll let the Hart County district attorney sort that out."

"But this is bullshit!" She marched up to me, which was just a couple of steps in the small room. Ayla only reached my upper chest but glared up at me like she was ready for battle.

I kept my tone level. "If I take everyone involved in that fight into custody except Ayla Maxwell's boyfriend, how will that look?"

"I told you. He's my driver, not my boyfriend."

"Not like I care either way." *Liar*, I told myself, but seriously, I was just trying to do my job. I wasn't the bad guy here. "Let's focus on one thing at a time. If you choose to bail Bryan out of jail later on, that's your choice."

"*Bail*? He didn't do anything wrong."

"That may be what the investigation proves in the end. But I can't show favoritism."

Her eyes flashed. "Then you can arrest me too."

"*What*?"

"Arrest me."

"I'm not arresting you."

"I was involved in the fight. Seems like favoritism to me."

"Settle down. There are no cameras in here, Ms. Maxwell. You're being dramatic."

Her cheeks glowed pink with fury. "And you're being an asshole, Chief Landry."

You want to see me being an asshole? I put my hands on my hips, willing myself to stay calm. But this was ridiculous. "Arrest you for what? You didn't throw any punches."

"For assault on a peace officer."

"You didn't—"

Ayla poked her finger into my chest. It didn't hurt. I'd had much worse from my nephew Ollie. It would've been downright cute if it wasn't out of line.

I stared at her for a moment. "You think this is some kind of joke?"

"Do I look like I'm laughing?" She poked me again, harder, directly above the nipple of my left pec. "Arrest me."

Ow.

Okay, that time, it kinda stung. And more than anything, it pissed me off. A burst of heat traveled up my center. A warning sign that I was about to lose my temper like she'd already lost hers, and no amount of yoga breathing was going to cool me down.

This diva insisted on testing my patience? I was about to show her *exactly* how much of an asshole I could be.

"Fine. You really want it to go down this way? You've got it, Princess."

"Don't call me princess!"

I spun her around and tugged her hands behind her back, reaching for my cuffs. The snick of metal was loud in the small room.

"Ayla Maxwell, you're under arrest."

EIGHT

Ayla

I WAS USUALLY PRETTY good at keeping my more extreme impulses in check. Example one: I hadn't decked that asshole earlier who told me to *show my tits*.

But when I got pushed too far, I couldn't help but react.

Something about Teller Landry just made me lose all common sense.

It didn't help that his firm touch as he put me in handcuffs ignited every one of my nerve endings like sparklers on New Year's. A flush spread over my skin.

"I hope this is worth whatever point you think you're making," he said.

"I did what I had to."

"Stay here and behave. Can you do that?" Teller turned me around and nudged me up against the bathroom wall. I wasn't sure when he'd switched from "Chief Landry" to "Teller" in my head. Maybe around the time that we shared a brief laugh about the gnome wallpaper.

"Yes, sir," I replied sarcastically.

Even now, his eyes betrayed a hint of amusement, even though his mouth remained in a stern frown. Those eyes were a pale green like cold sea glass, rimmed with thick light-brown lashes, and had no right to be so mesmerizing. Same with the broad shoulders and thick biceps that strained his dark navy police uniform.

If I'd admired Bryan's physique earlier, that was nothing to the chief's effect on me. Especially after spending the last ten minutes trapped in this tiny bathroom with him.

When he'd first carried me in here, I hardly knew what was happening. Yes, he'd been trying to get me somewhere safe. But I wasn't used to being manhandled. Teller had thrown me around like I was a doll.

I hadn't realized before how *big* Teller was. Not just his frame but the way he took up space, which was all about charisma. Fine lines traced the skin beside his eyes, and the scar down his cheek made his glower even more commanding. The touches of silver in his short dark-blond hair made him distinguished and somehow amplified his sex appeal.

I wasn't usually drawn to older men, but Teller Landry was no ordinary specimen. He was larger than life.

No wedding ring, either.

Why was I even noticing that? So what if he was attractive. Or single.

"*Stay*," he commanded. Then he unlocked the door and stepped out, leaving the spicy scent of aftershave in his wake. The bathroom suddenly felt huge and empty. And the gravity of what I'd done started to hit.

Oh, this was bad.

Every tabloid reporter would probably have a simultaneous orgasm when they heard about me getting arrested. My publicist was going to murder me.

Also, terrible example for me to set for Maisie. Except I did want her to learn to stand up for herself and for others. So there was that.

I'd just been so...*frustrated*. By the way my day got ruined. By how unfair it was that Bryan, one of the few men in my everyday life who I could trust, was going to jail because of me. And with

Teller being all bossy and gruff and intimidating, I just couldn't take any more.

I'd felt cornered. Like a rubber band pulled too far, I'd snapped. I chose violence.

Okay, I *did* regret that part. I shouldn't have put hands on Teller to make a point. Even if he *did* put his hands on me when he picked me up and carried me into this bathroom in the first place.

But now I was the one in handcuffs.

Also, my finger hurt from jabbing it into Teller's chest. *Ow.* He wasn't wearing a bulletproof vest under there, was he? It had felt like a solid brick wall.

How much muscle was he packing beneath that uniform?

The door squeaked as he returned to the bathroom a couple of minutes later. "We're going out the market's back exit. My SUV will be waiting. Someone's bringing it around. If we're lucky, no one will get any photos of you in cuffs, but I can't make any promises."

"I know. I, um, I apologize. I shouldn't have hit you."

He cocked his hip. "You didn't hit me. It was a poke."

"But there's no excuse for using violence. I'm sincerely sorry."

A smirk appeared on his lips, then smoothed away. "I accept your apology. But you wanted me to arrest you, so that's what I'm doing."

"I'll accept the consequences."

He dipped his chin in a nod. "Alright, Troublemaker. Let's go."

"At least *Troublemaker* is better than *Princess.*"

His lips twitched again.

Teller led me through the market. Rosie waved at me, while a few other shoppers gawked as I passed. I smiled sheepishly. Thankfully, nobody was taking any photos.

Maybe we could all laugh about this someday. *Right*? Because it was pretty ridiculous.

His Silver Ridge PD vehicle idled in the alley behind the market.

It was getting dark out, which meant most people were at dinner by now. Or maybe still distracted by the police activity out front.

"I lost my purse somewhere," I said. "And my shopping bags."

"Already spoke to Officer Nichols. She's got your belongings secured."

Then I remembered that I was supposed to be meeting Ashford and Emma and everyone else at Hearthstone any minute now. Crap. I didn't want to ruin the bachelor/bachelorette party.

Maybe I could get a message to them that something else came up, so they wouldn't worry when I didn't show.

"Could I use my phone?" I asked.

"We'll see once we get to the station. It's not far." He opened the front passenger door of his SUV.

"I'm supposed to ride in back, aren't I? I'm a prisoner."

Teller sighed. "Suit yourself." He closed that door, then opened the one to the backseat. "Get in. Justice awaits."

I slid into the back with difficulty, considering my wrists were still cuffed. Teller reached in to stretch the seatbelt across me.

"You do that for all your prisoners?" I asked.

"Just the extra troublesome ones." He smirked, but his large hands were gentle as they slid the seatbelt buckle into place with a click.

After getting in, he put the engine in gear and drove down the alley. "Might want to hide your face, unless you want someone to snap a photo."

Good point. I bent over and laid on the seat.

When we parked a few minutes later, I sat up tentatively. We were at the back of a sprawling, one-story brick building. Nobody was around as Teller got me out of the backseat and led me inside.

A couple of curious faces glanced over from open doorways, eyes going wide as we passed. I heard voices and activity elsewhere in the station.

I'd always wondered what it was like to get arrested. I just hadn't expected to experience it firsthand.

Would I get a mug shot for the media to splash all over the internet? Nausea churned in my stomach. If Teller wanted to make this painful for me, he could.

Yet when we'd been stuck in the bathroom, he'd actually seemed concerned about my welfare. I was pretty sure he'd even made a couple of jokes. He'd definitely made me smile, however quickly that moment had passed.

Teller led me down a hallway to an office with *Chief Landry* written on the door. He nudged me toward one of the chairs in front of his desk. "Sit there. Don't touch anything."

"Can I take my coat off?" My jacket was unbuttoned, but still too heavy for the temperature in here.

With another put-upon sigh, Teller fished a key from his pocket. "Alright. Turn around." He unlocked the cuff from one of my wrists, then tugged my coat off my shoulders, careful not to yank my hair.

The slide of his palms down my arms sent tingles dancing through me.

"I could've taken it off myself."

"I'm not trusting you to do much at the moment. Now sit down, Troublemaker." He tossed my coat onto the far seat. I sat in the closer one.

Then he took the dangling open end of the handcuffs, which were still attached to my left wrist, and fastened it onto the arm of the chair.

"I need to go handle some things. I'll be back."

"Prisoners are supposed to get a phone call, aren't they?"

"Just gonna have to wait. Try to be on good behavior."

"What about Bryan? How is he?"

"*Wait*." Teller gave me a wry look before he left the office.

Welp, here I was. In a police station under arrest. Taking a hard look at my life choices.

The chief's office was exactly what I would've expected of him. Everything nice and neat. He had a display case of challenge coins on one wall. Hardly any personal photos except for one with him, his sister Piper, and her son Ollie.

I was twenty-seven with a flush bank account, but I still barely felt like an adult. Teller gave off extremely grown-man vibes. Like he was too busy adulting to have much time to enjoy himself. Even in that family photo, he looked serious. As if he were contemplating the weight of the world.

Ashford had mentioned that Teller served as a Green Beret and had been wounded in action. He was the kind of guy my father would've pointed to and said, *Now there's a real man*.

Real men, according to the colonel, ruled their families with an iron fist and didn't put up with backtalk or independence from their women.

Who was Teller Landry underneath his scowl and his uniform?

My gaze continued to move around the room, taking in a bulletin board with photos tacked onto it. Some showed houses with broken windows. Another with red spray paint across a barn door. Next to the photos was a map with red pins on it, marking locations.

I wondered what that was about.

There was a knock, and the door opened. A uniformed officer in wire-rimmed glasses stepped into the office, balancing two coffee cups. "Uh, hello Miss Maxwell. I brought coffee. In case you'd like some. One black, one with cream and sugar, since I didn't know how you take it."

He held out both paper cups like an offering.

"That's nice of you. I'll take the sugary one. I could use a pick-me-up." I lifted my free hand, and he gave me the coffee. "Thanks."

"I'm Officer Duncan, but Seth is fine. I mean, if you want to call me that." He blushed.

Seth had medium-brown hair. Boyish features, though I guessed he was in his late thirties. His glasses made him look studious, but he was tall and leanly muscled. That kind of build could hide a lot of strength.

I sipped the coffee. *Yikes*. Too much sugar, but I swallowed a gulp anyway and smiled. "I appreciate it."

Seth glanced over his shoulder. "I can't believe the chief arrested you. This has to be some kind of misunderstanding, right?"

"You don't think I'm a hardened criminal?"

He sputtered a laugh. "I know exactly who you are. I mean, wow. You're...you're just, *wow*. Right here in real life."

I didn't remember him from my previous trips to Silver Ridge, so I figured he was new. Seth was all *ah-shucks* attitude. But then his gaze lingered a while on my dress, moving down my legs to my boots. I shifted, and the chain on the handcuffs jingled.

I'd known I was trapped here before, but now I truly *felt* it.

"Could I get your autograph?" he asked. "For my cousin in Denver?"

But before I could answer, a deep voice boomed from somewhere outside Teller's office.

"*Where is she*?"

NINE

Ayla

I KNEW THAT VOICE. *Ashford.* Relief flooded through me.

Then I heard Grace. "Where's Ayla? No, we will not wait for the chief. I want to see for myself that she's okay."

"In here," I called out.

Seth left the room, melting away like he'd never been there. A moment later, familiar faces appeared in the open doorway. Emma and Grace came in first. Emma's jaw dropped when she saw the cuff on my wrist.

I lifted my arm, shaking the chain. "Not my best look. How'd you guys know where I was?"

"Rosie from the market called Dixie, and Dixie called me," Ashford said, walking inside. "Word is spreading all over town that Ayla Maxwell was led away in cuffs."

Emma smiled ruefully. "The Silver Ridge gossip pipeline can almost be worse than the tabloids. *Almost.*"

"We still haven't gotten a straight answer about what you supposedly did," Grace said. "Not that it matters necessarily. I figure you've got lawyers, but Dane can have a top litigator on a plane like that." She snapped her fingers.

Dane up-nodded from the doorway. "Hi, Ayla. You okay? Do you need representation?"

"I'll be fine." I cringed. "But I'm so sorry I ruined tonight. We're supposed to be celebrating."

Emma reached for Ashford's hand. "You didn't ruin anything. This is going to become a classic story. How you got thrown in the pokey during our wedding weekend."

At least someone else could see the humor in this situation.

"Who the hell told y'all you could wait in my office?" Teller grumbled, pushing his way inside. "It's anarchy around here."

"Sorry, Chief!" a female voice said. An older woman with strawberry-blond hair popped in. "They snuck past me." Then she aimed a wink in my direction. Seemed like I had an ally.

Teller sighed. "It's fine, Susan. I'll deal with them."

Grace straightened up to her full height, all of five feet. "We're not leaving until you set Ayla free."

"Grace is about ready to stage a jailbreak," Ashford said. "She's serious, man."

Teller went over to his desk and sat behind it. His expression was neutral, but a vein at his temple twitched. The others gathered around me, taking up most of the space. It wasn't a tiny room, but it wasn't sized to hold this many people.

And they were all here for *me*. Not for the famous singer, but Ashford's sister-in-law. Maisie's aunt.

"What'll it take to make this go away?" Dane asked.

Teller squinted. "Not every issue can be solved with money, Knightly."

And then suddenly everyone was talking over each other. Grace asking Teller if I'd had the chance to call a lawyer, Emma reasoning that there were better ways to work all this out. Ashford demanding to know the charges against me.

Teller didn't say anything yet, probably because he couldn't get a word in. His gaze moved over to me. I took a sip of the over-sweet coffee. But it reminded me of Seth and his roving gaze, and I set it aside.

When everyone paused to take a breath, Teller said, "Are you all finished? Are you ready to give me a chance to speak? I arrested

Ms. Maxwell for her own good." Teller held up his hands before the others could get started again. "Because she was determined that was what she wanted."

"Is that true?" Grace asked me.

"Yes. I was trying to make a point."

Teller angled his head. "And you made it. I'm not actually going to book you."

The chain on my cuffs rattled as I sat forward. "Wait. You were going on and on about not showing favoritism. What about Bryan? If you're booking him, then you're booking me."

"Your bodyguard got himself arrested?" Ashford muttered. "That's concerning."

Emma playfully swatted her fiancé's shoulder. "I'm sure there's an explanation. He seemed great when we met him last night."

"Last night, I was busy trying to keep Maisie from sticking penne on all her fingers."

Teller's mouth twitched in that movement I was starting to think of as his version of a smile. "I'm not commenting on Bryan Krueger's case. The sooner you all get out of my office, the sooner we can sort this out and get on with our evening. I'm supposed to be watching Ollie right now. I'm half an hour late getting to Piper's. I already got an earful from my sister about this mess on the phone just now, so I don't need it from any of you."

I bit my lip guiltily and looked down at my lap.

"How about this," Emma said. "Everyone can meet at our place tonight instead. We'll grab some food, and once you and Ayla work things out, you can join us. I'll let Dixie know to bring Maisie over. And Piper can bring Ollie. It'll be more fun to have all of us together, including the kids. And you, Teller." She nodded at the chief. "Everyone."

I knew exactly what she was doing. Worrying that my presence would draw too much attention at the brewery after what had happened. She was probably right. But it didn't lessen the sting. "I screwed up your bachelorette party. I suck."

Emma squeezed my shoulder. "You didn't. We can hang out at Hearthstone anytime. But it's not every day I have the chance to get our whole group of family and friends together to celebrate. It'll be relaxed and comfortable, and we won't have to worry about any problems."

Such as tourists causing a riot over me.

"Okay." So much for spending this weekend feeling like a normal person.

They trailed out one by one. Grace was the last to leave, shooting Teller a disapproving look before Dane put his hand on her lower back to steer her on her way. "Make this right, Teller," she said.

Teller got up and crossed to the door, closing it. "I've even got Grace mad at me. Now I really know it's serious." He fished a key from his pocket and slid it into the lock on my handcuffs.

"It's hard to tell if you're kidding or not." I absentmindedly rubbed the wrist he just freed, though the cuff hadn't been tight.

"I get that I'm currently the villain in your story, but not everyone thinks I'm that bad."

"Still can't tell if you're kidding," I said under my breath.

Teller settled back into his seat across the desk from me. "I had a few words with Bryan Krueger. I've decided to consider him a witness and nothing more. We're going to turn him loose."

I exhaled out a heavy breath. "Seriously? He's not under arrest?"

"I've already seen a couple of videos recorded by bystanders of the street fight. It's clear Bryan didn't start things. Bryan also stressed that he doesn't want to press charges against the idiot who hit him."

Whoever had punched Bryan in the face deserved punishment, but I could understand. Bryan probably just wanted this to get resolved with as little fuss as possible.

"So you're letting everyone go free?"

Teller rubbed a hand across his square jaw. "I'm not okay with people brawling in the middle of Main Street. But the tourists who were involved say they'll be leaving town tomorrow anyway. They also said they'd make a public apology to you and your driver. There were no significant injuries. So this might be worth an alternative resolution instead of filling up my jail overnight. Saves me a hell of a lot of paperwork."

"Thank you," I breathed.

"But I've got one condition. You need to keep your head down for the rest of your visit here. Any minute now, those videos of the fight will get posted online, if they're not circulating already. Everybody in the world will know you're here. I'm willing to let things slide this time, but if Bryan is involved in another brawl? I won't be able to go easy."

His strident tone made me want to argue. But his point was valid. This weekend was supposed to be about Emma and Ashford, not me. "I'm leaving the day after the wedding. Then you won't have to deal with me anymore for a while."

"I think that's for the best, Ms. Maxwell. Don't you?"

Probably. It was a reminder that I didn't really belong in Silver Ridge, and that hurt.

But when it came to Teller Landry, I didn't know anymore *what* to feel.

TEN

Teller

By the time I finally reached Emma and Ashford's building, every light was on. It sounded like the party was well underway.

As I stepped inside, music and voices greeted me. The downstairs of the building was devoted to teaching spaces for Ashford's martial arts school and Emma's music lessons. They lived in the apartment upstairs. But tonight, it seemed like the impromptu party had taken over both floors.

I heard a laugh that might've been Ayla's, and the sound twisted around my spine, refusing to let go.

At the station, it had taken another two hours to square things away. We'd released Bryan Krueger and the other brawlers with strict warnings. If they stepped a toe out of line again, I was going to make them sorry they'd stayed in Silver Ridge. Ayla had waited for Bryan, and they'd left the station together.

A couple of brawling tourists had wanted to apologize to Ayla personally. But she didn't need to give those dumbasses more attention. So instead, I made them sit and write out a one-page, single-spaced apology essay. Mrs. Torkelson, my third-grade teacher, would've been proud.

I dodged as Stella loped by, ears flapping, followed by Ollie. My nephew changed course when he saw me, but didn't slow his speed. He lowered his shoulder and crashed into me like a defensive lineman. *Oof.*

"Uncle Tell, you're here! Finally! You're super late."

"Really sorry about that, buddy. Work stuff." But guilt closed its fist around my heart and squeezed. I hated disappointing him. Ollie already had too many disappointments courtesy of his father. "I'm here now."

Ollie's face scrunched up, dodging when I tried ruffling his hair. "We were supposed to work on the treehouse."

"Can't work on the treehouse when it's after dark, bud. We'll do that soon. I'm sure you've been having a blast here with Stella and Maisie."

"Yeah, I guess. But Maisie just wants to play with these dumb horses in her room upstairs. It's lame."

I arched an eyebrow. "That's not a great way to talk about your best friend."

"Sorry," he muttered.

Ollie was only nine, but he'd been shadowing the middle-school boys up the street lately. Any minute now, he wouldn't be interested in that treehouse at all. Time was always slipping by way too fast.

If not for that mess with Ayla, it would've been Ollie and me tonight. But Ollie needed more than just me and his mom. I needed more too. I'd been keeping to myself way too much, neglecting my friendships. Being antisocial. Almost arresting Ashford's sister-in-law hadn't helped with my standing around here.

I really didn't want to be the bad guy.

Piper appeared, carrying a longneck beer. "Teller, you made it!"

I stood up, ruffling Ollie's hair again, and he ran off after Stella. "Yeah, long day."

My sister shrugged. "I guess you had a decent excuse. Sounded a lot more exciting than my afternoon cleaning out the espresso grinder." Piper's hair was a similar shade of dirty blond to mine, slightly darker at the roots but paler at the tips. "Food's upstairs in the kitchen."

"Good, I'm starved. What about the bride and groom? I should say hello." And hopefully get on better footing with them.

"Living room, last I checked." She pointed her beer at me. "If you can get Ollie to eat some dinner, not just cake and chips, I will be forever grateful."

"Consider it done."

"He always listens to you. It's not fair."

"He doesn't *always*. But I do get a lot of practice convincing people to listen. Especially when they don't want to."

"I would love that superpower."

I smiled. "You feeling any better about the Danny situation?"

"It is what it is. But you're right. We'll get through it."

"We will." I lifted my chin. "Go have fun. I know the plan changed, but I can still be in charge of Ollie tonight." I would let my nephew run wild for a few more minutes, then find him and get him to eat.

"You're the best."

"I know."

I went upstairs in search of food. Passed through the living room and said hello to Emma and Ashford, who didn't seem so pissed at me anymore. Then continued on to the kitchen.

Callum, Ashford's younger brother, was there breaking open a bag of tortilla chips. "Yo, Teller. You want guac? My special recipe."

"I've never said no to guac, and I don't plan to start anytime soon. Need help?"

"Find a bowl for these chips. Aside from that, I just need you to stand back and let the master work."

I chuckled, grabbing the chip bag. "I'll stay out of the way. But can you set some aside with no jalapeños?"

"Because you can't take the heat? Surprised at you, Chief."

"No, for the kids. I have to make sure Ollie eats dinner."

"Then I don't envy you. But I'll keep the jalapeños on the side."

"Much appreciated."

Callum pointed at my clothes. "You look nice, by the way."

"Thanks," I said evenly. I smoothed a hand down my shirt. I was wearing dark jeans and a button-down. Something had possessed me to dress up a bit for tonight, since it wasn't just me and Ollie.

He cut into an avocado. "Can't believe you arrested Ayla, though."

I groaned. "I have to hear about that from you too?"

"Dude, you're going to hear about it from *everybody*."

The O'Neals had lived across the street from us when Piper and I were growing up. Piper and Grace had been best friends pretty much since birth, while I'd been closest to the oldest O'Neal brother, Grayden. Grayden and I had both been in charge, since our parents hadn't been around much. Grayden and I had also been the first to leave Silver Ridge for the Army.

What happened with Grayden after that was a very long story. Even I didn't know all of it. Grayden had reconnected with Grace in the last few months, or so I'd heard. Callum and Ashford still didn't talk to him.

I hadn't spoken to my former best friend in, what, ten years? Twelve? But if it didn't impact me or Piper, then I figured I should stay out of that drama. Wasn't my place.

Anyway, Ashford and Callum were like younger brothers to me as much as Grace was like another baby sister. I considered all of them family, but when it came to Ashford and Callum, we'd never been super close.

Callum was easygoing in all the ways I wasn't. He was a volunteer firefighter, so I'd crossed paths with him plenty of times in dangerous situations. He had a knack for keeping the mood light, which could make all the difference to a team's morale. Even if I hadn't been the police chief, I never would've been the jokester. But it took all kinds.

"I didn't *actually* arrest Ayla," I said. "I let her off with a warning." A few chips escaped as I dumped the bag into a serving bowl.

"Good thing. Otherwise, you'd have a team of scary lawyers flying in from LA as we speak to flay you alive."

I grunted my disapproval of that sentiment. That wasn't why I'd let Ayla, Bryan, and the others off the hook. "I'd be more worried about Grace, honestly. She was on the warpath."

Callum laughed. "And what about that guy who came to town with Ayla? You let the boyfriend go too, I hear?"

"Bryan's her driver and bodyguard, not her boyfriend."

Callum stopped his work on the cutting board and looked up. "I stand corrected."

I shrugged nonchalantly, as if I hadn't just snapped at him. "Just trying to be accurate. Facts matter."

He chuckled. "Got it, Chief."

I crossed my arms and glanced around. "Is Bryan here tonight?"

"You seem very concerned about Bryan's whereabouts."

"I'd like to know if a man I almost arrested is at a party with me."

"It *is* a small town. I'm sure it's happened before."

Okay, that was true.

Callum smirked like this was top-notch entertainment. "But no, I don't think Bryan's here. Ayla is, though. Nobody seems to know what she did to get arrested. She's not talking."

I rolled my tongue against my teeth. "She assaulted a police officer. Namely, me."

"Holy sh—" Callum dropped his voice to a whisper. "*Shit*. I knew Ayla was pretty fierce, but I didn't know she had that in her."

I'd gotten more than I bargained for with her, that was for sure. No wonder she'd built such a successful career. A lot of that kind of thing was luck, but there had to be countless hours of hard work behind it.

Ayla Maxwell was a whole lot of determination and a fierce attitude wrapped up in a gorgeous package.

Maybe I'd been wrong about her, and she wasn't the spoiled diva I had thought. But I doubted she would ever let me close enough to find out.

"She wanted to make a point," I said. "Whole thing was ridiculous, really. It got out of hand. Not sure if she has an issue with all police, but she definitely doesn't like me."

Callum turned thoughtful as he mashed the avocado in a wooden bowl. "You remember Ashford and Lori met on-base, right? Lori and Ayla's father was a colonel and a certified asshole." His voice was still low, so nobody else but me could hear him. "Colonel Hopkins was the reason Ayla ran away at sixteen. That's why Ayla and Lori didn't speak for so long. Ayla wanted a clean break from her family."

My brow furrowed. "Was their father abusive?"

"I don't know the whole story. But if she's got a problem with authority figures, that could be one of the reasons why."

Hell, I hadn't known that. Ayla had a way of pushing my buttons. I hadn't realized I was pushing hers right back without meaning to. No wonder she got so defensive with me.

Some people assumed I was a stereotypical cop who wanted to throw his weight around. Feel powerful. But that wasn't me. I just wanted to keep our town safe and thriving. My daily job had a lot more to do with community service than locking people in jail.

But it wasn't just the fact that I was a cop. The evidence of my military service was right there on my skin, the scars prominent for anyone to see.

Did I remind Ayla of a man who'd abused her?

Fuck, I hated that thought.

The past was never really gone, was it? You could tell yourself it didn't matter. But those old wounds still ached. And those old voices echoed.

ELEVEN

Teller

I WAS ABOUT to doze off when I heard someone climbing the step ladder to the roof of Emma and Ashford's building. A pale blond head appeared, glowing in the moonlight. "Oh. I didn't realize anyone was up here."

She turned to go.

"Wait, it's fine," I murmured, so I wouldn't wake the sleeping nine-year-old in my lap. "Not much happening, but feel free to join us."

Ayla stepped onto the roof. "I don't want to wake him."

"You won't. Ollie sleeps like a drunk in the tank. Hard part's going to be getting him downstairs and home to bed."

Ayla walked closer, her soft features coming into view. She had her long coat back on, along with the same cowboy boots from earlier, and a beanie on her head that she'd probably borrowed from Emma.

Wrapping her arms around herself, she turned her face to the sky and inhaled. "Wow. The sky is so clear. All those stars. Hard to believe there's a storm coming in a couple days."

I breathed in. "Smells like snow."

"But not like it's going to snow *now*, right? I thought it wasn't coming until Saturday."

"True, but forecasts change. Plenty of other unexpected things have happened since today started." Reaching down, I grabbed the extra blanket we'd brought up earlier. "Here. You're shivering."

"You don't need it?"

Ollie had one blanket wrapped around him, and he was keeping me warm. "Nah, I've got my own personal furnace right here."

After draping the blanket around her shoulders, Ayla sat in the chair beside me.

We were both quiet, glancing sidelong at one another. Like we were each waiting for the other to speak first.

Earlier, I'd convinced Ollie to eat a couple of chicken tacos with guacamole. Then we'd joined in while everyone played a trivia game. It got raucous, especially after Piper pulled out the Malibu rum.

Ayla had been there in the living room, and I'd given her space. Hadn't wanted to force an interaction, given everything that happened earlier. And given what Callum had told me.

I'd been constantly aware of her, though. Like I could feel her gravitational pull.

But then the kids had gotten bored, so I took Maisie and Ollie up here for some stargazing through Maisie's telescope. Half an hour ago, Ashford called Maisie down to get ready for bed, and since then, I'd been wondering how long I could sit with Ollie like this before my shoulder started giving me too much trouble.

"I assume Maisie's in bed?" I asked.

"Yep. I said goodnight." Ayla snuggled deeper into the blanket. "Thought I'd grab a few minutes of quiet. It's nice."

"It is." I forced myself to look away from her. I was staring.

"Ollie must really trust you. Letting you hold him like that while he sleeps."

"Or he's beyond exhausted from going nonstop all day. He used to be cuddly when he was littler. Lately he's been trying to act like the twelve-year-olds down the street. Skateboards and baggy jeans. He asked Piper to buy him hair gel the other day."

Ayla barked a laugh, hand flying to cover her mouth. "Oh my gosh. I feel the same about Maisie. They grow up too fast. Plenty of kids her age already have phones and social media. She's still a little girl now, but I dread the day I show up with a new toy and she scoffs at me."

"I get it. I never want Ollie to close himself off to affection based on what boys are *supposed* to do."

She tilted her head, turning those expressive eyes on me like she was curious. "I guess it's good he has you."

"I hope so."

My own father had definitely viewed things differently. If I'd reached out for my dad to hold me when I was older than four, my dad would've pushed me away. I could count the number of times he'd ever hugged me on one hand.

And dammit, that had me thinking about Ayla's father again. What she might have gone through.

"I've never seen you out of uniform before," she said.

"Contrary to rumors, it's not surgically attached."

"You're funnier than I expected. I thought you didn't have a sense of humor."

I looked up at the star-filled sky. "Despite my current reputation as the biggest boy scout in Silver Ridge, I was a hellion as a little kid. My kindergarten teacher's worst nightmare. I refused to be tamed."

"*Really*. So Ollie takes after you?"

I turned and gave her a sardonic look.

"I'm not criticizing your nephew! Ollie's as sweet as can be. Maisie adores him. But he does keep things exciting. He's... spirited."

I laughed. "Yep, that's what they call it these days. Ollie's got a big spirit and then some. But if he's acting out, that has more to do with his dad not being around. I had to grow up fast, and I don't want that for Ollie."

"Same," Ayla said softly. "I grew up way too fast."

And there went that fist in my chest, squeezing at the thought of Ayla hurting.

I knew almost nothing about this woman except what she'd revealed in her song lyrics, or what other people had said about her. And I wasn't dumb enough to believe that was the whole picture.

But I found myself actually wanting to know. I was curious about the real Ayla. She was more than I'd given her credit for.

Ayla gathered her hair over one shoulder, and I caught the scent of caramel. "I wanted to thank you again for letting Bryan go and not formally booking him. That would've been a mark on his record, and he might've gotten fired from the agency he works for. He has a wife and son to provide for."

"Not a problem." But I didn't mind hearing Bryan was officially off the market and not a potential love interest. As if Ayla's love interests had any relevance to *me*. "To be honest, I wasn't thinking that much about Bryan when I made the decision. I did it for you."

"For *me*?"

Shit, I needed to backtrack. That sounded like I was trying to make a move on her. "You impressed me with how tenacious you were. Defending your friend. Could've gone about it a better way—"

"No argument there. I still can't believe I put my hands on you."

I was holding my nephew, so I didn't let myself think about Ayla putting hands on me in a different context. "*But*, you convinced me I should be more flexible. Being a troublemaker isn't always a bad thing."

She didn't say anything, and she was looking down, so I couldn't see her expression.

Ayla was close enough that I imagined putting my arm around her, drawing her up against me. Which was a foolish urge.

This woman didn't like me. It was possible I downright scared her.

Yet she was sitting here with me. Relaxing in the quiet darkness. Like this wasn't such a bad place to be.

"Is Bryan feeling okay?" I asked. "He took quite a punch. He declined a visit to the hospital."

She glanced up. My gaze zeroed in on her lips as they pursed. "He mentioned he had a headache. Went back to his hotel. But he was a mixed martial arts fighter before."

I whistled. "Then he's probably been hit in the head in the past. If he's had concussions, that makes a subsequent one more likely."

She cursed, pulling her phone from her coat pocket. "I should call him."

"Better yet, I'll send an officer to check on him. If he's not doing well, they'll take him to the hospital."

"One of your officers would do that?"

"Barring some other emergency, yes. Of course. Hell, I would do it myself. But I'd prefer to delegate."

Ayla hesitated, then nodded. "Okay."

I carefully slid a hand into my pocket to extract my work phone and unlocked the screen. "Which hotel is he staying at?"

"I can text you the info."

I gave Ayla my number, and a moment later, a message popped up from her. A ridiculous part of me got a small thrill that I had Ayla Maxwell's phone number. Susan would give me so much shit if she knew, and I deserved it.

Using my voice-to-text feature, I sent a message to the department, asking anyone available to do a welfare check on Bryan Krueger. Since we were a small crew, we often did things informally. "Someone will head over to check on Bryan," I said. "We can go from there."

Ollie shifted around, but he didn't wake up.

"Thank you."

Then another potential issue occurred to me. "Bryan's supposed to drive you to Hartley tomorrow?"

"Yes."

"Well, if he has a concussion, that's not going to work. Plus, if the snowstorm does hit early, I don't love the idea of him driving you if he's not used to it. Same thing if you decide to drive on your own. Unless you have experience driving on icy roads."

She shifted around, pulling the blanket tighter. "I don't. That's why I have a *driver.*"

"Most everyone is heading over to Hartley tomorrow morning. Catch a ride with one of them. Emma and Ashford or Callum. Piper's driving Ollie. She'll have room."

Ayla's lips pursed again. "I don't need you to fix this for me."

"But I'd like to know that you're covered. Just tell me you'll ride along with one of them."

"I have other things I need to do. And besides, Bryan is supposed to drive me directly from the wedding hotel to the airport on Sunday." She cursed, rubbing her face. "Maybe the agency could send someone else. Another driver. I can't miss the wedding."

"You're not going to miss the wedding." I made the decision without allowing too much thought. "I'm going to drive you."

"You don't need to do that. I'll—"

"My plan is to leave tomorrow afternoon. I have responsibilities here before then. You can take care of the things you need to do." Whatever those were. "We'll be there for the whole day on Saturday. And on Sunday, I'll drive you to catch your flight back to LA." No doubt she was flying private, so it was the small regional airport.

"That's an hour each way."

"Yeah, it's nothing." Assuming the plows took care of the snow on the roads by then, but...one thing at a time.

"That's a service you commonly offer? The Silver Ridge Chief of Police drives random people to the airport?"

"You're not random. You're a family friend."

"Whom you can't stand."

Damn, she was calling me out, yet again. Why did I enjoy that so much? "I never said that."

"It was implied by that scowl on your face whenever you see me."

"Am I scowling now?"

Her eyelashes fluttered, and I felt a tug low in my belly. "I guess not."

"It won't be that bad." I pointed at Ollie. "Some people even like me."

"Seems you're not giving me any other choice."

"Don't make me take you back into custody. It'll be far less pleasant a drive if you're in handcuffs."

Her eyes widened.

The fuck are you doing, Landry? I asked myself. Almost sounded like I was flirting with her. Something I was extremely rusty at.

Ollie sat up. "Uncle Teller?" he asked blearily.

"Hey, bud. It's time to head home to bed."

"But the party."

"The party's over, and you're exhausted. C'mon." I nudged him, and his feet landed on the ground. My hand reached out to steady him.

"Don't try to argue, Ollie," Ayla said. "Your uncle is the bossiest man I've ever met."

Ollie half laughed, half yawned. "Yeah, true story."

"Hey!" I looked over at Ayla, and she was smiling back at me, and *fuck* that was a good feeling. Was there any possible way she was feeling it too?

Keep dreaming.

Ayla Maxwell could be with any man she wanted. Actors and rock stars and athletes lined up to date her. I had to put any attraction on my part out of my mind. She was a superstar in her twenties. I was a forty-year-old small-town cop.

But I could make sure she had a good trip, then send her safely on her way back to her glamorous life in Los Angeles. A life I couldn't begin to fathom, much less imagine being a part of.

Ollie wobbled toward the step ladder, so I jumped up to head him off. I had to help him down. "I'll pick you up tomorrow at five p.m.," I said over my shoulder. "Okay? Let me take care of this for you."

"Okay," Ayla whispered.

I saw something in her eyes then that I'd never expected. Trust. And if I reminded her of her father, of a past she wanted to forget, then I knew how much it meant that she was willing to try.

I wanted to deserve the trust Ayla was giving me. It felt like something precious, resting in the palm of my hand. Easy to crush if you didn't take the utmost care. I couldn't say where that image came from. But it felt like the truth.

Come hell or six feet of snow, I was getting her to that wedding.

Fuck. I wasn't sure I could get Ayla to the wedding.

"The mountain pass between here and Hartley will be closed within the hour," I said to my officers.

It was Friday afternoon. Hours before Ayla and I had been scheduled to leave. Overnight, the forecast had shifted, saying the storm would arrive earlier in Hart County than we'd expected. That was bad enough.

But the weather service had just issued another update, and it did not look good.

"This storm is moving very fast," I explained. "Once it hits the mountains, it's going to stall. The weather reports now say it'll be dumping two inches an hour on the pass by tonight. Conditions will be too dangerous for travel." The Department of Transportation had consulted with local authorities before making the final call, but I wouldn't have done anything differently.

"But Ashford and Emma's wedding," Susan said.

"Yes, I *know*. Thankfully, the O'Neals left earlier this morning. Same with Piper. She texted that she and Ollie arrived in Hartley an hour ago. But the pass won't open again until Sunday at the earliest."

And I had to break that news to Ayla. Why hadn't I listened to Jimmy Perkins when he was stocking up on toilet paper? Which was not a thought I'd ever anticipated having.

Seth put his hands on his hips. "We've got a lot of other people heading to Hartley. Both later today and tomorrow."

"Yep. Unfortunately, they won't be going anywhere if they haven't left already. Including me."

All our emergency services would be ready. We prepared regularly for situations like this, and we had major storms every season. But I already expected a flood of phone calls from irate Silver Ridge citizens, blaming me for the closure of the pass.

Then again, there was only one person in town right now who it killed me to disappoint. I remembered that look of trust in her eyes last night.

Surrender wasn't in my nature. There had to be something I could do. I'd given her my word, and I wouldn't break it.

After finishing up our meeting, I went to my office. But instead of going to my desk, I stared at the map of Hart County on my wall.

TWELVE
Ayla

"THANK YOU, Ayla. This has been an absolute pleasure."

I smiled into the camera on my laptop. "For me too."

"We'll have to do it again."

This reporter was from a prestigious magazine, one that managed to hold on to a physical circulation as well as an online following.

I'd been on the cover before. But after my last album's disappointing numbers, they hadn't asked me in a while. This was a big opportunity. A chance to get back to the front of the public's mind. Exactly what I was supposed to want.

"Maybe your publicist will let you answer all my questions next time?" the reporter asked.

"Hey, anything could happen."

He laughed, almost sounding sincere. Finally, the interview ended and the magazine reporter disappeared.

"That went fairly well," Cheryl said. She was still on the call. And she wasn't the only one.

"You were fantastic, Ayla. Just stellar. It's good to see you back at your best." Paul Ruxton sat behind his desk. The floor-to-ceiling windows behind him showed off a view of the beach. My publicist Beth was there too, hovering at the periphery and tapping at her phone now that the interview was over.

I was currently in the classroom where Emma taught music lessons. At least the interview was done, even though I wasn't off the hook just yet. I was a pro at putting on a smile when I didn't feel it. But on less than three hours of sleep? It was hard to care about anything when I was this tired.

Paul's eyes flicked down, focusing somewhere around my breasts, even though I was wearing a sweater. "We should've sent more wardrobe options for you, but the authentic look is good too. Giving your fans a glimpse of the real Ayla Maxwell."

As if Paul knew the "real Ayla Maxwell," whatever that meant.

Cheryl stood off to one side behind Paul, her arms crossed. Her bobbed raven hair featured a streak of silver-gray, and she wore a linen suit that straddled sophistication and elegance. She and Beth had gone to Paul's Santa Monica office for them to monitor my interview.

Paul was the newest and youngest executive at Ruxton Records. The son of the founder of the company. *Hello, nepotism.* Everything about Paul was slick, from the shiny fabric of his suit to his gelled hair.

He also had trouble keeping his eyes to himself. Female artists used to have to accept that treatment. But things were changing.

I was trying to reserve judgment on Paul, though. Several months back, he worked with another artist on a smash-hit album, far more successful than my last one. The label expected my next to put me back on the top. They claimed Paul would get us there.

And despite my past success in this business, I didn't have the clout to call my own shots entirely, thanks to the record contract I'd signed years ago. It would be another year before I could negotiate a new one.

Believe me, my team of high-powered lawyers would be all over that. But I had to be patient. No matter how difficult that was.

"You handled the questions about your sister's death with perfect poise," Beth said.

"Thanks. Since I'm in Silver Ridge, I figured the reporter would ask." I had deflected, while still pretending the questions didn't bother me. "At least yesterday's fight on Main Street didn't come up."

Cheryl's mouth tightened. "By some miracle, yesterday's incident has been quiet on social media so far."

Paul leaned back casually in his leather chair. "We're trying to keep a lid on it. I've made some calls. You don't think the police chief will make trouble about this, do you? Local cop trying to get attention, make himself look like a hero for showing you mercy and not going through with the arrest?"

I bristled. So Paul knew all about it. Cheryl probably felt like she had to warn him. "Teller? He wouldn't do that."

Paul scoffed. "You're on a first-name basis with the guy?"

I studied my fingernail, even though my instinct was to defend the chief. A pretty big turnaround from a day ago. I didn't feel like explaining it. "He's a family friend. Anyway, Bryan will need a ride out of Silver Ridge since he can't drive. Cheryl, the agency is sending someone to pick him up, right?"

"Yes. I've spoken to them to make sure."

Poor Bryan had a concussion. One of Teller's officers had taken him to the county hospital last night, but there'd been no way I could leave him all alone. He'd gotten hurt defending me. So after the party was over, I'd asked Ashford to drive me to the hospital. Thankfully he'd been sober.

I'd sat up with Bryan for half the night while the doctors ran tests. They insisted on keeping him there for observation, given his past history of concussions and his worsening symptoms. Then Ashford had to come pick me up *again* before he, Emma, and Maisie took off for Hartley.

I'd been on my own for the last few hours. Packing my things, then dealing with the magazine interview.

But in the background of my mind, ever since last night, there had been one constant refrain. Like a melody that appeared out of nowhere and I hadn't figured out yet.

Teller Landry.

"I hear there's bad weather headed to Colorado," Cheryl said. "Are you sure you don't need another driver? You're all set?"

"Yep, I am." She didn't need to know Teller was driving me personally. "Don't worry about it."

"I always worry about you. Especially when I sense there are things you aren't telling me."

Paul perked up. "Keeping secrets from us?" Beth's brow creased.

I forced a laugh. "No, there's nothing."

"You almost got yourself arrested yesterday," Cheryl said with a frown. "That's not nothing."

"Emphasis on the *almost*."

Cheryl looked at the window, as if she was calming herself by staring at the ocean view. A feeling I knew well. But I didn't like to feel that I was the source of her anxiety. I had enough of that on my own.

Paul's gaze remained directly on me, and I resisted the urge to squirm. "If anything else comes up, you'll let us know, right?" he asked. "Anything at all. We care. We're here to help you, Ayla. Help *us* help *you*."

How did Paul manage to make kind words sound so empty?

"I'll let you know when I get to Hartley," I said. "And I'll see you when I'm back in LA on Monday. Bye, everyone!" I rushed to end the call.

Gah.

Cheryl looked out for me, and I had to be grateful for that. My whole team looked out for me. I just didn't want to share anything about Teller, and certainly not in front of Paul. My record label didn't need to know every last thing about me. Though they clearly felt entitled to that.

I didn't want to think about Paul and his casual sleaziness.

Teller could be infuriating, but he was ten times the man Paul Ruxton would ever be.

My impression of Teller had changed completely since yesterday. Especially after seeing him on the roof with his nephew. The love between them had been so clear. And it seemed especially poignant since Teller wasn't Ollie's dad. Instead, he was stepping in because Piper's ex-husband wasn't the father Ollie deserved.

If only every kid had someone like that.

It made me wonder why Teller wasn't a dad himself. That was a deeply personal decision, of course. None of my business. Maybe he wasn't interested in having a traditional family. Or maybe he had a girlfriend and was getting ready to propose to her. How would I know?

Except nobody in Silver Ridge had mentioned Teller having a girlfriend. There had been some kind of spark between us yesterday. Would I have felt that if he belonged to someone else?

"You're ridiculous," I said to myself aloud.

I pushed back from the piano, putting the cover over the keys and grabbing my laptop.

I barely knew Teller Landry. And even if I wanted to know more, what was the point? He lived in Silver Ridge. I lived in LA, and I traveled constantly. We barely had anything in common.

Yet I couldn't stop thinking about what he'd said yesterday on the roof. *Let me take care of this for you.* He'd been straightforward and sincere. Everything a guy like Paul Ruxton wasn't.

I believed Teller. It felt *really good* to believe him.

Suddenly, music notes danced like snowflakes in my head. Pure and clear and just as fleeting.

That wasn't half bad.

I rushed to the piano, pushed back the cover, and let my fingers move. At first it was a quick repetition of notes. The beginnings of a melody. And then, it grew. Took on shape and dynamics.

"There you are," I murmured. "Stay with me."

Reaching for the sheet music I'd been using earlier, I flipped it over. Shit, a pencil. A pen. I needed something to write with. Frustration itched beneath my skin because I had to get this out. When inspiration hit me, it was a physical need. Undeniable, even painful if I ignored it.

Wait, my laptop. *Yes*.

I opened the computer and launched my favorite songwriting software as I hummed the melody. The notes started to become words as I worked. A story about a girl losing someone irreplaceable and eventually opening up to love again.

I only had the very beginning. No clue where it was going. But I always had an instinct when a song might be something special.

This one had promise. I just had to follow where the inspiration would lead.

I stood up to stretch and rolled out my neck. How long had I been sitting there? It felt like coming out of a daze. But when I was in the flow, I was hardly aware of anything except the music. Sometimes I forgot to eat or drink or use the bathroom for hours at a time.

Once, I was baking cookies in my Malibu kitchen, got distracted by a song idea, and almost burned the house down.

But it had been a while since that kind of inspiration had struck me. It felt amazing. Like the best high no drug in the world could ever replicate.

I was never happier than when I was creating.

My phone buzzed. I checked and found a message waiting from Teller. Oops, make that another message. He'd written me several.

> Storm's coming in faster than expected. You free? I have some updates.

We'll get to Hartley. I've been working on a modified route. No worries.

Free soon? We have to leave ASAP.

Sparks of anxiety hit my stomach. But I'd already packed my suitcase, and I had the rest of my stuff downstairs.

I was about to write him back when I noticed a new email message in my inbox. It came from someone who'd put *Biggest Fan* as their first and last name. Very few people even had my email address, which I rarely used for anything except business.

The subject was: *Smile for me.*

Dread slowly rose inside me like dark water. But at the same time, I had to see what this was. I had to know.

I clicked on the message.

To: ayla.m@email.com
From: BiggestFan@web.net
Subject: Smile for me

Dear Ayla,
Someday you'll smile like this for me. And only me. Until then, I'll be watching.

Love, your Biggest Fan

Below the message was a photo of me standing inside the baby boutique, smiling at Bryan. This photo had been taken yesterday, clearly through the shop window. Had this person been out there in that crowd?

My stomach flipped. The blood rushed from my head. Distantly, I heard a door open. Footsteps.

"Ayla?"

Teller walked toward me in his police uniform. I looked up at him, and the room seemed to swim and blur.

"What's going on?"

My knees went weak. I couldn't make my voice work to respond. He gripped my upper arm, while the fingers of his other hand touched my neck. "Your heart is racing. Can you tell me what happened?"

"I'm...I'm okay." I pushed the fear way, way down. I didn't want to think about it. *Couldn't* think about it.

"You don't seem like it."

My phone was still clutched in my fist. Then it was suddenly gone, and when I blinked, it was in Teller's hand.

His thumb flicked over the screen. "What in the *hell*? Who sent this to you?"

I grabbed the phone and turned it dark. "You had no right to do that." I tried to push away from him, but Teller held me there with a firm grip on my arm.

"Do you know who sent it?" he asked, so quiet and yet infinitely dangerous.

"It's a prank. Just someone looking to get a reaction from me."

"Seems like he got it."

"I forgot to eat lunch. That's why I was lightheaded." I stepped back. "Please let go of me."

Teller lifted his hands. But his pale-green eyes were still scrutinizing me. As if he saw right through me.

I had to smile. Perform. Make him believe it.

"Really, it was nothing. I get creepy messages sometimes."

"This has happened before?"

"It's an unfortunate reality of my job."

"It shouldn't be."

"How did you get inside? I thought I had the door locked." An aftershock of fear rippled down my back. What if the person who'd sent that message was in Silver Ridge? What if he'd gotten in?

"The electronic lock on the main door," he said. "I know the code."

I nodded rapidly, crossing my arms over my chest. *Stop*, I told myself. *Breathe*.

"Do you have a stalker, Ayla?" Teller asked softly.

I wasn't sure how to answer, so I just shook my head.

"If you want to talk, I'm here."

"Nothing to talk about. My stuff is ready. I just have to grab my suitcase from upstairs. Then we can go."

"Are you sure?"

"Yes. Just forget about it. *Please*."

At best, Teller would think he could fix this. Like I was a project. An obligation. At worst, he would find out how scared and alone I really felt and look at me with pity.

I couldn't deal with either one.

THIRTEEN

Teller

WHAT ON EARTH had just happened back there?

I mean, that email was creepy as fuck.

I wasn't sure what worried me more. The fact that she'd received that message, along with a photo taken on Silver Ridge's Main Street *yesterday*. Or the fact that Ayla claimed it was no big deal.

It was a very big deal. She'd been terrified. And no wonder. Was it an obsessed fan? Or somebody who actually knew her? A possessive ex-boyfriend?

If the guy had followed her to Silver Ridge, I would make him regret ever setting foot in this county.

But how could I do anything if she didn't open up and tell me the truth?

Ayla locked up the building while I carried her belongings out to my vehicle. I had come straight here after swinging by my house to grab my bag for the weekend. Hadn't bothered with changing out of my uniform. I could do that tonight once we arrived in Hartley.

I hadn't even had a chance to explain the new plan to her. She seemed calm now, and I didn't want to freak her out again. But I also had to let her know what was going on.

The air outside was frigid and bone dry. I opened the passenger door for her, and she climbed in, rubbing her arms over her coat to brush off the chill. Once I was in the driver's seat, I turned to her. "So the storm is arriving sooner than we anticipated. The weather service updated the forecast and increased the snowfall estimate."

"Right, your message said something about that. That's why we're leaving early." Her fingers tugged at the zipper on her coat, a nervous gesture.

I studied her briefly, looking for other signs that she was still in distress. Her pulse had been going like mad earlier. Then I snapped myself out of it. She was waiting for me to speak. "The Department of Transportation is closing the mountain pass between us and Hartley. It'll be blizzard conditions. Way too dangerous."

"What does that mean?"

"Means it'll be all but impossible for anyone else to get to Hartley who hasn't already left."

She jolted. "*What*? But—"

"But I've got another route. Skirts the mountain and comes around another way. Here's the thing, though. It'll take three hours." Also, my improvised route cut through a forest service road that wasn't exactly open to the public. If anyone had questions about how we'd made it to Hartley with the pass closed, well...too bad. I wasn't going to tell, and I doubted Ayla would either.

"Three *hours*?"

"Could be a little longer, depending on road conditions. We'll get to Hartley after dark."

"But we *will* get there, right?"

"Absolutely." I patted the steering wheel. "I've got 4-wheel drive and snow tires. I promised I'd get you to Hartley, and I'm a man of my word."

She relaxed against the seat. "Okay. I'll text Emma and Ashford so they know I'm still coming."

"Sounds good." I'd shared the rough contours of my plan with Susan. I was off duty for the rest of the weekend, though of course I'd be available on the radio or by phone if anyone needed me.

This wasn't ideal. But during my years as a Special Forces operator, how often had ops gone exactly to our original plan? Rarely.

Ayla stared at the overcast sky through the window. "It's not even snowing yet."

"Nope, but the snow is coming. No question about that." I turned on the engine. A haunting piano melody blasted through the sound system, and I quickly punched the button to turn off the stereo.

Ayla slowly turned to me. "That was one of my songs."

"Was it? Must've been on the radio." I put the SUV in gear.

"Looks like it was connected to your phone."

I was so busted. "It's one of those workout playlists. I lift weights in the mornings."

"Interesting. My upbeat songs are popular for workout playlists, but that was a heartfelt ballad."

"What can I say? I'm a sensitive guy."

"You enjoy a literal *and* figurative weight on your chest when you bench press?"

"See? You get me."

A smile ghosted over her lips, and after she'd been so upset earlier, it was a relief to see.

I didn't get flustered by anyone. But this woman... She did things to me.

First stop was food. Ayla had claimed she forgot to eat lunch. I didn't believe that was the sole source of her stress and lightheadedness earlier. Not even close. But I wasn't going to leave her hungry either.

Also, I could always eat.

"Do you have dietary restrictions?" I asked. "The travel stop on the highway out of town probably has an egg salad sandwich, but I can't vouch for the expiration date. The Sunspot Cafe has all kinds of wraps but it'll take half an hour for Betsy to make one."

"I'll eat whatever. Is there a drive-through?"

"You eat drive-through?"

"Are you kidding? In-N-Out is my go-to in LA. Or burritos."

"Didn't think a celebrity would eat fast food." I'd assumed she had a private chef or something.

"*Maybe* you don't know what I would and wouldn't do," she said teasingly.

"I'm realizing that."

"And stop side-eyeing me. I am *fine*."

"Alright. I'll take your word for it." For now.

"I appreciate you driving me, though. I really do."

"I'm happy to."

Once Main Street turned into the highway, I pulled off at the travel center, which had a drive-through burger place. I stopped the SUV in front of the menu board. "What'll it be?"

Ayla leaned toward me, blond hair spilling over her shoulder, and her caramel scent hit me. It sank into my lungs and then lower. Arousal pooled in my low belly. *Damn*. An involuntary reaction, but still, I needed to tamp that down.

"Ooo, I'll have the barbecue burger," she said. "That sounds great. And a mint shake."

"You want a cold drink on a snowy day?"

"It's warming up in here." She unzipped her coat and tossed it into the backseat.

It was definitely getting warm in here. We'd barely gotten started on the drive, and I was all too aware of her.

I pulled the SUV forward to the window. "Hey, Meredith," I

said to the teenager working today. She was a senior at the high school. Good kid. "How's your brother?"

"He's feeling a lot better, Chief. Thanks. I hear there's going to be more snow than expected."

"You heard right. Drive safe on your way home. Can we get two barbecue burgers, a mint shake, and two bottles of water? And would you mind grabbing me a big bag of salt-and-pepper kettle chips from the travel store? I'm addicted to those."

"Sure thing, Chief." Meredith looked past me and did a double take when she saw Ayla. "Um, anything else?"

I glanced at Ayla, lifting one eyebrow.

"No, but thanks Meredith," she said.

The teenager's eyes widened in shock, like she couldn't believe Ayla Maxwell knew her name. "I love your music. Like, *love* it. I listen to you all the time."

Ayla smiled. "Thank you. That's so kind."

Once she remembered what she was doing, Meredith gave me the total, then disappeared from the window to grab the chips. Normally I'd go inside the travel shop and get them myself, but I planned to give her a generous tip for saving me the trouble.

When I turned to Ayla, she was studying me. "What?" I asked.

"It's nice how you know everyone in town."

"Hazard of the job."

"And they clearly like *you*."

Meredith reappeared. "Here you go, Chief. And Miss Maxwell. This is so cool. Like, best day ever. I put in extra barbecue sauce." She handed me the food and the bag of chips, followed by the receipt. I passed everything over to my passenger.

"Wait." Ayla took the receipt, fished a pen from my cup holder, and signed the thin paper. *Thank you Meredith! Love, Ayla*. "Here." She reached across me again to hand the receipt to Meredith, who accepted it like a winning lottery ticket.

"Thank you so much!"

Then I drove off and got back onto the highway. "That was sweet of you," I said.

"She was a fan. It only took a second, so..."

"But it can't be easy. Giving so much of yourself all the time, not knowing if a fan's going to turn on you. Like the mob on Main Street yesterday."

Or that message earlier.

Her expression faltered, gaze moving to the window. Then she unwrapped her burger and took a bite. "Mmm. That's good." She swallowed. "I really was starving."

I was no genius, but I knew a blatant subject change when one came my way. Ayla wanted to keep our conversation light. Fair enough. I could oblige.

The winter landscape rolled past as we drove.

"Could you hand me my burger?" I asked.

"Do you need to pull over to eat?"

"Nah, I can multi-task. I've eaten many meals on the road."

"Same here. I also love kettle chips."

"Are you trying to steal my snacks?"

"I was hoping you'd share." She smiled and pulled my burger from the bag. "I would offer to take turns driving, but..."

"Sadly, I can't let you drive the department vehicle."

"Can I run the sirens?"

"Maybe."

"Wait, are you serious?"

"Not in the least, Troublemaker."

She barked a laugh, easy and carefree. My chest swelled with happiness and pride.

Fuck, I was an idiot. Hadn't been interested in dating a woman since becoming a civilian, and I chose a pop star for a hopeless crush? A pop star who needed a friend to have her back far more than she needed a guy lusting after her.

You're embarrassing yourself, Landry.

Ayla unwrapped the top half of my burger and handed it to me. I polished it off in a few bites without a single spill.

"That was impressive," she said. "Also scary."

I opened my water bottle one-handed and washed down my dinner. "Told you. Lots of practice eating on the road."

"I would've thought a police chief worked at a desk most of the time."

"In a big city, maybe. In a town like Silver Ridge, I'm out in the community."

"What's your favorite thing about being police chief?"

"The difference I get to make every day. Helping people through difficult times."

"Is it long hours?"

"Sometimes. I can always get called in, any time of the day or night. When I'm off duty, I spend as much time as possible with Ollie. And Piper, if she's around, but I'm happy to give her a break. Tough being a single mom."

"I'm sorry. It's great that she and Ollie have you."

"I do what I can." I set the water down. "What about you? What do you do when you're not working?"

"I'm always working. Except when I'm in Silver Ridge. This is my hot vacation spot. *Mostly*. Even on vacation, I still have interviews, calls with my manager. There's always something."

"Is that why you drove across the country that first time you showed up in Silver Ridge? To get a break from all that?"

She took another bite of her burger before answering. "Yeah."

"And then, when you got to Silver Ridge, I wasn't very welcoming."

"You, not welcoming? *Really*?"

I chuckled. "I deserve that. But I didn't know what to do with you. You showed up here with a whole lot of attitude and chaos ensued."

Her face fell. Shit, I was screwing this up.

"But that wasn't your fault," I went on. "You came to Silver Ridge needing help."

"You *did* help. You and your officers helped create a diversion so I could escape all those reporters."

"But I should've been kinder about it. That's what I'm saying. I've been told I can be intimidating, and I'm working on that. But if you ever need help in the future, any kind at all, I'll do whatever I can."

"I see what you're doing."

"I'm not trying to be subtle." I still wanted her to tell me about that screwed-up email. "I'd like to make sure you're safe."

Her finger traced a pattern in the condensation on the window. "Why?"

Because you're getting under my skin. Because there's something achingly fragile in you, and it calls to me.

"I like helping people. Probably explains my career choices."

She blinked, her jewel-green eyes meeting my gaze as I looked from her to the road and back. "Most people want something from me, even if they claim to admire me. Some see me as a mirror, a reflection of something I can't control, and they want to punish me for it."

The raw honesty in her tone slayed me.

Right then, the realization slid home. I'd been wrong about *everything* concerning Ayla Maxwell.

"You deserve people in your corner. I know you have Ashford and the O'Neal family. And probably a bunch of people in LA."

"Not as many as you'd think." She said this quietly, like it hurt her to admit.

"Then I'll be in your corner too. You owe me nothing, okay? You don't have to be *anyone* with me except yourself."

FOURTEEN
Ayla

THE SNOW STARTED about a half hour into the drive. About the time we would've made it to Hartley if the weather were clear. But I actually didn't mind that the trip was taking longer. Especially after that awful message had stirred up every old fear and negative feeling inside me.

Teller's presence was comforting. I never would've thought I'd say that about a broad-chested, bossy police chief, especially not *this* police chief. But I liked being around him, now that we understood each other better.

He had a hero complex. But was that such a bad thing?

For the longest time, I'd felt like everything I'd built could disappear in an instant. My childhood had taught me that. I had money and fame, but that didn't buy me peace of mind.

Ashford and I had a strong relationship now, but he was so busy with his family. Grace and Dane were also incredible friends, and Dane had even more resources at his fingertips than I did. But I didn't feel comfortable sharing my deepest insecurities with them.

Could I share those things with Teller?

I still didn't completely understand why Teller was so willing to help me. But I trusted that he didn't have any secret motives.

This was not a man who cared about social media exposure or getting his demo in front of a producer. He cared about the people in his community. His nephew and sister. He cared about being a good man.

You don't have to be anyone with me except for yourself.

I rested my head against the glass to watch the snow. It fell in perfect snowflakes that collected below the window. Tiny crystalline structures, each one unique.

"I used to love when it snowed when Lori and I were kids."

"Yeah?"

I picked up my shake and took a sip through the straw. Creamy, pepperminty goodness hit my tongue. The cold of the ice cream and brightness of the mint perfectly offset the richness. "Lori used to save her lunch money all week and buy a mint chocolate chip ice cream sandwich on the way home from school on Friday. We always shared it. She didn't even like mint, but it was my favorite."

"A good big sister."

"She was." Guilt poked at my heart, but it was an old feeling. A sadness that never fully went away.

"Where were you living then?"

Did he already know I'd been an Army brat and moved around a lot? That was a well-known part of my bio, though I never shared many details about it. "Our family lived on a lot of different bases over the years. You were a Green Beret, right?"

"Yes."

"You were wounded."

"I was. Received a medical discharge and came back to Colorado."

Suddenly my throat went tight. I didn't want to bring up bad memories for him, and I didn't want to get into my own. This was why I didn't usually talk about Lori or our childhood.

I'd been trying so hard to stay cheerful. To act like I was okay. But Teller made me want to open up about how frightened I was, and *that* only scared me more.

I needed my music. My safe space. "Um, I started writing a new song this afternoon. Do you mind if I work on it now? Would that be weird?"

His eyebrows lifted. "Not at all."

I *never* did this. Sharing a half-finished song with someone I didn't know well. While I had no problem singing in front of a stadium of thousands, sharing my creative process was different. Even with other songwriters I collaborated with, I liked to have a clearer vision in place first. But there was too much swirling around inside me, and I needed to channel it.

Somehow, I felt safe doing that with Teller here. Like he could be a safe space too.

Besides, we were stuck together for the next few hours. Couldn't exactly ask him not to listen.

Reaching into the backseat for my messenger bag, I pulled out my laptop. I'd had it plugged in earlier, so it was all charged up. I opened it, using my fingerprint to unlock the screen. The songwriting software program was already open.

"Here's what I have so far." I pressed play, and the program played back what I'd composed earlier. I hummed along, then played it again while singing the few lyrics I'd come up with.

"It's incredible. Really."

I glanced over at Teller, feeling my skin heat. This was why I didn't normally share a song so early. I'd written hundreds, yet every single one came from my heart. It was a vulnerable place to be in. The praise felt good, but it was intense too. Like the sun shining straight down on me. It could easily burn.

"It has a long way to go."

"I'm sure it'll be amazing when you're finished."

The corner of my mouth inched up. "Maybe you'll want to add it to your workout playlist."

He laughed quietly with his lips closed. "You got me there. I probably will."

I was smiling as I got to work. It was surprisingly effortless to find a flow. I almost forgot Teller was listening. My fingers moved over the tablet screen, jotting down different lines as I sang them to try them out.

More of the song took form. Would've been better to have a guitar or piano in front of me, but this was the next best thing.

When I looked up after a while, snow swirled in gusts outside. The view had expanded into a gorgeous winter panorama. Evergreens dusted with white, a broad valley. Mountains rose to our right, obscured by heavy clouds.

A large truck rattled past us going the other way. There weren't many other vehicles out. The heater was blasting, and yet the chill from outside made its way through the minute gaps around the door. The wind howled.

Teller had a look of serious concentration on his face. "That was beautiful," he murmured. "The song you're writing."

His compliment sent a tingle of pleasure down my spine. "Thanks. I have tunnel vision when I'm working. How long have we been driving?"

"About an hour and a half. I promise I can handle the driving part. Just don't ask me to write any music. Have you always been able to do that? Just...make it up that way?"

I grinned. "That's how it works. Sometimes I have to agonize over the bridge or the perfect outro or a rhyme that doesn't want to fit. But mostly, the music just comes to me, as long as I'm feeling inspired."

"Impressive."

"I appreciate you saying that. But to me, it's more like... sleeping or eating. Something I have to do to survive. When I was a kid, music was my escape."

Teller reached over and squeezed my knee, then quickly returned his grip to the steering wheel. His face morphed into a shocked expression, as if he hadn't expected himself to do that. Touch me that way.

I hadn't either, but I hadn't disliked it.

Instead, a feeling of longing raced through me. Teller made my heart rate speed up, but in the best way. Because there was still that sense of comfort underneath. A gentleness even when he was rough.

"Sorry," he muttered.

"I don't mind if you touch me."

His gaze slashed in my direction. "I should've asked."

"You didn't ask yesterday on Main Street when you carried me away from the fight. Or when you arrested me." Or earlier today, even, when he'd found me upset over that email.

He was watching the road again. The tip of his tongue traced his lower lip. "Maybe touching you meant something different before."

I sucked in a breath, unable to look away from him. Wanting his hand on me again. Wanting to confess things that I'd never told anyone, and why was that? I didn't even know him.

Why did Teller Landry have such an effect on me?

Then a bunch of things happened all at the same time.

Teller cursed and swerved the steering wheel. I looked up to see a huge, dark shape on the snow-packed road. I screamed.

The SUV bucked hard, then slammed to a sudden stop.

FIFTEEN
Teller

STATIC ROARED IN MY EARS. My vision blurred like I was underwater.

Gunfire. Screams.

Pain.

Then a whimper from beside me. *Ayla*. She was here.

I followed her voice like a lifeline back to the surface and out of my waking nightmare. Had to force myself to breathe. What had sounded like gunfire in my memory was just the ticking of the engine.

Shit. I hadn't experienced a flashback like that in over a year.

I shook off the haze in my thoughts and unbuckled my seatbelt. Reached over to unbuckle Ayla. Her head was bowed. She moaned.

"Hey, Troublemaker." My voice was hoarse. "You alright?" I carefully touched Ayla's neck, then inched my hands up to her face. "Can you look at me?"

Her head lifted. Green eyes blinked rapidly. But her focus was clear. "I...yes. I'm fine. Just shaken up."

Relief bled out of me. I brought my forehead to hers, my thumb stroking her cheekbone.

"Teller, are *you* okay?"

My heart thumped again, but for an entirely different reason. She'd called me Teller. First time that had ever happened, but maybe it was the shock of the near miss. Even so, the sound of it moved through me like the sweetest music, smoothing out my jagged nerves.

"I'm just fine. I didn't mean to scare you." My hands dropped away from her face, but Ayla reached over to grab my right one.

"You didn't." She tangled our fingers together. Our eyes locked and held for another couple breaths. "What happened?" she asked.

"There was a bull in the middle of the road. I swerved to avoid it. But we lost traction. I think we're halfway in the ditch." Not that we could see the ditch for all the snow.

"A *bull*?"

I chuckled. "A bull elk."

"That...makes a lot more sense."

"There are cattle ranches around here, but yes, your point stands."

She glanced around, but the elk was gone. "I guess that was a close call, right?"

"If we'd been going faster, I might have clipped him. He looked like eight-hundred pounds, easy. Maybe a thousand." I chose not to tell her about the fatal highway collisions I'd seen involving large animals. Gruesome for all parties involved. Even clipping the elk could've done major damage to the SUV and the animal.

But still, we'd slid on the ice and gone off the road. Now the SUV was tilted. I squeezed her hand. "I'd better see how things look out there. Then I can work on getting us back on the road." I had no idea how bad a situation we were in. But there was no point speculating.

"Is there something I can do?"

"Put your coat on. Stay warm." I grabbed my jacket and gloves from the backseat. "I'll be right back."

I had to push hard against snow to get the door open. Flurries blew into the cabin as soon as I opened the door. Jumping out, I shut it quickly, hoping to keep as much warm air inside as possible. It was damned chilly out here. The icy air stung my nostrils and ached in my sinuses. My boots sank into the snowdrift.

Wading a few steps away, I turned to survey our position.

This did *not* look good.

It took me several minutes to make my way around the vehicle and consider options. Frustration and disappointment sank into my bones.

Then I got back into the SUV, bringing a bunch of snow with me.

"Well?" Ayla asked.

I brushed snowflakes from my hair and shoulders. "There's an embankment to the side of the road that slopes into a ditch. We're partway into it. That's why we're tilted."

"Glad it's not just me."

I smiled halfheartedly. "Yeah, at first I wasn't sure either. Been a few years since I was wounded, but I was driving a Humvee when that happened, so car accidents can be…an unpleasant reminder."

Her brows knit. "Oh. Oh my gosh."

"I'm fine now. No worries." I cleared my throat. "We might get lucky, and someone will drive by who can tow us out. More likely, we'll need to wait for help to arrive. I'll radio in." My department vehicle was set up with a satellite connection.

"So we're stuck?"

"There's no driving out of here on our own. Not at this angle, with this much snow." Spinning the tires would just get us stuck even worse. I had plenty of supplies in my trunk, like a collapsible shovel and kitty litter to help create traction on slick surfaces. But none of that was going to magically fix this.

"Can one of us get out and, like, push while the other steers? That's a thing people do, right?"

My smile grew. Sometimes I forgot how little real-life experience she had. "That's a thing people do, yes. But I wouldn't make you get out and push the truck while I sit in here all comfortable. The pusher would be me."

Her cheeks pinked. "I work out a lot."

I can tell, sweetheart, I almost said. Thankfully I didn't.

"Under these conditions, even I'm not strong enough for that. Unless you have some superhero serum lying around. Ollie would love if I turned green."

Her gaze moved down, like she was assessing my chest and shoulders. I flexed involuntarily, as if she could see anything beneath my coat and uniform.

I'm an idiot.

"Don't worry," I said. "There's a lot of hours between now and the ceremony tomorrow. I'm getting you to that wedding. I'll carry you on my back if I have to. Lifting this SUV, no. Lifting you? I can manage that just fine."

"I think you've already proven that. Not that I doubted it. You're..." She gestured vaguely.

"I'm what?"

"Really big."

My cock twitched valiantly against my thigh, like he was getting ready to prove her right. Hell, no. That would not be happening.

I grabbed my radio and called in.

"Chief, you're breaking up. Could you repeat that?"

It was Finn Mackie on dispatch. "Finn, I narrowly missed hitting an elk but then slid off the road. Front wheels are in the ditch."

"An elk? Wow. Glad you avoided it. Remember that accident a couple months back where the drunk hit the elk head-on? Engine block of that car nearly cut the driver in half." He made a sound of disgust.

"I have a passenger with me, Finn."

A pause. "Whoops. Sorry about that, Chief. A passenger?"

Finn sounded curious. I assumed Susan hadn't mentioned my

improvised route to anyone else at the station, and I appreciated it.

"I'm going to need someone to tow me out of here."

"I'll work on it. But straight up, Chief, we just had a major accident get called in. Semi rolled over on several passenger vehicles east of town. State patrol is responding, and they've requested all units we've got available. Can't get anyone from Hartley with the pass closed."

"Dammit," I muttered. I was concerned about the people involved in the accident. Had anyone been killed? But I couldn't do anything to help. I was over an hour away, and Ayla was my priority. "We can wait. Just see what you can do."

"I'll call around to other departments and find someone for you. But with the accident and the storm, could be several hours given your location." My vehicle had a GPS tracker, so Finn could see my coordinates on the map on his screen.

Beside me, Ayla rubbed her chest. I wondered if the seatbelt had hurt her or if she was anxious. Or both.

"Whoever you talk to, tell them to be careful out in the storm," I said. "Won't help anyone if there's another accident."

I signed off.

"It could be worse," Ayla said, trying to smile. "I've had tour buses break down. One time, we were stranded waiting for repairs in middle-of-nowhere Kansas. Wound up at a twenty-four-hour diner where there was nobody under sixty, and not a single one of them knew who I was. We played songs on the jukebox and got the barflies to sing along with us to 'Hotel California'."

"Sounds like a good time."

"It was. Do you ever karaoke?"

"*No*, my voice is terrible. I'm not really a *late night at the club* kind of guy."

Her eyes sparkled. "Never would've guessed. You're fun, though."

"I'm *fun*? I've never been accused of that before."

"In a relaxed kind of way. The more time I spend with you,

the more I see it. Your sense of humor is subtle, but it's very much alive." She glanced down shyly, and that nearly did me in.

Ayla Maxwell wasn't shy, either in her performances or our interactions so far. But right now, when it was just the two of us, she was different. She was letting down her guard.

Was I having heart palpitations? Whatever was happening in my chest, it couldn't be normal.

"We have a few hours to kill," I said. "We'll make the most of it. We have the chips, plus I have MREs in the back with my other winter emergency supplies."

"It's getting cold in here already. I'm regretting the mint shake."

"Are you really?"

She thought about it. "No, not really. Mint ice cream is always worth it." Another soft smile, like it was made just for me.

I was in serious trouble.

I reached into the back. "I've got space blankets and hand warmers."

Ayla squeezed one of the hand warmer packs until it started to heat. We each wrapped ourselves in the thin, reflective space blankets, settling in as snow collected on the windows, already beginning to block the view outside. I resisted the urge to radio Finn and ask for an update. My department had enough on their hands with that traffic accident.

Nothing to do but sit still. Which wasn't easy for me. I preferred to be going places and getting shit done. In my Special Forces days, the most trying part of a mission had usually been the waiting before the action started.

Ayla seemed to be having a similar issue. She kept shifting around like she couldn't get comfortable.

"Hard to do nothing, isn't it?" I asked.

"Yes, but, um..." She turned two wide eyes on me.

"What's wrong?"

"Teller, I really need to pee," she whispered.

I barely kept my smile in. "You do?"

"I wasn't even thinking about it before, but now that I know we're stuck here for at least a couple hours, it's getting urgent. I don't think I can hold it."

"Okay, no problem. We'll act like we're camping. Come on." I went to open my door.

"But there's so much snow! I saw you out there. It came up past your thighs, and you're a lot taller than me."

"I'll help you."

She covered her face with her hands. "Oh lord, this is ridiculous."

A laugh snuck into my throat. I swallowed it down. "It's a basic bodily function. We're adults. Nothing to be embarrassed about."

"What if I get frostbite on my butt?"

A guttural snort burst out of me before I could stop it.

"You're laughing at me? What happened to us being adults?" She giggled. "Stop. If I start, I'll pee my pants."

"Wait, let me grab my phone. If I record this, I could sell it to a tabloid for a million dollars at least."

"Teller!"

"Okay, okay. Let's get this taken care of before there's an incident."

First, I ventured back out into the storm to get the collapsible shovel from the trunk. Snapping the handle straight, I did my best to shovel a narrow path away from Ayla's side of the SUV. Was *not* easy because of the slope of the embankment. But after a couple of yards, I dug out a little cave-like space in the snow. Like a makeshift restroom stall, giving her some privacy.

Heading back, I went to Ayla's door, opened it, and held out my gloved hand. "It's ready."

"You're going above and beyond."

"It's what I do."

Her eyes were round, stuck between the urge to laugh and sheer embarrassment. It was a cuter expression than you'd think.

The space blanket tried to blow away in the wind as she got

out. I stuffed it back inside the cabin and shoved the door closed. Ayla had to press up against me to go past. "Careful," I said. "It's awkward because of the slope."

"Not the only reason it's awkward."

I hung back, keeping an eye on her on my periphery. The hood of Ayla's coat edged along the path I'd made, then disappeared. "Okay?" I shouted over the wind.

"Yes!"

A minute or two later, she popped up again and made her way back toward me. Her creamy skin was bright pink, and I doubted it was just from the cold.

She was a few steps away when she slipped and, with a shout, vanished under a mound of snow.

"Shit!" I raced toward her.

By the time I had her upright again, she was completely caked with snow and was laughing so hard she hiccuped.

"Stay still. I'll brush you off." I swiped at her coat.

"I'm tempted to start a snowball fight, but it's too c-cold for that." Ayla's giggles turned into a screech. "Oh! Oh, it's inside my shirt! Teller, help!"

Then the wind picked up again and lashed us with sharp, icy flakes. I opened the door to the backseat. "Climb in. This'll be faster." I grabbed her hips and half lifted her to help her get in.

We both stripped off our damp coats and gloves and grabbed the space blankets from the front, huddling together. The SUV was still tilted at a slight angle, which meant the seat wasn't flat, but I braced my feet against the floor to keep us steady.

I had a package of wet wipes tucked into the pocket behind the front seat, and Ayla grabbed one, wiping off her hands. She shivered. "Please never, *ever* mention this again."

Laughter broke free from my chest like something I'd been holding for too long. She snickered, which escalated until the point of no return.

We were helpless. Shaking. Clutching each other. Tears coated her eyelashes.

I managed to take a breath. "I think my favorite part was the snow down your shirt."

Her mouth opened, eyes narrowing dangerously. Then she lunged, pushing her hands beneath the collar of my uniform. "Let's see how you like it."

"Hell, woman. Don't you have circulation in your fingers?" I tugged her hands down into my lap and rubbed them between my palms. "I'll warm you up."

She went quiet, the only sound her heavy exhales as she caught her breath. Her eyes were the soft color of moss, flicking between our tangled hands and my face.

It finally dawned on me how close we were. How her small body pressed against my side, still shivering, and tiny droplets of moisture dotted her hair and skin. Her pink lips looked unbelievably soft and full.

Hot, heady desire pumped into my veins.

Somehow, I had to stay strong. No making moves on the same woman I arrested just yesterday. That had to be in the department handbook somewhere, right?

But I wanted to push my face against that pale hair. Pull her all the way into my lap and run my tongue along her ear. Suck on the tender skin of her neck.

Warm her *all* the way up.

Despite the cold, my cock was thick and aching. *Fuck*. I was so close to the edge, about to tip over.

I lifted one of her freezing hands and kissed her fingertips.

SIXTEEN

Ayla

TELLER TOUCHED his lips to the pads of my fingers.

It felt like I was under some spell, just watching what he would do next. I'd been half frozen a moment before, but now, lines of fire traced up and down my limbs and into my stomach.

Something was happening between us, though I had no idea what it was.

Teller lowered my hands, placing them in my own lap. His gaze moved to the windshield, though there wasn't a thing visible with the snow covering it. "Better now?" His voice was tight.

When I spoke, I didn't sound like myself either. "Getting there."

It seemed like he was trying to give me some space. I thought of what he'd said earlier. *Maybe touching you meant something different before.*

But right now, it felt like the coziest place in the world was there in his arms.

I arranged my space blanket, but I snuggled up against his side at the same time. He had just seen one of my most embarrassing moments. I was feeling pretty shameless. Then his arm went around me beneath the blanket, pulling me deeper into the circle of warmth that radiated from him. My body went limp by a few more degrees. Like I just wanted to melt into him.

"This okay?" he asked.

"It's nice."

I rested my head in that small dip between his shoulder and his chest. It was getting darker in the cabin by the minute. We were both quiet, and I alternated between relaxing into the moment and nearly losing my breath from being so close to him. Like my body was at war with itself.

I settled somewhere between drifting off to sleep and tingling with excitement.

Very little about this drive had gone the way it was supposed to. And that whole disaster of going out into the snow because I was about to wet my pants? I'd rarely felt more ridiculous. But Teller had made me laugh through it. He'd actually dug me a path through the snow, plus my own personal bathroom area.

I mean, what guy would jump out and do something like that without even being asked?

Teller Landry, that was who.

On paper, he gave the impression of being a cruel, hard man. Like my father had been. Teller had come across that way the first few times we'd met. But that wasn't the guy sitting here with me right now. Or the man who'd held his nephew on the roof last night.

I genuinely liked this man. I couldn't decide if that was a good thing or a really inconvenient one. In less than two days, I would be leaving Colorado. I had no idea when I'd be back again.

But he was right here. Still larger than life, yet I felt completely at ease.

"Can I ask you something?" I said. "You don't have to answer."

He pulled back enough that he could look down at me. Pale green glowed in the dimness. "Go ahead."

"You mentioned being wounded in a car crash. Was that..." I raised my hand, meaning to gesture at his face, but my fingertips brushed the silvery scars on his cheek. The skin was a mix of bumpy and smooth.

He made a sound in his throat and caught my hand. But he didn't let go this time. "Yes. Are you asking how it happened?"

I nodded. "It's okay if you don't want to talk about it." I'd been around plenty of service members growing up. Many didn't talk about their deployments.

"It's not my favorite topic, but I don't mind telling you. Can't say much, though. It was a classified mission." His thumb ran across my knuckles. "I was driving. Another of our Humvees was in front of us, with four other operators from our unit. Another Humvee behind. One moment, everything was fine. The next, the first vehicle lifted in the air and crashed back onto us. They'd hit a concealed IED."

He'd spoken matter-of-factly, but his grip on my hand tightened.

"I was very lucky," he went on. "I was trapped and nearly bled out, and my shoulder got fucked up. But I survived and didn't lose any limbs. All of my friends in the first vehicle were killed. Same with the guy sitting next to me."

"How awful. I can't imagine."

"It was the worst day of my life. The days immediately after that weren't so hot either."

I squeezed his hand. "You left the service afterward?"

"Mainly because of my shoulder." He rolled his right shoulder a few times, the one closest to me. "It still acts up. Gets stiff. Especially when the weather's bad."

"I had my head on that shoulder! You should've said something."

His lips quirked. "You weren't hurting me."

"Does massage help?"

His Adam's apple bobbed. "Sometimes."

I shifted around so I could reach his shoulder. My hands seemed so small against him. I gently pushed into the thick muscle. "How's that?"

"Nice." The word came deep from his throat. I felt him watching me, but for some reason, I couldn't lift my eyes to meet his.

"Do the scars hurt?" I asked.

"Not anymore."

"Do you miss it?"

My question was vague, but he understood what I meant. "I miss the people I served with. Especially the ones who didn't make it home. Wish we could grab a drink, catch up, but we can't. The Army was my life for a very long time. But I enjoy being home, having so much time with Ollie and Piper. My family is what drives me. The guys I served with, the best ones, they felt the same. Family is everything."

I kept kneading his shoulder over his uniform shirt, but my eyes stung.

Geez, he was telling me important things about himself, things that were hard to talk about, and my brain was making this about me. My childhood growing up on Army bases, surrounded by men who looked like Teller. For all I knew, Teller could've been one of them.

But the man in *my* family back then, who was supposed to love us, protect us, only made me feel worthless.

Something hot and bitter streaked down my cheek.

I pulled back and turned toward the window, but Teller reached out, his huge palm cupping the side of my neck. "Ayla?"

I sniffled and wiped my face. "It's not you. I was thinking of something else."

"Your father?"

My body jolted. "What do you know about that?"

"Callum told me a little about it. You ran away from home at sixteen because of your father, the colonel. He hurt you."

Teller said that as a statement, not a question. Like he didn't need any confirmation, didn't have any *doubt*. He believed me already before I'd had to say a word. But still, I nodded. "Yes."

"I am so sorry he did that to you."

My skin was all hot and cold. Hot tears, cold from the air because I wasn't inside Teller's circle of warmth anymore. I edged closer, and he helped me pull the blankets around us both again. Teller's words from earlier repeated in my head.

You can trust me, Ayla. If you want to talk, I'm here.

A few days ago, even a few hours ago, that had felt impossible. But I found myself opening my mouth. And it all just poured out.

"The colonel wanted a son, but he got two daughters. After me, our mom couldn't have any more children. And on top of me not being the boy he'd wanted, I was always getting into trouble. Drawing pictures on my math worksheets and getting lost in the songs I made up when I was supposed to do chores. I cried too much. Felt too much."

"You were just a kid."

I closed my eyes. "Didn't matter. He was cruel to our mom and Lori, but the colonel *hated* me. He would stick me in the basement and call me stupid and lazy through the closed door."

"Jesus, Ayla." Teller stroked my back, holding me tight to his chest.

"The colonel never hit me, but his words were meant to hurt, and they did. I used to ask myself what I'd done wrong that he could hate me that much."

"*Nothing*," Teller said fiercely. "You did absolutely nothing."

I was shaking. I couldn't believe I was telling him this. I had never told *anyone* all of this, but it was leaching out of me like poison.

I needed it out of me.

"As I got older, I got more defiant. Every time we moved to a new place, I could try out being someone else instead of myself."

"Performing?"

"Exactly. Even Lori didn't know how bad it was for me. She had her own friends, like Ashford. It was even worse after our mom got fed up and left."

"She didn't try to take you girls with her?"

"The colonel would never have let her. I guess Mom just... decided to forget about us."

That was hard to say, but I'd come to terms with it. Mom hadn't tried to contact me, even after I got famous. I was grateful for that. It would've been so much worse if she showed up, armed with apologies and excuses, wanting money.

"Lori and I both stayed away from the house as much as possible whenever our father was around."

"Can't blame you."

"I babysat a lot. The little kids were the best. They looked at me like I was someone special."

"You *are* someone special." Teller was using that self-assured tone again. Like he knew exactly what he was talking about. Like he believed it down to his bones.

I smiled sadly. The words kept coming. A torrent that I could no longer hold back. "When I was sixteen, the colonel was stationed in Upstate New York. One night, I'd been babysitting next door. The family had a boy in middle school. The dad was a sergeant. Roy Carpenter. I thought he was nice. Sergeant Carpenter gave me flowers once for my birthday. But that night, the sergeant walked me to my door, and he...he tried to kiss me."

"*What?*"

"I punched him in the face."

"Good. He deserved worse."

"I thought about kneeing him in the balls too, but he backed off." A short laugh cut through my heartache again, then disappeared as the sadness took over. "My father must've seen through the window. He exploded when I got inside. Accused me of slutting around the base. It was so unfair. I finally told him off. Told him exactly what I thought of him. And...that was the last night I ever spent there. I left home before the morning came. Never went back."

"It took a lot of courage to leave."

"Didn't feel courageous. I sneaked away. Didn't even wait for Lori to get home. It felt like my only choice."

There was more to it than I'd said. But it just hurt too much to go through every horrible thing about that night. I'd never told anyone those details, not even my sister.

I was shocked I'd said as much as I had to Teller. My body trembled with the force of it.

"But you went to New York City, right? All on your own. That took guts. You survived, and you built a career for yourself. Now you're one of the most talented and respected women in the world."

"Yet a shitty anonymous message referring to my past can tear me down. Like I'm still that scared kid inside."

Teller's fingers hooked my chin. Lifted it so our eyes met. "I have never met anyone as resilient as you are. Or so determined. You're not afraid to make trouble when there's a good reason. I admire that about you."

"A lot of people might be surprised the chief of police approves of troublemaking."

"Well, sometimes I do. Your bravery blows me away. You stand up night after night in front of thousands of people and you show them who you are."

"Do I? What if I don't know who I am at all?" I couldn't believe I'd admitted that to him. Maybe it was the quiet stillness around us, the shadowed light. And the kind things he'd said.

"All I can tell you is what I see. You are...Ayla, you're breathtaking. No one can take that away from you."

A small whimper escaped my lips. Why did praise from him feel so much more significant than anything I'd ever received? "Thank you."

"I hope I don't remind you of someone who hurt you."

"*No.*" I shook my head emphatically. "You're pretty much the exact opposite. Military guys tend to make me nervous, not going to lie. That's been true for a long time. But I know you're nothing like him." Nothing like Sergeant Carpenter either.

Teller wasn't like anyone I'd met before.

"You didn't know that at first, though," he said. "When we met, I was kind of an ass."

I laughed, even though I still felt raw and vulnerable from everything I'd confessed. "I know you better now. You're one of the good ones, aren't you?"

"Trying to be. Every damn day."

I dipped my head, feeling shy again. "I might even like you."

"You like me, huh?"

"Might."

"Well, I like you too," he rasped. "Very much. Maybe too much."

"How much is too much?"

"Enough that I'm not sure I trust myself."

"I trust you."

"I know. And I know what an incredible gift that is. *You* are a gift."

The whole SUV was probably covered with snow by now. We were in our own tiny world, just us. My breaths were shallow, taking in the scent of him with every breath. Pure masculinity.

Teller was a very attractive man, and I'd noticed that before, but suddenly I couldn't think about anything else.

In my regular life, I was surrounded by good-looking men on a daily basis. Models and back-up dancers, movie stars and fellow musicians. But none of them ever made me respond this way. A flood of intense *want* that tightened my nipples and throbbed in my clit.

In my past, feeling small had been the same as feeling worthless. Weak. But not with him. Not even close.

Teller's size and his sheer presence overpowered me in a whole new way. He made *me* feel powerful because this strong, charismatic yet gentle man had every ounce of his attention fixed on me.

I could follow anywhere he would lead, and he'd make sure everything was alright. He would take care of me.

Tentatively, I brought my hand to his broad chest. Moved it

upward to his shoulder, where I'd been massaging him earlier. "You have scars here too?"

"I do."

"You said your scars don't hurt. But what do they feel like?"

"The skin is desensitized now. I can still feel plenty, though." There wasn't anything flirtatious about how he'd said that, yet another pulse of arousal made its way down my body.

"Does it feel nice for someone to touch you there?"

He pressed his lips together, and at the same time, his eyes darted down to my mouth. "Find out if you want."

I carefully touched his scarred cheek again, and Teller brought his hand up, covering mine. His head moved slightly, rubbing the skin of his cheek against my palm and making me shiver.

"Does feel nice. But how are your fingers still so cold?" he murmured.

"Maybe you didn't do enough to warm them up."

Without breaking eye contact, Teller brought my hand to his mouth. He closed his lips around my pointer and middle finger. His mouth was hot. His teeth nipped me.

Oh, *God*.

I whimpered again, but this one was a desperate sound made of pure lust. "*Teller*."

He groaned, eyes sliding almost closed. "When you say my name... You don't know what that does to me."

"Show me."

He came closer. Leaning in.

But at the last second, he stopped and wiped a hand over his face.

"Fuck. *Fuck*. What am I doing?"

"I thought maybe you were going to kiss me."

He bent forward, elbows going to his knees, and scrubbed his fingers through his short hair. "After what you just told me? And we're in my department vehicle. I'm in uniform, and I'm supposed to be looking out for you, not taking advantage of you."

"I wasn't objecting."

"That doesn't make it okay. I should have more control than this. I am so far over the line right now, Ayla. *Way* over the line."

"Then take me with you."

SEVENTEEN

Teller

"I WASN'T OBJECTING," she'd just said.

"That doesn't make it okay. I should have more control than this."

But I had never wanted any woman as badly as I wanted Ayla.

I'd meant to stay strong. All well and good when I was trying to make her feel better as she cried.

Ashford or Callum had mentioned that Ayla and Lori's father died, but if the colonel had been alive? I would've been eager to give the man someone closer to his own size to pick on. What kind of trash treated his daughter that way? How could her mother have left her in that situation?

And what about the man's superiors? Or anyone else on the bases where he served. Was it possible someone knew, and let it go on? It made no difference that her father hadn't struck her physically. He had hurt her deep. Same with that sergeant who'd tried to kiss the beautiful babysitter. Fuck that guy.

Ayla had scars every bit as much as I did.

I was humbled that she'd shared her history with me. All I'd wanted was to hold her and make her feel better. Show her that better men existed. She was safe with me.

But then she'd touched me, proving exactly how weak I was.

Not the kind of coward who would ever take out his anger or his lust on a defenseless girl.

No, I was the kind of idiot who got carried away when a gorgeous, brave woman pressed herself against me and caressed the places where I ached. A woman who had to feel vulnerable right now. She needed comfort. Not seduction.

"I am so far over the line right now, Ayla. *Way* over the line." I bent over, dropping my elbows to my knees to cover the obvious tent in my uniform pants. My cock had never been this hard in my life. I wanted to cup my bulge and stroke it to get some friction, and *seriously*? How was that even in my mind right now?

"Then take me with you," she said.

Slowly, I turned my head to look at her. Her blond hair, almost as white as the snow outside, was tousled around her delicate features. The green of her irises was bright. Beguiling and yes, vulnerable, but also completely sure.

She wanted this.

Our coats were still in the front seat, drying off from our outside adventure, and the space blankets were scattered where we'd let them fall. No wonder her hands had still been cold. Except that thought led me to the memory of her fingers in my mouth. How I wanted to drag my tongue over the rest of her, nip her with my teeth and kiss away the sting. Cover her with my body and keep her from anyone who might dare hurt her.

Keep her for myself.

And that selfish desire, that craving, that fucking *need* to have this woman, was so much stronger than any of my lofty ideals.

"Come here to me." I barely recognized the sound of my own voice. A low, bass rumble.

Ayla knee-walked across the bench, covering the foot or so between us. She didn't have far to go. We'd been sitting close to each other, cuddled up on the bench backseat until I'd retreated. But this was important. If Ayla wanted to cross this line with me, it had to be her choice.

When her bent leg brushed my thigh, my arm hooked her

waist. I swung her so she was in my lap, straddling me. Her palms landed on my chest.

"Put your hands here," I said, pointing at my collar. "On my skin, like you did earlier. Get them warm."

Her fingers tucked into the opening of my shirt and rested on my collarbones. The coolness of her hands felt good. Demanding my focus. It was my job to take care of her and make her comfortable, and I relished that. "Is that better?" I asked.

She nodded. Blond strands fell across her cheek, and her lips looked plump and pink.

"You want me to kiss you, Troublemaker?"

"Yes," she breathed. "Do whatever you want to me."

My hips wanted to move, but I kept myself still. I held onto her waist, squeezing gently. "Fuck, Ayla, you shouldn't tell anyone that. Especially me."

"I think you're exactly the person I can say it to."

She meant because she trusted me. I planned to deserve that trust. I wouldn't hurt her.

But I'd been holding back this part of myself for so long that I wanted a hell of a lot. I was like a starving man who'd been offered a feast.

I wanted to *devour* her.

"We'll just start here. And then we'll see." I'd admired her lips in the photos and videos I'd seen online. I was man enough to admit it. But Ayla in flesh and blood, here in my arms—she was *real* and better than any possible fantasy.

This was who I wanted. This was who I couldn't resist.

I circled my arms tight around her and brushed my lips over hers.

The next kiss was even lighter, slower, because I wanted to savor every second of this. If I was the starving man in front of a feast, then this was my first taste, when I had to stop and wonder if anything had ever been this good.

Then she sighed and rested her weight against my chest, her head tilting. Our lips fit together. The tip of my tongue slid along the seam of her mouth, and she opened on a whimper. Her tongue pushed against mine, and that made my cock jump in the too-tight confines of my pants.

My hands moved up her back. One rested at her neck, the other delving into her silky hair. She made a sound of pleasure, almost a purr, so I rubbed her scalp with my fingertips as I sucked on her lower lip.

Then I tightened my grip just enough to tug her hair strands a little. Her lips parted wide as she moaned.

"You like that?"

"Mmmm." Ayla's eyelids went half-mast. I directed her toward me again so I could keep kissing her.

I didn't ever want to stop kissing her.

I loved when she showed her eagerness, licking into my mouth and wiggling her behind on my lap. When she finally slotted herself all the way against me and felt my erection, she gasped. My chest lifted and fell as I breathed.

"You feel how hard you make me?"

That sweet look of surprise turned naughty and teasing. "Bet I can make you even harder."

A brief moment of disbelief flashed through my mind. I could hardly trace the chain of events that had led us here. At some point later on, I was probably going to have to think about it.

How was it possible I had Ayla Maxwell rutting herself against my cock right now?

But at the moment all my blood had rushed south. All my brain could process was how good she felt.

"Bet you can. Hold on. I'll make this better." Reaching between us, I adjusted myself to tuck my cock against my fly. I guided her forward to kiss me again as she rode my lap.

"You feel me against your clit, sweetheart?" I asked between pulls from her lips.

"Mmm. *Oh*. Teller. It's good."

Sounded like a yes to me.

How was this even happening?

The air in the cabin was steamy, the windows fogging with condensation. Ayla worked her sweet little body against my cock until my thigh muscles tightened. Her whimpers and moans only cranked up the heat running through me.

Molten pleasure dripped to the base of my spine.

Fuck. I was about to come in my uniform pants.

Then furious knocking against the window splashed cold water over the moment. “Chief? Hey, we’re here to rescue you!”

EIGHTEEN
Teller

SHIT. That was Susan's voice.

Really? Fucking *now*?

Ayla yelped and dove off my lap. Snow disappeared from the driver's side window as someone wiped it away, and a flashlight beam shone in, blurry from the fog on the glass. Ayla and I must've been so wrapped up in each other we didn't hear the engine approaching.

I opened the door. Icy air hit my face, cooling off my skin as fast as my erection retreated. It was still snowing, but not as much as earlier.

"Susan." I cleared my throat. "Thanks."

She smiled, her face pink from the cold. "You okay, Ms. Maxwell? Bet you're ready to get out of there!"

"Pretty much." Ayla had the space blanket around her, skin flushed. I lifted an eyebrow at her, and her lips made a straight line like she was trying not to laugh. Felt like we were two teenagers who'd gotten rousted from the local make-out spot. I just hoped Susan couldn't guess what we'd been doing.

The fogged windows might've been a dead giveaway, though, judging by Susan's odd expression. "Seems you've had quite the adventure."

"So to speak." I grabbed for the coats in the front seat. Ayla's was still damp from her dip in the snowbank, so I took mine instead and draped it around her. "You'll go out first. Susan will help you up the embankment to the road."

"I can manage."

"But it's a lot darker and the snow's deeper than earlier. I'll be right behind you."

"Good, I want you close," she whispered, her green eyes flirtatious as I secured the top button of the coat so it wouldn't fall off. It nearly swallowed her up. "Thank you, Teller."

Nngh. I bit back a growl. Seeing her lips all swollen from my mouth, and then hearing my name on them?

I desperately wanted to kiss her again. Almost did. But somehow, I restrained myself and lifted her over me toward the open door. Susan reached in to grab her.

"Okay, honey, you remember me? Officer Nichols," Susan said.

"Sure do. Thanks for coming to get us."

"Chief would have my hide if I didn't. He's a tyrant."

Ayla glanced back at me. "I know it."

My heart hammered, remembering how she'd crawled across the bench seat toward me before straddling me and riding my lap like a horny cowgirl.

Had that actually happened?

Susan cackled. "Let's get you up this slope, Ms. Maxwell. It's not that steep, but it's icy."

"You can call me Ayla."

"Then I certainly will. If you call me Susan."

Outside, it was that uncanny twilight that happens at night during a snowstorm. The headlights from a couple of vehicles waiting on the road added to the brightness. Looked like Susan's department SUV and a tow truck.

I greeted the tow driver, Earl, who offered to help get our bags from my trunk. By now, Ayla was already sitting in the front seat of Susan's vehicle, hopefully toasty warm. The engine was running.

"Chief, I figured you could take my ride," Susan explained. "So you can get safe and sound to Hartley. Just in case your vehicle got more banged up than you thought. We'll tow it and I'll ride with Earl back to Silver Ridge."

"I appreciate that," I said. "Good thinking."

"I tried to radio on my way to see if that worked for you, but I dunno, maybe the satellite was squirrelly."

"Could be." Or maybe we'd been so distracted I completely ignored everything but the woman in the backseat with me.

"You'll probably need a coat, though. Did something happen to Ayla's?" Susan batted her eyelashes innocently. "She looked very cozy in yours."

"Don't start. Her coat got wet, and it's drying off."

"Seems you *are* a fan of hers after all." Susan rested a hand on my shoulder. "Just don't get your heart broke, Chief."

Hell. Truer words. Susan had no idea how right she was.

Ayla looked so pretty sleeping. It was hard to wake her up. But we couldn't sit in the SUV all night. It was late enough as it was.

"Wake up, Ayla. We're here." I leaned over to kiss her forehead, unable to resist.

"Hmmm?" Her eyes blinked open. "Crap. I fell asleep. We're in Hartley?"

"Yep. The Last Refuge Inn. You've been here before, haven't you?"

"Yeah." She yawned the word, and that was damn cute.

The last couple hours of the drive had passed uneventfully. While the snow continued to fall, there hadn't been any more issues. No more elk in the road.

After we said goodbye to Susan and got moving again, I had

spent a good ten minutes on the radio checking in on things at the station. That big accident was cleared and things were calm back in Silver Ridge, even with the heavy snowfall. They had managed without me for a few hours, despite me going MIA on the radio while I was otherwise distracted. Not that I regretted a single moment I'd spent with Ayla so far today.

But by the time I was done checking in, she had drifted off. And after that, I kept glancing over at her, pleased that she was still wearing my coat and also clueless about where things stood between us.

We'd been extremely hot and heavy in that backseat. But had that been more about the emotion of the moment? All those things we'd confessed to each other. Being isolated together.

Obviously, we had chemistry. But that didn't mean Ayla would want to finish what we'd started.

I mean, I sure as hell did. But we were back to civilization now. I couldn't assume I knew what she wanted.

She sat up straighter, going to unbuckle her seatbelt. I beat her to it, pressing the button and gently lifting the cross belt. "Thanks," she said softly. "I should've stayed awake with you. That's like, a road trip rule."

"I didn't mind. But there *is* something we should still talk about. That email earlier. I might have some ideas for tracking down who sent it."

She nodded. "Okay. Not tonight though. I'm too worn out to talk about that."

"Later, then."

The inn was all lit up. The entrance building had once been the old ranch house on this property. Stone and rustic timber, with a generous porch. But the building beyond it was a more modern addition. Snow blanketed the peaked roof line. Smoke puffed from the chimneys against the night sky.

But the instant Ayla spoke again, I forgot about everything else. "You really didn't mind me falling asleep?" she asked. "You didn't miss me?" Her tone was flirty. Teasing.

Adrenaline and heat roared to life like a match struck against kindling.

I'd been getting tired those last miles, but now I was wide awake.

"Oh, I missed you. Had to keep my mind busy by replaying how you felt up against me." I reached over and rested my hand on her thigh. Then lifted it to stroke her chin. "What your kisses tasted like."

I was tempted to pull her into the backseat with me. We were late already, so nobody would know if we were out in the parking lot another half hour, right? How tired was she, really?

Except I didn't want this woman in the backseat of a car if we could stretch out in a bed. And I certainly didn't want to settle for half an hour if I could have her all night.

I imagined laying her out in front of a roaring fireplace. Kissing and touching every part of her while the flames cast dancing shadows over her naked skin.

Should I ask her to come to my hotel room after we checked in? I was so out of practice with this kind of thing.

She inhaled. "Teller—"

The front door to the inn burst open, and Grace and Callum came charging out. Grace wore a parka with a fur-lined hood pulled up around her face. She and her brother both waved as they crossed the parking lot toward us.

Shit, the universe kept having the worst timing today.

They went to Ayla's side of the car and opened her door. "You made it," Grace said. "We've been so worried."

Ayla jumped down, returning Grace's hug. "I'm sorry. We went off the road and got stuck. There was no cell service."

"No, it's fine. We know all about it. Officer Nichols called with updates. But how crazy is this storm, *right*? Wait, why are you wearing Teller's coat?" Grace slammed the door closed, so I didn't hear Ayla's response.

I dropped my head against the seat back.

After a few seconds, I realized Callum was staring at me

through the windshield, so I got out. "Long day?" he asked, rounding the vehicle with me to help me get the luggage.

"In some ways." I'd draped Ayla's coat in the backseat to finish drying, so I grabbed that too.

I needed to find a way to get her alone again. Pretty much my top priority at this moment, aside from breathing.

"You and Ayla were stuck together for a few hours there." Callum's tone held some kind of a question.

"Yep."

"Looks like you both came out unscathed."

"Oh, I don't know about that," I muttered.

NINETEEN

Ayla

THE INSIDE of the Last Refuge Inn was just as quaint as the outside. Lots of wood and warm, homey accents. Black and white historical photos adorned the walls. The place smelled like cinnamon and pine.

Over a year and a half ago, when I ran from all the pressures of my life and came to Ashford for help, he'd set me up here at Last Refuge for a few weeks to rest and recuperate in total privacy. No paparazzi, no media. Nobody but Ashford and Emma and their families had known where I was. The Last Refuge property also featured high-level security because they often housed women who were fleeing from abusive situations.

It had been exactly what I needed. The people here in Hartley had been incredibly gracious to me. So this place would always have a soft spot in my heart.

Yet Teller's embrace had felt pretty warm and inviting, too.

Grace ushered me to a sitting area in front of a roaring fireplace, her arm around my shoulders. "Are you hungry? Thirsty? Don't worry about checking in. We've got everything handled. Figured you would be exhausted by the time you made it here."

Piper appeared holding a mug. She placed it in my hands. "Hot toddy. I'm guessing you need this. I hope my brother wasn't too much of a bear to deal with." Her gaze darted to the coat draped around me. I'd gotten rid of the space blanket hours ago when we switched to Susan's vehicle, but I hadn't taken off Teller's jacket for one minute. I didn't want to now.

But his sister and Grace were watching me, and it was already toasty in here. I unbuttoned the coat and slipped it off, resisting the urge to press the collar to my nose the way I'd done a few times in the car.

"Teller and I got along pretty well, actually."

If getting along included making out like fiends, fogging up the windows, and dry humping like a couple of horned-up teenagers. Except I'd never been that turned on before in my life, especially not with some boy when I was in high school. Teller was a fully grown man in *all* the ways, judging by what I'd felt in his pants when I was wantonly gyrating my hips.

Okay, now I was overheating.

I took a sip of hot toddy, but that didn't help with the flush to my skin.

Teller and Callum joined us, setting down our bags over to one side. Teller held out my coat. "It's dry now."

"Thanks." Our hands brushed as I took my coat, and I was probably supposed to give his Silver Ridge PD coat back now. That would be normal. Even though I kinda wanted to curl up with it like a blanket before I went to sleep tonight.

Unless Teller was in my bed already. Keeping me warm himself.

Flutters shivered through my stomach.

I realized I was just standing there looking at him, and he was looking at me, and everyone else was observing this obvious tension. So I held out his coat. "I appreciate the loaner."

"Anytime."

"So, what's the coat switch about?" Piper asked, grinning. "Sounds like a story."

"A story?" Dane strode toward us, holding a couple more mugs balanced in one hand, a bottle of rum in the other. "I'm up for a story." He passed a mug to Teller. The second mug he gave to Grace, followed by a kiss.

Teller nodded at me, gesturing for me to go ahead, and I almost got lost in the wintergreen of his eyes again.

"Well, after we got stuck—" I began.

"Hold on," Callum interrupted. "You said something before about going off the road."

"We almost hit an elk."

There was a collective groan from all the Silver Ridge locals.

We all sat down. I squeezed onto a couch with Grace and Dane, while Teller was on a couch next to Piper with Callum perched on the arm. Nice and cozy, everyone sipping rum-spiked hot toddies, and I pushed aside my annoyance at Teller being so far away.

I told them how we'd narrowly avoided a head-on collision with a thousand pound animal, and then how I had desperately needed a bathroom. "Teller got out and dug me this little snow shelter to do my business in."

There was laughter all around.

After some prodding by his sister, Teller added to the story, explaining that I slipped beneath the snow on my way back to the SUV. "And then we just tried to stay warm and stay patient until Susan Nichols turned up with Earl and the tow truck," he finished.

I nodded, perhaps too emphatically. "Yep. That's pretty much the whole thing."

Don't look at him, I told myself. It was mortifying to think of both our families knowing about what else we'd gotten up to in that backseat. Probably because I wanted to do it again, right now, and a whole lot more. If the rest of them found out, they'd never let us hear the end of it.

Remember how you and Teller Landry had the hots for each other over the wedding weekend? Just because you were trapped together for a couple hours in that storm?

It was more than that. We had a connection. I'd shared things with Teller that I hadn't told anyone. He'd held me as I cried. Made me feel so cared for, so safe.

He kept insisting he wanted to help me with my potential stalker too, and that was a whole other issue. One that I could think about tomorrow.

But Teller and I *couldn't* be more than a weekend fling. Not realistically.

"How was dinner with Emma's family?" I asked.

"So much fun," Grace gushed. "Emma's little siblings are best friends with Maisie, and Ollie bonded with them too. We missed you, though. It's too bad you couldn't come with us this morning. Would've saved all that drama."

Dane affectionately pushed Grace's glasses up her nose. "But then they wouldn't have the story."

I glanced at Teller, which was a mistake. His look was soft and knowing, cutting straight to the heart of me.

"Ashford's having daddy-daughter time with Maisie tonight," Grace went on, "and Emma's staying with her mom and stepdad."

"And the other guests from Silver Ridge?" Teller asked. "Did people make it alright? With the pass closed, I'm sure there are some disappointed folks who couldn't get here." His default gruffness was in place, but his concern for everyone in his town showed through.

Callum grabbed the rum bottle and topped up his mug. "Actually, most everyone made it. Once the news about the storm spread, they got out of Dodge real quick this morning and got over the pass before the closure. No mishaps."

"Except for you, Landry," Dane said with a laugh. Teller frowned at him, and why did I suddenly find that so adorable?

Piper and Grace launched into an excited recitation of everything that would happen tomorrow. We were going to have brunch with Emma, her mom, and stepmom first thing. Girls only. Then it would be nails and hair, followed by helping Emma get ready.

"And the guys are doing their own male-bonding extravaganza," Piper added. "They have big plans."

"Not sure I signed up for that," Teller grumped.

I looked over at the men to see Callum subtly shake his head at Teller, like he was saying, *Don't worry about it.*

I set my half-empty mug on the little table between us. "Then maybe we should turn in early."

Grace clapped her hands. "You're right. We have so much to do tomorrow. Let's head up. You and I are on the second floor."

Crap, I had forgotten all about how Grace and I were sharing a room tonight. So we could enjoy the excitement and be completely focused on Emma tomorrow, and of course on Maisie too when Ashford turned her over.

Wedding festivities, *yay*.

Which was the whole reason I had come this weekend, not to sneak off and get naked with the police chief. There would be none of that tonight. No matter how much I wanted the man.

It was sweet how Grace wanted to make me a part of everything. I'd told her, *Treat me like a normal person. I don't need anything fancy or special.* If only I'd been more of a diva, demanding my own suite with a Jacuzzi, a bowl full of condoms, and soundproofing.

But tomorrow, Grace would be back with Dane. And very happy about it, considering the way she was kissing him goodbye.

"Okay." Grace threaded her arm with mine and led me toward the elevator. "Shall we? Dane, could you carry Ayla's bags?"

"I've got it," a different deep voice said, and my heart lifted when I saw Teller right behind us carrying my things. He stepped into the elevator with Grace and me, and she hit the button for two.

She smiled at him. "Thanks, Teller. *Very* thoughtful of you."

"I promised Ayla I'd get her to the inn. Just finishing the job."

Ugh, he was so close yet so far away. And as usual, he took up the bulk of the small elevator car.

I loved Grace, I really did, but I'd never wanted her to leave me alone more than I did *right now*.

The elevator doors opened on the second floor. Teller trailed after us. Grace sent a smirk my way, which I pretended not to notice. "Night, Teller," she said brightly after unlocking the door. "See you tomorrow. I'm going to head right in and brush my teeth, so you two can say goodnight, or...whatever."

My face burned. So Grace had picked up on the vibes between us. The tension in the elevator had not just affected me. Or maybe it had been the coat swap. But I wasn't going to admit to *anything*.

The bathroom door snicked closed, and I turned to Teller in the doorway. He'd set down my luggage just inside, but then he'd stepped back to the other side of the threshold.

"Thanks for getting me here," I said.

"My pleasure." He leaned against the door frame. At some point, he'd undone the top few buttons of his navy uniform shirt, which only reminded me of what he'd said in the SUV. *Put your hands here on my skin. Get them warm.*

Would Grace definitely notice if I sneaked out tonight? Maybe she was a deep sleeper. I really was tired though. I'd probably fall asleep in his arms, which didn't sound like such a bad thing.

"Tomorrow," he murmured softly, as if he knew just what I was thinking. "If you want."

"I want."

He reached out and cupped the back of my neck. Drew me in. But instead of bringing his lips to my mouth, he kissed my forehead, letting that contact linger. Like the last thing he wanted was to pull away.

But eventually, he did. "Night, Troublemaker."

"Goodnight, Teller."

"Be good."

"And if I'm not?"

He touched his fingertip to my lips, a silent promise, before dropping his hand. He stood there in the hall until I'd shut the door. Then I peeked through the peephole and saw his shoulders and chest move with a heavy exhale before he finally turned to go.

Tomorrow.

When I turned to open my bag and find my pajamas, I noticed that his coat was there, tucked underneath mine. He'd left it for me. My stomach swooped with pleasure.

I picked up his coat, pushed my face into the lining, and inhaled.

TWENTY

Teller

AYLA

How's the male-bonding extravaganza?

I SMILED AT MY PHONE. Beside me, Ollie shoveled chocolate-chip pancakes in his mouth. Dane and Ashford chatted across from us. Elsewhere at the long table, Emma's father and her stepdad both laughed at something Callum had just said. Emma's uncles were here too, Ashford's other friends like Judson Lawrence...a bunch of us. This event had taken over most of the inn.

ME

Male bonding has mainly been pancakes, bacon and coffee at the tavern. That's where I am now.

Before, there was optional deadlifting in the on-site gym. Army vs. Navy. There's a million of us around here who are Army, as you know. But Emma's dad Nash was a Navy SEAL. A strength contest was pretty much required.

AYLA

So, usual guy stuff.

Complete with grunting noises.

Did you compete? Was Army victorious?

I forfeited. Ollie's with me. Had to steer him away from the gym. He would've broken himself or someone else.

Good call. I bet you would have won though.

[muscle arm emoji]

[kissing face emoji]

Fuck me, now she had me sending emojis to make her smile. I'd never before been an emoji guy. But it was worth it for that kissing emoji she sent back. My inner caveman was very happy about the fact she thought I'd win that contest.

What was happening to me? Seriously?

It had been a good morning so far. I'd slept well. My room had been quiet, and I *liked* quiet.

But I also liked Ayla's laugh. And the cute snuffling sounds she had made while she was asleep in the car yesterday.

I craved seeing her again. Usually I was focused on family, on work, on Silver Ridge. Rarely on selfish needs.

Ayla made me want to be so fucking selfish.

She would also be leaving Colorado the day after tomorrow. This was beyond hopeless. It would be a lot smarter of me to forget this flirtation or infatuation or *whatever* right now. But that wasn't going to happen.

If this was stupid, then maybe being smart was overrated.

How was the girls-only brunch?

Festive and fabulous. Maisie and Emma's little sister were princesses holding court. Nails and hair for everyone except Emma are finished. Mom and stepmom have only cried three times, but luckily, they haven't done their mascara yet.

I bet you look pretty.

[blushing face emoji]

When can I see you today?

Turn around.

I glanced over my shoulder and saw a flash of pale blond, just visible beyond the doorway between the tavern and the lobby. My pulse accelerated. "Ollie, can you stay here with Uncle Callum for a bit? I'll be right back."

"Okay." Ollie looked like he was contemplating a jail break.

I got up and clapped a hand on Callum's shoulder. "Cal, make sure Ollie doesn't go anywhere? I'll be back in a couple minutes."

He up-nodded. "I got 'im."

"Thanks."

I stuck my hands in my jeans pockets and made my way toward the lobby. Didn't see her at first when I strolled around reception, but then I spotted a small figure waiting in a quiet side hallway.

"Hi there." Ayla wore a simple pair of gray sweatpants and a loose shirt, yet somehow she made it look like designer fashion. Her hair fell in soft, styled curls around her shoulders, begging for me to run my hands through it. Light makeup highlighted her features.

"See? I knew you looked pretty."

Smiling, she ran a finger down the row of buttons on my chest. "You're wearing a Henley today? That's just unfair."

"This shirt's called a Henley?"

She laughed.

"Why is that unfair?" I asked.

"Because it makes your pecs look huge. Drives the girls crazy. I don't think you have a clue how attractive you are, Chief Landry. I might get jealous."

I braced a hand on the wall by her head. Ayla Maxwell was jealous? About *me*?

"There's only one girl around here I care about attracting."

Ayla smiled and looked down, just like that blushing emoji she'd sent me earlier.

I ran my fingertip along her cheek to her chin. "You must've put a spell on me yesterday," I murmured. "I don't get like this. I barely slept."

"You wish this wasn't happening?"

"Didn't say that."

In fact, I'd never felt so alive.

Her gaze fell to the carpet again. "I brought your coat into the bed with me last night. I hope you don't mind. I made sure Grace didn't see."

My cock swelled as I thought of her in bed snuggled into my coat. I growled with frustration, wanting to wrap her up and kiss her breathless.

How was it possible I could feel this wild about a woman who, two days ago, had hated me?

"I don't have long," she said. "I snuck away since Emma's getting her hair done, and Maisie's occupied with her grandmas."

"I don't either. Ollie's waiting for me at the table." My body leaned involuntarily toward her, but I heard voices and footsteps nearby. They might see us. Then again, if I didn't touch her, I might not survive.

I reached out and took her hand, running my thumb over her knuckles.

"I want you to be my date for the wedding," I blurted out before really thinking it through. Which was not like me. I wasn't going to take it back though. My chin lifted, and I waited for her response.

"Your date?"

"We don't have to make a public thing out of it, if you don't want. But people have a tendency to hook up at weddings. I need to know that, if you spend the night with anyone this trip, it'll be me."

I couldn't remember the last time I'd moved on a woman this way. But I hadn't wanted anyone like this before.

"You think I plan to hook up with some other guy? After what happened between us on the way here?"

I closed my lips on a growl. "I'd prefer not to think about it. But if you do, be forewarned, the guy might happen to disappear into the woods by Monday and never be heard from again. Purely by coincidence."

With a smirk, she angled her head, lips pressing to my jaw as her hand rested between my pecs. Barely any contact, yet she conveyed so much passion and anticipation in those little gestures that I had to order my cock not to get hard.

"Does that answer your question?" she asked.

My fingers found her hip. "So you're mine tonight?"

Mine, mine, mine.

She nodded. "Wish we had more than a couple minutes right now."

"Me too. But now that we have *that* out of the way... Maybe we should use these minutes to discuss the stalker situation. I had some thoughts about how we might track down who sent you that email."

She huffed and dropped her head back, groaning. "*Really*? I can think of more fun ways to spend two minutes."

Like two minutes would be enough for anything I had in mind. But besides that. "This is important, Ayla. I want to know you're safe when your plane takes off tomorrow."

Because no matter what happened this weekend, it would

come to an end all too fast. I couldn't forget what else was going on. My sense of responsibility wouldn't let me.

Her eyes clouded over. So did her expression. "What do you suggest?"

"You know Emma's uncle Aiden?"

"Yes, I met him before when I stayed here."

"Then you know Aiden and his friends are good at investigating problems that require discretion."

Understanding dawned on her beautiful face. "You want them to look into the creepy email."

I nodded. "Forward the message to me, and I can share it with Aiden. I already mentioned this morning that I need a private chat with him."

"Unofficially? Not as Silver Ridge Chief of Police?"

I touched her chin, a brief slide of skin on skin that only left me wanting more. "I'll just be asking as Teller. Your date for the wedding who's looking out for you."

Ayla blinked at me with those long lashes.

Then she said, "No."

Damn. She had every right to tell me no, but I'd thought we were past that. "No?"

"You don't have to fix this for me. If you're talking to Aiden about me, then I want to be involved. We can talk to him together." She pulled her phone from her pocket, checking the time. "How about an hour from now?"

"I'll check with Aiden and text you to confirm."

"Okay." She started to step away, but I caught her hand. After checking we were alone, I brushed a kiss to the inside of her wrist, feeling the delicate throb of her pulse.

"I'm glad you're trusting me to help you."

She whispered, "I'm really glad you're here."

TWENTY-ONE

Teller

AN HOUR LATER, Ayla met me in that same hallway. I whistled quietly. "You were pretty earlier, but you've left *pretty* behind in the dust. Wow."

Ayla wore a long-sleeved emerald-green dress. The wide neckline swooped to reveal a hint of enticing cleavage, and the skirt flared out at the waist, showing off the curves of her hips and ending just below her knees.

She touched the lapel of my sport coat. "You clean up well." Beneath the coat, I'd worn a striped button-down tucked into dark gray slacks. It was nothing special. Not in comparison to her.

"You nervous?" I asked.

"You can tell?"

"When I'm paying attention." Now that I was getting to know her better, it was impossible to do otherwise. I linked our fingers. "It'll be okay. We'll get through this, and then we can focus on the wedding again."

She nodded. I started to let go of her hand, and was surprised when her fingers tightened on mine. "You'll stay with me the whole time?" she asked.

"Of course." Again, I marveled at the shift between us. But at the same time, it felt natural to be this close to her. Even if it was just a temporary thing.

We went to the end of the hall to the door marked *Office*. I knocked. It opened right away. Jessi Shelborne, half of the duo that owned the inn, stood there with a curly haired toddler on her hip. "Ayla! It's wonderful to see you again. And you too, Chief Landry."

Ayla gave her a hug, then patted the toddler on the head. "And who's this munchkin? You were in your mama's belly last time I was here."

"This is Zoe. She was just giving her dad a goodbye kiss because it's naptime. Thank goodness we hired an event coordinator. Otherwise I'd be running around with my hair on fire." Jessi glanced down, noting our linked hands, but there was nothing more than fondness in her gaze when she smiled. "I'll see you both at the ceremony."

Aiden gave his wife and daughter another kiss before they left. A pang of something bittersweet hit me. But I brushed that aside as we stepped into the office and shut the door.

Aiden nodded a greeting at me, then held out his hand to Ayla. "It's been a minute," he said.

Ayla laughed. "It has. Your daughter is adorable."

"Not going to argue with you there." He hooked a thumb at the other man in the room, who'd been leaning casually against a wall and watching us with a lopsided smirk. "You remember River Kwon? Chief Landry mentioned you had an issue involving computers, and River's our computer guy."

"Yeah. Hi, River."

"Ayla. Lovely to see you again."

I bristled at his familiar tone. Which was ridiculous, because both Aiden and River were happily married. River's wife was the Colorado lieutenant governor.

But Ayla was the most beautiful woman in existence. I mean, they had to have noticed. She was exquisite, and as far as my possessive instincts were concerned, she was mine.

At least for today.

Ayla's fingers squeezed my hand. "It's possible I have a stalker. Teller offered to help, and he knows how important privacy is to me. I..." She swallowed, and I rubbed my thumb over her skin. "I want to keep this quiet."

"Quiet is my specialty." River gestured at a leather couch set against the wall. "Grab a seat and tell us what's been going on."

Ayla glanced at me like she was seeking reassurance. Given how brash and gutsy she could be, that just showed how uncomfortable she felt, even though she knew these men. And, truth be told, that soothed my flare of possessiveness. No matter how ridiculous it had been in the first place.

Aiden's network of friends had some next-level skills, and it was a long story how they'd all ended up in Hart County. Their group provided security for Last Refuge, but they were hardly your run-of-the-mill security guards. River had been a Navy SEAL and then CIA.

They handled delicate situations, and not always with entirely legal means. But that was all unconfirmed rumor, and it was better for us law-enforcement types not to know any specifics.

I knew we could count on Aiden and his friends, though. I would never have brought Ayla's problem to them otherwise. Dane Knightly had talked up his New York investigator, but we had assets of our own here in Hart County.

We both sat on the couch, and I let go of Ayla's hand, moving to wrap my arm around her shoulder instead. "Start at the beginning," I said softly. "Yesterday wasn't the first concerning message you've received, was it?"

Ayla leaned into me. "The first time was last September. I was in Toronto for a show. My team vets gifts and flowers that fans send. Same with letters and cards. I get my share of hate mail about how I'm corrupting the youth." She rolled her eyes. "I had never received anything dangerous or really concerning, as far as I know, anyway, and my manager Cheryl would tell me. But then in Toronto, I received a flower arrangement with a card."

She closed her eyes. I rubbed her shoulder.

Then she recited, "*You don't even know how beautiful you really are. I've always been your biggest fan.*"

A thread of uneasiness worked its way down my neck like a cold drop of water.

"Gives *me* the creeps," River said. "That's for sure."

"Fans say those kinds of things to me all the time. My team must've thought it was innocent. But there was a photo tucked inside. A photo of me at fifteen or sixteen, in front of the house on the Army base where I lived then. I think my sister Lori took it."

"A private photo?" Aiden rubbed a hand over his beard. "Something that wasn't publicly available?"

"That's right. It seemed...*dark*, like the message had something to do with my past. My childhood was not good. That's not something I talk about publicly. *Ever*."

Shit, no wonder it had been upsetting. Now I knew exactly how awful Ayla's life had been before she got away from her father. I exchanged a look with Aiden, and his brow knitted sympathetically.

"I asked my manager to find out who sent it. But according to the florist, the person paid over the phone with a cash gift card that was untraceable."

River perched on the edge of the desk across from us, hands clasped in his lap. Trying to make himself less intimidating. I'd used similar techniques plenty of times when interviewing crime victims. "Did your team contact law enforcement? Or a private investigator?"

"No. I've worked with investigators before, like after Lori died, but not this time. I didn't want to, even though I was still pretty shaken up. Didn't want to invite interest in my childhood for...reasons."

River nodded along like this didn't surprise him in the least.

"I didn't receive anything else suspicious in the months after.

I thought it was a one-off. I hoped it didn't mean anything at all." She took a heavy breath. "Until the email yesterday. Another message, another photo."

Ayla took her phone from her pocket, unlocked it, and handed the device to River. He studied the screen. I hadn't forgotten what it said, and fury rose in my throat as I recalled how frightened she'd been.

Someday you'll smile like that for me. And only me. Until then, I'll be watching.

Love, your Biggest Fan

River held the phone to show Aiden. "It's more threatening," River said. "Suggests an escalation.

Exactly my thought. "We have no idea how long this person has been trying to contact Ayla," I added, "or how long he's been watching her, planning his next move."

She shuddered. The last thing I wanted was to add to her fear, yet I also had to stress how serious this was. She couldn't just ignore it and hope it went away.

We didn't have a ton of stalking incidents in Silver Ridge, but it happened. I knew the progression. An obsession could start slow. Develop gradually inside the stalker's head. But once things escalated, it could get very bad, very fast.

"Was this photo taken recently?" River asked.

"Two days ago in Silver Ridge. I was in a store on Main. There was a crowd outside, watching me. Maybe someone from the crowd posted it online, and this creep downloaded it?" She shrugged. "I have no idea."

"Unless your stalker himself was in Silver Ridge that day," Aiden said.

"I considered that too," she whispered.

She seemed to fold into me, her head dropping to my shoulder. As if she wanted to disappear. The vulnerability of that gesture plucked every last one of my heart strings. I kissed her temple, knowing Aiden and River were right there, but at the current moment? I didn't care. They could think what they wanted.

Maybe she wasn't mine to keep. But right now, I was going to take care of her.

"I'll start with a reverse image search," River said. "If that photo was already posted online, I'll find it. See whether or not I can trace it back to the stalker." He held up Ayla's phone. "Mind if I keep this a few hours? I want to pull what I can from your email account. I'll return the phone later and go from there."

Ayla nodded, and her hair brushed my neck. "You really think you can trace the message to who sent it?"

"That's complicated. If this is the same guy who sent you the flowers in Toronto, he's got some idea of how to cover his tracks. But I'm pretty good at what I do." River winked. Which seemed unnecessarily flirty to me, but Ayla relaxed. "We'll help you through this. I'll go get started."

River stood up, and he left the office.

"I'm sure it wasn't easy to tell us that, so thank you," Aiden said to Ayla. "Take as long in here as you need. See you at the ceremony." He stepped out and shut the door.

"How you doing?" I asked.

"I'm trying not to smush my face against you, because my makeup will ruin your shirt."

Chuckling, I kissed her head again. "I can find another shirt."

She snuggled in closer, mouth curving. "I already said this. But I'm *really* glad you're here. Thanks for making me do that."

My arms closed around her. "We need to take this seriously, but you're not dealing with it alone. You are *not* alone."

Ayla lifted her head. "I didn't know they made men like you in real life."

"I'm just me."

"You're not *just* anything."

At this moment, I'm just yours, I thought.

"Kiss me?" she asked.

I dipped to press my lips to hers. My tongue slicked inside her mouth, and she answered with a moan, somehow fitting herself even tighter against me.

And my heart kept spinning in my chest, wondering when I was going to come to my senses.

TWENTY-TWO

Ayla

It was almost time for the ceremony. Guests were streaming into the event space, and the bridal party was waiting nearby for their cue. I'd just left Emma, Grace, and Maisie. All of them in great spirits, with no clue about the turmoil raging inside me.

The meeting with Aiden and River had taken a lot out of me. I still didn't want to believe I had a stalker, especially someone who might know things about my past. Thank goodness Teller had been there. So strong and gentle the entire time.

Sexy too. He acted like he didn't know how handsome he was. The way he'd looked in that Henley earlier, the soft fabric stretched over his chest? *Yikes*. He probably wasn't super lean or cut like a gym bunny. The type of guy who flexed in front of a mirror.

No, when Teller held me, he felt solid, with just enough give to make him an incredible cuddler.

I wanted to find out how he felt skin to skin.

Last night, I really had slept with his coat draped over me like another blanket. I'd slept more soundly than I had in a long time. I wanted to get back to that feeling, instead of this tangled-up sensation inside me. Like I was being pulled in too many different directions.

How long had Biggest Fan been watching me? And would he really escalate to something even worse?

"Miss Maxwell, would it be terrible if I asked for an autograph?" A woman with curly red hair, who I recognized as Rosie from the market in Silver Ridge, held out a postcard.

"Not at all. I'm happy to."

A scruffy man with a ponytail stood next to her. "Rosie loves your music. Won't play anything else. She's obsessed."

"Oh hush, Jimmy, you'll scare her off."

Rosie and her man weren't the first to come up to me today, and I truly didn't mind. Most of the wedding guests here were people I'd seen in Silver Ridge before, people who'd been nothing but kind to me.

A lot of people all over the world had claimed to be my "biggest fan." They talked about being obsessed with my music. With *me*. Almost always, it was harmless.

Yet I couldn't stop a sliver of fear from working its way under my skin again. Wondering if my stalker had actually been in Silver Ridge the other day.

If he could be here at the wedding right now.

Then I looked over and saw Teller with Ollie. He was all the way across the room, yet he had his eyes on me like he could be at my side in an instant. He wouldn't let anything happen to me here.

I rarely let myself lean on anyone, and it was so tempting to do that with him.

But when I got home tomorrow to my house in Malibu, he wasn't going to be there. He said I wasn't alone, yet all the safety I felt here with my family, with *Teller*, would disappear when I got on that plane.

"Thank you," Rosie gushed. "You've made my day."

I nodded, watching them find seats in the audience for the ceremony. Then a hand rested on my arm. "Ayla?" It was Dane, looking dapper in a suit. "Got a second? Ashford wanted to talk to you."

My stomach swooped. "Everything okay?"

Dane laughed. "Better than okay. Ashford's finally calmed down. But I think he's getting sentimental."

This I had to witness.

I followed Dane to the office where I'd met with Aiden and River earlier. Except now, Ashford was inside, handsome in a white suit and pacing the floor. Dane gestured for me to go in, while he hung back in the hallway.

Ashford had his hands tucked into his pockets, brow pensive, but he smiled when he saw me.

"Good, Dane found you."

"What's going on?"

"Before I go out there, I needed to say this."

"Yes?" I waited.

"I love you."

I was probably making a very strange face, because he snorted and kept talking.

"I love you like a sister. And a friend. But I don't think I've ever actually said those words, and I realized how shitty that is. After all those times you reached out to me, tried to call, and I shut you out."

I waved a hand dismissively. "We've both forgotten about that. It's not important anymore."

"It *is*, and I had to say it. In some ways, you might be the reason Emma and I got together."

"Me?"

He shrugged. "Sometimes, people need a little push. Or a not so little one. You showing back up in my life turned my world upside down, but that just made me realize how much I wanted something different. For me and Maisie both. Does that even make sense? I don't know. You're the poet, not me."

"I think I get it." My heart felt too big for my rib cage. A common problem when I was around my niece, but Maisie's dad could do that to me too, it seemed. "I love you too. Now let's get out there. You're about to get married, and I don't think you'll want to keep Emma waiting."

Ashford turned. But I put a hand on his arm. There was one more thing I needed to add.

"Lori's looking down on you and your family today. And she's really happy for you. I know it."

The seats were filling up. Teller and Piper had already found spots, placing Ollie between them. But there was a free seat next to the chief.

I worried for a split second that I'd be crashing their family party if I sat there. But then Teller's gaze found mine, like he'd been watching for me. His brow lifted subtly, and he nodded at the empty seat beside him.

When I sat down, Ollie pulled on Teller's sleeve. "Uncle Tell, she's really pretty," he whispered. It was a kid-whisper though, so I could easily hear him over the voices in the room.

"She is." Teller turned to me, his arm nudging mine. "Where'd you go?"

"Just having a sisterly chat with the groom."

"All good?"

Ashford and Dane walked to the front of the room, taking their places by the huge bank of floor-to-ceiling windows that showed the winter landscape outside. All snow-capped purple mountains in all their majesty, tall evergreens, blue sky. Ashford could hardly contain his smile. The man was practically vibrating with joy.

"Yep," I said. "All is well."

Despite the turmoil of the last couple of days, all the ups and downs, that felt like the absolute truth. Ashford was about to get married with Maisie by his side, and I was here with Teller. I didn't know what we were to each other, but this felt too good to fight it.

Maybe everything would be different tomorrow, but right now, all was well.

The music started up. The remaining guests took their seats, everyone turning to watch the aisle. Emma's little brother Thompson appeared first, adorable in his tiny suit and carrying the rings on a purple pillow. Then Emma's little sister Kelsea, followed by Maisie, both flower girls smiling wide.

Maisie's lavender dress flounced with every step. She looked so happy and proud of herself. My sister's baby girl. My heart swelled.

Grace came next, elegant in a darker purple dress and holding a bouquet of dahlias.

And then there was Emma, with her dad Nash escorting her. A collective hush of awe fell over the room. Her dress, a confection of lace and satin, followed the curves of her body. Her dark hair was swept back, and a long veil flowed around her as she walked.

She reached Ashford, and the look they shared was filled with so much love.

Tears burned in my nose and throat. This was exactly the moment they deserved. All three, Ashford and Emma and Maisie.

As the ceremony began, too many emotions twisted around inside me. I wished Lori had been able to be here, because Ashford had been her best friend, and she would've been just as happy as I was to see this. Such a beautiful, perfect occasion.

And yet my heart was cracking because I missed Lori *so much*. So damn much.

I would *always* regret the years we lost because I was so desperate to get away from the colonel that I'd avoided her too.

Teller put his hand next to mine and linked our pinky fingers. It was like he'd shown me the way out of the storm.

I held on to that small point of contact until my sadness faded to a distant ache. Lori wouldn't want me to be sad right now.

We clapped as the bride and groom kissed. Stood and cheered as they walked the aisle again as husband and wife, but with Maisie holding each of their hands.

I felt the gentle pressure of Teller's fingers against my lower back. "That was beautiful," he said in my ear. "Your sister would've been very proud."

I nodded, grateful beyond words that he'd somehow known what I was feeling.

Ashford and Maisie's happiness, after the loss they'd endured, was miraculous. But Teller was something of a miracle too. A week ago, I would've thought he was the least likely man to understand me and say exactly what I needed to hear in this moment.

Maybe I should've had doubts about how close we'd grown over just a few short days. But instead, I wanted to sink into it. Sink into *him*.

Just enjoy it for the last several hours we had before my plane would take off tomorrow.

TWENTY-THREE

Ayla

AFTER THE CEREMONY, it was time for photos.

Ashford and Emma had saved the pictures for afterward, since Emma hadn't wanted him to see her dress. A little touch of traditionalism that Piper, Grace, and I agreed was adorable.

"We need one with the Lonely Harts club," Piper announced after the many portraits of the combined O'Neal and Jennings family were done.

"Do we really?" Ashford muttered, and Emma playfully teased him about being grumpy at his own wedding.

I'd heard plenty about the Lonely Harts club during my prior visits to Silver Ridge. Piper had started it as a joking play on the spelling of Hart County. The *lonely* part wasn't accurate anymore for several of the members. But still, Ashford, Emma, and Grace gamely stood in front of the windows, with Callum, Piper, and their friend Judson Lawrence gathering around them.

"Ayla, get in here," Piper said. "Teller, you too."

Her brother shook his head. "I've never been a part of this weird club of yours."

Ashford arched a brow. "If I have to do this, so do you, man."

I stood next to Judson, and Teller squeezed in behind me.

"Now I feel left out," Dane complained. We all waved him over, then posed while the photographer took at least a dozen shots.

Teller's hand found my hip. I leaned back against him.

Then his palm trailed downward until it rested on my ass through the fabric of my dress, while I tried not to react in a way the camera would see.

My heart rate had tripled. My thighs clenched together, and I struggled to catch my breath like I'd just run up Refuge Mountain instead of calmly standing here. And my cardio was top-notch. Had to be to sing and dance for hours on end during my concerts.

Moving slowly, I put my hand behind my back and found the inner seam along Teller's pants. Followed it up his inside thigh. He made a half-coughing, half-choking sound.

"You okay, Tell?" Ashford asked.

"Mmhmm. Fine." But he widened his legs a little, letting me tease upward along his pants seam while he rhythmically squeezed my butt cheek. My pinky brushed against his bulge.

Lord.

Finally the photographer announced we were finished. "Are we eating soon?" Callum asked, loosening his tie.

I was hungry too. *Starving*. But not for dinner. I glanced back, catching Teller's eye. His stare was hard and ratcheted my pulse by a few more beats per minute.

He clasped his hands in front of his crotch.

A tiny wrecking ball crashed into me. "Aunt Ayla, did you see me dropping the flower petals? I stepped in time with the music, just like you showed me."

"I know. You were amazing." I shook off the haze that Teller had induced in my brain. We were in the middle of a wedding reception, surrounded by our families.

But last night, he'd said tomorrow. And that was now today.

If you spend the night with anyone this trip, it'll be me.

At some point, I had to get that man alone for an extended stretch of time, and I wasn't sure how much longer I could wait.

I made it through the buffet. The Last Refuge Inn lived up to its reputation for outstanding cuisine. Then it was cake and toasts and happy laughter as we all celebrated with the bride and groom.

I sat next to Maisie, while Teller was at a different table with Piper and Ollie. Yet I was painfully aware of the police chief at every moment. Exchanging hot glances.

Of course, I managed to focus my attention on Maisie too. Had to make sure my niece was having the time of her life. But Teller remained on a low simmer in both my body and mind. I could feel his eyes on me like the sunlight streaming through the windows.

Even though the tension with Teller had been *killing* me, I was also having a wonderful time. The wedding guests were treating me like any other member of Ashford's family. No more requests for autographs or awkward stares.

Ashford and Emma had their first dance, followed by Emma with her father Nash and Ashford with Emma's mom. Then her stepmom and stepdad. When it was time for everyone else to join them on the dance floor, Callum asked me to dance, followed by Judson.

Teller stood by the tables, sipping a glass that looked like whiskey with his eyes fixed on me. He was the only guy here I actually wanted to dance with.

"Thanks for taking a turn with me," Judson said when a slow song ended. He was wearing his cowboy hat, and he tipped it politely.

"My pleasure." As soon as Judson stepped away, I glanced around for Teller. But Maisie appeared and grabbed my hands.

"Aunt Ayla, you have to dance with me now. You're the best dancer in the world."

How could I say no to that? I twirled Maisie around until she was dizzy, followed by little Kelsea and Thompson. Ollie joined our dancing circle.

A large hand touched my back, lingering a bit longer than a simple friend's would. "You're having all the fun over here," Teller said.

There went my pulse again. "You should join us."

It took another three or four songs before the kids got tired and ran off on some other adventure. And I was finally back in the warm circle of his arms.

"Dance with me." The gentle command in his voice reminded me of the backseat of his SUV yesterday.

Desire wrapped around me and refused to let go.

"Are you finding this as impossible as I am?" I whispered. "Waiting until we can sneak away and be alone?"

His grip tightened on my waist. "I think more. Especially when I have to see you dancing with any man but me. You're supposed to be my date."

"But nobody else knows that," I said teasingly.

He made a growly sound in his chest. I felt it more than heard it. "You're playing with fire, Troublemaker."

This possessive side of Teller was a surprise, but I was here for it. "Judson's the one who asked me to dance. Not my fault."

"Next time I catch him speeding, he's not getting any favors. He's getting the damn ticket."

I laughed and tucked my head against his chest. I had no idea if anyone was watching us or what they thought. It didn't matter.

Later, it could be embarrassing for the chief of police if his constituents found out he'd hooked up with the wayward pop star. And I didn't want to deal with the tabloid media speculating about us.

But on this dance floor, we had a little bit of freedom to get close. I had to take advantage of it. If only because I couldn't make it much longer without his hands on me.

"You've got your room to yourself tonight?" he asked.

"Yes. Grace will be with Dane, and Maisie's staying with Nash and Madison Jennings and their kids."

"Good. Ollie's joining their sleepover too. Piper's doing her own thing. Nobody will notice if we slip away after this song ends. If you're sure you want this."

"I want *you*."

"Then I'm yours."

Excitement bloomed like a firework in my belly. Did he just mean for tonight? Anything else was beyond the realm of possibility, considering our jobs and our schedules. But maybe the wedding had me feeling wistful.

The music faded out, and another song took its place.

"Meet me by the back stairwell," Teller whispered. "Ten minutes."

He slipped out of the room right away. It was agony to wait. But it allowed me time to give Maisie another hug and yawn in front of Emma and Grace.

If anyone asked later, I went to bed a little early. Never mind the fact that I was still set to Pacific time and it was even earlier there.

After nine minutes and thirty seconds, I checked that my room key was in my dress pocket, then walked through the lobby. A couple other wedding guests smiled and waved.

I ducked down a hallway, went past the elevator, and looked for the stairwell. The door was cracked open. I didn't see Teller, but the moment I went into the stairwell, I found him waiting.

"Thought you'd never get here." He shut the door behind me and crowded me up against the wall, hands going to my hips. His gaze was pure, lusty fire.

"You told me ten minutes."

"Aren't you a good girl, listening to me."

Then Teller's mouth crashed onto mine, and there was only *him*.

The pull of his lips and the needy strokes of his tongue. His hands raising to tangle in my hair. We hadn't even made it to a room yet. Any moment, another wedding guest could stumble upon us in this stairwell. But it was impossible to pull away from him.

"Want you so bad," I panted.

"My room or yours?" His tongue licked from my neck to my ear.

"Which one's closer?" I asked.

"Fuck," he muttered. "Can't think. All my blood's in my cock. I'm so hard I'm dizzy."

I needed Teller's hard cock inside me. Needed it bad. Wasn't sure I could survive much longer without it. "My room. Second floor."

He grabbed my hand. We dashed up to the next floor. Teller had enough brain power to check that the coast was clear.

I found the keycard in my pocket and dropped it on the carpet, but Teller scooped it up. He held me in front of him, his stomach to my back and an arm around my waist, as he waved the card to unlock my door. I felt his thick length against me through our clothes.

When the latch clicked, he walked us inside.

The moment the door closed, he reached down to grab my legs and lifted me up. My back hit the wall, and his mouth crashed down on mine again. We kissed frantically until we had to come up for air.

The room had a sitting area with a couch near the door and two beds closer to the window. Neither was a king-size, but I hardly cared right now. Any bed would do as long as Teller and I were naked in it.

Then my eyes caught on something new in the room. A flower arrangement on my dresser. I went still.

"Something wrong?" he asked, lowering me so my feet touched the floor.

"Those flowers. They weren't here before."

A glower darkened his expression as he followed my gaze. "You're sure? The housekeeper didn't leave it?"

"I don't think so." My body went cold, fear creeping in where before I'd only felt desire. "I have no idea where that came from."

TWENTY-FOUR
Teller

I STORMED over to the dresser and grabbed the flower arrangement, sending petals flying. After a quick inspection, I found a card with Ayla's name, but no other message. Nothing to indicate who'd sent them.

"Could it have something to do with the wedding?" I asked. "Did Grace bring them in?"

"After she stayed here last night, she packed her things and left the key with me."

I set the flowers by the door and took Ayla's hand, guiding her to the sofa to sit. "Okay, then let's call the front desk." There was a hotel phone here on the side table.

She picked up the receiver and held it to her ear. I pulled her into my lap and draped my arms loosely around her.

"Hi, this is Ayla in room 203. There's a flower arrangement here. Where did this come from? Do you know who sent it?"

"I'll check on that for you," the clerk downstairs said. I was close enough I could hear the voice, but couldn't recognize it. "Just a moment."

Ayla was trembling. I kissed her hair, and she rested her head between my neck and shoulder until a voice spoke on the other end of the line again.

"Ayla? This is Jessi. You had a question about the flowers?"

"Yeah." She gripped the phone receiver in both hands. "Where'd they come from?"

"They arrived a few hours ago for you, just before the ceremony. Same florist who did the wedding flowers. I was shocked the delivery made it here with the snow. I had our security guys check them over and then sent them up to your room. Is there a problem?"

"I...I'm not sure. It just surprised me." Ayla shared a glance with me.

"I'm so sorry. I would've asked you directly if you wanted them, but with the wedding—"

"No, we were all busy. That's alright. The security team looked them over?"

"Of course. I wouldn't just pass something along to you. You probably get fans trying to send you weird things."

I tucked a strand of hair behind Ayla's ear. "Yeah," she said. "But the card didn't say who they're from. If you could ask the florist, that would be great. Or I could have my assistant call, or..."

"I'm happy to. I'll let you know."

"Thanks, Jessi." Ayla set the hotel phone on its cradle. But at the same time, I was pulling my device from my pocket.

"Glad to hear they checked over the flowers, but I want to give the arrangement to River, just in case."

"Just in case what?" She pressed her lips together.

"It's an abundance of caution. That's all." I sent a text, and a few minutes later, River knocked on the door. Ayla stayed on the couch while I answered, holding the flower vase.

River was dressed casually, since he hadn't attended the wedding. He eyed the flowers. "Landry, you shouldn't have."

I leveled a glare at him. I'd already explained in my message that the flowers could be from the stalker, so I wasn't in the mood for his humor. "Just get them out of here, would you?" I muttered. "And see if there's anything hidden in there."

"Will do." He took the flower arrangement in one arm, then

pulled Ayla's phone from his pocket. "Please return this to Ms. Maxwell. And let her know I ran that reverse image search. Looks like a female tourist visiting the ski resort took the photo of Ayla on Main Street and uploaded it on social media. Still investigating, but I didn't get any indication the original poster was tied to Biggest Fan. I think Biggest Fan simply saw the photo and saved a copy. I'll keep working."

I nodded. "Thanks for the assistance."

"That's what we're here for."

I closed the door, returning to the sitting area. "You heard all that?" I set her phone on the table. The couch cushion dipped as I took my place beside her again.

"I did." Her gaze was distant, her mind somewhere else. And I couldn't blame her. That flower arrangement had poured ice water over the heat building between us earlier. And yeah, that was disappointing, but I was far more concerned with what she was feeling right now.

Ayla made me want to be selfish, but I couldn't do that with her.

"What do you need?" I asked. "If you'd rather I head back to my own room, that's okay."

Emerald green flashed, her focus returning. "Are you kidding? You'd better not go anywhere. I thought you were mine tonight."

"I am." However she wanted me, I was on board.

"I was just thinking." She bent her legs and folded them beneath her. "I appreciate Aiden and River helping me. And you especially. But I'm not the kind of girl to sit back and wait for other people to make things happen."

"I have no doubt of that. But this is a different kind of situation. We could be dealing with a dangerous person. He went months with no contact, and suddenly it's twice in a matter of days."

"And I refuse to sit here and cower in fear. I spent too many years of my life afraid of my father. I won't live that way. Not anymore." With a sudden burst of energy, she grabbed her phone.

"I'm going to write back to that email. See if the guy responds and gives something away that we can use."

"No, you are *not.*" I put my hand over hers. "That's not a bad idea in theory, but let River handle it. He's the computer expert. Or hell, I'll write the creep back. You're not subjecting yourself to that. You need to leave this to us."

Her gaze was pure steel. "If I backed down every time a man said that to me, I wouldn't have a career. I'd be some pinup puppet without a brain or a voice of her own. You'd better get used to that, Teller Landry. Because I'm not changing. I'm not fading into the background. Not for anyone, including you."

Damn. Alright then.

"I apologize." I moved my hand, and she unlocked her phone. "Will you at least show me what you're writing to that asshole?"

Ayla side-eyed me. "Yes." She scooted closer, halfway in my lap again, as she opened her email app and started on a message. Her thumbs paused on the screen keyboard, and she took a deep breath. Preparing herself.

I decided to stay quiet for now and let her think. It was clear how important this was to her. Ayla was taking back her agency, and I'd been a fool to try to stop her.

So long as she didn't walk into a far more dangerous situation later on. But she was smart. And I didn't really have a right to boss her around, did I? No matter how much I cared about her safety. Whatever this was between us... I had no idea if it would last beyond tomorrow.

She wrote, *I have a lot of fans. What makes you different?*

Her finger hovered over the send button. "I can practically hear your brain working. Go ahead and say it."

I dragged my tongue across my teeth, considering my words. I didn't love this. Would the stalker take her message as a provocation? A challenge to do something more dramatic to grab her attention?

But the stalker probably wouldn't be able to resist writing

back to her question. Would Ayla really let me and River know when that happened?

I figured River would make sure he had access to monitor any such replies. The guy was a hacker. I didn't know the specifics of all his skills, but from what I'd read between the lines, they were impressive.

And it made me feel slightly shitty that we might have access to Ayla's email without her knowing. I would have to tell her.

Eventually.

"It's good," I said. "Short enough that he can read what he wants into it. Well done."

"I don't need your approval. But...I don't mind it either." She hit send and put the phone facedown on the table. A vicious smile played at her lips.

"Feel better?" I asked.

"Yes. I can't wait for that asshole to write back."

"It's possible the stalker will escalate again. You'll have security when you're back in LA? Bryan's going to be out of commission for a while with his concussion. Do you have someone else you can trust?"

"Bryan works for an agency. They provide security at my home in addition to driving me around."

"So they're all trained bodyguards at this agency?"

"Yep. That's why I hired them." She caressed my jawline, smiling. "It's sweet how you're fussing over me."

"Just want to make sure you'll be okay without me."

A hint of uncertainty passed across her pretty eyes. Then it was gone. "I've managed up until now. But I'll tell the agency I may have a stalker. I don't want to share anything else about the messages. It's too personal."

"The wisest course would be to inform the LAPD and the local station where you live. So they know about the danger."

But she shook her head. "The police might leak it to the media. I already have to deal with the paparazzi. More bodyguards means more restrictions. I don't like feeling caged in. You know? I don't like feeling watched and followed all the time, even though I *am*."

"I get it," I said softly, stroking her hair. "Not saying I understand what you face every day, but I get why you need to protect your freedom."

Of course she didn't like feeling trapped. That made perfect sense, especially considering her childhood.

Fury gathered in my chest as I remembered what she'd told me about the colonel. How he'd made her sit alone in the basement as a kid and berated her through the door. How screwed up was that? It made me sick that anyone had treated her that way, especially the man who should've cared for her the most.

Ayla moved so she was sitting on my lap, her back resting on my chest. She picked up my hands and crossed my arms over her body.

"I like when *you* cage me in though. I like..." Her voice faltered. Dropped low, like she was shy about saying this. "It feels completely different with you."

I pushed my face against her hair. Tightened my grip on her. Ayla turned her head, and I kissed her a few times, slow and deep. Sucked on her lips while I squeezed my arms around her, feeling her sigh. Ayla relaxed against me, as if all the remaining tension was leaving her.

"When I get home to LA, I'll give you the details on my security setup," she murmured. "If you want. And if there's a response to my email, I'll send it to you and River."

"Thanks. I'm relieved to know that. I just want to help. But for the rest of tonight, I'd rather not hear any other man's name on your lips."

She nodded languidly. "Yes, Teller."

I growled again. "It gets me so hot when you say my name like that. You're taking full advantage, aren't you?"

Her lips quirked. She definitely knew.

The lights in her hotel room were low. Just a couple of lamps switched on in this room.

Then I glanced up and realized we were perfectly centered in the large mirror across from us on the wall. How had I not noticed that before? Probably because I'd been entirely consumed with the woman on my lap. Making sure she was okay after the fresh reminders of her stalker. But she didn't have to stress about that anymore. Not tonight, not with me.

The mirror gave me a new view of her. Of *us*. My cock jerked, and she must've felt it, because she squirmed in my lap.

Ayla's eyes found mine in the mirror and widened slightly, like she'd just noticed the view as well. My arms were crossed over her like bonds, pinning her arms down. She looked small and precious. Stunning in that green dress that perfectly matched her irises.

"You are so fucking beautiful," I said. "I don't mean just on the surface. I mean every part of you. You're the most breathtaking woman. It blows my mind that you're here with me right now."

"This is exactly where I want to be."

I kept one arm cinched over her, but with the other, I trailed my fingers over her stomach and up between her breasts. The fabric of her dress was thin enough that I felt her soft skin beneath. The wild beat of her heart against her ribcage.

"When we were stuck in the storm, you said I could do anything I wanted to you. Is that still true?"

Her cleavage lifted as she inhaled. "Yes. Please, Teller."

I cupped my hand over her breast. It seemed like her dress had a built-in bra of some kind, because there wasn't anything else beneath. Just the sweet give of her body under my palm.

Using one finger, I tugged the scooped neckline down, exposing her breast. The nipple was already beaded, and I flicked it gently with my thumb. Playing with the rosy nub.

"*Yes.*" Her head fell back against my shoulder, her spine arching. I dipped to kiss her neck.

My touch turned rougher as I tugged her neckline further. The fabric slipped down both shoulders. Both her breasts were naked now, lifting and falling and swaying slightly with her heavy breathing.

My gaze stayed fixed on us in the mirror. She was beyond gorgeous. A sensual work of art.

My cock protested at the restrictive confines of my pants, but this was going to be worth the wait.

I used both my thumbs to rub circles over her pink nipples. She turned her head again, seeking out my mouth and kissing me back with passionate fervor. When I tugged her peaks between my fingers, she gasped and looked at the mirror again. Her lips parted, expression dazed.

"We look amazing, don't we?" I asked.

Her reflection smiled. "Want me to put on a show for you? Is that what you want?"

I dragged my nose across her temple, inhaling her honeyed scent. "You are incredibly good at that. But you don't have to perform for me, Troublemaker. You've got all my attention already. This is a duet, and it's for you as much as it's for me."

TWENTY-FIVE

Ayla

I HAD LOVED when Teller trapped me in his arms. I'd never felt as safe as I did with him.

But the scandalous way he was staring at me in the mirror while he played with my nipples? Oh my… That was pretty great too.

I couldn't remember ever being this turned on. As if that feeling of security amplified my arousal. I truly did trust him to do whatever he wanted to me.

Teller was so steady, so upright. A classic knight in shining armor. But he'd already shown me he could get filthy and dominant when he wanted to.

That was what I craved. Teller Landry, unleashed.

For now, I was losing my mind from how good this felt. Every tug on my nipples sent a jolt of liquid desire down into my belly and between my legs. I whimpered when he pinched them once more, then let go.

He worked the top of my dress down the rest of the way to my waist, helping me extract my arms from the stretchy sleeves.

"Stand up and take your panties off. Keep facing the mirror." That demanding tone in his voice gave me excited chills.

I got up on shaky legs. Reached beneath my dress to grab the elastic of my lace panties and worked them down, shimmying them off. Given my job, I'd spent more time in front of mirrors than I'd ever wanted to, and I knew all my different expressions. The fake ones and the sincere ones.

But the sheer *want* I saw in my face right now. The open hunger. That was new.

Also, I didn't usually stand in front of mirrors with nipples deeply pinked from being touched, wearing half a dress and nothing else. Teller's words caressed my spine and slid under my skin.

You are so fucking beautiful.

How many people had said similar things to me in my life? How many men? Whether I'd welcomed the attention or not.

None of them, *ever*, had said it the way he did. None of them had really made me feel it. Not like this.

I heard the rustling of fabric. A belt buckle. A zipper going down and the slide of more fabric on skin. I started to turn, and Teller playfully pinched my butt cheek through my dress. "Don't turn around."

"I want to see you."

His shoulders were broad enough behind me that I could see he'd taken his shirt and undershirt off. His pants were still on, but I assumed he'd pushed them down to his thighs. I couldn't wait to eat him up with my eyes. Touch him and kiss him everywhere. Every scar his history had left on him.

"You will. Soon enough." He reached for my hips and guided me backward. "Sit on my lap again. On your knees."

I did as he asked, a knee finding the couch cushion to one side of him, then the other. It was a little awkward moving backward like that, watching myself in the mirror instead of facing him, but Teller's hands added silent instruction to his verbal ones.

This was fun. Not knowing what he had in mind, but putting myself fully in his hands.

He pushed up my skirt to expose my bottom, though the

fabric stayed down in front. Tugged my hips until I was resting fully in his lap.

I gasped when I felt his hot, hard, bare cock on my pussy. Not starting to push inside me, but under me and positioned up against me and between my legs. "Oh, Teller," I moaned.

His arms pinned mine at my sides, his hands splaying flat on my chest and belly.

I felt his warm skin on my back. The bulk of his muscles.

Then he shifted beneath me a little, and the smooth length of his erection slid against all my sensitive parts. I moaned.

"Good?" he rasped.

"So good," I breathed. "Oh my God."

Teller kissed the side of my face and my neck. He rocked his hips in a soothing rhythm, not moving all that much, yet I felt every subtle motion so intensely. I was sitting in his lap, my breasts exposed in front of a full-length mirror as he held me against him. Yet everything else was hidden beneath my dress, and somehow that made it even hotter.

When I couldn't take it anymore, I leaned forward enough that my clit got even better contact.

Oh, that angle. Wow.

His grip on my upper body loosened. "That's it. Rub yourself on me. Get yourself wet and ready to take me."

I rested my palms on his knees and undulated my hips wantonly, rubbing myself on his cock. My clit throbbed. The flared edge of his tip caught against that bundle of nerves, and I cried out. The sound I made was almost feral.

"Look at you. You're desperate for this, aren't you?"

"Need you inside me."

"Do we need protection?"

"No. Just need *you*. Please."

He put a hand on my hip to steady me. I felt his thick tip notch at my opening. But he didn't push all the way into me, his grip keeping me from moving, and that sensation of not-quite-full threatened to drive me crazy. "*Please,*" I begged.

"I've got you," he whispered. "Look at me. Not the mirror. At me."

I turned my head. He was so close, his bright gaze hypnotic. So real. His free hand grabbed my chin. Slowly, he pulled me down onto his shaft as he kissed me.

He fed his tongue and his cock into me at the same time.

"Good?" he rasped.

I made an agreeable sound. All I could manage.

When I was fully seated against his thighs and so perfectly stretched with him inside me, his arms held me tight again as he kept up those deep kisses. I sucked on his tongue.

The taste and scent and feel of him was everywhere. My whole world, at least for a little while. While we were here together like this, connected, sharing what we could give each other.

I tried to rock against him for more friction, but he kept me still.

"I'm not going to rush this," he said against my lips. "You feel spectacular on my dick, Troublemaker. So snug and hot. You have no idea."

"So Chief Landry is a secret dirty talker. Never would've guessed."

"All your fault. I can't control myself around you."

"Good thing I can take it."

"Yeah? You can take it?" His hips pulled back, his cock withdrawing by an inch before he thrust back into me. Not as much movement as I wanted, but still enough to make me moan.

"Teller, *please*."

"You want me to use your body however I like? Make us both feel incredible?"

"Mmmm." That wasn't even coherent, but the message got through. He started to lift and lower me. I rested my hands on his knees again, finding that angle I liked.

He bounced me on his lap. I looked shameless in the mirror.

I looked like a woman taking a muscular man's big cock and *loving* it.

With a wild groan, Teller pulled out of me and tipped me over onto the couch. I landed on my hands and knees on the cushion. The movement was so sudden, I barely registered him kicking off his pants and boxer briefs the rest of the way. He shoved my dress up to my waist, then sank his cock back inside of me from behind.

Now the view in the mirror was *so* much more explicit.

His slick erection moving in and out of me. He had one leg bent, knee on the couch behind me. His other foot flat on the floor. His fingers dug into the flesh of my hips as he pumped into me. The muscles in his chest and stomach and his thighs flexing with every thrust.

I lowered to my elbows. Surrendered to the moment. To *him*.

An orgasm hit me fast, shocking a cry out of me. Teller grunted a curse. "Hot damn, Ayla, you're gripping me tight. I can't hold back."

His fingers squeezed my hips, and I felt the hot pulse of his release inside me as shudders of pleasure kept racking my body. Extending my climax. He thrust languidly a few more times.

Then Teller collapsed onto the carpeted floor, pulling me down on top of him. We were a pile of half discarded clothes, shaking limbs. "Didn't want to make a mess of the hotel couch," he panted.

I giggled. "Very responsible."

"Somebody around here has to be."

We both dissolved into laughter. I burrowed against his broad chest, and he held me around the waist, and I never wanted to leave this spot.

Or at least...never leave this county.

I let myself think, for the first time, about staying in Silver Ridge. Really think about it instead of pushing that idea away like some forbidden fantasy. I imagined what it would be like.

Seeing my niece's sweet face every day, hearing her laughter. Spending time with the O'Neal family, *my* family, and the friends I'd made in Hart County the last couple of years. Writing and recording music while surrounded by so much inspiration.

And maybe, seeing Teller more. Spending nights with him like this, tangled up in each other. Talking. Getting to know everything about each other. Kissing and laughing. Sinking into the warm, solid embrace of his arms. A restraint that somehow made me feel freer than I ever had.

Being *happy*.

But then I recalled what happened just a few days ago in Silver Ridge. A mob started a fight in the middle of Main Street and gave my friend a concussion. Emma and Ashford had to cancel their evening at Hearthstone Brewing because I would've caused too much of a scene.

The occasional visit worked out okay because I never stayed long. The town probably breathed a sigh of relief whenever I left. As chief of police, Teller had to feel the same. Could I really blame him for that?

It was his job to care for the whole town. I brought chaos. *Trouble*.

I didn't belong here.

So I had to enjoy what little time I had in Hart County. If tonight was all I got to have with Teller, then I planned to savor it.

TWENTY-SIX

Teller

Eventually, I tapped my palm against Ayla's naked butt cheek. "Come on. Let's get cleaned up."

It was late, and we were sweaty and sticky and sated. Her dress was still bunched around her middle. I hoped it wasn't ruined because she'd looked damn good in it. Those LA dry cleaning companies probably knew how to work magic.

She rolled off of me, and I admired that expression of relaxed bliss on her face.

And then I had to kiss her some more, since she was irresistible.

But finally, we made it into the hotel bathroom. Ayla stripped off her dress and tossed it through the doorway into the bedroom, while I switched on the water to let it warm up.

"I have to wash my makeup off," she said, grabbing a bottle from her toiletry bag. Probably fancy stuff. "My hair is *wild*. Like I got mauled by some animal."

"This animal enjoyed every second of it."

"I did too." She smirked at me in the mirror over the sink.

I braced a hand on the glass shower wall and watched her. Fully naked for the first time in front of me. Blond hair a messy halo, miles of perfect skin. My cock felt heavy between my legs. Not firming up again so soon, but definitely interested.

Ayla dabbed her face with a towel, then walked toward me across the expanse of tile. Once she was close enough that I could touch her, I trailed my hands down her sides, following her curves, then back up to cup her ample breasts. At the same time, her eyes roved over me just as appreciatively.

Ayla reached around to squeeze my ass. "You really are big everywhere, aren't you."

I barked a laugh. "I assume that's a compliment."

"Very much so. I like how you're so much bigger than me. All this muscle. The guys I've been with before weren't this...substantial. Some of them were leaner and prettier than *me*. But that's LA for you."

My chest rumbled with a growl as I hooked her waist, walking her into the shower through the open glass door. The air inside was already steaming up. "What did I say about mentioning other men?"

She bit her lower lip. "But it's so fun to watch you react."

"I'll just have to make you forget about anyone else."

"How will you do that?"

The water was nice and warm. I angled the shower head lower, so it would be the right height to hit her body, then nudged her forward into the spray. I stood directly behind her, hand on her stomach to hold her naked body to mine.

"By taking extra good care of you. You're not lifting a finger the rest of tonight."

Pumping some shampoo into my palm, I worked suds into her hair. Scrubbed my fingertips into her scalp. Ayla moaned and let her head fall back into my hands.

This woman was incredibly responsive to my touch, and that just urged me on.

She'd been the same a few minutes ago on the couch. Grinding herself on my cock before I was even inside her. That had been the sexiest experience of my life, watching her features contort with sheer pleasure in the mirror.

I probably could've come from that alone. And it had been decades since I'd had a hair trigger.

Then pushing my cock into her tight heat, taking control of her exactly the way we both wanted. I liked the idea of making her forget any man but me. Yet Ayla had already wiped every past sexual partner from my memory. A supernova blotting out the other stars from the sky.

No one could compare to her. And probably, no one else ever would.

I spun her and rinsed the shampoo from her hair, careful to keep the suds from her face. Her long hair hung like a waterfall down her back. Next was conditioner, which I rubbed into the ends, followed by another scalp massage since she'd liked the first one so much.

I wrapped the long tail of her hair around my fist and tugged gently. Her lips opened on a groan.

She kept making sounds of pleasure as I washed her body. Especially when I delved between her legs. The haze of steam and arousal in the shower almost reminded me of the backseat of my SUV, except we were both naked and soaking wet.

I stroked her clit until she pushed my hand away. "No, it's your turn now. I'll wash you."

"I'm supposed to be doing all the work. You're supposed to relax."

Her wet lashes fluttered. "Please, Teller? I want to."

I held her chin between my thumb and forefinger. "Okay, sexy thing. I can't say no to you."

She snorted. "You say no to me all the time."

"Well, I'm not *now*."

Ayla lathered body wash in her hands and smoothed them over my skin. I kept in shape and had a flat stomach, but I hadn't boasted a six-pack since my Army days. Ayla didn't seem to mind.

Her eyelids were heavy, and she kept whimpering the way she'd done when *I* was the one doing the touching.

"You're so sexy," she murmured. She hadn't even gotten to my cock, but it started to fill.

Then her fingertips moved over the twisted web of scars on my right side. Worst around my shoulder, trailing in silvery lines up my neck and face, down along my ribcage and across my pec.

I wasn't self-conscious about them. Yet I hadn't been with many women since the injuries. Some people could be weird about that kind of thing, either disgusted or a little *too* interested.

Ayla was neither. She touched my scars the way she did the rest of me. Like I turned her the hell on.

I wasn't used to standing around and being admired. Wasn't all that bad.

I wasn't expecting the question she asked next. "Why aren't you with anyone? A girlfriend or a wife. I have to think some lucky lady in Hart County would want to lock all this down."

I smiled, but it faded when I considered my answer. "I was engaged once."

Her green eyes lifted, flaring in surprise. "Really? To someone I've met before?"

I rested my hands on her hips. "No. My ex doesn't live in Colorado."

Ayla shrugged one shoulder, like she didn't care either way, but that hint of jealousy in her tone had given me a secret thrill. "What happened?" She reached for another pump of body wash.

"I'd been a soldier for a couple years when I met her. We clicked. A year later, I asked her to marry me."

"You were pretty young, then?"

"Early twenties." Only a few years younger than Ayla was now. I chose not to dwell on that. "I wanted to get married right away, before my next deployment, but she kept saying we should wait. Maybe that was a warning sign."

"What did she do?" Ayla asked angrily, which was unbelievably cute.

"We'd been together almost six years when she told me she didn't want to be a military wife. Also, she'd met someone else. That was a bigger problem."

"She *what*? Are you kidding me?" Ayla balled her fists like she was ready to throw down on my behalf.

I caressed her face. "Relax, Troublemaker. It was a long time ago."

She pushed me under the spray to rinse off. Her arms went around me, her forehead resting between my shoulder blades. "I'm sorry. Your ex was an idiot who didn't deserve you. But if it was so long ago, why aren't you with anyone now?"

I rubbed the suds from my skin, remembering how hard the break-up had hit me. Ancient history now, but I'd sworn I would never make the mistake of falling in love again.

Several years later, a fiery explosion nearly killed me and made romance an even lower priority.

"After I was wounded, it took a while before I was interested in sex again. Things were...rough. Physically and mentally both. The flashbacks were pretty frequent the first couple of years afterward. They've faded now, mostly. Talking to a therapist helped."

"I'm sorry you went through all of that." Ayla hugged me again. It felt nice. How could I have known she'd be this sweet?

"These days, my options for dating are limited as chief of police," I said when she pulled back. "If I so much as think about going on a date, half the town hears about it and wants to know the details." I scrubbed my face under the water. "I've got my plate full with work and with Piper and Ollie."

Ayla pressed a kiss to my shoulder blade. "I guess it's good you're single. Worked out great for me this weekend. The women of Hart County have no idea what they're missing."

This weekend.

Because that was all we had together. She was leaving tomorrow, and whatever *this* was, it would have to be over. Ridiculous to even imagine another scenario.

Superstar musical artists didn't date small-town cops. I didn't date *period*.

But it still made me nauseous to acknowledge that she might fall for some rich actor next month. Or even next week. As much as she felt like mine right now, she wasn't. She would never be.

So I had to leave her with plenty to remember me by.

I turned around and cupped her face, dipping to drag my tongue across her lips.

"Wait, I haven't washed your hair yet," she said.

"Later," I grunted before I claimed her mouth, kissing her deeply until she went soft and pliant under my hands.

I backed her up against the tile, caging her in with my arms while we made out. My mouth lowered, kissing my way down, teeth grazing her nipple as I bent to one knee. She gasped. My tongue darted out to her breast to soothe the sting. My other knee dropped, and I pushed my face into her stomach, my tongue licking into her belly button. Her fingers raked through my damp hair.

Drawing one of her legs up and draping it over my shoulder, I kissed along her inner thigh. Anticipating my final destination.

Then I had to sit back and get an eyeful of the mouthwatering cleft between her legs. Every inch of her was so stunning. So precious.

I brought my thumb to her clit. Dragged it lower to her opening.

"*Teller*." Her head fell back against the shower wall.

"How does that feel?" I asked, fingers stroking.

"Unbelievable."

"It's about to get a lot better. I need to taste you."

"Doesn't the tile hurt your knees?"

I smirked up at her. "I can take it."

She laughed, since I was just repeating what she'd said to me earlier. And take me, she had. She'd taken me so well.

Laughter turned to moans when I leaned forward and teased the tip of my tongue at her clit. Circling and flicking.

I drew my lips together and kissed her most intimate places, licking and sucking. Coating my taste buds with her sweetness. Oh fuck, that was good.

My daily life as a Green Beret, and later as police chief, had always been about keeping my cool. Staying in control, even if the world spun out around me. But Ayla made me lose it.

She made me feel like a *beast*.

I grabbed her other leg, draping it over my shoulder, my hands cradling her behind to hold her up. She cried out in surprise.

Ayla was braced against the shower wall and held entirely in my grip while my tongue pushed inside of her over and over. My cock was so hard it could've been forged out of steel.

"Teller, I'm going to... *Oh*, that feels..."

My tongue and lips kept working until she was trembling and moaning so loud her voice echoed on the tile. When her seemingly endless orgasm finally stopped, I carefully lowered her legs so her feet could touch the shower floor.

She didn't stay standing, though, sinking down along the wall. I sat back against my heels. My erection jutted out, aching and throbbing for some attention. And that was exactly where her gaze fell.

Ayla's hand tried to close around my shaft. I covered her grip with mine. Together, we stroked.

"Faster," I grunted, showing her how I liked it. I was already so damn close.

I groaned as I came hard enough to make my vision white out, my release spilling over our hands and her stomach.

My shoulders sagged, and my palm smacked against the tile as I caught my weight against it.

That had been...*ungh*.

"We'll have to clean each other up again," I said. "Whoops."

She looked up at me through her lashes and grinned.

TWENTY-SEVEN

Ayla

SUNLIGHT HIT MY EYELIDS. Whimpering, I rolled over and met a solid expanse of warm, smooth skin and thick muscle. I draped an arm and leg over him, snuggling in. The last thing I wanted to do was check a clock and find out what time it was.

The previous time I'd done that, my phone had said four in the morning. Teller and I had stayed up almost all night. It had been *so* worth it.

But I had a flight scheduled at midday, and I didn't want to leave this bed.

Then again, did I really want to sleep away the remaining hours I had in Colorado?

Yawning, I blinked my eyes open. Teller's handsome face was smushed against the pillow, and he was still out cold. I decided to take the opportunity to sneak over to the bathroom.

Carefully pulling away from him, I scooted across the mattress and pushed back the covers to get up.

In the bathroom, I freshened up. Combing through my hair with my fingers, brushing my teeth, and taking care of business. My body was worn out in the very best way.

Teller was over a decade older than me, but that man was *not* lacking in stamina. Or libido.

Since our epic shower, we'd been naked the rest of the night. We'd laughed and talked and kissed.

That had been the best night of my life. Even better than when I'd won a Grammy, or the nights I'd sung in front of a hundred thousand fans screaming for me. Because I'd shared the messy parts of myself with Teller, my imperfections, and he'd pulled me closer. Cared for me. Made me feel pleasure I'd thought was impossible.

When I opened the door and stepped into the bedroom, the bed was empty. "Teller?" I said.

Two strong arms swept me up from behind. "Who said you could leave the bed?" He kissed my neck. "I woke up and you were gone."

I felt my smile slip. I would be gone for real soon, and we both knew it. "Nature called, and I didn't need you to dig a path through the snow to find a bathroom."

"Good thing. We'd both have frostbite if we were naked in that kind of weather." My feet left the ground as Teller picked me up, tossing me slightly in the air, and carried me back to bed. "Stay here. I'll take my turn in the bathroom."

A few minutes later, we were under the covers, kissing and touching. Teller tasted like minty toothpaste, and his short dark-blond hair was disheveled.

He shifted us so I was flat on my back, and his heavy body stretched out on top of me. His hard cock nudged my hip, leaving my skin sticky with his arousal.

"You're ready to go *again*?" I asked.

"If you are."

"You're the one who's trouble, not me. The people of Silver Ridge would be scandalized that their beloved Chief Landry is a sex maniac."

"Can't help it. You inspire me." He kissed a line down between my breasts, and I felt his smile against my skin.

My breath caught. Teller inspired me too. I couldn't get enough. An ache of longing built in my low abdomen, as if he hadn't been inside of me just hours before. He rubbed his naked body over mine until I was panting and begging.

"Need you now," I said.

"How bad do you need me?"

I groaned, my legs cinching around his hips. "I think it's obvious."

"No, I want to hear it. How bad do you need my cock?"

"Bad enough that if you keep making me wait, we might have a problem."

"Uh oh. The diva's getting demanding." He laughed joyously. I loved that sound, especially because I'd heard him laugh so rarely before this weekend. I suspected that Teller almost never let himself fully relax.

But he was now. He sprawled out beside me on the mattress. "Here I am. Your turn to do whatever you want."

I licked my lips, admiring him some more. Long limbs, thick muscle. And his perfect cock lying on his stomach, hard and straining. We'd both lost any remaining inhibitions at some point during the night.

I swung my leg over him to straddle his hips, my palms going to his pecs to brush over his chest hair. His nipples peaked as I used my thumbs to play with them.

Teller moaned, and his gaze raked over my body. His hands went to my thighs, his fingers gripping me. "Fuck, Ayla. Still can't get over how incredible you are."

A lump suddenly formed in my throat. *How can this be ending when it's just barely begun?*

"Wanna watch you ride my cock," he growled out.

I lifted up. Teller gripped his shaft, and I lowered myself onto him. He filled me inch by inch. The stretch had taken me by surprise every time since last night. Now was no different. I was a little sore, but that faded quickly.

When I was all the way down, I rocked my hips with him inside me. Moving nice and slow.

I couldn't rush this. It might be our last time.

This man had me in a trance. On a knife's edge of pleasure that just kept building. His eyes locked on mine like he didn't want to miss one single second, while his hands explored my skin like there was so much of me he still needed to discover.

Our hips rolled as our bodies met. Teller brought his fingers to my mouth, and I sucked on them to muffle how loud I was moaning.

The pace quickened, and so did our breaths. His cock surged upward into me. Slick and hot.

"You're being so good for me, sweetheart," he purred. "You're riding me like a pro. I need to feel you come. Can you do that for me?"

I nodded, my eyes rolling back. Teller held tight to my hips and thrust. The base of his cock hit my clit exactly the way I needed him, and then I was shuddering and gasping through another earthshaking orgasm.

Then suddenly he flipped me over, rising above me. He gripped my knees and forced them wider. Pumped his cock deep, and somehow it felt even thicker and harder than before.

A few moments later, I felt him spasming. His handsome features were drawn with ecstasy.

I went limp. He lay down beside me, and I put my cheek against his chest as my head swam.

Then the hotel phone blared. Teller looked over at it, while I sat up, my spine going rigid. "No," I whined. "Not now. Go away."

Teller smiled and caressed my cheek. "You don't have to answer it. Whoever it is, they can wait."

I lay back down and snuggled into him.

But the hotel phone rang again a minute later. *Dang it.* "I probably should answer it."

"I've got it." Teller scooted out of bed. He grabbed the cordless handset and carried it to me.

I answered, putting the line on speaker. "Hello?"

"You have a visitor at the front desk who insisted we call you. Cheryl Traynor."

"*Who*?" Teller mouthed.

"My manager," I whispered, covering the handset.

Cheryl knew the fake names I used to register for hotels. That was how she'd gotten the front desk to pay attention.

"I have no idea what she's doing here." I closed my eyes, racking my brain for a way to avoid her. I wanted to stay in bed with Teller and enjoy what was left of our morning together. Moving my hand, I said into the phone, "Could you ask her to just—"

Cheryl's voice came through the speaker. I imagined her leaning over the hotel's front desk, nearly shouting so I'd hear her. "Dear, would you please answer your cell? We've been calling all morning trying to get ahold of you."

Crap.

"Ask her to wait for me in the lobby. I'll be down as soon as I can." I hung up the phone.

"Did you expect her?" Teller asked.

"*No*. I have no idea what this is about. Cheryl wasn't supposed to be here at all." And my brain just registered that she'd said '*we*'. *We've been calling*. Who did she mean?

Teller put on his boxer briefs while I checked my notifications. I'd set my cell phone to *Do Not Disturb* last night. Cheryl had first written around dawn this morning.

> Hope the wedding was fun. Some updates for you. First, Bryan is resting well at home with wife and baby. I stopped by his place yesterday to make sure, since I know you've been worried.

I was glad to hear it. I'd meant to call Bryan's wife Mikaela yesterday, but between the wedding and crap about the stalker and spending time with Teller, I'd been fully booked.

I read on.

> Second, I know you said you'd figure out your ride to the airport today. But since the jet was leaving to get you anyway, Paul and I decided to hitch a ride. I hear there's snow in Hart County, so we'll come fetch you and make sure you reach the airport safe and sound.

"No," I groaned. "Paul too? *Why*?"

Teller sat beside me. "Paul? Who's Paul?"

"My least favorite label exec, who's in charge of my next album. He's here in Hart County with my manager. They decided last minute to come here and escort me to the airport, since I lost my driver."

"You didn't mention to them that I was going to drive you myself?"

"It wasn't their business."

My phone rang in my hand. *Cheryl*. And I was still sitting on the bed completely naked. Grabbing a pillow to cover me, even though it was just an audio call, I pressed the green button on my screen.

"I didn't see your messages earlier," I said without preamble. "I was up late celebrating the wedding."

Also having the hottest sex of my life, not that I planned to share a single one of those details.

"I figured you would be. This was a last-minute thing."

Teller brought over a fluffy bathrobe, helping me put it on while Cheryl kept talking in my ear.

"You needed a ride to the airport, and this is the perfect opportunity to discuss a few things."

"With *Paul*?" I asked testily. "I'm not working this weekend."

She sighed, because we both knew how ridiculous that was. I was always working. "Shall I come up and help you pack? What's your room number?"

"No, I've got it. I'll be down soon. But I have to say goodbye to my family and friends first." I ended the call, my fingers rubbing at my breastbone, as if that would calm my racing heart. "I'm so sorry about this. I had no idea they were coming here."

"Doesn't your manager work for *you*?"

"Yes, but...it's a little more complicated than that."

Teller sat on the mattress and patted the space beside him, urging me to sit back down. When I did, he cupped the sides of my neck, his thumbs brushing my jaw. "Hey, look at me. You don't have to rush. They'll wait until you're ready."

"I wanted more time with you."

His lips parted, those vivid sea-glass eyes softening. "Me too." He pulled me into his lap, then tipped me backward onto the bed. His fingers delved beneath the soft edges of the bathrobe to brush against my collarbone. His lips followed, dropping kisses. My tension melted, though I couldn't relax completely.

"I need to shower," I said weakly.

"We showered last night." His lips closed over my breast and gently sucked.

"*Mmm*. Yes, but we got dirty again after." I had the evidence all over me.

"I like that you have my scent on you. Especially around this *Paul* guy from your label."

I whimpered. On second thought, forget the shower. I wanted Teller's scent on me. Marking me. That scent would fade all too soon, so why not keep it for today, at least?

He kissed his way back up to my mouth, hypnotizing me with the smooth glide of his tongue. Then he pulled back enough to lock eyes with me for several long moments. My heart ratcheted in my chest.

"I'll never forget this weekend with you," he said.

Flutters moved through my stomach, goosebumps over my skin. "I won't either."

"You'll let me know if you hear from the stalker? Or if you need anything else? Doesn't matter what it is."

"I will." I enjoyed the weight of him on top of me for a little longer. Then my phone buzzed with another text.

We were out of time.

TWENTY-EIGHT

Ayla

I CLEANED UP A BIT, and then we each got dressed. I braided my hair to make myself presentable, while Teller smoothed out his own messy strands.

Then Teller helped me pack my things. He stopped every so often to kiss and touch me. Like he was as eager for these last few moments together as I was.

I checked my other messages. There hadn't been any formal plans for breakfast this morning, but I'd missed a few texts from the O'Neals. "I wanted to see Maisie one more time and give her a kiss and hug goodbye."

"Go find your niece," Teller said. "I'll carry your things down to the lobby for you."

"Thanks. Do you want to go to your room first to change? Someone downstairs might notice you're in the same clothes from the wedding."

He tilted his head like he was thinking about it. "Nah. Actually, I don't have the energy to care about that. Unless you mind."

"I don't. Just thinking of your reputation. Don't want your constituents to see their chief on a walk of shame."

"No shame here." He smiled and pressed his lips to my forehead.

I wasn't ashamed either. I didn't plan to publicize our night together, but I was on the same page as Teller. He'd wiped me out last night and this morning, and I'd loved it. I didn't have it in me to worry about the Hart County gossip mill just yet.

Maisie was playing with Emma's little siblings again. I gave her as many hugs as I could fit into five minutes, then said another goodbye to Emma and Ashford, who wouldn't leave for their hot springs honeymoon until tomorrow.

I felt rushed and didn't like it. But I probably would've felt the same if I'd spent the entire morning with them.

And I couldn't regret the hours I'd spent with Teller last night and this morning, either. It had meant a lot to me. So much that I still struggled to wrap my head around what I was feeling for him.

But there was no time to ponder it. Not until later, when we'd be hundreds of miles apart.

In the lobby, Teller stood off to the side with my bags. Cheryl paced by the fireplace, decked out in a designer tweed pantsuit with long necklaces layered over her silk blouse. She stuck out here like a giant sign declaring, *This doesn't belong!* But Cheryl was always herself, and I appreciated that about her.

She crossed the lobby to me as soon as I stepped out of the elevator. "So that's the chief of police?" She nodded at Teller with a frown. He regarded her coolly right back, though he stayed where he was.

"Yes? So?"

Cheryl pulled me a few feet from the elevator, away from the wedding guests milling around the checkout area. "I recognized him. A few more photos of the altercation in Silver Ridge have made it to social media. Him carrying you out of there."

I shrugged, hoping that my cheeks weren't turning red.

"And now he's got your luggage. I recognize your suitcase. I also know the look of a man who just rolled out of bed and is wearing the same clothes from the night before. Just how close are you two?"

"That's not important," I whispered. "I want to know why

you're really here. This wasn't necessary, showing up with no notice like this."

"I did give you notice when I texted this morning. I was concerned about you when we talked on Friday, after your video interview for the magazine. You were evading my questions, and I don't like that."

"But it's not your job to—"

"It *is* my job, Ayla." The pure calm of her tone was so infuriating. "Are you forgetting how you got so overwhelmed that you suspended your tour less than two years ago and then disappeared altogether? Ran away to Colorado? Trust me, the media hasn't forgotten. Your label has not forgotten either. They've invested too much in you."

"Right. I'm an asset, not a person. Is that why Paul is here somewhere? To protect his investment? Is he waiting in the car because the Last Refuge Inn is beneath him?"

She sighed like an indulgent mother dealing with a wayward child. "Paul is here because it's his job. Just like me. Dear, I know you hate some aspects of this business. So do I. But we work within those boundaries. That's why you hired me after you returned to work and made a fresh start. To help you navigate these issues. To step in when I see you need help so we avoid future hiccups. I'm on your side."

My past mental health episode was a *hiccup*? I took offense at that. But everything else she'd said was true. So I swallowed down my annoyance and my disappointment at my time with Teller being cut short.

But I wasn't leaving without a proper goodbye.

Teller picked up my bags as I approached him. "Everything alright?" he asked under his breath. I knew he meant with Cheryl.

"Mostly. Yes." *She was worried I'd run away again and refuse to leave Colorado*, I added silently.

Had I been tempted to stay? Maybe a little. But I'd decided all on my own to take the wiser course. I wasn't running away from my career again.

"Will you walk me outside?" I asked. "I was hoping for a goodbye kiss." I would ask for a kiss right now except for the people strewn around the lobby, watching us without any subtlety.

But the way Teller smiled at me was filled with such an intense mixture of affection and scorching heat, no one could fail to notice. Including Cheryl.

"You think I'd let you leave without one?" Teller rumbled as he helped me put on my coat.

We walked outside with Cheryl wedged next to me like she really thought I might bolt. Teller followed us with my bags. Thankfully, she and Paul had parked their rental—a Mercedes G-wagon—off to the far side of the lot, out of sight of the inn's entrance.

And there was Paul, leaning against the driver's side door in a Burberry coat, immersed in his phone. He flashed a cocky smile when he heard the crunch of our footsteps on the half-melted snow and gravel. "Ayla, there you are." His grin shifted to suspicion. He must've noticed Teller behind me. "A police escort? That seems unnecessary."

"I'm here in a personal capacity." Teller put an emphasis on the word *personal*.

Paul's jaw flexed. His gaze shifted to me. "You kept us waiting, Ayla. We should get to the airport. They said they can move up your scheduled departure window."

Teller's heat warmed my back. "Why does this guy talk like he's your boss?" he said in my ear. "Like he owns you."

"Because he kind of *does*." I didn't have time to explain the nuances of record contracts, or the fact that I had to play nice with my label until my renewal came up.

But Teller's resting grump face was out in full force. Every bit the intimidating police chief even though he wore his rumpled clothes from last night. It was freezing out here, and he hadn't bothered with an overcoat.

Teller strolled to the G-wagon's trunk, opened it, and placed my bags inside. Then he walked back to me, held my face in his hands, and kissed me.

There was no hesitation in this kiss. Anyone could've seen us, but Teller didn't care, and neither did I. His tongue teased me with slow, deep strokes that left me shivering as I remembered his cock moving inside me just an hour ago.

A throat cleared. Paul muttered something. But Teller kept kissing me until I was dazed and breathless.

He pressed his lips to mine one last time and said, "Goodbye, Troublemaker."

"Bye, Teller."

He kissed my forehead. Let go and walked backward by several steps. My heart beat at a reckless pace, like it wanted to leap right back into his arms.

"Ayla," Paul said sharply. "Let's go."

I stood still another moment. What choice did I have, really?

I had to get back to LA. Back to my regular life. No matter how much I loved my visits to Hart County, there was always an end.

Teller stood in the parking lot until we pulled onto the road. We turned a corner, and then I couldn't see him anymore.

Paul was driving. "It's good to have you back," he said brightly.

I kept my mouth shut and watched the trees pass by in the window.

Cheryl sat in the backseat, typing on her phone. I received a text notification.

CHERYL

I know it's difficult, but you have to put the police chief out of your mind. Don't get any romantic ideas. Can you imagine if the media sniffs out that you had a tryst with the man? Especially with the whispers already swirling about how you almost got arrested by him? They wouldn't leave him alone.

I paid Cheryl to tell me the rough, unvarnished truth, but right now? I kind of hated her for it. Which wasn't fair. She hadn't made the world the way it was.

My presence in Hart County made Teller's life harder. I didn't see any way around that.

Another text appeared on my phone.

TELLER

I miss you already.

My heart lodged in my throat.

I reacted with a heart to his message but didn't write back, simply because I had no clue what to say. Instead, I squeezed my phone in my fist and held it to my chest.

Every time I left Colorado, I felt like I was leaving a piece of myself behind. Before, it was about Maisie. The O'Neal family. And that emptiness was still there right now, because I would never be able to participate in their lives as much as I'd have liked. Not if I wanted to keep the career I'd fought so hard to build.

But after this weekend, Hart County had carved another chunk out of me. The part that wished I was someone else.

A girl who belonged with a man like Teller Landry.

I would *never* forget what we'd shared. He'd said he wouldn't either.

But it would've been easier for us both if we did.

TWENTY-NINE

Teller

Two. Weeks.

Fourteen days.

No, make that fifteen days since I'd last seen Ayla. Today was a new day.

Work had been keeping me busy, at least physically. But that was no blessing. Another vandalism had occurred last night, this one on the outskirts of Silver Ridge.

I was sitting at a kitchen table across from Donna Zanetti, a young mother whose husband had gone to visit his sick father out of town. She had a baby carrier strapped to her chest with her six-month-old asleep inside.

"Take your time," I said. "Tell me what happened."

"I heard the noise at 2:15 in the morning. Breaking glass. I grabbed my phone first thing. Called 911."

I reached across the table to place my hand on Donna's arm, but that didn't stop her trembling.

Susan had been on duty, and she'd made it here within ten minutes of the call. She'd called me after she confirmed that the suspect was gone and the scene was secure.

Donna rubbed her daughter's back. "I stayed in my bedroom with the baby. She must've known something was wrong. She was crying. And then I saw the shadow moving outside the bedroom door. I knew he was out there."

Shit. This was much worse than any of the previous vandalisms around the county. No one else had reported that the culprit went inside an occupied house.

"Did he try to open the bedroom door?"

"I don't think so. I had it locked anyway, since my husband is gone."

"Was it one person? Could it have been more than one?"

"Definitely just one. I heard his footsteps."

The vandal had left red graffiti in the shape of a flower on the outside of the house, exactly like the previous incidents. He'd broken windows and smashed some toys and equipment the family had left outside. Nothing was missing, either outside or inside the house. This hadn't been a robbery.

This behavior was designed to scare the homeowners. Always women alone.

But actually going inside the home? That was new and extremely concerning.

"I never thought..." Donna shook her head. "I've heard about those other incidents lately, but I never..."

I patted her arm gently. "I know. That must've been terrifying. But we're going to find who did this. We'll have someone check for fingerprints and other forensic evidence. The sheriff's office and the other departments around the county are involved in the investigation. We're taking this very seriously."

I finished interviewing Donna. Susan and our other officers wrapped up their photos and notes, and I had someone stay behind to wait for the crime scene techs. As a rural county, we didn't employ any of our own. The forensics techs worked for the state and traveled to scenes in the region whenever they were needed.

Susan and I headed back to the station. When we arrived, I waved her into my office.

She sat heavily in the chair across from my desk. "Well, that was awful. I've known Donna since she was a baby herself, and I was there at her daughter's christening. Chief, we have to figure out who's doing this. It's just mean and nasty."

"You're preaching to the choir."

"I already got a text from Dixie. She's setting up a meal train to help out Donna, along with volunteers to stay with her and the baby. Donna's husband will probably head back sooner after what happened. But people are going to be talking about this. They'll want to know what we're doing to catch this creep."

"Yes, Susan," I said calmly. "I know." I was well used to receiving calls daily from my citizens.

"And that red spray paint nonsense?"

"It's his signature." I was assuming the suspect's gender was male, but would a woman do this? I doubted it. "He's doing us a favor. We know for sure it's the same person, even though we haven't gotten any physical evidence or camera footage yet to confirm it."

"What's that design supposed to be, anyway?" Susan took out her work phone. She had some pictures from the scene today on it. "Those swirls." She held it up. "A flower?"

I nodded, my sense of unease growing. "Yes. It's a flower."

"Creepy as all get-out."

"The escalation..." I drummed my fingers on my desk. "It's a bad sign."

She put her phone away. "Madness. I swear there's something in the air. It's the pollen spores in spring, I swear. They mess with the noggin."

I almost smiled. "It's March. It'll be a while until pollen season really hits." It would be spring soon, and we had a few more months of chaotic weather ahead of us before the relative calm of summer. Though I'd seen snow here in June and July. At least the Colorado sun melted the snowfall from the roads and trees between storms year round.

But thinking of snow just brought Ayla to mind, and that was a bad idea. I'd already spent plenty of sleepless nights lately obsessing over her.

"Yes, I realize it's not spring just yet," Susan said. "But people have been acting strange. Like Seth being out sick today for the third or fourth time in a couple months."

I'd noticed that. I'd had so much on my mind that I hadn't checked up on him, but I should have.

"And *you.*" Susan pointed a finger at me. "I'm not the only one who's noticed your surly moods lately, mister."

"I'm not *surly.*"

"You're in a funk. Have been ever since the wedding. And I've heard a few rumors about what went on in Hartley. Don't think I haven't."

I gripped the skin between my eyes. "No idea what you mean."

Of course, I knew *exactly* what she meant. And Susan's smirk said she knew that too.

Everyone seemed to know about that goodbye kiss with Ayla in the parking lot. Granted, I hadn't been discreet about it. I'd lingered with our lips together, trying to imprint her taste in my memory. The feel of her under my hands. The way she'd worn my scent on her skin...

Hell, I wasn't supposed to be thinking about that.

"I heard you got very cozy with a celebrity who shall remain nameless. I suppose that's only natural, since you two had to snuggle up when you were trapped in that snowstorm."

"Susan..."

"*But,*" she went on, "those pollen spores must be going to your head if you're this distraught over a little weekend rendezvous." Her eyes narrowed. "Unless it's more than that?"

I put my hands flat on my desk. "We're at work. I'm not going to indulge your need for gossip. But regardless, I have nothing to say about any celebrity or otherwise. You have reports to file. You may exit my office, Officer Nichols."

"*See?*" she muttered to herself on her way out. "*Surly.*"

Fuck me. I needed a drink.

Around midday, I pulled up a stool at the end of the bar at Hearthstone. Callum walked toward me, draping a bar towel over his shoulder. His brown hair stuck out haphazardly from beneath his backward baseball cap.

"Chief, you're in here early."

"Just for lunch."

"You sure? You look like a guy who could use a drink."

Geez, he had it right. Same exact thought I'd had earlier. But I couldn't. "A beer would be nice, but I'm on duty."

Yet I'd still come here to a bar, as if I wanted to torture myself over what I couldn't have.

He winked. "I won't tell."

I really hoped Callum wasn't that irresponsible. I decided to assume he was kidding. "I'll have a root beer and a burger. Hold the onions."

"You got it." He went to enter my order.

Callum usually worked all day on Wednesdays. I knew way too much about people's schedules around town, but that was my habit. Making sure things in Silver Ridge worked like clockwork and, when they didn't, stepping in to help fix the problem.

At this current moment, though, I was the one who was messed up.

It was long past the lunch rush, and Hearthstone was nearly deserted. Callum brought over my soda. "I heard a rumor," he said.

I tensed. "What about?"

"Another vandalism last night. That true?"

I exhaled, not even sure what I'd been bracing myself for. "Yeah, unfortunately. We're devoting a lot of resources to finding the culprit."

"I'm sure. They've all been outside of the town centers, right? More isolated areas?"

I nodded. Otherwise, I'd be worried about Piper living alone with Ollie. But they were close to Main Street.

There wasn't much more I could say about the vandalism case. We were keeping the details as confidential as possible.

"I've hardly seen you since the wedding," I said, changing the subject.

Callum's brow creased. "Yeah. But trivia night with the Lonely Harts club isn't really your scene."

Okay, fair. Callum and I didn't usually hang out much. I had my long hours at the station, and he had his bartending gig and volunteer firefighting duties.

Yet we'd known each other our entire lives. He went through life more flippantly than I did, but he was a good egg. A doting uncle to Maisie, brother to Grace, friend to Piper.

Maybe he could help, because I couldn't go on like this.

"I need some advice," I spit out.

"From *me*? What about?"

"A woman."

"*Ah.*" He drew that one syllable out like a full sentence. "I heard some interesting things about you and Ayla at the wedding."

"Careful," I growled.

"Ease up, killer. I wasn't going to say more than that. *Ashford* might. She's important to him. But I think the gossip skipped him and Emma because they were off on their honeymoon until last week."

I took a long sip of soda, frowning. This felt ridiculous. Asking anyone for dating advice, much less Callum O'Neal. But Callum dated constantly. Always seemed to have a different tourist on his arm. I wouldn't go to him for tips on long-term relationships, but surely he could interpret the basics of female communication. Right? Ayla was twenty-seven, and Callum was far closer to that age than I was.

Yes, I was really this desperate.

Cal pulled off his ball cap and combed his fingers through his hair. Pushed the hat back into place. "I'll just assume this is a *hypothetical* woman you need advice about. Okay? Tell me what's going on. The love doctor is in."

I suppressed an eye roll. But I'd already started this, so I might as well see what he thought. "So, this woman... We spent time together. We clicked. On many levels."

A crooked grin started to slide up Callum's face.

"*No*," I barked. "Whatever you're thinking, don't."

He pressed his lips into a flat line. "Got it. Go on."

I'd spent some late nights torturing myself by watching her videos, scrolling her social media. Not exactly healthy. And also unsatisfying.

Her talent was mind-blowing, yet the version of herself that she revealed in the media wasn't the woman I'd held in my arms at the Last Refuge Inn. The woman who'd opened up to me, laughed with me.

Who'd whimpered and cried out when I made her come.

That was who I wanted. The truth of her.

I'd replayed the moments we'd shared in my head like my favorite movie, even as I'd refused to confirm or deny any of the gossip. Those memories were private. Something that belonged just to the two of us. If any man had dared to make a snide comment about Ayla, he would've quickly found my fist in his face. Even Callum.

Deep down, Ayla still felt like mine.

I didn't know how to stop feeling that.

"We had to say goodbye. We don't even live in the same state, and we have almost nothing in common beyond some very intense chemistry. But I still can't stop thinking about her."

"Sounds rough."

"It's becoming a problem." I leaned forward on my elbows, rubbing my eyes. "My temper is shorter than usual."

"I hadn't noticed."

I glared. He thought he was cute. "I can't *sleep*, Cal. It's bad."

He nodded. "Okay. Have you reached out to her?"

"Yes. I've texted to check in on her."

"Have you heard back?"

"A few times."

I'd been texting her every few days to check in, and she wrote back often enough to suggest the communication wasn't unwanted. But beyond that, Ayla had gone quiet on me. No updates yet on the stalker situation.

"Does she write back to every message?"

"Not exactly."

"What does that mean? Not *exactly*?"

I took out my phone, glancing over the messages I'd sent. "She doesn't always reply, but she always likes my messages."

"Wait." Callum grimaced. "With a thumbs up?"

"With a heart."

He nodded, relieved. "A heart is promising. We can work with that."

"Yeah? I have no idea what to think."

"Show me what you've written. We need to check your tone."

"*What*? No. I'll check my own tone." Holding my hand over my screen, I scrolled back through my texts over the last couple weeks.

ME

Hope you're well.

AYLA

I am. I hope you're well too.

I am. Just been thinking of you.

She responded with a heart to the message. Then, a few days later.

Day off today. Spent time with Ollie and Maisie at the park. They were up to their usual antics.

Wish I could've been there.

I wish that too.

Sending a photo

Another heart. Then a couple more days. I remembered agonizing over whether or not to write, starting and stopping several texts before I sent the next one.

Heard one of your songs while I was driving today. Got so distracted Finn had to radio me three times before I responded to dispatch. Embarrassing. 🙄 [eye roll emoji]

☺️ [blushing face emoji]

And just yesterday, from me:

Missing you.

Fuck. I scrubbed a hand over my face.

"That bad?" Callum asked.

"What is wrong with me? I sound like I'm *obsessed*."

He grinned. "From you, Teller, that's saying something. And it's a pleasant surprise."

"Doesn't feel pleasant."

When Ayla and I had been together in person, the chemistry between us flowed naturally. But it ended when that weekend was over. It *had* to end, and we'd both acknowledged that. Logically, I knew it.

But the rest of me just wasn't listening.

I was all twisted up over Ayla, and I had no idea what to do about it.

I put my phone away. "I'm so fucking out of practice with this kind of thing."

"What exactly do you want to happen with her?"

I rapped my knuckles on the bar top. "Something that's... impossible. But I still want it so fucking much." I'd been cursing a lot more lately too. Probably went without saying.

He nodded slowly. "It kinda sounds like you might be falling for her."

Oh hell.

Hell.

No. That could not be it. Ayla was incredible, breathtaking, every superlative. But *me*, falling that way? After one weekend together and then two weeks of sheer misery without her?

Could a weekend be that life-changing?

The muscle in my chest reacted, thumping out an answer that I felt in my bones, my skin. My face fell into my hands.

"What's happening to me?"

I didn't do this kind of thing. Chase a woman who was unattainable. I didn't chase women at all.

I'd spent the last ten years devoted to causes bigger than myself. That hadn't left room for anything else. But now there was suddenly a hole in the middle of my life. A lack I hadn't even realized was there. Until Ayla Maxwell filled up that space for a few life-changing days and showed me just what I'd been missing. Laughter and connection and intimacy. Plus epically hot sex.

Did I just need to find a girlfriend? A more realistic prospect than a superstar?

The very thought of touching some other woman made me nauseous. No, this was about Ayla. The most incredible woman I'd ever met.

A better question: what the hell was I going to do?

"Maybe it's just an infatuation," Callum said. "You wouldn't be the first guy to fall for the girl on the cover of the magazine. She must have men chasing after her all the time."

Remain seated, I commanded myself. *Do not launch across this bar and strangle your friend.* "Stop talking about her with other men. Unless you want me to lose my shit."

"Okay, okay, I'm sorry." Callum held up his hands. "That was a test, by the way."

"And?"

"You're an intense guy all the time, Teller, but you're extra intense about her. Seems like it's something real. Look, it's a long shot, the two of you working out."

I scowled. We'd both dropped the fiction that this wasn't about Ayla. "I don't need a reminder of that fact."

"*But*, if you feel that strongly about her, you shouldn't give up. Just don't jerk her around. Or yourself. Only do this if she's worth it to you."

My response leaped to the tip of my tongue without a moment's hesitation. "She's worth everything."

I had no idea what I was doing or where this was going. But Ayla was the kind of woman who was worth burning down the world for.

THIRTY
Ayla

Ricky, my makeup artist, spun me around to face the mirror. "What do you think, lovely? The green shadow with touches of gold and matching eyeliner, which I call Naughty Forest Spirit, or the darker Va-Va Vixen palette?"

"Um, what was the first thing again?"

He bowed his head. "You didn't hear a word I said, did you?"

I bit my fuchsia-painted lip. "Not a single one. Sorry."

Ricky's boisterous laugh filled my bathroom. "You're probably writing a song in your head right now. Which is totally fine. Don't mind me. I'll take lots of pictures and let you decide later which palette you prefer for which event."

My neighbor Hayleigh popped her head into the room. "He's right. You've been super distracted lately." She gave Ricky a look. "We had a brunch date last Sunday, and I had to drink three mimosas waiting for her late ass to show up."

"I said I was sorry. You guys make me sound like the worst. Also, how did you get in here?"

She shrugged. "Bryan let me in since Ricky was already here. Your security guys love me."

We were in my house in Malibu. Ricky had come over today

to test out some new makeup looks. My assistant had been in and out, doing the things she always took care of for me.

As for Hayleigh, she showed up whenever she wanted since she lived in the next house over. She was the daughter of a famous movie director and a legendary actress. Her parents funded her lifestyle, and Hayleigh hadn't decided on a career yet. Every month, it was something different. Screenwriter, fashion designer, wellness influencer.

Being friends with Hayleigh wasn't really a choice. She just *happened*.

As for Bryan, he was back to work after his recovery from the concussion, and he'd been a constant presence on my security detail.

Ricky put his hands on my shoulders. "You're my favorite client by far. I'd let you get away with any number of crimes, fashion or otherwise."

"If anything, you should be *less* approachable," Hayleigh said. "You're always the sweetest. As long as nobody interrupts your calls with Maisie."

I smiled. "Thank you for noticing."

"But I have to admit, I'm curious about what's going through that talented head of yours," Ricky added. "The next Grammy winner for album of the year?"

Lately, I'd been wrapped up in my music. That was true. Inspiration had grabbed hold of me since my return from Colorado, which was a relief in some ways. I'd spent hours in my recording studio here at home every single day. Bits and pieces of new lyrics and melodies came to me constantly. My songwriting notebook lived on my nightstand for middle-of-the-night surges of creativity.

Yet I hadn't finished a single song.

My potential stalker remained in the back of my mind. So far, he hadn't replied to my email trying to draw him out. The flower arrangement I'd received at the Last Refuge Inn had been another dead end. No idea who'd sent it.

But it wasn't really the stalker that had me so distracted. It was the rest of what happened during Ashford and Emma's wedding weekend.

It was *him*. Teller. How his body had felt on mine... All the things he'd said...

You're the most breathtaking woman. It blows my mind.

I'll never forget this weekend with you.

Two and a half weeks now since Cheryl and Paul piled me into that G-wagon and we drove away, Teller Landry in the rearview.

"I've been writing a lot," I said. "But I wasn't thinking of a song just now. Something else."

Hayleigh came further into the bathroom and perched on the counter. "Something you want to share? Entertain me, please. That's why I'm here."

I stuck my tongue out at her.

Teller had been texting me every couple days, and his messages had been a lifeline. Little bubbles of happiness that popped way too soon. I'd tried to write back, but it was hard. Not knowing what to say. Not even knowing what I felt about him.

I suspected my brain was trying to channel all those mixed-up emotions into my music. But that didn't mean I had answers. Just a lot of heartfelt verses filled with aching longing and zero conclusions.

My heart was scraped raw. Great for inspiring my music. Really dang painful to experience.

I needed someone to talk to. I trusted Hayleigh and Ricky both. Ricky had told me about his boyfriend troubles, and even though Hayleigh still hadn't decided on a career path, she'd always been supportive.

"There's...a guy," I admitted.

Ricky gasped. "Has he been wooing you? Please tell me he has."

"He's been texting me a lot. Saying he's thinking of me. He's very protective. I've never felt safer than when I'm with him."

Hayleigh fanned her face. "I have tingles."

"But we both agreed we can't be a thing. I mean, we didn't discuss it outright, but it was implied. A relationship would be too complicated."

"Is this Paul Ruxton?" Hayleigh asked breathlessly.

My face scrunched up. "Absolutely *not.*" A tabloid story had popped up recently, speculating about me and Paul. He'd made sure paparazzi snapped pics of us outside one of LA's hottest sushi restaurants, though it had been nothing but a business dinner.

But it wasn't worth getting upset over made-up stories.

"This guy isn't in LA, and he's not in the industry. I feel like I can be myself with him."

Hayleigh nodded along. "That's the dream, right there."

"But I don't even know when I'll see him in person again. Kinda hard to date someone I never see." I was aware that people dated long distance, but it didn't seem realistic for me.

"You're Ayla effing Maxwell," Ricky said. "He should be moving heaven and earth for the mere chance to grovel at your feet."

I smirked. "That line has potential as a song lyric."

Ricky winked. "It's all yours."

After Ricky finished testing makeup looks and we decided which were my favorites, I asked him and Hayleigh to stick around for dinner. We had takeout on my balcony. After my usual bedtime call with Maisie, my friends and I snuggled into my oversized couch with microwave popcorn and fuzzy blankets to watch a movie.

The time I'd spent with Teller in Hart County made me realize how lonely my everyday routine in LA had gotten. I'd told myself that my music, my frequent calls with Maisie, and the occasional hang-out with my few trusted friends kept me fulfilled. But that wasn't enough for me anymore.

I wanted to *live*.

And I was *Ayla effing Maxwell*, right? Didn't I deserve that?

After Ricky and Hayleigh left for the night, I found myself glancing over Teller's text messages again. Then I opened that photo taken at the wedding reception of the Lonely Harts club. I zoomed in on me and Teller, and my body recalled with a rush of goosebumps how he'd been touching me while this photo was taken.

Which had been very exciting, don't get me wrong.

But tonight, I missed the emotional closeness we'd shared. Having someone to confess my innermost thoughts to. I had shared more with Teller about myself, my *past*, than anyone before.

I'd avoided having a real conversation with him since leaving Colorado because I'd thought it would just make this harder. I was supposed to move on.

But he'd said he missed me too.

I went back to our messages and was about to start typing when a text popped up from him, beating me to the punch.

TELLER

Just heard from River. He has an update on the stalker investigation. Any chance you're free to talk with us?

I'm free now.

A couple minutes later, a video call came in. I quickly ran my fingers through my hair, feeling silly about my self-consciousness, then accepted it on my iPad. Good thing I'd washed off all my crazy makeup hours ago.

Teller was in his office at the station. Hair neat, handsome in his uniform. He looked *so* damn good.

"Ayla," he said softly. "It's great to see you."

Meanwhile, I could hardly breathe. I was nervous, and it wasn't so much about the stalker.

This man. Did he have any idea what he did to me?

"You too. It's almost midnight in Colorado, isn't it? You're working late."

"Busy day at the station."

I frowned. "Anything bad?" Silver Ridge was a small town, but terrible things could still happen there. It made me dizzy to think of him being in danger.

He glanced to the side, and I could tell he was holding something back. "It doesn't involve anyone you know. I'm sure you're anxious to know what River found. I'll add him to the call."

"Okay."

Actually, I would've preferred to talk with Teller for a while longer before we got to the stalker updates. It was the first time I'd seen his face in weeks. But I didn't want to keep him up later than necessary if he'd had a difficult day. Teller had so much responsibility on his shoulders.

Made me think, oh-so-briefly, about what I would've done if I were in Silver Ridge. Like stop by the station to bring him dinner. Massage those tense shoulder muscles, kiss away his pensive expression...

I shook off that sliver of fantasy.

Another window popped up on the video call, and River appeared. He was wearing black-framed glasses, and it looked like he was in a dark apartment, his face lit by the glow of his computer. We greeted each other, and then River got right to his news.

"I've been working on tracking the sender of the email you received, Ayla. As we discussed in Hartley."

I nodded, remembering the creepy message from Biggest Fan and the attached photo of me shopping on Main Street. "You found something?" I prompted.

River adjusted his glasses. "It's taken longer than I would've liked. Your stalker took some elaborate steps to hide his identity.

There are anonymizing programs you can download on the dark web, and unfortunately they're easy to access. But after a lot of tracing back through different servers, I narrowed down his IP address to the west side of Los Angeles."

I blinked, feeling that knowledge sink in.

Teller had a more obvious reaction, his fingers running through his hair and roughing up the short strands. "So he's definitely in LA?" Teller asked. "Not Silver Ridge?"

"When the stalker sent the message, he was in LA," River clarified. "Ayla, if he writes you again, I'll be able to get a more current location, and hopefully I can narrow it down further. I'd rather the guy leaves you alone, but the more data points we have, the better. I've been monitoring the email account you showed me before. I assume he hasn't tried to contact you some other way?"

Teller looked at me like he wanted to ask the same question.

"No contact at all," I said. "Nobody on my team has mentioned anything either." I hadn't given my new security guys or Cheryl the exact details about the stalker, but if something suspicious had come up, they would've mentioned it.

Then my mind backtracked over what River had said. "Wait, you've been checking my email?" I asked. I rarely used email for anything. Definitely nothing sensitive or personal. I didn't really care if River or Teller could get into the account. But I was still surprised. "I thought I was supposed to let you both know if the stalker wrote me."

River shrugged. "I maintained my access to the email account so I would be able to keep an eye on it. If you'd rather I don't do that..."

"No," Teller cut in sharply. "We shouldn't change anything at this point. River's already made progress. If the stalker writes back, then River should be able to run with it immediately."

"Fine by me," I snapped. But my insides were all bunched up, and I didn't even know why.

River's eyes darted over his computer screen, his gaze dancing between me and Teller. After a pause, he said, "Okay then. I'll let you know if I find out anything else."

"Thanks, River."

"Of course, Ayla. Have a good night."

River's window disappeared, but Teller's stayed. His hand rubbed over his jaw. "You're upset about the email thing."

"No, I'm not."

"Are you sure?"

"Yes." But *something* felt weird. "It just would've been nice to know that you could access my account."

"I haven't been reading your email, if that's what you're worried about. I don't have access to it."

"But you knew River did?"

"I...yes. I figured."

I wasn't even mad about the email. I didn't freaking *care* about email. "It just makes me feel like you don't trust me to make choices for myself."

"Of course I trust you to decide things for yourself. I know I don't have any right—"

He cleared his throat. Color had crept into his face beneath his late-night stubble.

"I should've mentioned it," he finished. "But you've been busy, and I can't imagine how stressful it's been for you lately. Still not knowing who the stalker is."

I shifted, unable to get comfortable. "I guess. I've had a lot to focus on."

He flinched. What was *that* about?

I wanted to understand what this was between us. Where things stood. And I didn't.

"Teller—"

"Are you seeing that guy from your label?" he blurted.

It took a moment for me to catch up. "Do you mean *Paul*?"

Teller's face flushed. "Yes." He said the word carefully, but there was a distinct flare of something possessive in his eyes, in his tone. Something *dark* as he leaned forward toward the camera. "Are you?"

"I would never date Paul. There was that tabloid story a day or two ago about us, but it's nonsense."

The muscle in his jaw pulsed. "What about anyone else?"

I shook my head, my throat going dry. "I'm not dating anyone. What about you?"

"There is no one else I want," he rasped. "No one but you."

His words hung in the sudden silence between us.

No one but you.

My heart was beating fast, all those mixed-up emotions at war again inside me. "Oh," I whispered.

"Does that honestly surprise you?"

"I just wasn't sure. With how we left things when we last saw each other."

He huffed, a sound halfway between a laugh and pure despair. "I can't stop thinking about you. As if the million texts I've sent didn't make that obvious. And then I saw that article about you and Paul." He shook his head. "I know I don't have a claim on you. You don't owe me anything."

"But?"

"When I saw that story, it *gutted* me." His fingers kept tracking through his hair, splaying the ends. "You didn't write back to most of my messages the past couple weeks."

"Only because I was trying to move on."

"Do you *want* to move on?"

I hesitated. What did I want?

"Please give me some kind of sign." He managed a weak smile. "You're killing me."

That smile said he was kidding, but his gaze was pleading.

"I miss you," I said. "I've been thinking about you. All the time." I swallowed the thickness in my throat. "Every day."

"That's something, then." He leaned toward the camera. "Tell me how you've been."

I told him about my progress on my new album. Movie night

with Ricky and Hayleigh. Teller shared his latest stories about Ollie. Then told me about the series of vandalisms over the last several months all over Hart County.

Thinking about him on duty and facing danger felt different now. He'd been doing those things for years, of course, yet now the idea of Teller getting hurt made it harder to breathe.

After a while, we took a break so he could head home. I changed into my pajamas and got ready for bed. "I'm going to call back though," he said. "Half an hour."

I smiled. "If you don't, I will."

When Teller called back, he'd changed from his uniform to a T-shirt. "Are you in your bedroom?" I asked. It looked like there was a headboard behind him.

"Yeah. You?"

I nodded. I was lying against my pillows with the overhead lights dimmed. It felt intimate, the two of us in our beds and talking quietly.

The position reminded me of being in bed with him at the Last Refuge Inn. Naked beneath the covers.

Talking with him was wonderful too, though. This was almost perfect, actually. Just getting to see him, hear his voice, know what he was thinking about. This felt *right*.

I really liked him.

Before I knew it, hours had passed. I yawned. "We've talked almost all night. Don't you need to go to bed?" I asked.

"I don't like saying goodbye to you."

"Me neither."

We were both lying on our sides, facing one another through our cameras. Like he was really here with me.

"There's something I should tell you," he murmured.

I nodded sleepily. "Yeah?"

"I've..." He swallowed. "I've never felt like this." His voice was deep and rough. "I've been distracted at work. Downright impossible, if you ask Susan. You've got me so messed up, Troublemaker. I don't know what to do with myself."

His desperate tone. The look in his eyes. It was like the straight-laced, confident, fearless police chief was coming apart at the seams.

I felt it too. But I'd had no idea Teller was feeling this torn up about *me*. It made me ache that he was hurting.

"Then what do we do?" I asked.

"I'll work on figuring it out. If you're willing to give me a shot."

I hardly knew what we were talking about. We both felt something for each other. That was clear. But what was he hoping for?

"A shot at what, exactly? Another hot weekend together? Because we'd end up with the same problem."

And it might hurt even worse. Being that close to him again, just to say goodbye. I'd never felt like this before either.

It scared me.

He blinked those thick lashes at me. Teller conveyed more sincerity in a single glance than anyone else I'd met.

"No, Ayla. I want a shot at winning you. To make you mine for as long as you'll have me."

THIRTY-ONE
Ayla

TELLER WANTED TO *WIN ME*. That sounded romantic. But I didn't know exactly what to expect.

Until he showed me.

The next few weeks were amazing. And also the worst kind of torture.

He texted religiously every morning and night, and sometimes in between. Mostly with sweet messages like *missing you more than ever today*. Or pictures from around Silver Ridge. Like melting icicles on the eaves of his house. Maisie and Ollie clutching cups of hot chocolate in their mittens. Or Stella the dog prancing through snow.

At night, after my usual calls with Maisie, I called Teller and chatted with him, sometimes for hours. A few times, I'd gone to sleep to the sound of his deep, melodic voice and had the most relaxing, comforting dreams.

The rest of my days were spent in the recording studio. Either mine at home, or the Ruxton Records studio in Santa Monica, where I'd started to share my new songs with my producer and favorite collaborators. Everyone was thrilled with what I'd come up with so far. Together, we'd actually finished a couple of the compositions, though I still wasn't completely satisfied with them.

But my new album was actually taking shape. I couldn't remember another time that I'd been this happy, even though I longed to see Teller again with every fiber of my being.

He kept insisting that he didn't want any definitive answers from me. Teller said he only wanted a chance to prove himself. I already thought he was worthy. I definitely didn't want to see anyone else.

How a relationship between us was supposed to work logistically, though? I still didn't know.

When I was home one afternoon, a call came in from Bryan. "Hey, we have a delivery here. Something perishable. Delivery guy says it's...ice cream?"

Bryan and the other security guys knew about my possible stalker, though not all the gritty details. But the stalker hadn't bothered me once in the five weeks or so since Emma and Ashford's wedding. As if he'd vanished from the face of the Earth, and I was all for it.

I set my songwriting notebook on the coffee table, jumping up from my seat on the couch. "That must be from Teller." His text that morning had said, *Expect a surprise today. Sending some cold to you since there's no real winter in LA.*

"Yep, just checked," Bryan said. "Delivery sent by Teller Landry. We'll bring it in."

"Thanks." I ended the call and hurried to the front door.

Two minutes later, Bryan and the other security guy on duty carried two boxes inside. Frost dotted the tops of the cardboard. They set them on my kitchen island. When we opened the boxes and saw what was inside, the guys looked confused.

But my heart was bursting.

"Mint chocolate chip," I said. "He remembered."

Teller had sent me two cases of mint chocolate chip ice cream sandwiches. While we were stuck in the snow, I'd told him how my sister bought these when we were kids.

"That mean something to you?" Bryan asked.

"It does." It meant Teller was incredibly sweet.

I gave the guys a couple of ice cream sandwiches, then stacked the rest in my freezer. When that was finished, I unwrapped one and video-called Teller.

"Hi." He was in his office. He grinned when he saw me on the screen, but his expression turned to pure lust when I licked along the edge of the ice cream sandwich.

"Delicious. This is an amazing present. Thank you."

Eyes heated, he got up from his desk and went to close his office door. "You're welcome. But you better stop licking your treat so suggestively or I'm going to get hard at work."

"Should've thought of that beforehand, Chief Landry. I have enough ice cream sandwiches to send you a sexy dessert video every day for the next month."

He laughed. I loved it when his face lit up that way. "I miss you, Troublemaker."

"Miss you too."

My heart ached. This was getting dire. If we both didn't have work responsibilities, I would've been on a plane already to see him.

How could I miss someone this much when, overall, we'd spent only a few days together in person? I didn't get it.

I also still didn't know the endgame that Teller had in mind. But he was winning me over more and more every day.

Making me want to fall for him.

During one of our nightly conversations, I told him I didn't like watching TV, but I was a huge fan of reading. Sometimes Hayleigh and I cruised the shelves of our local bookshop and left with a haul. I secretly kept a Little Free Library by the Santa Monica Pier stocked with my old books.

But what I really wished I could do was while away an afternoon at a bookstore myself without being recognized. Without having to go after hours or ask the owner to keep people away from me.

A few days later, Teller wrote me to expect another delivery. It arrived while Ricky was doing my makeup for that night's event.

Hayleigh dashed into my spacious bathroom, where Ricky had spread his supplies over the vanity counter. "You're not going to believe what just got here," she squealed. "I saw the truck drive past my house and hurried over as quick as I could."

We all went out to my living room, where Bryan was wheeling boxes inside with a dolly. "Landry strikes again. Warn him we're going to need hazard pay for carrying all these delivery boxes. Geez." Bryan grinned.

As it turned out, Teller had asked the clerk from the local independent bookshop to send me a copy of every single current bestseller, plus a selection of the bookshop's recommended favorites.

I mean, *what*?

Ricky picked up a hardcover and thumbed through it. "This guy is going all out for you. Is he your boyfriend yet?"

"If you don't marry him," Hayleigh said, "I want his number."

I just stared in awe at the books that now filled my living room. There had to be a hundred at least. "I don't know what we are. But he's pretty incredible, isn't he?"

"Surprised he hasn't bought you an entire flower shop yet," Ricky said.

The thought of flowers gave me an uneasy shudder. My stalker had ruined flower arrangements for me, at least for the foreseeable future, and Teller understood that without me needing to say it.

Plus, a bookstore delivery was far more creative.

But I was guilty about how much Teller must've spent on this. Thousands?

I slipped into my bedroom and called him. "I can't believe you sent a bookstore to me. Thank you so much."

He was in uniform in the driver's seat of his department SUV, maybe on his way home given the hour. It looked like he'd pulled over to answer my call. "So you like it?"

"I do. It's over the top in the best way."

He grinned.

"I just...I don't want you to feel like you need to spend money on me." It was no secret that I made a lot more money than he did. I could've asked the bookshop to make a bulk delivery myself. Of course, I wouldn't have thought of it, and it wouldn't have been nearly so special.

Teller smoothed a big hand over his sharp jaw. "Sweetheart, don't worry about that. I like doing things for you. Thinking of ways to make you smile."

Ugh, this man. "Thank you," I said again. "This made my day."

When had someone done anything like this for me, ever?

I'd had boyfriends who bought me diamonds and exclusive, expensive trinkets. But nothing that truly meant something to me. Teller knew how to speak directly to my heart.

He wanted to show me that he listened. That he cared. I cared about him too. More with every passing day.

I touched my thumb to his face on the screen. "I really need to see you again."

He sighed and said, "Soon."

Unfortunately, I didn't have much time to talk before I had to jump back in the makeup chair and get ready for my obligatory appearance that night.

On Paul Ruxton's arm, no less.

But I took a sexy selfie before getting dressed. My hair and makeup were styled, but I still wore my bathrobe. I draped it down around my shoulders, showing the tops of my breasts and giving a sultry pout to my phone camera.

ME

You might see pictures online from the event tonight. But this one is only for you.

TELLER

Wow. 🔥 Will you be thinking of me at your event?

Every minute. Especially later when I'm alone in my bed.

You make me so hard, Troublemaker. Good thing I just got home, because the tent in these gray sweats is very much NSFW.

Gah. Shivers of desire made me rub my thighs together.

While we spoke every day and flirted and teased one another, we hadn't done more on our calls. Teller could say such dirty things in that commanding tone of his, but he also had a gentlemanly streak. It seemed like he wanted to wait for more sexy times until we could see one another in person again.

Just one more form of delicious torture. As soon as we could find a few days to get together, I planned to jump him and spend the whole time naked.

Why couldn't I be doing that tonight instead of this stupid party?

The gatehouse at the edge of my neighborhood called ahead to my security guys, letting them know that Paul had entered the neighborhood.

I heard the loud rumble of an engine before I stepped out my front door. Paul was in his bright orange Lamborghini.

I'd dressed in a wide-legged jumpsuit, sliding my feet into a pair of Jimmy Choo heels. The event was a pre-release party for another artist on my same label. Not even an actual release party. It was being held at a fancy restaurant in Beverly Hills. And because Paul insisted on escorting me, he was driving.

Bryan opened the passenger door for me. "Let us know if you need anything tonight," he murmured.

He would be following separately and parking down the street from the venue, just in case. I'd agreed to ride with Paul to the event so we could step straight onto the red carpet together, but I wasn't going to be stranded with the man.

"Thank you," I whispered to Bryan, then slid into the low leather seat.

"You look gorgeous," Paul said as I got in, his eyes roving.

Teller said that to me all the time. How did Paul manage to sound infinitely sleazier?

He smirked. "Ouch, no compliment for me in return? Tough crowd."

I hid my eye roll. "You look nice too." He was wearing the same designer clothes as usual. And too much cologne.

"That's more like it." The engine roared as we pulled away from my house. "I've been looking forward to tonight. I've hardly seen you lately. It's like you've been hiding from me."

Cheryl's voice intoned in my head. *Be nice.*

"We were at that business dinner just the other night," I pointed out. "And I've seen you at the Santa Monica studio."

He'd been inviting himself to my sessions with my collaborators. It was his job to show up and monitor how I was doing, offering advice and smoothing the process. But I didn't have to do whatever he said.

Or accept his suggestions of grabbing a private dinner or drinks after my recording sessions.

"Yes, but that's work." Paul's smarmy grin inched up his face. "This is much better. You're my date tonight. We can finally get to know each other on a personal level."

I almost choked.

I'd been thinking a lot about what Teller said that last day in Hartley, after he met Paul. *It's like he owns you*. I remained under contract with this label for another year.

But playing nice didn't mean rolling over and playing dead.

"Tonight is business, not personal," I said. "I have a boyfriend. Just so you know."

Paul's smile froze. Turned ice cold.

He blasted music for the rest of the drive. When we reached the red carpet, I stepped out to shutters snapping and cameras flashing. Paul raced around the side of the car to put a hand on my back as we walked. I smiled for the posed pictures and video segments and entertainment reporter questions.

This was publicity for my upcoming album. It would be worth it. Or that was what I kept telling myself.

But as soon as we got inside the restaurant, I slipped away from him. After weaving through the crowd, I dove into a conversation with some musicians I knew and liked.

There were more cameras and reporters here, so I posed. Performing for the audience like I always did. But there was no way I'd pretend to be Paul's date.

Hell *no*.

Sometimes I loved these types of events. Getting dressed up, chatting with other artists and meeting their partners. Which made me wonder what Teller would think of it. Would he ever want to come to something like this with me? Would he hate it? He would definitely hate the red carpet.

Yet he was so sweet and thoughtful that he'd probably tolerate it all, for me. I could just imagine his deadpan responses to reporter questions and industry small-talk.

I smiled, picturing it, even as sadness dulled the fantasy. Teller would be giving up a lot to be with me. His privacy first and foremost.

God, how would this ever work? A sudden wave of despair had me reeling.

When I'd mentioned my "boyfriend" to Paul, it made me realize how much I wanted that. To call Teller my boyfriend. To be with him whenever we wanted. Share what I felt about him with everyone we knew.

But was there any possible ending where we could both have the life we wanted and still be together?

I missed him more than ever, so much right now it was painful. Finding a quiet corner, I went to open my text messages. Just needing to talk to him. Remind myself how much Teller wanted this too. *Us*.

But then I noticed a new email notification. The restaurant started spinning like I had vertigo.

It was from *him*. Biggest Fan. Tonight, about half an hour ago, he'd finally replied.

To: ayla.m@email.com
From: BiggestFan@web.net
Subject: Re: Smile for me

Dear Ayla,
You asked how I'm different. It's because I know the real you. Because I'm always watching. Someday we'll be together, and you'll understand how perfect I am for you.

Love, your Biggest Fan

There was another photo attached. One of me outside the Santa Monica recording studio this past week, probably taken through a telephoto lens.

My hand trembled. Bile rose up in my throat and coated my tongue. I was going to be sick.

"So here's where you've been hiding," Paul said in a sing-song voice. "What's so interesting on your phone?"

I stuffed the phone back into my clutch purse. "Nothing."

"Don't give me that. What's the matter?"

"It's not your concern." I didn't even try to hide how upset I was. I just had to get out of here. "I'm not feeling well. I need to go."

I needed Teller.

When I tried to weave around Paul, he blocked me. "Ayla, I can help."

"No, you *can't*. I'm going to call my driver to pick me up."

"If you need a ride, I'll take you. But let's go back to my place. Have a drink and talk this through. Babe, I'm here for you."

Babe? "Absolutely not. I'm not your *babe*."

"Wait a minute." Paul's hand seized my shoulder, keeping me from walking away. "Look, I heard about that Biggest Fan guy. Why won't you just let me in? Let me help you."

Chills seemed to radiate from where he was touching me, slithering along my limbs. "How the hell do you know about that? *Nobody* knows about that." Except for River, Aiden, and of course Teller. None of them would've shared it with another soul.

Paul laughed nervously, glancing around at the faces turning toward us. "We should talk somewhere quieter." Raising his voice, he said, "We're just having some creative differences. We'll be back." I opened my mouth to tell Paul where he could stuff his *creative differences*.

But he pulled me down a hallway before I could get a word out. I struggled to pull free. "How do you know about the stalker?" I demanded.

"I didn't really. I guessed. You just confirmed it."

"Bullshit. You knew he calls himself 'Biggest Fan.' Don't play games. How did you know?"

Names flew through my mind. Could Ricky or Cheryl have whispered something in his ear? They'd been there at the concert venue in Toronto when I first got the flowers. But a lot of other people had too. Nobody knew about the emails or the flowers I'd received in Hartley...*right*?

I hated that I could never fully trust my industry friends. Always had that inner doubt.

Paul let go of my arm, but cornered me against the wall. "It's my job to be aware of what's happening with my artists. You could've come to me. I just want to be here for you."

"It's not your business."

Paul's fingers squeezed on their way down my arm. "Ayla, why are you being so difficult about this? We could be good together. If you just stop fighting it and give this a chance."

For a moment, I was so shocked I couldn't even respond. This guy was such a stereotype of a toxic Hollywood male. Like he had no idea what a sad, tired cliché he was. I was *done* with it.

He chose that moment to lean in, puckering his lips.

I slammed my knee into Paul's crotch. His eyes bugged. He made a high-pitched squeak and slumped into the nearest wall.

"Those creative differences can be rough, can't they? Come near me again, and I'll creatively separate your balls from your body."

Texting Bryan to pick me up, I marched for the nearest exit.

THIRTY-TWO

Teller

Breathe, I told myself. I shifted into downward dog, feeling the muscles in my shoulders bunch and my hamstrings stretch.

I'd been doing yoga for about a year and a half. I still felt uncoordinated. This didn't come naturally to me, unlike running five miles in my sleep or banging out deadlifts. After my injuries, I'd worked my ass off to get fit again. Though I couldn't do as many pull-ups as when I'd been in the Army, given my shoulder.

Yoga was not my favorite thing. But tonight, I needed all the help I could get with staying calm.

Ayla was at that event with Paul, and I didn't like it. After everything she'd told me about him, plus my impressions from meeting him in Hartley, I didn't trust him.

Didn't help that I'd already seen photos online of them arriving together. His hand on her back like he thought he had some claim on her.

Fuck, why had I even looked at social media?

As if I could've stayed away. That algorithm had me figured out. My feed was all Ayla Maxwell, all the time.

I was no stranger to being away from the woman I cared about. Deployments had taught me patience on that front. But this thing with Ayla was a whole new experience. Seeing her in the media with another guy. It was surreal. My heart didn't understand why I couldn't just be there. Telling the label exec to take his sleazy hands off her.

And then I would wrap her up in my arms and kiss her and make sure she had everything she needed. Show her what I felt. Because my craving for her was getting extreme. It was difficult for me to think of anything else.

Especially at a time like this, when I was supposed to be focused on yoga breathing and staying in the moment, when instead I couldn't stop wondering what Ayla was doing right now.

I shifted into one of the warrior poses. If only this could give me some clarity.

I fell out of the pose when my phone rang. Grabbing for it, my excitement dulled when I saw it wasn't Ayla. And then guilt washed in.

"Hey, Piper. You okay?"

"Why do you think something's not okay?"

"Because you never call me in the evening unless you have a problem."

A pause. "Oh my gosh, you're right. I suck."

I chuckled, sprawling on the yoga mat and looking at the ceiling of my living room. "No, you don't. You're a single mom and business owner with a lot going on."

"Yeah, true. Also, I'm a delight most of the time."

"You are. Now tell me what's up."

"Actually, I was calling to see how *you* are. Which I don't do enough, clearly."

"I'm fine," I grunted. "I'm always fine."

Sure. That sounded convincing.

"You said that the last several times I've seen you. I want a real answer. Something's been weird with you for the last month or so. I'm not the only one who's noticed."

That was...fair.

Last weekend, when Ollie and I were working on his treehouse, I nailed the wooden door shut before realizing what I was doing. Just a few days ago, Susan made a huge deal out of the fact that I forgot to shave two days in a row. Apparently I had dark circles under my eyes too.

Which was what happened when a guy couldn't sleep.

Before, I couldn't sleep because I was tearing myself up over a woman I thought I couldn't have. But lately, I'd been staying up late to talk to Ayla for hours on end. Or brainstorming what I could send her next to brighten her day. Not an easy feat when her net worth outpaced mine a hundredfold.

It was killing me not to be able to see her. But I had just as many responsibilities in Silver Ridge as ever, and of course that mattered to me too. My head was all fucked up over how to make this work.

I had to have Ayla in my life. There was no longer any other option.

But *how*?

"I know you do that usual manly thing where you refuse to talk about your feelings," Piper said. "But you're also the uncle who tells Ollie that boys are allowed to cry. I need you to be real with me. Are you hung up on Ayla?"

Of course Piper had heard that gossip. I was surprised she'd waited this long to confront me. Maybe because she figured I would deny it.

Before, I would have. But I was determined to win Ayla over. I wanted a relationship with her. This was going to impact my life. *Our* life. It was past time that I admitted that to my sister.

I blew out a breath. *Just say it.*

"Ayla and I got close during Emma and Ashford's wedding weekend. We both tried to move on after, but that wasn't happening. A few weeks ago, I told her how I feel. More or less."

"Wow. That's major. What did she say?"

"She's open to it. We talk every day."

"And how exactly do you feel about her, big brother?"

I hesitated, and Piper must've heard something in that silence.

"Tell, are you in *love* with her?"

My pulse thrummed in my throat. Guts twisting, heart rate taking off. "Pretty sure. Yeah."

I had no idea how I'd fallen for Ayla this fast. It had been bad a few weeks ago when I went to Callum for advice.

But now that we were talking every day, it was so much worse.

Every conversation drew me deeper. Convinced me all the more that I had to have her. No matter how difficult it was.

Maybe that explained the sparks between us each time we'd interacted before the wedding. The way she'd made my blood heat and my defensiveness rise up. I'd known, down to some primitive, instinctual part of me, that she was supposed to be mine.

I hadn't wanted to fall in love. But with Ayla, how could I not?

"It's brutal," I finished.

"Teller," Piper whispered. "No, it's not. It's wonderful."

"How do you figure that? I don't know how to make this work. Aside from Ayla, everything else that matters to me is here. Especially you and Ollie. This could impact you both."

Piper cursed. "Please tell me you aren't sacrificing your own chance at love because of me. I don't want that. It's not your fault my ex was a shitty husband and father."

"I know. But I would never abandon you either."

"It's not just you and me. How can you not realize that? It never has been. We've always had Ashford and Callum and Grace. And now, Emma and Dane. Judson and Dixie and Rosie. Plus so many other people who love us in this town."

"I do know that, but—"

"No. Stop right there. You've been my hero for a long time. Ollie's too. Your whole life has been about sacrificing what you need and putting other people first. But it's your turn now. If you love Ayla, then get out there and go after her."

I huffed a laugh. "You don't think I'm foolish, hoping someone like her will end up with a small-town guy like me?"

Ayla was incandescent. The kind of person everyone wanted to get close to, but she burned brighter than them all.

Who was I to think I could hold on to her?

"You don't have to give her the whole entire world," Piper said. "You just have to give her yours."

I was back on the yoga mat and trying to get my thoughts in order when Ayla finally called. She was using a secure video call app that River had recommended.

I answered with a big smile already painted across my face. But when I saw her expression, the rest of the world disappeared and all my attention narrowed to her.

"What happened?"

She was in the backseat of her usual car. I recognized the lux interior and the leather seat. Light and shadow played across her skin. She wore the same outfit from earlier, but her hair was disheveled, and she looked distraught. Skin too pale, eyes too wide.

"It was a bad night. I'm not even sure where to start."

"Are you safe right now?"

"Bryan is driving me home. I have the privacy screen up so you and I can talk." She took a shaky breath. "I don't want to talk to anyone but you."

"*Sweetheart.*" Something furious buzzed under my skin. "Let's start with *who did this.* If someone did something to hurt or upset you, then I should know who I need to destroy."

Ayla rubbed her eyes, lips curving. "It makes me feel a little better to laugh. Thank you."

"I'm not kidding."

She inhaled, yellow light pulsing over her face as they drove.

"Was it Paul?"

A nod, eyes to the side.

It took all my training and willpower not to reveal the nuclear explosion detonating inside me.

I had to stay calm. It wouldn't help her if I started flipping out.

"What did he do?"

Because I had to decide whether to just maim him or outright kill him. In that moment, I probably would have. Not ideal for a law-upholding chief of police. But that was what Ayla did to me. Turned around all the assumptions I'd made about myself.

And I suddenly realized that I wouldn't want it any other way.

"I didn't let things get too far. It started with..." Her eyes closed. "There was something else even before Paul came at me with his bullshit."

A text came in while as she was talking. The notification crossed the top of my screen.

RIVER

Ayla got a response from Biggest Fan. Let me know when we can talk.

I'd have to write him back later. "Did you get an email from the stalker?"

She blinked, and tears dotted her lashes before she rubbed them away. "You saw it?"

"River just texted me. He must have some kind of automated monitoring system on your email account." I doubted he was staring at it every minute, and River was nothing if not resourceful.

"I'm sending you a screenshot." Ayla fiddled with her phone.

"Alright, but keep talking. Tell me what happened after you got the email."

"Paul came up to me. It was obvious I was upset. I told him I was leaving, but he wouldn't let me. He pulled me into a hallway and admitted he knew about my stalker. Biggest Fan. Somebody had told him about it. He claimed he wanted to help and got mad when I refused him."

"Okay," I rumbled. *Calm*. I was totally calm.

"Then he said we could be good together if I stopped fighting it. And tried to kiss me."

That settled it. Paul Ruxton was dead. Would Dane loan me the money for a hit man? No, that wasn't good enough. Dane could loan me the funds to pull off the hit myself...

Her frown turned vicious. "I kneed him in the balls and told him I'd cut them off if he ever touches me again."

"Good. That's my Troublemaker. Are you almost home?"

She glanced at the window. "Yeah. I want to lock all the doors and just be with you, however we can."

She was tearing my heart out.

I stayed on the call with Ayla as she reached her house. Heard her talking to Bryan and the other security guard on duty. Then she went inside, making sure everything was locked up and all her curtains were closed. I wished I could be there doing all of that for her.

Especially as she stood in her kitchen making a mug of herbal tea. "I wish I could make that for you," I said.

"Yeah?" She smiled weakly. Her eyes were glazed.

"If I were there, I would draw you a bath and bring your tea when it was ready. Then afterward, I would carry you to bed and hold you and kiss you."

"That would be perfect."

"Do you want to change clothes? Put on something more comfortable?"

She nodded.

"Go do that. I'll be right here. And when you're back, your tea will probably be ready."

"Okay." Ayla disappeared to change into comfier clothes. She left her phone on her kitchen island.

I took the opportunity to glance at the screenshot she'd sent. Another creepy-as-hell message from Biggest Fan and a photo of her. Probably to prove he was "*always watching*." Asshole.

The photo had been taken on a public street, at least. Could've been downloaded from a paparazzi site.

I sent a quick text to River.

Can you run a reverse image search on the photo attached in the latest stalker email? See if this one is publicly available?

RIVER

Already done. It came from a tabloid site. He claims he's watching her, but all he's doing is following things other people have posted online.

"You're frowning," Ayla said, once she'd returned to the kitchen. She picked up her phone, and her face filled my screen again. "Were you looking at the new email from the stalker?"

"I just did. I was texting River. Do you wanna talk about that? Or would you rather wait and deal with it tomorrow? It's your call."

She sipped from her mug. "Tomorrow. I want to spend the rest of tonight feeling good. You always make things better."

I was so damn glad to hear it. Ayla was plenty strong enough to handle her problems herself, and it was a privilege to know she was letting me help.

"Should we go to the bookstore together?" I asked. "You can pick something out."

"That is the absolute *best* idea. It's a date."

Ayla carried her mug and the phone into her living room, where she put some relaxing music on her stereo.

I moved to my couch, dimming the lamps.

Her living room was absolutely covered in stacks of books. The tables, the floor, the other side of the couch. I hadn't thought that part through, but she didn't seem to mind.

On the video, she showed me each one. Flipping the pages of the ones she liked and reading the descriptions. I loved seeing the smile on her beautiful face.

Ayla set aside another hardcover. "Thank you again. Can't

believe you did this for me." I could tell her worries still sat heavily on her heart, but at least she'd relaxed some.

"You're welcome. Have you picked a favorite?"

"More like fifteen. Which do *you* like?"

I shrugged. "Probably something non-fiction."

"Let's find one. I'll give it to you when I see you next."

We talked about the books for a while longer. Then she said, "This is the best date I've ever been on, and we're not even in the same state."

"Just wish I could give you a proper kiss goodnight."

Her teeth tugged at her bottom lip. "It's getting late, and it's an hour later for you than it is for me. I don't want to keep you up. You have work in the morning. You've been staying up late with me all the time."

"I don't sleep even when we're not up talking. You're the one who should be exhausted from how much you've been running through my head."

A laugh bubbled out of her. "That line was terrible. So clichéd."

"Made you laugh, though. That was my goal."

She pushed books out of the way to lie on her side on her couch, just like I was lying on mine. "But please tell me you're not serious, Teller. I don't want you losing sleep over me."

"You want me to lie?" I propped my head on my hand. "I told you before that I think about you constantly. It's only getting worse. I miss you. Every minute."

She groaned. "I think about you all the time too." Her lashes fluttered, her gaze heating. Two emerald-green flames. "I think about the things we did together in my hotel room."

"Do you?"

"I have a vibrator. A *big* one. I make myself come and pretend it's you."

Fuuuuck. Now that was a change of subject.

I'd definitely be lying if I claimed sex wasn't on my mind. Her sweet little body underneath me. How she'd tasted. I was desperate to be inside her again. Get her begging with my tongue, then bounce her on my cock.

Grrr.

But I'd been holding back the filthier parts of my mind lately in favor of romancing her. We'd had a *lot* of sex during our one weekend together, and I didn't ever want her thinking I viewed her as an object.

If my girl was needy, though, I couldn't deprive her.

"You want to show me?" I asked.

She nodded, biting her lower lip again.

"Then take me to your bedroom, sweetheart," I rumbled.

THIRTY-THREE
Ayla

I CARRIED my phone to my bedroom and switched on my bedside lamp, filling the space with a warm glow. When I glanced at my phone screen, Teller was closing the door to his bedroom too. I couldn't see much aside from his chest in a white T-shirt and the blue wainscoting on his walls.

We'd given each other video tours of our homes before. We'd had many long conversations while lying in our respective beds. But this was the first time we would be getting extra personal.

I couldn't *wait*. I'd never been so sexually pent up in my life.

My mattress dipped just slightly as I knelt on the covers. Next I propped my phone on my nightstand so he would have a good view of me.

All the fear and uncertainty I'd felt earlier had vanished while we were talking. I wanted this. To feel as close to him as possible.

"What should I do first, Chief Landry?" I played with the edge of my slouchy oversized top.

He sat on his bed up against the wooden headboard, all broad shoulders and sexy confidence. "Where's the toy you use to make yourself feel good? Get it for me."

Grabbing a key from its hiding place, I unlocked the drawer

of my nightstand. Since I had people in and out of my house pretty often, I was careful to keep some things private.

From inside the drawer, I pulled out a box and opened it. "Here it is." My vibrator wasn't quite as big as Teller, but it did the job.

His eyebrows lifted, and a wicked look crossed his handsome features. "Set that down for now. Take off your top for me. Nice and slow."

I pulled my arms inside my sleeves, then eased the top over my head and tossed it onto the floor. I had on a cotton bra underneath, and I felt my nipples brushing at the fabric.

"Wish I could touch you," he murmured.

"What would you do?"

"I'd start with your breasts. Playing with your nipples just the way you like."

"Like this?" I rubbed my thumbs over the white fabric of my bra. It was thin, almost translucent. My skin so sensitive beneath.

"Mmm. Just like that. Except without the bra in the way. I'd tear that off you."

I giggled, pulling the bralette off and then cupping my exposed breasts. My nipples tightened even more in the cool air as I imagined his warm tongue licking them.

"Lower your hands," he rasped. "Let me see how pretty you are."

With just a touch of self-consciousness, I moved my hands away from my breasts. His eyelids were heavy as he looked at me. I wondered if he was hard.

"Now take off those little shorts and your panties. I want to see all of you." His bossy, *Chief Landry* tone of voice gave me happy shivers. And also wiped away any last hesitation on my part.

I got onto my knees and playfully inched the rest of my clothes down over my hips. Giving him a sexy show.

I'd never done anything like this before. Never wanted to. Thank goodness for this fancy encrypted video app. Normally I was paranoid about explicit images of me leaking to the media. A vengeful ex-boyfriend might sell me out to make a quick buck. But I knew I was okay with Teller.

He made me feel safe enough that I could be as wild as I liked. He was my sanctuary.

He told me to lie back and run my hands all over myself. I closed my eyes and listened to his voice, not worrying about anything except his next command. It was relaxing. Like the tension I'd been holding bled away, leaving only trust and pleasure.

"Do you want me inside you?" he asked.

"Yes," I moaned. "I need it. Need to feel you."

"Are you wet for me?"

Teller's intense gaze through the screen had me enthralled. Despite the distance between us in reality, he felt so close. Right here in the room with me.

I brought my fingers between my legs. "Dripping for you."

"Get your toy."

I reached for the vibrator. He kept talking as I switched it on and massaged the head over my clit. Teller directed the pressure, the speed.

"Use it like it's my cock, sweetheart."

I couldn't believe I was doing this on camera. But it felt so good.

When I pushed the toy inside me, it really felt like Teller was giving this to me. Making me so perfectly content and secure even as the pleasure wound me up and sweat glistened on my skin.

I turned my head to look at him on the screen. His hand was in his sweats, stroking. Sweat shone on his forehead too, and his chest lifted with each heavy breath.

"I want to see you," I begged. "Please?"

Propping his phone, Teller yanked his shirt over his head and shoved his sweats down. He wasn't wearing underwear, so his cock slapped his stomach. He fisted his shaft.

It was the most erotic, enticing sight I'd ever seen. The man could've been a model or a movie star, but I wanted this view only for me. And I loved the way his eyes moved possessively over his screen like he was thinking the same about me.

"Teller, I'm..."

His fist moved faster. "Come with me. Show me how good I make you feel."

My entire body seized, pleasure overtaking me. But I kept my eyes open to watch as Teller moaned, his hips bucking as he painted his stomach.

Whoa.

Maybe I should've recorded that. He was a work of art.

We just stared at one another as we came down from the high. But when Teller shifted like he was going to get up, I said, "Don't move yet. I need to finish uploading this to the fan site I'm making about you."

"A fan site, huh?"

"Yep. About the hottest police chief in existence. He acts grumpy, but inside he's really a big marshmallow." I giggled. "A sexy marshmallow."

Teller grinned. "Somebody's drunk on endorphins."

"Just drunk on you," I whispered. "I hope I dream about you tonight. So I can feel you next to me."

His brows tightened, crinkles appearing around his eyes. "I want that too."

If I thought too much about the miles separating us, I might cry. So I wasn't going to do that.

We both got cleaned up and ready for bed. I left my phone on the nightstand, and when I crawled under the covers, Teller was relaxing in his bed on the screen.

I brought him over to my pillow. I loved when we talked in bed like this. We'd been doing it nearly every night, yet it felt new every time.

"I don't want to fall asleep yet," I said, even as my eyelids drooped. It had been a very long day. "But you have to get up earlier than me."

"Don't worry about that. I'll stay with you as long as you like."

We talked awhile until he was the only one keeping up the conversation. He murmured sweet nothings as I drifted off.

Then Teller said something that almost pulled me back to consciousness. But I was too far gone. Couldn't stop sleep from washing over me.

I was probably just dreaming.

But it had sounded like he said he loved me.

I had a hangover. Not from alcohol, since I'd had less than one glass of wine at the event last night. Nope, I had a man hangover. A bossy, thoughtful, dirty-talking man who I couldn't get enough of.

A man who had my heart *aching*.

I'd had enough of this distance. I had to see him again. I *had to*. This wasn't a want anymore. It was a dire need.

I was expected at the Santa Monica recording studio today to work on my album. When I arrived, I tracked down Cheryl. I'd asked her to come in today so we could talk.

I found her in one of the flexible office rooms, her laptop open on the desk. She stood up when I came in. "Morning," Cheryl said. "I just got your text. You wanted a chat?"

"Yeah, about a few things." I leaned against the door frame. "First off, my schedule. I'm going away this weekend."

"*This* weekend?"

"Yes. Tomorrow's Friday. I'll leave in the afternoon." I could arrive in Hart County by the evening. Maybe stroll into the Silver Ridge PD station. *Surprise, Chief. I'm here.*

Just the thought had my heart racing.

Cheryl scurried back to the laptop. "Wait. I need to check some things. We have a lot on the burner."

"I don't care what else is going on." I'd already resolved that I wouldn't take no for an answer. I wasn't a pushover, yet I'd let my career dictate far too much of my life.

Yes, this next album had to succeed. But there would always be something else. The industry always wanted *more*. I wanted more too. More of the things that made me happy and fulfilled.

"I'm going to Colorado."

Cheryl seemed to sense my inner resolve. She didn't argue, though she looked like she wanted to. "Then I'll make it work. If you promise I'll get more advance notice next time."

"Thank you," I said on a sigh of relief. "The second thing is about that flower arrangement I received in Toronto back in September."

She looked confused for a moment. "The one last year? With the photo of you when you were a kid?"

"Yes. Did you ever discuss that with Paul?"

"I...I might have mentioned you were upset, and we were trying to figure out who sent it. But that was a while ago. Why?"

Well, that explained how Paul found out. But Cheryl only knew about that first flower arrangement. Paul had sounded like he knew about the emails too. How?

I'd have to figure that out later.

"Just something Paul said to me at the event last night. Which brings me to the final thing I need to chat about."

"Paul?" Cheryl's gaze shifted to look past my shoulder.

A throat cleared behind me in the hallway. "Ayla, can we talk?"

Shit.

I turned around. Paul stood there, looking red-faced and sheepish.

"You said plenty at the event yesterday," I snapped.

I heard Cheryl getting up from her chair and coming toward us. "What happened yesterday?"

"Please, Ayla," he whispered. "Let me apologize in private. I'm begging you."

I didn't want to spend another minute alone with this jerk. I'd been about to tell Cheryl I wouldn't work with him any longer. Screw my contract. If the label didn't replace him, then I would refuse to perform. End of story.

It was time for me to step up for myself. Be the *boss*.

But maybe I could get Paul to move aside on his own. Let him choose the easy way instead of the hard way.

"I'll give you five minutes," I said.

He wiped a hand down his face. "Thank you. Come with me. We'll talk somewhere quiet."

"No. We'll talk here. Cheryl, can we have the room?"

She put a hand on my arm. "You're sure?"

"It's fine." I gave her a reassuring smile. "Five minutes. That's all we'll need."

After aiming an uneasy glance at Paul, Cheryl left the room.

He went to close the door, but I shook my head. "This is all the privacy you're getting. Your five minutes are ticking down." Nudging Paul out of the way, I left the door cracked by several inches. Not totally open, but not isolating me with him either.

Then I spun to face him, arms crossed and head held high.

He put his hands on his hips, pacing. Almost a full minute passed. I started to wonder if he'd say anything at all. "Paul, I don't have a lot of patience. What do you want?"

"Look, I'm sorry about last night. I came on too strong."

I barked a laugh. "That's one way of putting it."

"I'm here to beg you to forgive me."

"No."

"That's it? After all the months I've devoted to you and your next album? You won't forgive one mistake?"

"Was it really one mistake? If I start asking around, will other female artists have stories about you?"

His eyes narrowed, mouth sinking into a scowl. "Are you forgetting who I am?"

This guy was unbelievable. "I don't care if your father is the head of Ruxton Records or the damn King of England. You have two choices. Admit to the label what you did so they can deal with you. Or I'll tell them *and* leak it to the media. Either way, I'm never working with you again. Your choice how ugly it gets."

I stepped toward the doorway. But Paul moved faster. His fingers clamped down on my arm, and he shoved me up against the wall. "No fucking way," he hissed. "I'm not letting a replaceable little slut like you ruin me."

I sucked in a breath to scream. At the same time, loud voices shouted in the hallway.

"Mr. Landry, you can't go down there. *Hey*!"

Suddenly the door pushed open. A tall form loomed. Took a split-second look at me pushed against the wall, Paul with his hands on me.

"The hell are *you* doing here?" Paul sneered.

Teller crossed to us in a single long stride.

Then he smashed his fist into Paul's face.

THIRTY-FOUR
Teller

THE MOMENT my knuckles connected with Paul Ruxton's chin, chaos erupted. People rushing into the room behind me, shouting.

But all I could see was Ayla.

She stared at me with wide, shocked eyes. "You're really here? Teller. Oh my God. How? When?"

"Just now." My cab had only pulled up to the address of the recording studio about five minutes ago. "I'll explain everything later." I caught her and hugged her when she launched herself into my arms. The sweet scent of caramel filled my nose like a drug.

Mine.

But just as quickly, she was wrenched away from me, and I found myself shoved against the wall. Some huge security guy yanked my arms behind my back.

Ayla's manager Cheryl had followed me in, shaking her head. "Landry, I told you to wait. This isn't helping."

This was one of the more reckless things I'd ever done. Not just showing up in Los Angeles unannounced to visit one of the most famous singers in the world. But also, the part where I'd just rearranged a rich recording executive's face.

"I'm bleeding," Paul whined, cupping his split lip and sore jaw. "I want him arrested!"

Another security guard was trying to lead Ayla out of the room, but she scrambled away. "Then I want Paul arrested too," she snapped. "For harassment and assault."

I turned my head to glare at Paul. "You're lucky you're still breathing."

"Everyone heard that, right? He's *threatening me*."

Cheryl waved her hands in the air. "Everyone, *calm down*. Before some paparazzo figures out what's going on in here and news vans start forming a parade down Wilshire Boulevard. None of us needs that."

A few minutes later, somebody led Paul away with a bag of ice on his face. Cheryl ushered me and Ayla down the hall and shoved us into a posh sitting area. "Both of you, wait here. Let me sort this out."

"This is not Teller's fault. He was defending me. Paul tried to kiss me last night, and today he was trying to intimidate me into staying quiet."

"That's what you wanted to discuss with me? Shit on a stick." Cheryl dug her manicured fingers into her perfectly styled hair. "Just stay here and give me a chance to untangle the mess. Okay?"

We sat heavily on the couch, sinking into the cushions. Ayla leaned into me. She reached for my hand, examining my knuckles, which were swelling up. At least the skin hadn't broken. I'd only gotten in one punch.

"Oh, Teller. I'll go ask for some ice. They better not have used it all on Paul."

"No, I'll worry about my hand later. I need to hold you, sweetheart."

"I need that too." She buried her face against my chest. "I'm supposed to be the troublemaker, not you."

I wrapped her in my arms and kissed her hair. "Yeah. But I'd do anything for you."

"Like suddenly teleporting almost a thousand miles right when I need you most?"

"You'd have dealt with Ruxton like you did last night." Though of course, I hated that she'd had to face that without me. "Don't sell yourself short."

"I don't. But I *do* need you. You have no idea what a relief it is to have you here. To be able to touch you." Her thumb traced over the scar on my cheek.

"I've got a pretty good idea, based on what I'm feeling."

"How did you get here? I could've sworn you were in your house in Silver Ridge when I went to sleep a few hours ago."

"Really want me to explain it all now? Or do you want me to kiss you?"

Her soft lips formed a small O. "The second one, please."

I took her mouth with firm strokes of my tongue, lips caressing. A play of hot and sweet. It had been a month and a half since I'd had the pleasure of kissing this incredible woman. Too long.

And it meant something different now. This kiss was a confirmation. A promise.

You're mine, and I'm yours.

We got lost in each other's kisses for a while. But then she dropped her head to my shoulder with a sigh, tucking her forehead against my neck. I smoothed my palm down her back. "After we spoke last night, I knew I had to come here. Had to see you."

She hadn't asked outright for me to do this. But she'd said she needed me. In that moment, nothing in this world would've kept me from her.

As soon as Ayla had fallen asleep, I swallowed my pride and made a call.

"*Landry*?" Dane had sounded groggy. "*What's going on*?"

"*Is that Teller*?" Grace asked in the background.

"*Sorry to wake you and Grace.*"

"*Nah, don't worry about it. If you're calling this late, I'm sure it's urgent.*"

"*It is. I need a favor.*"

I recounted that conversation to Ayla. How I packed a bag, called the station about needing to make an emergency trip, and jumped in my car.

She sat up, blinking at me. "You flew out here on Dane's jet?"

I nodded. "I'm lucky the timing worked out, and the jet was already in Colorado with a crew available on short notice. I would've driven to Grand Junction and flown coach, but that would've taken a lot of extra hours. I had to get to you as soon as possible. Would've done pretty much anything. Even given Knightly a get-out-of-jail-free card. I owe him now."

Ayla smiled. "What do you think he'll ask for in return?"

"So far, he's made me promise to sit in the dunk tank at the summer fundraiser for the Silver Ridge Children's Center."

"You in the dunk tank? I'll have to be there to witness it."

"I hope so."

"But what about work? Piper and Ollie? I know how important they are to you."

I tucked a lock of blond hair behind her ear. "You're important too. Piper knows where I am, and she knows how I feel about you, and she's already given her blessing. It turns out I might've been overplaying my role as protective older brother."

"*You*? No."

Her sarcasm made me chuckle. "Only reason I didn't call you this morning was in case something came up, and somehow I didn't make it. Didn't want to disappoint you." I never wanted to disappoint her. Men in Ayla's past had let her down. I refused to be one of them.

"You are full of surprises, Teller Landry."

When we were talking last night, Ayla had mentioned that she would be in the Santa Monica recording studio today. I did some detective work while I was on the plane to find the address. Then took a cab from the airport straight here.

I'd spent several minutes standing on the sidewalk, wondering how the heck to get in. The studio was unmarked, like they didn't want random people walking in from the street.

Go figure. I'd been about to call Ayla and say I was right outside.

But then Cheryl had stepped out, lighting a cigarette and looking harried. Good thing I'd met her once back in Hart County.

Cheryl had recognized me too. Hadn't exactly been happy to see me, but she agreed to escort me inside past the studio's security. Told me to wait in the lobby until Ayla was available.

But of course, I hadn't waited. I'd heard Ayla's voice down the hall. So I followed the sound and barged in through an open doorway, seeing absolute *red* when I found Paul with his hands on her.

"They really don't need you at the station?" Ayla asked. "You told me about the vandalisms going on."

"That's definitely on my mind, but Sheriff Douglas is heading a task force to pinpoint the suspect. It's not all on me." As Piper reminded me yesterday.

Ayla kissed my cheek. "How long can you stay?"

"A few days. Through the weekend." Frustration bled into my voice, because I couldn't stay for long, and I couldn't pack her up and smuggle her back to Silver Ridge either.

I had to focus on the present. Be in the moment. Like those yoga videos always said.

Ayla put her arms around my neck. "Earlier, I told Cheryl that I needed the weekend to myself. I was planning to head to Silver Ridge to visit *you*. I wasn't going to take no for an answer."

Damn. We'd been thinking the same thing. That gave me hope, more than anything else she'd said lately, that I wasn't fooling myself. That I actually had a shot at keeping a woman like her.

"Then I take it you're free this weekend," I said.

"I am."

"What about today? Assuming I don't get hauled away in cuffs for smacking Paul around. If that happens, I might need help with bail." How the tables had turned.

"They'll take you away over my dead body." Her frown was adorable. Especially that little crease when she scrunched her nose. "I'll stage a protest. They can arrest me too."

"I believe it. I've seen firsthand how difficult you can be."

"That's not ever going to change." She leaned in to nuzzle at my jaw, and I nuzzled back.

"Glad to hear it." Because I wanted the real Ayla. Opinionated and authentic. Even if things got messy. Her talent bowled me over every time I heard one of her songs, but her passion was even more addictive.

I still barely understood how this had happened to me. Falling for her so hard and so fast, and having even a fraction of those feelings returned. But there was no turning back. Not for me. I planned to be in her life for a long while.

In fact, I had my sights set on forever.

THIRTY-FIVE

Ayla

Paul finally backed down, agreeing not to press charges against Teller. In exchange, I agreed to give Paul a few days to prepare before I called the heads of the label and the media.

My stance hadn't changed. I would not be working with Paul again, and I refused to be silent about it. But if Paul needed a long weekend to figure out what to tell Papa Ruxton of Ruxton Records, he could have it.

If only I could use this to get out of my contract. That was less likely. The label would probably assign me a different executive.

But in the meantime, recording my new album was on hold. I planned to spend every minute of the next few days with Teller. And I was going to enjoy it. That meant putting Paul out of my mind.

Same with the stalker. River was working on tracing the new email from Biggest Fan, and he would let Teller and me know when he had any new updates.

In the secured parking lot behind the studio, Bryan greeted Teller with a huge smile and a firm handshake. "Chief Landry. Good to see you again. Especially since I'm not in handcuffs." I knew Bryan didn't bear him any ill-will since Teller had let him off the hook after that street fight thing. Also, I'd dropped plenty of hints that Teller and I were more than friends.

"I'm off duty and way outside my jurisdiction. You can call me Teller. How's the concussion? Giving you any problems?" Teller's brows drew together with concern.

"It's better, thanks. I'm not a hundred percent. But you know how it is. I had to get back to work." Bryan lowered his voice. "My boss is kind of a monster. She's working me to an early grave."

"I believe it. High maintenance, this one." Teller's hand trailed from my hip down to my butt and squeezed.

"Hey," I protested. "You're both spreading lies." In fact, I'd offered to help Bryan with money so he could rest at home for longer. When he refused, I offered a loan. But the man wouldn't accept.

Laughing, Bryan opened the back door for us to climb inside the vehicle. "My other problem is that Ayla's man keeps sending heavy boxes for us to lug inside her house. The guy is obsessed with her."

"You'd better be talking about me," Teller joked in a grumpy voice. "I'm definitely obsessed."

Bryan put up the privacy screen as we drove home. Probably because Teller and I couldn't stop kissing.

"This reminds me of being in the backseat in that snow-storm," I said. "Remember?"

Teller smirked. "When you almost made me come in my pants? Yes, I believe I do remember."

I walked my fingertips up his jeans-clad thigh. "Want to try again? Let me finish the job this time?"

He picked up my hand and kissed my knuckles. "I do love it when you're bad, but doing that on a busy highway in Southern California seems a touch riskier than a rural, snowed-in road in Hart County."

I pretended to pout. But I'd been teasing him. My house wasn't that far from the recording studio. Just a quick drive up the PCH. "Then I'll have to drive you out to the middle of nowhere the next time I'm in Hart County. See if I can make you lose your mind."

His eyes softened, and he stroked my cheek, his thumb brushing over my lips. "I would *love* that."

A thrill of both excitement and nervousness lifted my chest.

Teller was throwing around that *L* word an awful lot.

When we reached my house, I introduced Teller to the other security guys on duty. And then we headed inside. He'd brought a duffel as an overnight bag, which he had slung over his shoulder while his other hand held tight to mine.

"Well, this is it," I said, tugging on his hand. "My place. Let me show you around."

The entrance led into a sunken living room with spacious, low sectional couches. Currently dominated by the bookstore delivery. A gourmet kitchen, butler's pantry, formal dining room and guest rooms occupied one wing of the main floor. My bedroom suite occupied the other side.

Downstairs was my home recording studio, media room, and workout room. And along the length of the house, huge spans of windows overlooked the cliffside decks and the ocean below. The glass was tinted on the outside for complete privacy.

"I bought the house for myself when I first hit number one on the billboard charts." I couldn't remember if I'd mentioned that before. "My big indulgence. Plus, the gated neighborhood is nice."

"You deserved it. This is even more impressive in person than on video."

I studied his expression, wondering what he was thinking.

I'd put a ton of time and effort into decorating here. Making it mine. Yet I'd never had anyone to share it with except for a few friends. The O'Neals in Silver Ridge hadn't visited yet, mostly because Ashford was such a stick in the mud about leaving Colorado.

Maybe it was silly, but I wanted Teller to like it.

"It probably seems extravagant," I said.

"It's beautiful. It suits you."

"I'm equally comfortable in Ashford's guest room in Silver Ridge, though. Just in case you're thinking..."

Teller spun me to face him, holding my waist and looking into my eyes like I was the only thing that truly mattered. "Ayla, don't make yourself smaller. *Never* do that, especially not for me. I know you have more money than I ever will. A hell of a lot more talent too. I see who you are, and that's exactly who I want."

I sighed, and Teller swallowed up the sound with a kiss that stole my breath away.

He picked me up and set me on a counter. We were downstairs, in the open lounge area with the view of the ocean spread out behind us.

"You're who I want too," I said, feeling more vulnerable than I maybe ever had.

It was such a relief to know he wasn't jealous of my money or anything like that. Men could be weird about that kind of thing, as I'd experienced the times I'd dated a guy with a lower income. Or even men who were richer than me. They'd felt a constant urge to prove it.

Of course, I should've known Teller was different. I *had* known. He was so impressive in his own right. Confident, intelligent, charismatic. His dominance had nothing to do with money and everything to do with his inner strength.

His kisses went from heated to downright steamy. My breaths came faster, shallower. He lifted the edge of my slouchy top to run his warm fingers over my skin beneath.

I wrapped my legs around him to draw him closer, while my hand worked between us to cup his growing erection.

Suddenly, we were both desperate. Kisses urgent. I fumbled with the buckle of his belt, and he took over, opening it and unbuttoning his jeans with quick movements.

I tilted my hips so he could pull off my linen pants. Then my silky panties beneath.

I cried out when his cock pushed inside me. My hands braced against the counter. He grabbed my hips and held on as he thrust.

It had been weeks since I'd felt him inside me, and I'd *so* needed this.

It didn't matter where we were. Nothing else mattered but the two of us. This intense connection that had somehow only been increased by the time apart.

This was where I belonged. With Teller kissing me, treasuring me while we gave each other pleasure.

When we both came, Teller hunched over me with his forehead pressed into mine. Then he kissed me again as he caressed my face and we panted to catch our breaths.

"How did I get this lucky?" he whispered against my lips.

"I'm asking myself the same thing."

Now that Teller had seen my home, I wanted to show him more of my life here. "Would you be up for meeting some of my friends?" I asked.

"Absolutely. I can't wait."

We'd cleaned up and were upstairs now, cuddling on my living room couch with books surrounding us. "You might want to brace yourself for Hayleigh, though."

"Your neighbor? You said she's enthusiastic, but I'm sure I can handle it. I've got Piper for a sister."

"We'll see. Hayleigh's sweet, but she can be a lot." Ayla spoke with pure affection. "She's one of a kind."

Within five minutes of receiving my text, Hayleigh barged in through the front door. "Where are you, Maxi-pad?"

Teller snorted.

"We're in the kitchen making snacks," I called out.

Hayleigh swept in wearing a zebra-print caftan and waving a giant bottle of white wine. It was only half full. "Like, good snacks? Or healthy crap we have to pretend to like? *Oh.*" She stopped in her tracks when she spotted Teller. "Hello there. So this is Mr. Bookstore. We finally meet." Turning to me, her eyebrows pumped, and she mouthed, *Hot.*

I know, I mouthed back.

Teller's face flushed. But he smiled and greeted Hayleigh warmly. "Nice to meet you."

"Sauvignon Blanc?" She held up the wine bottle. "It's good. I've sampled it thoroughly."

I wondered if Teller would ask for beer or whiskey instead. Except for a few sips of champagne at the wedding, I'd never seen him drinking wine. But he didn't. "Sure. I'll have a glass. Why not?"

Within thirty minutes, Ricky and some others had arrived. They exclaimed over the bookstore explosion in my living room and insisted on helping organize. I couldn't wait to order some new shelves to house my collection, so it would *really* feel like a bookshop in here.

The afternoon went by in a blur of laughter, and our happy hour turned to dinner. Roasting a chicken, sipping white wine, and telling stories about life in LA. We invited the security guys too, and they took turns grabbing plates of food while the other manned the gate. No alcohol, since they were on duty.

Teller hadn't left my side for more than a few minutes at a time. His fingers trailed down my arm, or he dropped a kiss at my temple, or slid his hand over the back of my neck. Small touches that gave me chills every time.

My friends had noticed, too. They kept giving me pointed looks. My cheeks hurt from smiling so much.

They grilled him with questions about Silver Ridge and police work, while Teller asked about their lives and listened attentively to their answers. He laughed off the predictable jokes about him being older than me and gave them hell right back.

I couldn't believe how easily he fit in with them. Like the hard edges of the man I'd met in Silver Ridge, the grumpy police chief, had smoothed out and softened.

Yet he was still Teller. He went quiet at times, all broody and intense. He stood with his back ramrod straight and hid his sense of humor beneath a deadpan tone. He chivalrously topped up wine glasses and carried heavy pans. And his butt looked great in those jeans while he did it.

How was I supposed to survive without him again at the end of this weekend?

Partway through dinner, I noticed the time. "Hold on, everyone. I need to take ten."

"For what?" Teller asked.

Hayleigh propped her elbow on the table, leaning over. "Video call with Maisie. Shouldn't you know that?"

"I *should* know that. You're right."

I pushed my chair back and stood, then held out my hand to Teller. "Want to come? We could call your nephew too."

He arched an eyebrow, asking a silent question. *You sure*?

I nodded, so he got up with me. A murmured *awww* went around the table.

"Be right back," I called out as we left the room.

"We'll get dessert going," Hayleigh said. "If you take too long, we'll eat it all."

"They might be filling up on other things," Ricky quipped.

Laughter followed us down the hall. I pulled Teller into my office. Not that I did a lot of "office" work here. But I kept important papers in the stylish desk I'd bought in Denmark during my last European tour.

The door snicked closed, and I held on to both of Teller's hands. "Can I tell the O'Neals about us? Would you be okay with that?"

Teller laced our fingers. "Much more than okay. But, ah..." He looked sheepish. "They may not be surprised. Emma and Ashford, I mean."

"Why?"

"Rumors have been going around about you and me since the wedding. Someone saw us kiss in the inn's parking lot before you left Hartley."

I clapped my hands over my mouth. "Everybody knows?"

"Not *everybody.*"

"So, not *all* of Hart County, but everyone who was at the wedding and all their friends?" I asked sardonically. "Like Callum and Dixie and that guy with the ponytail who's dating the woman from the market?"

"Jimmy and Rosie? Yep, they definitely know. Plus my officers, the fire department... Susan's been giving me shit about it. I've never confirmed anything, but people think what they want to."

I snorted a laugh. He'd mentioned earlier that his sister knew about us too. I guessed that made it easier. Fewer people to tell.

Though I wasn't even sure what we *should* tell them. That we were dating? In a long-distance relationship?

Then my phone started ringing, and I pulled him toward the loveseat.

"Aunt Ayla!" Maisie exclaimed when we appeared on the screen. "And Uncle Teller. What's he doing there?"

"He's visiting me. Teller is..." I shot a glance at him. "My boyfriend."

He twined our fingers together again.

Maisie erupted in giggles, and Ashford's head popped into view behind her. "So we're talking about this now?"

"You don't know anything about it, Ford," I protested, using Lori's old nickname for him.

"Not anything I can mention in front of my daughter."

"Daddy, it's not your turn." She pushed him out of view.

Maisie told me about her day, and we sang a song together as usual. Then she dashed off to brush her teeth, and Emma and Ashford popped on. They were curious. I could tell they both had a lot more questions than they were asking.

But I was grateful Emma kept the conversation light. She kept saying, "It's fun to see you two together," eyes sparkling.

"We didn't expect you to take off for LA, Teller," Ashford said, a slight accusation in his tone.

"It was last minute. Just for the weekend. But I couldn't stay away."

"Thank goodness you didn't," I whispered.

After the call finished, I turned off my phone screen. "Ashford's the closest thing I have to a brother."

"I'm aware. I expect him to interrogate me when I get home. Which should be amusing."

I grinned, snuggling into his arms. "Will he ask for your intentions?"

"If he does, I'll tell him I'm serious about you."

"Yeah?"

"Very serious." Teller pressed kiss after soft kiss to my lips. I loved how affectionate he was. The tenderness in his touch and in those pale irises as he gazed at me. Kissed me like I was the most captivating thing he'd ever encountered.

I had millions of fans who screamed my name at concerts. Followed my every move on social media.

But this was the first time I'd ever truly felt *adored*.

THIRTY-SIX

Teller

I COULD KISS Ayla like this all night. All month.

For the rest of my life.

But her friends were waiting for us in the dining room with dessert. Even though the sweetest thing in the world was already here in my arms.

"We should call Ollie next," she said.

"Yeah, he'd love that." My nephew had a little crush on her. "We'll make it quick."

Ollie was excited to hear from us, getting shy when Ayla asked him questions. Piper said hi as well. Ayla was bubbly with smiles and happiness as we talked to them, and hell, so was I. The glow in my sister's eyes suggested she could see it.

Ayla was supposed to be with us. Part of our family as much as she was part of the O'Neals'. It felt so obvious to me now.

After ending the video call, we returned to her guests, socializing for another hour or so. I enjoyed seeing Ayla in this new context with her LA friends. She seemed a little hesitant with them, like these friendships were still new. She'd told me how difficult it could be to find true friends given her fame. How people had betrayed her in the past. I was proud of her for letting

Hayleigh, Ricky, and the others into her life, despite the fact that she'd been hurt before.

Of course, I was also scrutinizing her friends in my own way. Making sure they deserved her. They were completely different from me in almost every way, but they had good hearts and good intentions.

And hey, they seemed to think I was an okay guy too. Imagine that.

After they left, we confirmed with the security team that we were in for the night. I went around to double-check that all the doors were secured. No more interruptions tonight.

I looked forward to having Ayla all to myself.

The more stubborn parts of my brain drifted back toward Silver Ridge. I was used to worrying about the town's residents. My sister and nephew. I was used to them *needing* me. It took some faith to trust that other people in Silver Ridge could step in and take my place.

But Ayla needed me too. And with her, I wasn't okay with being replaceable. I intended to be her number one.

There were a few dishes left, so I rinsed while Ayla loaded the dishwasher. A simple domestic task that I enjoyed sharing with her.

Then I placed her in front of me, with her facing the kitchen island, and massaged my thumbs into her shoulder muscles to work out the tension of the day. Her head lolled back. "That's nice. Should we go to bed?"

"Soon." But there was something else I'd been wanting. "I enjoyed hearing you sing with Maisie. I'd love to hear more."

That four-letter *L* word kept slipping into my sentences. Making it obvious how I felt. I wanted her to know, and at the right moment, I planned to tell her.

For a few beats, she didn't say anything. Her profile appeared as her head swiveled to see me. "You want me to sing for you?"

"I can think of few things that would please me more. Only if you're up for it. If not—"

"No, I'm always up for music." Her eyelashes splayed shyly as she smiled. "Yeah. I'd like that. Let's go downstairs to my studio."

We held hands down the open-riser staircase to the lower level. The house followed the shape of the cliffside, so we didn't lose the ocean views. I spotted the counter where I'd taken her just a few hours before, and a flare of desire heated my insides.

I wanted her again. But I let that simmer. We had all night.

The sun had set. Moonlight danced over the waves below.

There was a cozy, open sitting area with a grand piano and a half dozen guitars, some acoustic and some electric. Beyond, through a glass door, there was a soundproofed booth with a microphone and recording equipment.

Ayla selected an acoustic instrument and sat on a stool, one foot propped on a wooden rung. Her guitar draped gracefully over her lap. I took a seat on the couch opposite her.

"Do you invite a lot of people here?" I asked as she tuned the strings.

"Hardly any. I could probably do more of my recording here, but I tend to be choosy about who I bring home."

"I feel special."

"You should. What shall I sing for you?" she asked coyly.

"Whatever you like."

"This was your idea."

Hell, that flirty tone of hers went straight to my cock. She knew the kind of power she had in this position. And I loved seeing that confidence in her. She deserved every bit of success, every accolade, and more.

"How about the song you were working on in Silver Ridge? How's that going?"

She shifted on the stool. "It's not finished yet. But I can play what I have so far."

Her fingers moved over the strings. She started to sing.

And instantly, I was *gone*. Pulled into her orbit like a satellite around the sun.

Time seem to stand still. Was my heart even beating? Definitely a few skips.

I'd heard her sing countless times in recordings. Heard her sing in person before too, even today. But nothing, *nothing*, compared to the experience of Ayla singing directly to me.

Some people seemed to think they were entitled to pieces of her. Paul, her more zealous fans, the stalker—they believed they owned her. Didn't they see the gifts Ayla gave to the world with every note and lyric?

I had to catch my breath when her fingers left the strings.

"See?" she said. "Not quite finished yet. But it's getting there."

"That was...beautiful. You're unbelievable. Thank you for sharing that with me."

"Thank you for listening."

She set the guitar aside and crossed to sit next to me. I turned my body and put my arm out, trying to fit her as close as possible against my side. "I'm already a super fan. I have been for a while."

"You don't need to exaggerate."

"Not kidding. I've memorized every one of your songs. All your albums are downloaded on my phone."

"Not just on your workout playlist?"

"On all my playlists. And I've watched all your music videos. But only around a thousand times."

Ayla belly-laughed, and my entire body glowed with satisfaction. I loved making her laugh. Making her happy.

"I'm glad you like what I do," she said. "That means a lot."

"You should be so damn proud of everything you've accomplished, sweetheart."

"About that. I like when you call me sweetheart. But what happened to calling me Troublemaker?"

"You're that too. My Troublemaker." My lips brushed the tip of her nose. "You've shaken up my whole world. I never thought I would have this. Someone like you." I didn't mean her physical beauty or the fame or anything material that came along with it. I meant that inner light that shone from her. Drawing me in. Showing me, in sharp relief, everything I'd been missing.

"Neither did I." She touched my face, her gaze every bit as adoring as mine.

This was the moment. It felt right. I had to make sure she knew what I felt.

"Ayla, I love—"

She jolted away like a spooked rabbit. Frightened eyes stared back at me.

Shit. Not the reaction I'd hoped for. It had been obvious what I was about to say.

"Is it too soon?" I swallowed my disappointment.

"No, I… I just…"

Before I knew it, a tear streaked down her face like a falling star.

"Hey," I murmured. "What is it?"

"I need to tell you something." Her voice shook. Whatever this was, she was already broken up about it.

Like she'd been holding it in for too long.

"You can tell me anything." I pulled her fully into my lap, Ayla straddling me. Scooting my hips forward on the cushion, I reclined so she could rest her weight against me. Getting as comfy as possible.

It was a solid minute before she spoke again, her face hidden against my shoulder. "I'm a liar."

THIRTY-SEVEN

Teller

"A LIAR? WHAT DO YOU MEAN?"

"I didn't run away."

Confusion kept me from responding. But maybe I wasn't supposed to say anything yet.

She struggled to get the words out. "That night. When I was sixteen. The night I left. The colonel, my dad, when he saw me on the porch with Roy Carpenter..."

"I remember you telling me about it." I petted the back of her head, thinking what Ayla had shared already about the night she left home. How she'd babysat a neighbor boy. Sergeant Carpenter, the kid's father, walked her home afterward. Tried to force a kiss on her.

"The colonel called me names." She swallowed, as if she wanted to push the words back down, but they kept coming. "*Trash* and *slut* and *whore*." Her body shook like each one was a blow.

"Sweetheart," I whispered. Wishing I could take that pain away.

"And then he told me...told me that was the last straw. Told me to pack a bag and be gone by the morning. I wasn't welcome there. He kicked me out. Threw me away." She was crying.

I held her tighter. Kissed her hair, so she knew I was here. I was listening.

"I felt like the shame would swallow me up. I couldn't bear to tell Lori. That's why I didn't wait for her to get home. I wrote her a note, saying I was running away, but it was a lie. People think I made some brave choice, chose my music, but I didn't. I left because my dad didn't want me. I've been lying ever since."

"Nobody could blame you for that. You protected yourself."

"But that night still lives inside me. This...shadow over me. That's why the first message from Biggest Fan terrified me so much. The photo of me from back then. I didn't want anyone to know."

I could imagine Ayla at sixteen. She'd probably had something magical about her, even then. Roy Carpenter saw her light and tried to steal it for himself. And the colonel, in his twisted way, was jealous of his daughter. Wanted to snuff her light out and escape it.

"You didn't let those men smash your dreams. You kept going."

"But no matter how successful I am, how many adoring fans are screaming my name, I still hear my father telling me to get out of his house. How he never wanted to see me again. He didn't *love me*."

Oh, hell. I understood now. The best I could understand, anyway. What it would mean to Ayla if I said I loved her.

Fans and admirers said they loved her on a daily basis, but they didn't truly know her.

If I ever changed my mind, took my love back, *threw her away*, then it would destroy her.

"Ayla? Can you look at me?"

Slowly, she raised her head. Revealing bloodshot eyes and tear-streaked cheeks.

"You didn't do anything wrong."

"Teller—"

"Shhh," I soothed, rubbing circles into her back. "You did the best that you could. Every step of the way."

"How do you know that?"

"Because I see you. You're brave and passionate and you never give up. That's why I fell in love with you."

She shuddered as she inhaled. "You can't say that unless you—"

"I'm sure. I love you. I love Ayla Hopkins, Ayla Maxwell, every version of you. I'll never hurt you, and I'll never leave you or push you away."

Silent tears poured down her face. "How can you be real?"

"I'm sitting right here."

"I want to believe you. I really do."

I wiped her tears. "I hope you believe it. But everything I said is true either way." My fingers stroked through her hair. "Now, I'd like to take you upstairs and be good to you. How does that sound? Nothing but pleasure for you for the rest of tonight."

"Perfect," she said on a sigh. A stuttering breath followed. She was worn out from crying. "I've never felt better than when I'm with you."

That settled it. I had to find a way for us to be together. I'd already known that in theory. I'd wanted it.

But now, it was essential.

I was never going to leave this woman. The rest of the world would have to bend, because I wouldn't.

"Arms around my neck," I said. I picked her up, switching off lights along the way as I carried her upstairs.

Her bedroom was spacious, decorated in neutral colors, with artwork on the walls and potted plants hanging in planters by the windows. Carrying her into the en suite, I set her on her feet and started the faucets in the huge tub. I got rid of my T-shirt, tossing it through the doorway into the bedroom.

Then I went to my knees in front of her. Reminded me of the time I'd knelt on the tile floor of the shower in Hartley and buried my mouth between her legs. I loved worshipping her. Craved it.

Somehow, I'd never felt like more of a man than when I was on my knees for this woman.

I eased down her pants. She stepped out of them. I lifted her loose top and reached up to help her pull it off. With more of her skin uncovered, I pressed kisses to her belly, thighs. Ran my hands over her. Ayla held on to my shoulders and whimpered, but it was a sound of contentment.

When I unhooked her bra, then tugged her panties down her hips, my touch was more caring than sexual. I mean, my cock was rigid against the fly of my jeans. Uncomfortably constricted. But this was about Ayla. Showing my love while expecting nothing in return.

Another kiss to her stomach. "I love you," I murmured against her skin. She stroked my hair and shivered. "You're mine, sweetheart. I take care of what's mine."

Standing, I picked her up and set her in the warm water of the tub. Ayla relaxed immediately, eyes sinking closed. I switched off the faucets. Had her lie back to wet her hair, then grabbed a bottle of shampoo. She moaned softly as I massaged suds into her scalp.

Caring for her this way was an indulgence for me too. Watching the open, unguarded expression on her face. How beautifully she responded to me.

After washing her body and rinsing her clean, I helped her out of the tub. Wrapped her in a big, fluffy towel. We both brushed our teeth to get ready for bed.

Then I carried her to the bedroom, set her on the edge of the mattress, and switched on a bedside lamp. Ayla seemed more tired and quiet than usual, which made sense. Her confession had taken a lot out of her. I just hoped she was taking comfort from me.

"Which drawer are your pajamas in?" I asked. "I'd better get you dressed and under the covers."

"Wait." Ayla pushed the towel from her shoulders, letting it pool around her hips. Revealing her gorgeous curves. "I want to feel you."

Arousal flooded my veins. My cock swelled again. "You're tired. We have all weekend."

"No, I need this." She brought her hand to my bare chest, palm flat over my beating heart. "Teller, would you make love to me?"

Fuck. I unbuttoned my jeans. Pushed them off with my boxer briefs, my cock long and thick, my desire for her so clear to see.

Ayla lay back on the bed, knees parted.

"I'll make you feel me," I murmured gently, my tone blunting the force of my words. My fist closed around my shaft and gave it a few strokes, my thumb teasing over the head as I crawled onto the mattress and between her open legs. "I'll spend the rest of my life making love to you, if you want me."

Then I covered Ayla's naked body with mine and slanted my mouth onto hers with a deep kiss.

In that Hartley hotel room, weeks and weeks ago, we'd been wild together. The sex we'd had that weekend had been the best of my life. Today was different.

And somehow, even better.

We touched each other for ages. Until neither of us could wait any longer. She gasped as my cock stretched her. Ayla's legs gripped my waist, and her arms clung to me as I circled her with mine and held her as tightly as I could.

We were a tangle of limbs and sweaty skin, our edges blurring. No beginning and no end.

Just shared heat. Movement. Pleasure.

I wanted this to last. The two of us locked together, holding back the rest of the world.

I lifted onto my hands, arms straight, so I could stare down at her. Watch my hips thrusting, our bodies linked in such perfect harmony. "You ready to come for me?"

The pointed tips of her nails raked down my back. "I'm so close. *Please*. I—I need—"

"I know. I've got you." I held her thighs beneath her knees, pushing her legs up to her chest as my cock glided in and out of her.

Hell, that was tight. Her damp hair splayed over her pillow, drying into blond curls. Her eyes were hooded, lips plump and pink from our kisses. She stretched her arms over her head to brace against the headboard.

"My good, sweet little Troublemaker," I whispered.

The way she gave herself to me was so beautiful.

But this union, the wholeness that I felt with Ayla, like we were two incomplete pieces that were meant to fit together—that was even more incredible.

Her mouth opened on a cry of ecstasy. Her body clenched on my cock. Tingles raked down my spine.

My orgasm moved through me like a strike of lightning. Sudden and hot, then washing over me like rolls of thunder. I pumped my love into Ayla. Marking her as mine. No one else's.

That beat of possessiveness in my heart, in my brain, raised the pleasure even higher.

And I was hers. All of me.

Always.

THIRTY-EIGHT
Ayla

"I'll walk you home, Ayla," Sergeant Carpenter said.

Smiling, I pocketed the money he'd just paid me for babysitting that night. His son was reading comics in his room before bed, and Mrs. Carpenter was relaxing on their couch watching TV.

"It's just next door. You don't have to."

"No, it's late. Want to make sure you're safe. It's no trouble at all."

We walked through the Carpenters' front yard, past their planters of flowers. Red daisies grew in a pot on the side closest to my house. The same red daisies the sergeant had left in a bouquet on my porch for my birthday.

He was a nice man. A good father. Proof that some of those existed in the world, unlike the colonel.

Whatever. The less time I spent dwelling on my dad, the better. I had to deal with him enough in person. I couldn't wait until I was old enough to get out of here and live on my own.

We stepped onto my house's front porch. The light was off, both of us mere shadows. "Goodnight," I said, but Sergeant Carpenter didn't go. Instead, he stepped closer.

"You know, I never got a chance to enjoy my teenage years. I

became a dad way too young. What I wouldn't give to be sixteen again."

"Okay." I shrugged, not sure why he was telling me this. "I promise, it's not that great."

"You're special, Ayla. You could have the world in the palm of your hand. You have no idea how beautiful you really are."

The sergeant pulled something from behind his back. A red daisy. He held it out, reaching toward me.

The daisy melted into his palm, turning to blood that spilled over his skin and onto the porch.

I screamed, and the door burst open behind me. My father stood there, so tall he could barely fit in the doorway. "I knew you were a worthless little—" He grabbed my shoulder, yanking me into the darkness.

I jolted upright in the bed, a scream still on my lips.

My hands fisted the sheets. Someone else was here, broad shoulders in silhouette, and I cringed away from him.

"Sweetheart, it's me," Teller said softly. "You were having a nightmare."

"Teller." *It's him. Just him.* Somehow, I managed to breathe. I crawled toward him, folding myself into his arms. "I'm sorry."

"Don't be sorry. You're okay. I just didn't want to touch you until you were fully awake. I know how nightmares can be."

He was right. In my fear and confusion, I'd almost pushed him away.

"Have some water." Teller grabbed the water bottle from my nightstand, and I took a few gulps.

That had been so awful. It took me a couple of minutes for my thoughts to become coherent again and my stomach to settle.

"Did you have nightmares?" I asked, voice hoarse. "After you were wounded?" He'd told me before about his flashbacks.

"Yep. I did." Teller rubbed my back. "Still do, every once in a while."

I burrowed as close to him as I could. "I had a lot of bad dreams around the time Lori died. I'd wake up in a cold sweat." I would dream about the basement. My father yelling at me through the closed door.

But dreaming of Sergeant Carpenter, of that night… I hadn't played out those details in a very long time. Either asleep or awake.

"Did you have one because of what we talked about last night?" Teller asked. "Is that what your nightmare was about?"

How did he understand me so well? Better than anyone else I'd ever known. "Yeah. Sergeant Carpenter was walking me home. It was the night he tried to kiss me, when my father threw me out. But the nightmare was different. The sergeant…"

I inhaled, sitting up as I remembered.

"What is it?"

"I dreamed that he gave me a red daisy. His wife grew them in the summer. I forgot about that." My gaze found Teller's in the dimness. "The flower arrangements from Biggest Fan had red daisies, too."

Teller sat up, reaching for my hands. "Both of them? You're sure?"

I nodded. "Do you think that means something?"

"Do *you* think it does? You would know better than me."

"I don't know what any of it means." My breathing started to speed again. Like I might hyperventilate.

Could Sergeant Carpenter have something to do with Biggest Fan? But how? *Why*? After all these years?

"Come here." Teller sat against the pillows and opened his arms. He pulled me so I was between his legs, lying back against his chest, and he held me tight. Just the way I liked. "We don't have to figure it out right now. But we will."

I turned my head to breathe in his scent from his bare skin. Letting him calm me again. This was much better than when I usually woke up from a nightmare alone.

I wasn't alone anymore.

I kept repeating it to myself. *You're not alone.*

Teller grabbed the blanket and pulled it around us. This felt so good. Being skin to skin with him, nothing between us. No more secrets.

I'd barely begun to process what Teller had said to me last night. That he loved me. I'd been overwhelmed by memories, by the need to confess my deepest secret to him. So he knew I wasn't as perfect as he seemed to think.

I'd felt like a liar for so much of my life. Pretending to be somebody important who mattered when my own father didn't want me around.

But that hadn't made any difference to Teller. He'd said everything that I'd needed to hear, and I'd known it was the truth. At least, the truth from his perspective. Those old wounds were still raw. But Teller was healing them even now. It meant everything that he saw the real me, knew my past, and he still loved me.

I was falling for him too.

I'd been on my own for so long after leaving home. I'd trusted the wrong people. Gotten hurt. But all of that had led me to Silver Ridge. To Teller.

How could I stand being away from him again?

I pressed my face to his chest. "I don't want you to go. I need you to stay with me."

Teller's grip on me tightened, his body tensing. Immediately, I regretted what I'd said. I hadn't been thinking.

"I didn't mean that," I said. "Not literally. I wouldn't ask you to—"

"It's okay. I want you to be honest with me."

"I know you only have this weekend here. I'm grateful for that. I promise."

He lay his palm over my cheek. "I could find a way to stay. Not permanently at first. But maybe I could arrange a leave of absence from work. Susan has years of experience in the department. She could—"

I sat upright. "*No*. Don't even say that. You're not giving up what's important in your life for me."

"*You* are important. That's what I've been telling you. I love you."

Unshed tears ached in my throat. "Maybe I could come to Silver Ridge for a while. I've thought about it."

"You have?"

I nodded. "Maisie and the O'Neal family are there. It's always hard for me to leave when I visit Colorado. But I cause problems when I'm in town. Remember the riot over me last time? What if you resent me for that? What if you don't want me around anymore? Because I'm too much trouble."

His expression crumpled like my words had given him physical pain. "Ayla, I hate that I've ever made you feel that way. I was an idiot. You don't cause problems. It's other people, and that's on them, not you."

"But when the media finds out we're together, they'll put you in the spotlight. You know that, right? They'll write articles about you. They won't leave you alone."

"It took me a while to figure it out, but the kind of trouble you bring to my life is *exactly* what I want. I'll deal with whatever that entails. The more important question is, would you be happy not living in LA? You've worked so hard for what you have here. This house, your friends."

I hesitated before I answered. Other musicians lived in small cities or towns, and they found a way to make it work with their careers.

"I do like it here. Being near the ocean. I've got the industry at my fingertips. And my friends are important to me too, especially because I know how hard it is to find genuine ones. But I like Silver Ridge and the people there a lot. I like you most of all."

Teller grinned. "Do you?"

"I think I'm falling in love with you," I whispered.

He took my hand and kissed the end of each of my fingers. "Then I won't let anyone or anything keep you from me," he said, voice low and rumbling. "Not anymore."

We didn't make any final decisions yet. It was only Saturday, and we still had Sunday to talk things through. Figure out our next step. But we both knew one thing for sure.

Somehow, we would find a way to stay together.

We got out of bed, showered, and slipped on loungewear for a relaxing day together. Made breakfast and had coffee. My view of the Pacific was pretty great, but so was Teller in nothing but gray sweats. His sexy chest and arms on display, along with the scars that spoke to his history. Something about his bare feet in my kitchen was intimate and adorable.

Then we went to the living room. I'd picked up a fast-paced techno thriller yesterday, with a plot as far from my real life as possible. As I sat down to read, Teller picked a non-fiction book and snuggled in beside me.

I glanced at his book's cover. "A parenting manual? Is that for Ollie?"

He shrugged. "Sure. I know I'm not his parent, but I like to put in a good effort at whatever I'm doing."

Of course he did. "Would you ever want to have kids?" I asked, trying to be casual. As if this question hadn't been burning in the back of my mind.

He set the book on the coffee table and turned to me. "I used to see kids in my future. Then I figured Ollie was the closest I would get. I love being in his life. I would never want to change that. But...if I had a chance to have kids of my own too? Yeah, I would like that. What about you?"

"I never gave it much thought before."

He pinched my chin playfully. "Because you're in your twenties."

I smiled. "But Maisie makes me want kids of my own." I put my arms around him and kissed his collarbone. "I think you would be an amazing dad."

He kissed the top of my head. I glanced up and found Teller gazing down at me, so much love and hope in his eyes. My heart did somersaults in my chest.

Furious knocking pulled me from a dreamless sleep. "Ayla, you need to open up."

It was Bryan, banging on the front door. Teller and I had dozed off on the couch in each other's arms, books in our laps. I started to get up, but Teller held my wrist.

"I can go see what he wants."

"It's fine. I'll go. It must be important." I grabbed my cell from the coffee table and checked my notifications as I strode to the door. Whoops. Bryan had called a couple of times in the last minute, but my phone had been on silent.

I threw the door open. Bryan's fist was raised like he'd been about to knock again. He lowered it. "Sorry to interrupt, but you weren't picking up your phone, and I decided to skip the landline and come straight to your door."

"Why? What's up?"

"There's a delivery driver here. With flowers."

I held my breath. Teller's warm hand rested on my back.

"At first I wondered if you sent them," Bryan said to Teller. "Since you send Ayla presents all the time. But the sender is anonymous."

And I'd told Bryan and the other guards about my stalker. They didn't know many details, but they knew about the flower arrangements and the need to carefully vet deliveries.

"Is the driver still here?" I asked.

Bryan nodded. "Yeah, we stopped him. We're keeping him at the gate. Want me to call the police?"

"Not yet. I want to see the flowers. Are there red daisies?"

Bryan frowned, clearly confused. "I don't know. I could go look, but why—"

Teller stepped past the threshold, putting himself in front of me. "Hold on. First, I want to talk to this delivery guy." He glanced back. "If that's okay with you, sweetheart. For all we know, this could be the stalker."

I gripped Teller's arm. "Then I don't want him near you. What if he's got a weapon? What if he tries to hurt you?"

"That's something I'm trained to deal with. Bryan, are you armed?"

"No doubt. I'm fully up to date on my training. The agency requires it."

"Good. You and I will talk to the guy. Depending on what he says, we can decide whether to call the police."

Bryan lifted his chin. "Works for me."

Teller went inside briefly to snag a T-shirt. He tugged it on over his sweats, not bothering with shoes, and he brought me a hoodie to cover my tank top. The hoodie said Silver Ridge PD across the front.

"Be careful," I said.

Teller kissed me. "I will. You be careful too. Stay back and out of sight. I don't want him seeing you."

We'll see about that, I thought, grumbling to myself about being left behind while Teller walked into danger. Potential danger, anyway.

No, there was no way I could just wait patiently for my man to return. That wasn't me.

I slid into a pair of shoes. Tiptoeing across the stone pavers outside my door, I approached the long, tall hedge that hid my house from view of the driveway and the road. When I reached the edge, I peeked around the bushy plant wall.

"Hey, man, I've made my delivery," an unfamiliar voice was saying. "Can I have my ID back and go? I have a lot more flowers and traffic to deal with."

"I haven't seen your ID yet," Teller said. "I want to know who the hell you are."

Teller, Bryan, and another of the security guys were spread out, surrounding the delivery driver. I'd never seen the man before. A truck with flower decals was parked beside him.

I spotted the flower arrangement on the ground. Bigger than any of the others I'd received so far. The splotches of bright red were visible from here.

Red daisies. Shit.

There was a small card stuck into the new arrangement. I had to know what it said.

"Why are you people making such a big deal about this? I deliver the flowers. That's it."

Bryan handed the ID to Teller, who studied it. "So you work for the florist, Christopher?"

"Yeah, that's what I've been telling you."

Whatever was going on, I didn't believe this guy was my stalker. Biggest Fan had been too careful in the past, never revealing his identity even when he'd ordered those flower arrangements to be sent.

Teller had asked me to stay out of sight, but that just wasn't going to work for me. He was my boyfriend and the most important man in my life, but I'd already told him that I wouldn't fade into the background. That would never be me.

I marched across the driveway, right into the middle of their huddle, and grabbed the card from the flowers.

"Dude," the delivery guy exclaimed. "You're Ayla Maxwell."

Teller was at my side like a shot. "What are you doing out here?"

"Finding out what I need to know." I tore open the envelope. There was a card inside with a handwritten note, I assumed written by somebody working for the florist.

He'll never be good enough for you.

A folded sheet of paper sat behind the note. I opened it. Yep, another printout of a photo. But this one showed Teller in his police uniform.

Heavily scribbled Xs blacked out his eyes.

Anger flooded my bloodstream. The previous messages had been bad enough. But this one seemed to be threatening Teller.

"You're Christoper, right?" I asked the delivery driver. "I want to know who sent this. It's extremely important."

Christopher shook his head. "I don't know. The order was called in yesterday, and the person gave a lot of instructions about printing out a photo or some shit, which is definitely weird. But it's not our job to ask a bunch of questions."

"Really? Even when somebody sends a photo like this?" I turned the image toward him.

Christoper's eyes bugged. "Dude, that's creepy."

"You think?" Bryan asked.

Teller's face was impassive.

"Somebody else prepped the order, and they probably figured it was a joke," Christopher said. "I didn't know."

Teller pulled out his phone. Took a photo of the man's ID. Then held the card out to return it. "Mention any of this to anyone, and we'll know it was you. We're going to call your employer and check your story."

"Whatever you want. I don't want nothing to do with this creepiness. I'm just going to make my deliveries and keep my mouth shut."

He got in his truck, backed up, and drove off.

I pointed at the flowers. "Red daisies."

Teller nodded. "I noticed."

"What does that mean?" Bryan asked.

I waved a hand. "Don't worry about that. Can you check the flowers? Make sure there's nothing hidden inside? Unless you two want to call a bomb squad or something."

Teller arched an eyebrow at me. "Not funny."

"I'm not laughing either." Bryan grabbed a pair of gloves and carefully poked around. "It's clean. Nothing here."

Like the others.

I was so damn sick of this.

Bryan stood up, backing away from the flowers. "You want me to toss them? Or—"

I charged over, picked up the arrangement and started tearing the stems out. Once all the flowers were scattered on the driveway, I stomped them into the concrete. Last, I dropped the terracotta planter. It cracked in half.

"Sorry about the mess."

Bryan and the other security guy just stared.

"Did that make you feel better, Troublemaker?"

"It did, actually."

Teller put a hand on my shoulder. "Come on. Let's go back inside."

THIRTY-NINE

Teller

THE MOMENT WE GOT INSIDE, I hugged her to me.

"You're not mad I came out there, are you?" she asked.

"I don't like that you put yourself at risk, but I'm not surprised." I kissed her temple. "I love that you're you. Are you mad at *me* for being protective?"

She smoothed down my shirt. "I love that you're you."

I smiled fondly. "Watching you trash that flower arrangement was something to see. Good thing I took a picture of it beforehand."

Ayla made a sheepish face. "I was pissed off. I'm so tired of this nonsense. And now that awful picture of you with your eyes marked out? What the hell? Seems like he's threatening you."

"Let him. It's not going to change anything. Nothing is going to keep us apart."

"But how does he even know about you? What if it's leaked to the media that we're dating?"

"Then we can handle that too." I pulled her over to the living room couch, where we'd been napping peacefully less than an hour ago. "Let's take a look and find out."

Using my phone, I googled Ayla's name. There were the

pictures from the event she attended with Paul a couple of nights ago. But nothing in the news since. Nothing at all about me.

I set my phone down, thinking it through. "The photo of me was taken from my department's public website. How he knows we're dating, I have no clue." It was concerning. Hardly anyone knew about us, except our closest friends and family and a few people who worked for Ayla.

And a lot of folks in Silver Ridge. At least, they suspected.

"His last email said he's watching me." She shivered, and I tucked her closer.

"But if that's true, why wouldn't he send a photo that's not publicly available? Every pic this guy has used was online already, including that paparazzi shot from outside the recording studio."

"Not the very first one. The first flower arrangement I received in Toronto. My sister took that photo of me, and it's never appeared online."

Dammit. That was right. "So, he somehow got access to a private photo of you as a teenager. He used it like an opening gambit. Trying to get your attention. Which worked."

"But then, why the large gap in between sending the flowers to my Toronto concert venue, and then the flowers and email when I was in Silver Ridge? It was almost six months in between."

"We're probably not talking about a sane individual."

And I couldn't forget what Ayla had shared with me earlier today about Sergeant Carpenter. The red daisies.

If I'd had access to my office computer, I would look up Carpenter using my law-enforcement databases. But I couldn't do that with just my work phone. I could ask Susan to do it for me. But that would mean sharing personal things about Ayla. I didn't want to do that unless we had no other options.

"Can we talk to River?" Ayla asked. "See if he's made any progress on tracing Biggest Fan's latest email?"

"Good idea. I've been meaning to check in with him. Should inform him about the latest flower delivery."

ME

Ayla received another flower arrangement from the stalker.

He wrote back almost immediately.

RIVER

Sorry to hear that. I know it's not pleasant for her. But I've got an update myself and was about to text the both of you. Want to call Ayla and conference me in?

Actually, I'm with her in LA right now.

Nice. You two are official?

As far as I'm concerned, yes.

Put a ring on that finger. Don't let her get away. That's what I did with mine, and it's working out great.

I snorted.

"What?" Ayla asked.

"Nothing. River's being his usual self." I video-called him. After the usual friendly greetings, Ayla held up the new photo we'd received.

River whistled. "Somebody doesn't like you, Landry. Luckily, I have a pretty good idea of who."

Ayla sat forward, getting closer to my phone screen. "You traced the email?"

River had his glasses on, his hair messy and clothes rumpled like he'd been at his computer all night and all day. "I was triple-checking my work. Had to be sure. You recall the previous email that you received from Biggest Fan in Silver Ridge? I was able to narrow down the origin to the west side of Los Angeles, but couldn't get a closer pin than that."

"I remember," Ayla said.

River's mouth quirked at the corner, a devious half-smile. "Biggest Fan messed up this time. Used his personal phone to send the email. It was sent from the same restaurant you were at for the event. The phone is registered to a Paul Ruxton."

Ayla flinched like a bolt of electricity had just gone through her. "You are *fucking. Kidding. Me.*"

River twisted back and forth on his swivel chair. "Afraid not. I did some quick background on him. He works for the label that owns your recording rights?"

I was struggling to stay calm. But darkness feathered at the edges of my vision.

Paul Ruxton. That piece of shit. I should've done more than give him a split lip.

I hadn't lied before about wanting to destroy anyone who'd hurt her.

Ayla nodded. "He's been working with me on my new album. But why would he do this? It's...beyond bizarre. It's pathological."

"Because he wants you," I bit out. "It's obvious he's wanted you for months. He set up this stalker fiction in the hopes you would go running to him for help and he could play your hero."

"Do you think Paul seemed especially desperate at the event the other night?" River asked. "Enough that he'd ignore all caution and email you directly from his personal phone?"

Ayla's hand flew to her mouth. "I told him I have a boyfriend. He seemed angry."

I reached out for her hand, though honestly I was trying to soothe my own fury. Remind myself that I couldn't just storm the streets of LA to hunt Ruxton down.

"I ditched him once we arrived at the restaurant, and that's when the email came in. Then he got in my face right after. Said he knew about the stalker and wanted to help. Tried to kiss me. I thought Cheryl must've told him about the flowers, but he didn't need that. Because the asshole sent them himself. He invented the whole thing. This is sick."

I thought back to Silver Ridge. How the email from Biggest

Fan had arrived at the start of the wedding weekend, then the flowers, then Ruxton himself the next day. The bastard must've expected to find her terrified about her stalker. Instead, I was there.

No wonder he'd gotten increasingly desperate.

And shit, the flowers today with the defaced photo of me. Yeah, the man was no fan of mine. Explained how the stalker knew about us dating, though.

Ayla let go of my hand. "I need to call Cheryl. Right away. She needs to know."

"Do you want me to be there?" I asked.

"No, I can handle it." She picked up her phone and walked to the hall. I assumed she was heading toward her office.

River was still on the line, swiveling in his chair as he waited for what I'd say next.

"Thank you. This would've been much harder to figure out without your help."

"No problem."

I glanced toward Ayla's office, then back to River on my phone screen. "There's a loose end, though. Something maybe you can look into, since I'm away from my office computer and my database access."

River's fingers poised over his keyboard. "Hit me."

"I need you to find a Sergeant Roy Carpenter. He was stationed in Upstate New York about a decade ago, when Ayla's family lived there. He could be a different rank now, or might have left the military. I want to know where he is and what he's been doing."

"You think he's got some connection to Paul Ruxton and this stalker business?"

"It's possible. Hard to imagine their paths have ever crossed. But Paul got that photo of Ayla as a teenager from somewhere. There are other reasons to think Carpenter has a tie to this stalker situation too. Won't know until we have more information."

"Then I'm happy to do what I can. That's what I'm here for."

"Let me know if I can return the favor for you or any of your friends at Last Refuge."

"I'm sure we'll think of something."

I found Ayla sitting in her office and staring into the distance, deep in thought. She looked up as I came in, not quite smiling at me.

"How are you doing with all this?" I held out my hand and helped pull her up, drawing her close.

"I'm angry. Aside from that, it's still too fresh. Cheryl doesn't want to believe Paul really did this, but she's coming around. She's heading over here right now. She wanted to call my publicist too, but I can't deal with all of that right now."

I smoothed my hands down her shoulders. "I'm glad you're speaking up for yourself."

"I'm trying to. I thought I'd made so much progress toward being independent. I can't believe how easy it was for Paul to manipulate me."

"Not your fault." It was a good thing Paul wasn't smart enough to go too far with his mind games. In the end, he'd been so obvious and arrogant that he gave the whole thing away.

Ayla played with the hem of my T-shirt. "But if he tries to do anything to you," she said, "I'm going to grind him into the ground."

"Unless I get to him first." I smirked. "I'm not worried about him, though. Defacing my photo and sending it, when he knew I was here with you, was his petty attempt at revenge for us both embarrassing him. When he's not hiding behind anonymity, he's a coward. Not a real threat."

She nodded. I trailed my fingers down her side and squeezed her hip.

"You look great in my hoodie, by the way," I said. "But if you want to get changed before Cheryl arrives, I don't blame you."

"Yeah, that does sound good. I could use a few minutes to collect myself."

"Then you go ahead. I'll tidy up in the main room and answer the door when she gets here. She can be patient until you're ready."

Also, that would give me the chance to have a little chat with Ayla's manager.

Bryan called the landline to announce Cheryl's presence about half an hour later. I answered the door to let her in. She was dressed in a fancy suit like yesterday and draped in jewelry. Meanwhile, I hadn't changed out of my tee and sweats.

"Landry. You're still here."

"I am." I stepped aside to let her pass. "Ayla will join us in a few."

"And you're standing sentinel at her door? I thought your job was chief of police in Silver Ridge. Ayla has enough bodyguards already."

"Yet until I showed up, she didn't have the protection she needed." I wasn't interested in a verbal sparring match. I preferred to speak plainly. "You're supposed to be her manager. You should've protected her from a predator like Paul Ruxton."

Her face flushed red. "I had no idea. I feel terrible about what happened. But Ayla didn't even tell me she had a stalker. I only knew about the first incident, and she downplayed it. How was I supposed to—"

"Not another word. Don't you dare put this on her."

Ayla was already in a vulnerable place right now. If she heard Cheryl blaming her for what happened? No. I would not allow it.

"When Ayla comes in here, you're going to listen to everything she has to say. You're going to do whatever she asks. And you're going to use this bullshit with Paul Ruxton to get her out of her recording contract with Ruxton Records."

Ayla had told me, during one of our late-night conversations, about that iron-clad contract. How much she wanted out of it, but she had to wait another year to renegotiate. Even Paul's attempt to kiss her probably wouldn't have been enough.

But after this stalker madness? Give me a break.

Cheryl tightened her jaw. "I can try, but—"

"No buts. Work with her lawyers and make it happen. I know I seem like just a small-town cop, but I can make your life difficult if it comes to that. I love Ayla, and there are no limits to what I'd do for her."

Cheryl edged away, eyeing me like I was a feral animal. But then she said, "Good. Ayla deserves that. I suppose I can learn to get along with you."

"If you still have a job after Ayla decides what to do with you. Never forget that you work for *her*, not the other way around."

Cheryl blanched, but she nodded.

When Ayla came in, she pulled me aside and quietly said she'd like to speak with Cheryl on her own.

"I get it," I assured her. "Just let me know if you need anything." I'd already said my piece to her manager. Ayla was a successful businesswoman without any of my help. I just wanted to make things a little easier for her if I could.

While she was busy, I went downstairs and sat on the balcony overlooking the ocean. Called the station to see what was going on, then texted with Piper.

"Hey, handsome." Ayla stepped out onto the balcony. The sun was setting, lighting up the sky and the waves with vibrant oranges and reds.

"C'mere." I patted my thigh, and she slid into my lap, her arms going around my neck. "How'd it go with Cheryl?" I asked.

"She promised to confront Paul. She even offered to go to the police, but I'm not sure about that. I don't want to bring River into this. I just want Paul to admit what he did, and I want the label to fire him."

"Do you think that's likely?"

She sighed. "I don't know. Since his father is the owner?

Maybe not. I can still go to the media. But I told Cheryl that I'm definitely done with Ruxton Records. I want out of my contract, and I don't care what she or my lawyers have to do to make it happen."

"And what did she say?"

"She was surprisingly supportive. I'd expected a lecture about how difficult the legal battle could be, but she said it was as good as done. She also apologized that she hadn't realized what Paul was doing."

I fought a smile. "Good."

"You said something to her, didn't you?"

I barked a laugh. "Guilty. But *not* because I don't trust you to handle your own career. You obviously can. I just care about you. I want you happy."

She leaned in for a slow kiss. "Thank you for being in my corner. You told me you would be, way back on the day we got stuck in that snowstorm. You're a man of your word."

I was glad she thought so.

My fingers slid into her silky hair as we kissed again. The sun was sinking fast into the horizon. "Do you think I'm a fool for sticking with this job?" she asked, so quietly I almost couldn't hear her. "After everything?"

She was thinking of the paparazzi attention. The way her value was judged based on her appearance and the money she brought in. The betrayals by friends and employees she trusted. And of course, the latest manipulations by Paul, not to mention his outright harassment and threats.

It would be too much for many people to deal with. Much less someone who felt things as intensely as she did.

I sat back enough that I could look her in the eyes. "The strength you've had to find within yourself, every single day, to survive in this industry is unbelievable. But you give something special to the world with every single song. I truly believe that." I didn't even know how to convey how beautiful her music, her *talent*, was. How much her art meant to so many people.

"Is it worth it, though?"

"That's a decision only you can make for yourself."

"I know. Doesn't make it easier." She sighed, looking out at the ocean. "I'll go to Silver Ridge with you tomorrow. I'm going to take some time to think. And be with you. More than anything, I want to be with you."

"Then that's what we'll do. I can't wait to take you home."

FORTY

Ayla

THE MEDIA still hadn't found out I was dating Teller yet. It was inevitable they would. But I wanted to keep that secret for as long as possible. To have a sliver of peace and privacy for while it lasted.

That meant only a small circle of people could know I was leaving LA.

Before dawn on Sunday, we grabbed our bags and sneaked over to Hayleigh's house. She was the one who drove us to the private airport, where Dane's jet would take us back to Colorado. She was giddy as she drove with Teller and me in her backseat.

"Maybe I should try being a ride-share driver," Hayleigh said, tapping the steering wheel to the rhythm of the stereo. "I would be good at this."

I exchanged an amused glance with Teller. The windows were tinted, so we didn't have to worry about being spotted in the backseat.

I'd told Bryan I would be gone for a few days, but I hadn't wanted to bring any bodyguards with me. I would be sticking close to Teller and keeping out of sight in Silver Ridge. No strolls along Main Street. We were going to be careful.

I didn't want to spend my life in hiding, but I could handle it for a few days. Especially given what we had learned about Paul.

I was still trying to get over the shock of learning he was Biggest Fan. But in a way, he'd done me a favor. His behavior had been so egregious there was no way the label could refuse to let me out of my deal. Stalking me in order to push me into a romantic relationship had to count as a breach of contract.

I was full of nervous excitement as the jet landed, and we got into Teller's SUV, which he'd left at the airport a few days ago.

After so many weeks, I was finally heading back to Silver Ridge. It felt like no time at all, and yet it also felt like forever. Because so much was different.

I had a wonderful man who loved me, and I was quickly falling for him.

Ducking down in my seat, I waited for Teller to give me the go-ahead that we'd passed through the town. "There's Dixie," he murmured. His arm moved. I guessed he was waving.

"People must know you were gone for the weekend. What are you going to tell them?"

"The truth, if you're okay with it. That I went to see you. I'll just leave out the part where you came back with me." His hand ventured over and rested on my arm. "You sure you feel comfortable being alone while I'm at work?"

"Totally."

We'd already discussed this, and I'd given it a lot of thought. Teller lived in a quiet, woodsy area without any visible neighbors. No reason for anyone to know he had a guest. He'd also told me he had a security system. Since very few people even knew I'd left LA, we had nothing to worry about.

I was taking a break from recording, but I planned to work a lot on my next album. In fact, I was already bursting with ideas, my fingers itching to get them down.

If Ruxton Records agreed to let me go without a long legal fight, then I would be *free*. That also meant no record deal to distribute and promote this album. But I had *me*. My own determination. I had direct links to my fans through social media.

Plenty of other artists had released independently, so why couldn't I?

And I had Teller. It was going to be amazing waking up next to him every morning. Enjoying a quiet dinner together and making love in his bed.

Maybe the world would figure out where I was sooner rather than later. We would deal with that when it happened.

But no matter what, this album was going to belong to *us*. Nobody else.

"Okay." He patted my shoulder. "We're clear."

When I sat up, we were just pulling onto a long driveway with pine trees on either side.

"Teller," I breathed. "This is...stunning."

His house was set into a clearing with a babbling creek. Woods surrounded the clearing, cut through by just the driveway and a bridge that crossed the water. The home itself wasn't giant. It had a small footprint with an attached garage, everything about it quaint and inviting. A combination of timber and stone, with a stone chimney rising over the shingled roof.

"I love it so much."

He beamed with pride. "I'm glad."

We both got out, not bothering with the baggage yet. I wanted a better look around. "How far are we from Main Street?" I asked. It was like we'd stepped into another world. Yet it was somehow still quintessential Hart County.

"A fifteen-minute drive. I didn't want to be too far from Piper and Ollie. They live right near the center of town, close enough for Piper to walk to her coffee shop and to Ollie's elementary. But I also wanted privacy."

"Because everybody in Silver Ridge is always in your business otherwise?"

"They are. I don't have my constituents spying in my windows when they walk by. Anybody who's out here came here on purpose."

I laced our fingers together as Teller showed me around the

rest of the property. He'd done a lot of work on this place. But there were still unfinished projects. Like a messy shed and a half-built picnic table. "The table is a project with Ollie," he explained. "Lately we've been focused on building the treehouse at Piper's place. Otherwise Ollie's going to grow out of the treehouse phase too soon."

The mention of Ollie made me think of Maisie. How close she was right now.

And somehow, Teller knew just what I was thinking. He lifted my hand and kissed my knuckles. "We can invite family over later. Surprise them. If you want."

"*Yes*. That would be amazing." Even though I wanted my visit to stay quiet as far as the bulk of the town was concerned, I had to be able to see Maisie and the O'Neals. That was nonnegotiable.

"But first, I'm taking you inside." Teller swept me off my feet and into his arms, bridal style. I laughed in surprise.

The interior of his home was just as quaint. Simple decor, lots of warm wood. An updated mountain cabin feel. All of which I'd seen on video during our calls, but homier than a screen could convey.

"Take me to your bedroom? I want to see it in person."

His smile was heated. "I know what you want, Troublemaker."

"If you're thinking I want to get naked and horizontal in your bed, then yes, you're correct."

I'd shared my home and my bed with him, and now I was getting to enjoy his. LA and Silver Ridge were so different, yet Teller and I were a perfect fit in both locales.

I could get used to this.

"Teller Landry, hosting a party," Ashford said. "Now I've seen everything."

I hid around the corner in Teller's kitchen pantry as the O'Neals arrived. Laughed silently as Teller greeted them. But when I heard Maisie's voice, I couldn't hold back any longer.

I stepped into the living room. Maisie did a double take. Gasped. Then she barreled toward me. "Aunt Ayla!" she screamed, loud enough to hurt my eardrums. *Ouch*. But worth it.

"Hey you." I caught her when she leaped at me. She was too heavy for me to carry around at this point, but I squeezed her thoroughly before easing her down.

Stella loped over, tail going a mile a minute as she licked all over my face.

"Good to see you too, Stella," I said, laughing and wiping my wet cheek.

"What are you doing here?" Maisie asked. "Is it 'cause Uncle Teller is your boyfriend? Do you live with him now?" She bounced excitedly.

"Um, no, I don't live here. But I did come to visit him for a while. And visit you too."

"But then why aren't you staying at my house with Daddy and Emma and me?"

"Monkey, Aunt Ayla can stay wherever she wants." Ashford came over for a hug next, followed by his wife.

"I can't believe you're here," Emma said. "You look great!"

"So do you. How's married life?"

"Amazing." She laced her hand with her husband's. "Never thought I could be this happy."

Neither did I, I thought. Thank goodness I didn't say it aloud. Teller and I were nowhere near ready to make that kind of commitment. But it was nice to think about.

He'd changed everything for me.

Grace and Dane showed up, both of them far less surprised to see me. Then Callum, Piper and Ollie. Everyone had brought food for the party. It was cold but sunny outside, warm enough for Teller to fire up the grill and make hot dogs and burgers for lunch while the kids played fetch with Stella.

We hung out with our families. Teller and I had our arms around each other, my head on his chest. The first time we were *together* in front of them. I loved it.

"We're out of potato salad." I picked up the bowl. "I'll be right back."

"I can help," Grace announced. She trailed behind me. Once we were in the kitchen, she perched a hand on her hip. "So, you and Teller are cute together. I can finally spill that he's had a crush on you for ages."

"What?" I paused with a spoon in the potato salad container. "Are you sure?"

She cackled. "It was obvious to those of us paying attention."

I gave her a sardonic look, and she only laughed louder.

"Trust me, that man has been so into you for so long. Even if he didn't know it himself. Thank goodness he figured it out." She leaned in. "I would love to hear sometime how it all happened. Did it start with him arresting you? Was that your version of foreplay?"

I winked. "Someday, I just might tell you."

Grace took the spoon from my hand and took over filling the salad bowl. "You know, my brothers and I grew up with the Landrys. Now that you and Teller are together, the uniting of our two families is just about official, since you're pretty much an O'Neal."

"Aww, thanks. I'm glad to be. It feels good to have both our families here. Seriously...I couldn't have made it through the last couple years without all of you supporting me."

"It was no hardship." Her lips twisted, bright eyes turning sad behind her glasses. "The only person who's missing is Grayden. The oldest O'Neal brother. And I'm still working on that."

"Let me know if I can help." I knew how hard it was to be estranged from a sibling. Grace had reconnected with her oldest brother recently, but Ashford and Callum weren't so sure about doing the same.

"We'll get there." Grace pushed out a breath, shaking off the change in her mood. "For now, I'm thrilled that you'll be around more. I assume so, anyway. Are you thinking of moving to Colorado? Even just part-time?"

I glanced toward the door. Everyone else was still laughing and having fun outside. "I don't know," I admitted. "We want to be together all the time, but it's hard to figure out how that will actually work."

She nodded sympathetically. "Dane moved to Silver Ridge to be with me, but his job is pretty mobile."

"Dane still travels though, right? He goes back to New York a lot."

"Sure. He does. I go with him when I can."

Even if I made Silver Ridge my home base, I'd have to travel a lot. Would Teller want to come with me? But I didn't see how he could if he continued serving as police chief.

"You'll make it work," Grace said. "I'm sure of it."

"Let me borrow some of your hope and optimism?"

She laughed. "Ever since Dane and I fell in love, I've had plenty to go around."

That night, after everyone went home, Teller and I crawled beneath the covers. Our families had promised not to blab to anyone about my presence in town. Of all of them, Maisie and Ollie were the most likely to let something slip. But they loved the idea of being spies, like they were helping me keep a secret identity or something.

Teller tilted my chin to kiss me. "You're comfortable here? At my place?"

"Very." I sighed as I relaxed into him.

During Ashford and Emma's wedding weekend, I'd briefly imagined making a home in Silver Ridge. I'd dismissed that idea quickly. Thinking Teller and the O'Neals wouldn't want to deal with the problems my fame brought to their door. But now, I knew Teller wanted me here. Ashford and Emma had also reassured me.

Did I really want to move here permanently though? What about my life in Los Angeles? My house and kooky friends. The ocean.

What if Teller and I could truly unite our lives? Neither of us having to give anything up?

I imagined how perfect it could be. Somehow traveling back and forth between here and California or wherever I was on tour. I still, even now, didn't see exactly how it could work given our jobs. But I had to hope. Teller had said he wouldn't let anything keep us apart.

Maybe we really could have it all.

I was starting to drift off when Teller grunted, picking up his phone from the nightstand. "New text from River. I'd asked him to look into Roy Carpenter, just in case there was a connection to Paul Ruxton."

"Really? Did he find something?"

"Take a look." He showed me the text.

RIVER

Sergeant Roy Carpenter passed away six years ago. Lung cancer.

Six years ago. Before I'd even signed with Ruxton Records.

I certainly didn't miss Sergeant Carpenter, but he was another part of my past that was dead and gone. Yet those red daisies...was that just a coincidence?

And the old photo of me as a teenager. Where had Paul gotten it?

"You okay?" Teller murmured, stroking my hair.

"I will be."

It didn't actually matter where Paul had dug up that old photo of me. We'd outed him as Biggest Fan. His sick little game was over, and he couldn't hurt me.

FORTY-ONE
Teller

I WOKE SLOWLY. Ayla was wrapped around me, her hair all over the place. Smiling, I rested a hand on her head and blinked at my bedroom ceiling. Same old view I'd had every morning for years since I bought this place. The faint imperfections in the plaster visible in the morning light.

Yet Ayla Maxwell, the love of my life, was now lying in bed with me. How had we gotten here? I mean, I knew in theory, but I never could've seen any of this coming.

And don't think for a second I'd missed the part yesterday where she asked about whether I wanted kids. Said I'd be a great dad.

Every one of the dreams I'd given up could still come true. All because of her. Hell, I was ready to build a white picket fence around this house, even though it wouldn't quite match the woodsy mountain vibe.

But I loved this woman with my entire being. I had to protect her from the Paul Ruxtons of the world.

"Hi," she said sleepily and wiggled against me. My morning wood twitched and thickened.

"Hey."

"I missed you."

A grin broke wide across my face. "You missed me while you were sleeping?"

"Mmhmm." She moved so she was lying on top of me. She'd worn one of my T-shirts last night and nothing else. I had a pair of flannel pajama pants on, which did nothing to hide my erection. She wiggled again, grinding herself on me, and I groaned.

I rolled her over and thrust against her hip a few times.

"It's Monday," she said. "Don't you have work today?"

Another groan from me, this one far less happy. "Probably." I checked the clock on my nightstand. Thankfully it was only six thirty. We'd woken up early. "I have a little time."

"Shower?"

"Okay." Perhaps we could knock out more than one thing.

We gave each other hot, meaningful looks as we stripped. The moment we hit the spray, she was pulling me down to kiss me and reaching for my cock. She hitched one leg up, wrapping it around my hip. My fingers played between her legs. I had to bend way over given our height difference, but I wasn't complaining.

Before Ayla, I'd rarely had sex. I hadn't felt much need for it. Maybe because of the aftermath of my injuries, or maybe just that I was getting older. Even in my younger years I'd never had a high libido.

Yet with her, I'd been insatiable since our very first time together. Always wanting more of her. Any excuse to touch her, to watch her face light up with pleasure and then do filthy things to her with my cock. Ayla had called me a sex maniac before. With her, it was kinda true.

I couldn't get enough.

And the thought of having a baby with her someday? Getting her pregnant with my child? My hips bucked, pushing my erection into her hand as I imagined it. I wanted that so badly.

A family with her. Everything with her.

After we both came, I lathered up and washed Ayla's body, simply because I loved doing it. Then I washed myself while she shampooed her hair.

I dressed in my uniform. She pulled on jeans and the Silver Ridge PD hoodie she'd stolen from me yesterday. In the kitchen, the coffee machine gurgled, and I pulled some breakfast items from my fridge. The milk from a few days ago was still good. "Eggs and toast okay?"

"Sounds great. I'll toast, you scramble."

"Perfect." I handed her the loaf of bread and pressed a quick kiss to her mouth.

She slotted two pieces into the toaster. "What's your usual morning routine?"

I cracked eggs into a bowl. "I work out. Usually lifting weights at the gym near the station, but sometimes I do a yoga routine. There's a channel Piper subscribed me to. It's not my favorite, but—"

"Chief Landry." Ayla's tone was accusatory. "How is this the first I'm hearing about this? You do *yoga*?"

"Is that so hard to believe?"

"It's sexy, that's what it is. I'm just imagining these big glutes up in the air." She reached around to my ass and squeezed. "I love yoga."

"Do you now." I made sure the stove was on low, then backed her against the counter, one hand on either side of her. "I can think of a few poses I'd like to try with you."

"Are you all bendy?"

"Not at all. I'm still a beginner, actually. How about you? Are you bendy?"

"I am. I'm pretty advanced when it comes to yoga, if I say so myself." She lifted onto her toes to kiss me. "Also Pilates. I have to be in great shape to sing and move around for hours during my concerts. I can hold myself in some *very* interesting positions."

A growl rumbled out of me. I pressed my body flush against hers. Could I be late to work? That had never happened before, but damn it was tempting.

I'd been serious about not wanting to be away from her. Even the eight-plus hours of my workday seemed daunting. For a workaholic like me, that was saying something.

"What have you done to me, Troublemaker?" I murmured between kisses.

My cell rang. The personal one, not work. So I was a little slow digging it out of my pocket.

"It's my sister."

"Answer it," Ayla said. "I'll keep working on breakfast. We need to get you out the door soon, Chief. Silver Ridge is counting on you."

"Yeah, yeah. I know." I accepted the call. "Hey, Piper. How are you this morning?"

"Teller?"

Immediately, all my inner alarm bells clanged at the same time. Piper's voice was shaking. Terrified.

"Tell me what happened."

Ayla spun to face me with a wooden spoon in her hand, features morphing with concern.

"Someone broke in. Tell, he was in the house while we were asleep. I just called 911, but I need you here. Please."

"Yeah. I'll leave right now. Let me just—" My eyes lifted, meeting Ayla's.

"Oh, God, I forgot about Ayla being there. I'm so sorry." Piper sounded like she was crying, and on the verge of falling apart completely.

"No. Everything's going to be fine. I'm on my way, okay? Let me head out to my SUV. I need to check in with the office. Then I'll call you back and stay on the line with you. Okay? You and Ollie are safe right now?"

Another call came in, this one on my work phone. That was probably the station.

Piper sniffled. "We're locked in my bedroom. Please hurry."

"I'll be there soon." I ended the call and stuffed it in my pocket, then grabbed my work cell. Missed call from Officer Nichols. Susan.

"Something happened with Piper?" Ayla asked.

"Break-in while she and Ollie were asleep."

Was it the vandal who'd targeted other women living on their own? I'd never thought he'd go after someone living in the middle of town. I'd been wrapped up in my own happiness. Ignoring my duties, thinking about *sex*, while some piece of shit broke into my sister's house and terrorized her and my nephew.

Ayla swallowed, as if she was mastering her own fear and dismay. She grabbed a piece of toast and wrapped it in a paper towel. "Eat this on your way. You need something in your stomach."

I had to get to my sister. But to do that, I was leaving Ayla here alone. That seemed far riskier than it had an hour ago. Should've brought Bryan or another bodyguard here with us from Los Angeles. And wouldn't *that* have been romantic.

Why the hell had I believed I could do this? Have everything I wanted, protect everyone I cared about, with zero repercussions?

I shook my head at the toast Ayla tried to hand me. Food was the last thing on my mind. "You're going to Ashford's house."

"What? No."

"Don't argue with me." I shoved my wallet into my pocket.

"But our plan was that I'd stay here while you were at work."

"That was before. I can't leave you alone."

"If I go to Ashford's, it's more likely someone will notice I'm in Silver Ridge. I don't need Ashford to babysit me. If I have to be cooped up, I'd rather be here."

"I don't have time, sweetheart. I just need you to listen." Keys. Where were my keys?

She scowled. "You have an alarm system. I'll be fine. I'm not a child. Just go, alright? Get to Piper's."

I didn't want to argue with her. Didn't want either of us to lose our tempers right now. I pulled her in and kissed her forehead roughly. Spotted my keys on the counter and grabbed them. "Stay inside," I commanded as I strode out the door.

As I slammed the SUV door shut and put the engine in gear, I realized I hadn't said I loved her. That would just have to wait until later.

I called Susan. "On my way to Piper's," I said without preamble. "Talk to me. What do I need to know?"

"I'm here at her place. Got here a couple minutes ago."

"Shouldn't you be off shift by now?"

"Yes, Chief, but Seth Duncan didn't show up for work today."

I cursed. "Is he sick again?"

"I don't know. He didn't answer anyone's calls. I was about to go check on him, but then Piper's 911 call came in. Now I'm working a double, but that's fine. Luckily I put my big-girl panties on last night before I went to work."

I was grateful for that too. Thank goodness for Susan.

"Officer Bradley is with Piper, getting an initial statement. She and Ollie are shaken up, but I'm sure it'll help when you get here. Chief, I think it was the same guy." Her voice had lowered. "The vandal. Left a red flower spray-painted on the side of the house."

I'd already suspected it was him, but the confirmation had my pulse in overdrive. "I'm almost there."

Red flowers. That reminded me of the red daisies in the flower arrangements Paul had sent Ayla. An eerie similarity, but it couldn't possibly be anything more than a coincidence. Right?

As I sped down the road, I radioed the station. I made sure the officer on the front desk contacted Sheriff Douglas's task force to inform them about the link to the string of vandalisms.

We were going to need the regional crime scene techs. Every officer and deputy the sheriff could spare. Not because the latest victim was my sister, but because the guy had once again struck while the homeowner was there asleep. And he'd changed his M.O. Not just hitting rural areas, but a denser neighborhood.

Another escalation. He was getting more reckless. All the more likely he would get violent.

He'd been inside the house with my sister and nephew.

Fuck.

When I pulled up to the curb, Susan had created a perimeter and was speaking to a couple of Piper's neighbors. I threw my door open, not bothering to turn off my flashers. My boots hit the ground hard, and I charged toward the house.

Then I saw it. Looping red spray paint. A roughly drawn flower. Where the paint had dripped down the siding, it looked like blood.

FORTY-TWO

Ayla

I WANTED to call Teller to find out how Piper was doing. He'd been so stressed out when he left. Not that I could blame him.

But he'd seemed angry with me. Did he regret that I was here?

Stay inside, he'd ordered. As if I would've done anything else. I usually like his protectiveness, but I didn't appreciate him speaking to me like I was exasperating him.

Like I was a burden.

After I made sure the alarm was set and every door was locked, I tried lying down in Teller's bedroom. But I couldn't stay still. So I got up and paced the carpet.

Ugh, it was awful that someone had broken into Piper's home. I wished there was something I could do. But I also suspected that Teller's guilt about taking care of his sister and Ollie had reared its ugly head. He didn't want my help. Didn't want me to cause *trouble.*

You're more trouble than it's worth.

"Stop," I said into the silence.

Teller was upset, with good reason, but he loved me. We loved each other. Nothing would change that. Not even our first real fight as a couple.

My phone rang, and my heart leaped, hoping it was Teller.

But it was someone else. Someone who made my head pound just looking at his name.

You're kidding me.

Paul Ruxton was calling. What on earth could he have to say to me?

Well...maybe it would be useful to talk to the man. Just so I could ask where he'd gotten the old photo of me, because that still nagged at my mind. And the thing with the red daisies.

Better yet, I could record this call. I had an app for that on my phone, considering the calls I sometimes received from reporters. There were laws about recording people in California. Something Cheryl had mentioned to me. But I wasn't in California right now, so I wasn't going to worry about that.

I opened the app, then hit the record button before answering. "Paul?"

"*Ayla*. Thank you for picking up." He sounded out of breath.

"You're lucky I didn't block your number." I paced across Teller's bedroom carpet again, stopping to look at the trees through the window. "I should have, after what you've done."

"Please. I need to talk to you. In person."

"No, you need to answer my questions. First of all, what the *hell* is wrong with you?"

"I don't know. I screwed up. I realize that."

I almost laughed. "You stalked me."

"No! It wasn't real. You know that, right? I wasn't stalking you."

"You sent me those emails. You said you were watching me."

"But I swear Ayla, the whole time I was trying to help."

He was even more despicable and clueless than I'd thought. The man cared about no one but himself. "Which part was helping me? Where you invented a stalker to mess with my head? Or where you planned to use that to get me to sleep with you?"

"If you would let me explain. Do you realize how badly this is fucking over my career? Cheryl called my father. He *fired me* from Ruxton Records. His own son."

"Good. That's what you deserve." Actually, I was impressed. Not enough to stay with the label. But maybe I wouldn't trash Ruxton Records in the media.

"Look, I get that you're pissed off. But you'd be smart to sit down with me and hear me out. You don't even know what's really going on."

I shook my head. "Yeah, I thought I could do this, but I was wrong. You can talk to my lawyers."

"Just give me a chan—"

I hung up, feeling sick to my stomach. That asshole. I hadn't even gotten to my real questions, but what was the point? Why should I believe anything Paul said?

Just talking to him made me feel gross.

I went out to the kitchen. Poured a glass of water. Then I heard a knock at the front door. A shadow crossed the windows.

"Ayla!"

Oh, no. No way.

Paul was outside. *Here*.

My heart rate skyrocketed. Dashing out of the kitchen, I made sure he couldn't see me from the front windows or the door. I didn't know what to do. My first instinct was to call Teller. But he was already busy taking care of Piper. He would completely crash out if he learned Paul was here. Piper needed her brother right now. I wasn't the only person who mattered in Teller's life.

My phone rang. Paul again.

"*Think*," I said to myself.

Should I call Ashford or Callum? Was that even necessary? The alarm was set, and the doors were locked. Paul wasn't the type to break a window or kick his way inside. He was a record producer, nowhere near the size or strength of someone like Teller or Bryan.

And why should I call a man to come save me, anyway? Last time, I'd gotten away from Paul with a well-placed knee to his groin. I could handle him myself.

When Paul's number rang on my phone again, I answered,

pressing my back to one side of the hallway. "What are you doing?" I asked through gritted teeth.

"I told you I want to talk in person. That's why I'm here. I know you're inside Landry's house."

"What makes you think that?"

"I bribed one of the security guards who works at your house in Malibu. Cost me ten thousand dollars."

My eyes closed. *Please tell me it wasn't Bryan.*

"The guy said you and your boyfriend had both left LA, and it wasn't that hard to guess you'd run off with him to Colorado. That's what you do, Ayla. When shit gets bad, you run to that small town. Not that hard to figure out."

Perhaps he had a point there.

"I flew in last night." Paul was talking loudly enough I could hear the drone of his voice both through the phone and out on the porch. "You're not the only one with access to a private jet. Which won't last long with my father threatening to cut me off completely. I drove here in a rental and waited down the road. I was about to try calling you. Then I saw Landry drive off in his police car with the lights on."

"I'm not at his house. I'm with my brother-in-law."

"Liar. I saw you through the window when you ran out of his kitchen. You're hiding."

I cursed under my breath.

"I just want to talk, okay? Please. I'm begging here. I came all this way. Just let me explain some things, and you'll see..."

"What. What will I see?"

"That I made a mistake, but I'm not that bad of a guy." He knocked on the front door again. "I have information that you'll want."

I scoffed. "And you think you can trade something for it, is that it?"

"Pretty much. Open the door, and I'll tell you. You'll definitely want to know this. It's important."

Temptation whispered at the back of my mind. What if he really knew something? Was it about the old photo of me?

But there was absolutely no way I'd give Paul what he wanted. I wished I could march outside and knee him in the balls again. Then break his nose. He was stronger than me, though. I didn't have a gun or the training to use one.

There was only one real choice. "I'm going to call the police." Maybe another officer would respond, and Teller could stay with his sister.

"*No*! No, no, no, just let me speak, okay? I'll tell you. You have a real stalker, Ayla, but it wasn't me. I never sent the flowers in Toronto! Do you hear me? I never sent those."

I froze, my finger hovering over the *End Call* button. Between the phone speaker and his voice on the porch, I could still hear Paul clearly.

"Cheryl told me about the flowers and what the card said. Yes, I sent the emails calling myself Biggest Fan," he went on. "But I just borrowed the name."

I lifted the phone to my ear again. "Why? Why would you do that?"

"To stop you from making another stupid decision. You went off the rails a couple years ago, and then your last album flopped. I was supposed to mastermind your big comeback. The return of Ayla Maxwell to the top of the charts. You'd gotten those creepy flowers before, so I decided to capitalize on that."

"But why send the email when I was in Silver Ridge for the wedding?"

"Because Cheryl and I were both worried you wouldn't come back from Colorado. That place has some kind of hold on you. That's why Cheryl and I both came there to get you. I just took it a step further. I thought...I guess I thought if you were afraid of a stalker, you'd be more willing to do what we asked."

"More willing to fall into your arms, you mean." My stomach twisted. I wanted to retch. "Then you sent more flowers. And that disgusting photo yesterday with Teller's eyes blacked out. You're pathetic."

"I didn't send any of the flowers. That's what I'm trying to tell you. None of them. I only sent the two emails. And the second one was only because I panicked at the event the other night."

"Why should I believe you?"

"I fucking swear, Ayla. On my grave and, like, my bank account."

Wow. Under different circumstances, I would've laughed. Paul was truly a shining example of the worst LA had to offer. He'd sent the emails from Biggest Fan to swoop in and play my hero, just like Teller had thought. As if Paul could be a hero to anyone except in his own mind.

But if he was telling the truth, if Paul hadn't sent those flowers, then...

Who?

"Shit," Paul said. "You really called the cops on me? Is that your boyfriend, here to attack me again just for trying to tell you the truth?"

What was he talking about?

I emerged from the hallway and looked through one of the front windows. A police SUV had just driven up the driveway. But that wasn't Teller behind the wheel.

The vehicle's brakes squealed as it stopped. The driver's door flew open.

An officer I'd never seen before jumped out, a hand on his gun holster. He was young, early twenties, with messy light-brown hair. A Silver Ridge PD uniform. He approached the porch. "Sir, can you identify yourself?"

Paul shifted from foot to foot. "I was just trying to talk to her!"

"Were you harassing Miss Maxwell?"

Had Teller sent this officer here to watch over me? I wasn't surprised.

Annoyance rose briefly inside me. I'd told Teller I didn't need a babysitter.

But...okay, I did need help getting rid of Paul. I'd been about to call the police anyway.

Quickly, I disabled the home security system and opened the front door, stepping outside onto the porch in my bare feet. "Paul was just leaving, Officer..."

I looked at his name badge. *Officer Duncan.*

"I've met an Officer Duncan before. Are you related to him?" But this guy looked nothing like the officer I'd met on my last trip to Silver Ridge. The same day Teller had arrested me. That man had wire-rimmed glasses. Seth, I remembered. Officer Seth Duncan.

The officer suddenly drew his gun and pointed it at Paul. Paul lifted his hands, shouting.

A gunshot rang out.

I stared in utter shock as Paul collapsed. Blood spread beneath his head. It had all happened so fast. My brain couldn't catch up.

Then the officer pointed the gun at me, and his hard expression faltered.

"Ayla Hopkins. I've been waiting a long, long time for this."

FORTY-THREE

Teller

"WE'RE OVER HERE!" Piper was standing near the back of her house with my officers. Ollie ran toward me the moment he saw me, and I scooped him up as we collided. He put his arms around my neck, tight enough to choke me. Dropped his face to hide it like a little kid.

"You're okay, bud," I said softly. "I'm here now."

I felt an ache of longing for Ayla too. I hated that I'd left her with those harsh words on my lips instead of I-love-yous. As soon as I had a spare moment, I would send her a text.

But I had to do my job right now. Not just as a brother and uncle, but as Chief Landry.

While carrying Ollie, I went over to Piper. She hugged us both. "Hang out with Officer Nichols a few minutes?" I asked Ollie, nodding at Susan. "You remember her. I'm just going to chat with your mom."

Reluctantly, Ollie let go of me. But Susan asked about his favorite superheroes, and that helped. She'd had three boys of her own who were grown.

That left me and Piper to chat quietly. "What happened?" My arm went around her shoulder. Her hair was up in a messy ponytail, and she wore a sweatshirt over her flannel pajamas.

"I woke a little after seven. Went to Ollie's room to get him up and ready for school. Like normal. When I got to the living room, I saw the back door was open." She pressed a hand to her mouth, eyes filling with tears. "Muddy shoe prints on the floor. Somebody had been inside. He picked the lock. We didn't hear a thing."

"What about your security system?"

She shook her head. "I don't always turn it on. I'm sorry. Ollie's set off so many false alarms going outside if he wakes up before me, and..."

"Hey, I know. It's okay. Any windows broken? Things missing?"

"No. But the intruder could've... Teller, he could've done *anything*."

Acid rioted in my stomach. "Let's check your cameras." Even if the alarm hadn't been armed, she had cameras on the exterior perimeter. I'd made sure of that when I helped her set up the system.

A check of the footage revealed a man of average height and build, wearing a bulky black jacket, a black balaclava over his face, and wraparound sunglasses. Gloves too. The guy had been careful. There was nothing identifiable about him. Not yet, anyway. The crime scene techs would get images of the shoe prints.

The vandal hadn't spent much time here. Hadn't risked making a lot of noise. It was like he'd simply wanted to cause terror. Prove what he *could've* done. And leave his spray-painted signature.

Like a taunt. Not just at Piper. But at the police.

While Officer Bradley, one of my reliable veterans on the force, interviewed neighbors, Susan and I took Piper and Ollie to the station. Sheriff Douglas had sent over one of his trusted deputies, Keira Marsh, to help out. She worked for the sheriff's office in Hartley, but Deputy Marsh was a Silver Ridge resident herself.

After I gave her an update, Deputy Marsh volunteered to play board games with Ollie in our break room. A huge relief. We couldn't have him running around the station. After Piper was done with her interviews, she joined in the game. I made sure they had food and warm drinks and then returned to my own office.

When I had a few minutes, I sent Ayla a quick text.

I love you. Piper and Ollie are okay. I'm at the station working. Let me know if you need anything?

She didn't read the message or write back immediately. I didn't know if she was frustrated with me over the way I'd spoken to her earlier. Or maybe she'd gone back to sleep.

But I had an app for my home security system on my phone. Did it constitute spying on her if I looked at it?

I decided I didn't care. A quick check of the app showed the security system was activated. *Good*. Ayla was fine.

After chatting more with Piper and some group texts, we all decided that Piper and Ollie would stay in Emma and Ashford's guest room tonight. I'd offered my own spare room, but Piper and Emma agreed that the kids would have fun together. And Piper wanted to stay close to the coffee shop. Keep things as normal as possible until repairs were finished at her place.

There. At least that was taken care of.

I checked my message thread with Ayla again. She still hadn't read my text. Shit, she really was mad at me, wasn't she?

Susan knocked on my office door, which was partway open already. "Chief? Can we talk a minute?"

"Of course." I put my phone away.

Susan came in and shut the door. "I tried calling Seth Duncan again. Still no answer, which is odd. Usually when he's sick, he at least picks up the phone or responds to texts."

"Maybe it's just one of those days," I said, thinking of how Ayla hadn't written me back either. "Spring pollen season messing with people?" I joked.

"Yeah, I know I was harping on that before. But this might be more. Finn Mackie didn't come in for his dispatch shift, and the dispatchers had to scramble to cover for him. And Finn lives next door to Seth."

"Right." I'd known that. They'd both been newcomers to Silver Ridge in the last year. Finn had moved here for his first job out of college, while Seth came to join my department as a second career. He'd been an accountant before deciding to pursue law enforcement.

They'd been an odd pairing as friends. But neither of them had any family in town.

"So, you think they're both sick?" I asked.

She nodded. "Finn isn't answering his phone either. It's got all my instincts screaming. Something ain't right, Chief. I'm sure of it."

We didn't need this today. A serious illness going around?

"We can head over there and do a welfare check," I suggested.

"Exactly what I was thinking."

Finn and Seth didn't live too far. A ten-minute drive. They each had a small bungalow in a row of them. I'd driven, and I pulled my department vehicle up to the curb out front. Susan and I got out.

She rang Seth's bell. Opened his metal screen door and knocked on the wood. "Seth? It's Susan. You in there?"

Nothing.

She glanced at me, worry creasing her forehead.

We went around to the back and did the same. Knocking and calling out. Same lack of response. The windows around the house were closed, so we couldn't see inside.

"Try the back door," I suggested. "Maybe it's unlocked." Which would be odd for a police officer, but this was still a small town. And Seth had been behaving strangely.

Susan pushed the door handle. It opened.

Officer Duncan's body lay prone on the tile, arm reaching like he'd been going for the door.

"Oh, dear lord," Susan muttered. "Oh, Seth."

I glanced inside. That was enough to confirm that no medical attention would fix this. Not much smell, no insect activity. Probably happened within the last several hours.

I shut the door. It was important now that we not destroy any evidence. "Looks like a GSW. Get started on securing the scene. I'll call it in. We're going to need to contact the district attorney and the CIRT." The regional Critical Incident Response Team, since this involved the death of an officer. Looked like he'd been shot in the head. We'd need the coroner and the state CSI team as well.

Her wide eyes pinned me. "But Chief, what about Finn?"

Hell. We had to check on him too. My pulse roared in my eardrums as I imagined what else we might find.

My personal phone rang. It was River. I didn't have time right now to find out what he wanted.

Then a text came in about a minute later. I yanked my phone out again.

RIVER

Need to speak with you. URGENT. News related to Roy Carpenter

Dammit, why was everything happening now?

"Chief?" Susan asked.

"Yeah, coming." I just didn't have time for River at the moment. A Silver Ridge dispatcher could be injured in his home. If Finn was still alive, we had to get him help.

We went next door. Knocked on Finn's front door, went around to the back. Same routine. "Finn? This is Chief Landry. Answer us if you're inside." But when we heard nothing, I wasn't going to mess around any longer.

"It's locked," Susan said, trying the knob.

"Stand back."

Susan and I both drew our weapons. I lifted my boot and kicked at the lock. It burst open. The door slammed against the doorstop, rattling.

No sign of anyone inside.

"Finn?" I shouted.

Susan and I made quick work of clearing the home. Nobody was here. Finn was gone.

I had about ten thousand calls to make. But River had said his news was urgent, and coming from a man like him—a former CIA operative—that meant something very serious.

He picked up on the first ring.

"Make it quick," I said. "I've got a major situation on my hands. Officer dead, likely murdered."

"I did some more digging into Sergeant Roy Carpenter and his family. He had a son. Jarod Carpenter. Jarod was still a minor at the time of his father's death. Had a few minor run-ins with the law. Then a few years afterward, his online presence vanished."

"River, *please*. Get to the point."

"Then I checked Jarod's mother's maiden name. It was Mackie. I just found a record of a name change, processed by a court in Colorado. Jarod Finnegan Carpenter's name is now Finn Mackie, and according to DMV records, he lives in Silver Ridge."

What. The. Fuck.

I was standing in Finn's kitchen. Susan ran into the room. "Chief, you need to see this."

"Landry?" River said through my phone, but I'd dropped it from my ear and held it at my side.

I couldn't breathe.

I followed Susan down the hall to Finn's bedroom, where I'd been a few minutes before to check for signs of him. The place was neat as a pin. Bed made, nothing out of place.

But then Susan opened Finn's closet door, and I got a better look at the photos decorating the inner surface of the wood.

So many photos.

Still images from Ayla Maxwell music videos. Paparazzi shots of Ayla from LA and other locales. Even from Silver Ridge. There were news articles about her. Tabloid pieces.

A photo of a teenaged Ayla, smiling at the camera. That had

to be the image she'd told me about. The one of her outside her father's house on the Army base.

But below them, I spotted photos of the sites that had been vandalized all around Hart County. The spray-painted red flowers. The broken windows.

"This is not normal," Susan said. "But I don't get it. What's it all about?"

The truth slammed into me.

"Finn is the vandal. And he knew Ayla when she was younger. He has some connection to Ayla's stalker."

"*What*?"

But I didn't see how it all fit together. It didn't make sense. "Secure the scene here and at Seth's place. We have to assume Finn could be a suspect in Seth's murder."

Susan gasped. "How on earth do you figure that? This looks bad, but—"

I strode toward the back door, lifting my phone again. "River? You there?"

"Yeah. I heard snippets. Enough. What do you need?"

I needed Ayla safe. I needed her in my arms right fucking now or I just might lose my mind.

"I'm heading to my house. Could you get to Silver Ridge? Bring anyone from Last Refuge that you can. Maybe you could call Sheriff Douglas for me too." I knew he and River were very close. "I'd do it myself, but—"

"Consider it done."

"We're about to have a manhunt on our hands. But Ayla—I left her at my place, I have to—and she hasn't been answering my messages—"

The words died in my chest along with my breath.

"Get to her," River said. "I'll be on the road as soon as possible."

The next few minutes were a blur. I sped toward my home, eyes more on my phone than on the road. Ayla still wasn't answering my calls.

I checked the app for my home security system. It was disabled now. The front door was open.

When I checked the live camera footage on the app, I nearly swerved off the road.

God, please, I prayed. *Please don't do this to me. No, no, no.*

My tires squealed as I tore up my driveway and hit the brakes. I threw my door open and flew toward the house.

Paul Ruxton lay in a pool of blood on my front porch. That was shocking enough, but I didn't have time to dwell on it. Jumping over him, I went through the open door and inside.

"Ayla!" I screamed. But she wasn't here.

The camera. I had to see what had happened.

With shaking fingers, I pulled up all the recordings from my doorbell camera from the last few hours.

I saw Paul Ruxton appear on the porch. Running his mouth and knocking, but Ayla didn't come outside.

Good, sweetheart, I thought, and kept watching. Listened to a little of what Paul said. That he'd never sent the flower arrangements. There was another stalker...

I skipped the footage forward. The camera showed one of my department's vehicles pulling up to the house. Finn Mackie got out, dressed in a uniform. Seth Duncan's uniform? Because Finn sure as hell wasn't a sworn officer himself. Then Ayla came outside, clearly believing it was safe.

With increasing horror, I watched as Finn shot Paul.

And then...

"No," I whispered. And fell to my knees.

I was in the middle of a nightmare, one far worse than anything I'd ever encountered. Worse than the day that IED had nearly killed me. Worse than all the pain that had followed.

He'd taken her.

FORTY-FOUR

Ayla

THE POLICE SUV's trunk was totally enclosed. Dark. I heard the wheels rolling over asphalt.

It smelled like metal and oil back here. There were doors to storage areas, maybe for police equipment or guns, but they were all locked tight. There was nothing in here I could use as a weapon or means of escape. I felt around for a latch to get out, but there was nothing. He'd taken my phone.

My breaths started to come faster. Shallower. I hated being cooped up like this. Trapped. Like the basement when I was a kid...

Teller, please find me. Thinking of him calmed me. I imagined his arms holding me tight.

All I could do was wait.

The SUV drove for a while. Enough time that I had nothing else but my thoughts and my imagination to keep me company.

This man had to be my real stalker, right? I assumed he wasn't actually named Duncan. But how had he gotten Officer Duncan's uniform?

At first, I'd refused to get in the trunk when the man ordered me. But the black circle of his gun's muzzle had been aimed at me.

The sharp smell of the previous shot that killed Paul lingered in the air.

His hands had shook as he held the gun. "*In the trunk, Ayla. I'd rather not hurt you, but if I have to...*"

So I'd done as he asked. I had to stay strong. Stay in one piece so I could fight back and escape.

Every one of my senses had been heightened as I climbed into the SUV's rear compartment. I was surprised my kidnapper didn't tie me up or handcuff me, but maybe he thought I'd be secure enough. He'd made me lie down, then closed the door.

Who was he?

He was young, early twenties. I racked my brain, trying to remember if I'd seen him in Silver Ridge before. At the station?

Yes, that had to be it. I'd seen him at the station the day Teller arrested me. Seth Duncan had come into the office to chat with me, but this younger man had been on the fringes. One of the onlookers when I walked through the station in cuffs.

He worked for Teller. Or at least, worked at the same building.

Then my kidnapper's features struck a deeper chord of recognition inside me, especially given my dream from just a couple nights ago.

The one of Sergeant Carpenter.

I realized, with a terrible sinking feeling, who my kidnapper reminded me of.

The SUV came to a stop, and the engine shut off. A door opened. Footsteps crunched over gravel. The door to the trunk lifted, and I blinked at the sunlight.

"We're here," he said. "Climb out."

I did what he asked, eager to be out of the dark and the stale air of the trunk. My bare feet hit the gravel. Ouch. "Where are we? Is this your house?"

He shook his head. "It's somewhere safe. Don't run. There's nowhere for you to go."

I tried for a smile. "But you said you don't want to hurt me."

"I don't. I'm not stupid, though. You can't trick me, okay?" His voice wavered, a contrast to his words.

Unlike Teller's home in the woods, this place was in a valley with open meadows of grass all around. No other buildings in sight. The home itself was a classic farmhouse style. Cream-colored siding, a large porch. It looked deserted.

A huge blotch of red spray paint marred the side of the house, like a wound. A looping abstract flower.

I turned back to my kidnapper, studying his features. Was I right? Was this really the boy I remembered from all those years ago?

I had one play. Should I use it now? Or wait until I was alone in that house with him? Then again, the thought of going inside with him had me nauseous. I had no idea what he wanted from me.

"I know who you are," I said softly. "Jarod."

His eyes shone, the gun sagging in his grip. "You...you remember?"

"I do now."

The boy next door who I used to babysit. I hadn't seen him since he was twelve years old. Had barely even thought of him.

I saw the resemblance now. Jarod reminded me of his father, Sergeant Carpenter, but with features I'd once believed were innocent and kind.

So carefully, I took a step toward him. Tears pressed at my throat, welled in my eyes. "Jarod, I don't understand any of this. Whatever it's about, we can figure it out. Please. We can talk. But you have to put down the—"

"*No.*" He raised the gun, aiming it at my chest. "I'll tell you everything. But only after we go inside."

Dammit. I really had no choice.

He gestured for me to go first. I walked toward the house. My eyes stuck on the spray-painted flower. "Did you do that, Jarod? The graffiti? The vandalisms?"

"You know about that?" He scoffed. "Of course you do. *He* told you, didn't he? The chief."

"Jarod, why would you do it? You scared people." I tried to keep my tone steady and mildly disappointed, like I was still his babysitter, and he'd simply broken a house rule. Like I hadn't seen him murder Paul right in front of me a half hour ago.

"They weren't safe on their own, Ayla. I had to show them how easily someone awful could come and hurt them."

Someone as awful as you? I wanted to say. But I couldn't risk making him angry.

"You mean the women?" I asked. "They were home alone, so they weren't safe?"

"Like you were alone back on the base when we were kids. Of all people, you should understand what I was trying to do."

I wanted to scream at him. Tell him this was all madness. But he had a gun pointed at my back.

I led the way inside the house.

The interior was warm, lovingly cared-for. There were baby bottles on the drying rack by the sink, a high chair at the kitchen table. A family lived here. But from the lack of any other cars outside, it seemed like they'd left. Or...*oh, please tell me Jarod didn't hurt them*. I hoped they'd left because of the vandalism.

"Keep going," Jarod said. "The door up there on the left."

I reached the door. Opened it. A rough wooden staircase led down into darkness. Stark walls. An unfinished basement.

"No," I whispered. "Not down there."

"Ayla, go." The muzzle of the gun nudged my back. "This is important."

"But my father used to lock me in the basement in the dark." Panic started to claw at my throat. I wasn't claustrophobic, but I still couldn't stand being trapped. And down there, in an actual basement? "Please."

"I know. You told me about that a long time ago. You used to trust me, remember?" He reached to flick the light switch. "See? It's not dark anymore."

"But I don't want to."

The gun pressed harder into my back. "You won't be alone for long. Wait for me down there. And before you know it, I'll come to you. We can finally be together. Like we were always supposed to be."

FORTY-FIVE

Teller

Half an hour after I'd discovered Ayla was missing, I sat in a conference room at Silver Ridge PD with a hum of activity around me.

I could not afford to let myself fall apart.

Personnel had flooded the station. We had two murder investigations underway, that of Seth Duncan and Paul Ruxton. A kidnapped woman who happened to be a world-famous celebrity. A manhunt for the suspect, Finn, one of our own dispatchers. Someone who knew our procedures well.

And no leads.

I'd found Ayla's cell phone discarded on my driveway. Finn's appeared to be off. No way to track them using cell towers.

Ayla, I'm so sorry. I dug my fingers into my hair, yanking at the short strands. *I swear I'm going to find you.*

I'd been on and off the phone almost constantly. Calling in every officer from every nearby department. State authorities. The DA. Some of my reinforcements had arrived, while others were speeding toward Silver Ridge. Several people were already tacking up all the info we had onto a board here in the conference room.

I stared at each piece of evidence, yet none of it gave me the answer I needed.

We'd already run a trace on Officer Duncan's department vehicle. The GPS tracker had been disabled. I had no idea where Finn Mackie—Jarod Carpenter—had taken Ayla. They couldn't have gotten very far yet. But Hart County was a big place.

Where would he take her? Where would he hide?

Finn had to know he'd be the top suspect in the murders and the kidnapping. What did he have planned for Ayla? What would he do to her?

When I thought of him hurting her, it was like being flayed alive. Like someone was tearing the skin from my body.

I had to get my shit together. Falling apart wasn't going to bring Ayla home.

My personal phone rang, and I glanced at the screen. Ashford O'Neal. Piper and Ollie had gone over to his place, and I'd already confirmed they were secure. He had to be calling about Ayla.

I was surprised he, Callum, and Dane hadn't stormed the station by now demanding to know what was happening. We hadn't made any public statements about Finn Mackie's one-man crime wave or Ayla going missing. But this was Silver Ridge. Word would spread fast that shit was going down.

I had to let Ashford's call go to voicemail. I would check it in a moment, just to see if he had anything important. But otherwise, there was nothing he could do. If I'd needed somebody's ass kicked, Ashford could've handled it with his martial arts skills. But this was a police operation.

When I spoke to Ashford next, it would be to tell him Ayla was safe.

Then Susan tapped on my shoulder. I hadn't even noticed she had entered the conference room. "Chief, Sheriff Douglas just arrived, along with some friends of his. River Kwon and Aiden Shelborne?"

"Take them to my office. I'll be right there."

After a few more words to the people in the conference room, I strode to my office. Three large men waited inside.

"Chief Landry." Sheriff Owen Douglas wore his signature

cowboy hat. He held out his hand. "I'm so sorry. River and Aiden filled me in." They stood behind the sheriff, nodding at me in sympathy.

"Owen's deputized us," River said. "I usually love when that happens, but these are not the kind of circumstances I would call fun."

"Riv, *please* shut your yap for once," Aiden muttered.

The sheriff ignored them. "Deputy Keira Marsh was already keeping me posted on the break-in at your sister's. Is it true you suspect the same guy of kidnapping Ayla? One of your dispatchers, the same guy River was investigating for you?"

I quickly updated them on everything else we knew. It sounded worse the more I repeated it. Finding Seth Duncan's body. Then the horrifying shrine to Ayla in Finn's closet, along with the photos of the vandalism scenes.

The red flowers had been the link all along. Though I still couldn't begin to fathom Finn's motivations for everything he'd done.

All this time, Ayla's true stalker had been here. Working in my building. A man I'd taken under my wing. Sharing laughs, coffee breaks...

"He's taken Ayla somewhere," I said. "Finn has no family in Hart County. He was driving Officer Duncan's vehicle, not his own. He'll know we've put out an APB and that state patrol will be looking for him. So he must've holed up somewhere."

Sheriff Douglas nodded. "Just tell us what we can do."

Having the sheriff and the guys from Hartley here reminded me of all the assets I had at my disposal.

Ayla, sweetheart, I'm coming for you.

"I need your eyes," I said.

I took them to the conference room. We went over the evidence yet again. Step by step. There had to be some clue. Some small hint of where Finn would go.

But it was Officer Susan Nichols who gasped, finally making the connection we needed.

"Chief. I have an idea. You remember Donna Zanetti? The young mom whose husband was out of town, and the vandal struck her place about a month ago."

"Of course." I thought of sitting with Donna and her baby at their kitchen table. "That was the first time he'd broken into the home instead of just vandalizing the outside."

Finn had done that. It was still a shock to imagine.

The break-in at Donna's had been just a couple of weeks after Emma and Ashford's wedding weekend. Had Finn heard the rumors about me and Ayla? Had he been jealous, and that was why he'd escalated? But why strike out at an innocent woman like Donna?

"Well, I spoke to Donna last week," Susan said. "I was checking in on her, making sure she was doing okay. She said she'd been having trouble sleeping, and her family was going away for a while. They took off over the weekend. Finn could've heard about that. He might be drawn back there. We know suspects are often compelled to return to the scenes of previous crimes."

"Seems worth a check," Sheriff Douglas said. River nodded along.

"I agree." Then I remembered a certain feature of Donna's home. I'd seen it when I was there after the vandalism.

An unfinished basement. A cellar, really. Not uncommon around here.

But Ayla's home in New York had one too, when she'd lived next door to the Carpenters. Maybe... Could that have reminded Finn of his former home, when Ayla was his neighbor?

"That's it. Susan, you're a damn miracle."

"I am?"

I jumped up, heading for the door. "I need as many people as we can mobilize in the next five minutes."

FORTY-SIX

Ayla

THERE WAS a washing machine and dryer down here. A set of heavy dumbbells and a workout bench. Not much else. My lungs constricted from being trapped in this small space. The damp smell was too familiar.

Terrible memories surfaced in my mind.

Teller, please find me, I thought for the thousandth time. *Please hurry.*

I heard the floor creaking upstairs. Jarod was up there, but what was he doing? I had no idea when he'd come down here. Or what he had planned.

Could I pick up one of the dumbbells, wait for him to step into the room, then knock him out? But wouldn't he see that coming?

My eyes scanned the small basement. Looking for a tool maybe, anything small I could hide in my clothes and use as a weapon. But the place was stripped clean.

After a while, the door at the top of the steps opened. "Ayla? It's me. I'm coming down." He'd spoken as if this was a normal visit. But then he paused on the steps, the gun pointing down. "Come to where I can see you. Show me your hands."

I stepped into the light coming from the exposed bulb. Held out my open palms. I hadn't found anything, anyway.

The stairs creaked as Jarod made his way down. He'd changed out of Officer Duncan's uniform. His hair was damp like he'd showered. Like he'd wanted to look nice for me.

"I've been waiting so long for this," he said, repeating his words from earlier.

I backed up against the wall, while Jarod sat on the bench, still pointing the gun at me. At least he didn't make me sit next to him. "What do you want?" I asked.

His gaze slowly moved over me from head to foot. "You said you wanted to talk. Let's start there."

The bitter taste of bile hit my tongue. "You sent the flowers to me in Toronto, didn't you? With that old photo of me."

He nodded. "Lori gave me a copy of the photo. That was after you'd left. I missed you so much. The night that it all happened, when my dad tried to kiss you..."

"You knew about that?"

"I snuck out when he walked you home. I'd seen the way he looked at you. The way he looked at other girls around the base. I didn't trust him. I saw him try to kiss you, and you hit him. That was so badass."

A smile lit Jarod's face. He looked so normal. I could imagine how he'd managed to fool everyone in Silver Ridge, pretending he wasn't unhinged.

"But then, when you went inside, your dad was yelling at you. Saying all those terrible things. I'm so sorry, Ayla. I wanted to do something, *anything*, to help you. But I was just a kid. I was scared."

A tear streaked down my cheek. I wiped it quickly away. Maybe it would gain more sympathy from Jarod if I cried, but I had to hold them back. Keep my strength. *Focus.*

"I watched you through your bedroom window afterward," he continued. "I saw you packing a bag. I knew you were leaving, and I wanted to go with you. Ran home to pack a bag of my own.

But my dad caught me. He made me stay in my room, and I fell asleep. By the time I woke up and got back to your house the next day, you were already gone. I tried calling your phone, but you didn't answer."

"I left it behind."

"Yeah. You had to leave a lot of things behind. I was in love with you back then. I even gave you that bouquet of daisies on your birthday. I left them on your porch. I was too nervous to do it in person."

Jarod looked so sad and small. Like the twelve-year-old I'd once taken care of. And yeah, I did recall letting some things slip. Confiding in him a little when I was really upset after my dad was awful to me.

But I'd had no idea about his feelings for me. I'd thought his father Sergeant Carpenter left the birthday bouquet. I should've known the man wasn't that thoughtful.

"I was heartbroken when you left," Jarod went on. "I didn't blame you, though. I blamed *myself*, for not being able to stand up for you. Nobody stood up for you. Your mom had left. Lori was always off with her friends. You were alone. That's why my dad thought he could kiss you. And why your dad thought he could treat you the way he did."

I crossed my arms, hugging my middle. "I did feel alone. But I went to New York City and made something of myself."

"I know. When I first heard your music and saw your picture and realized it was *you*, I was so proud of you. You'd turned out okay. I was happy for you." His expression darkened. "But then a couple years ago, everything fell apart for you. You suspended your tour. Ran away from that rehab facility. I realized you were still lost. As lost as *I* felt. You needed my help."

My skin crawled.

"At first, I tried contacting you on your social media. But you never responded. I guess my voice got drowned out by all the other people wanting your attention. I was taking some college classes already, so I got a transfer to a school in Denver. My plan was to move here, to Hart County. Silver Ridge. So I'd be closer to you."

"I've never heard of a Jarod Carpenter living in Silver Ridge, though."

"Because I changed my name. I'm Finn Mackie now. I..." He glanced guiltily to the side. "I had some issues back on the east coast. Misunderstandings. Some women thought I was following them around, watching them. After I got to Colorado, I filed the paperwork to take my Mom's last name. And switch my middle name to my first."

So he'd had a history of stalking. Not remotely surprising.

"Then late last year, I saw the job opening for a dispatcher in Silver Ridge. I applied. It was so perfect. And I thought it was time to reach out to you in a way you couldn't overlook."

"You sent the flower arrangement to my concert venue last fall."

"I didn't want to tip my hand just yet. Just...get your attention. Get you thinking about your old life and people you used to know. That's why I included the photo."

The words of the message played out in my memory. *You have no idea how beautiful you really are. I've always been your biggest fan.*

"And the red daisies?" I asked.

"I picked an arrangement that had them. So you might guess it was me. I had this fantasy that when you finally saw me in Silver Ridge on one of your visits, you'd recognize me. You'd remember everything. You'd know, right then, how much you meant to me. But you didn't." He squeezed the gun, fingers going white. "Chief Landry brought you into the station after that street brawl, and I smiled at you, and you looked right through me."

Dread seeped into my veins. "It wasn't on purpose."

"But it still hurt. That weekend, I sent flowers to the Last Refuge Inn using the wedding florist. No card that time. Picked another arrangement with daisies, and I thought that was message enough." He rubbed his free hand against his navy pants, scowling. "Wanted you to know I wasn't giving up. We were meant to be together."

"But you've also been vandalizing houses around Hart County for months."

"Because of the *pressure*," he shouted.

I cringed, flattening myself against the wall.

"I was sitting around, waiting for you to come to Silver Ridge and notice me. I wanted *someone* to notice me. Women would call 911, and I'd get to help them. Make them feel better. When I realized how many women around the county were alone all the time, I knew I had to do something. I didn't ever hurt them. Just scared them, so they would know how dangerous it was to be all alone."

Chills made me tremble. The innocent kid I'd once babysat was gone. Finn Mackie was truly twisted.

There was no reasoning with him. I had to get out of here.

"I heard about you and Chief Landry. You thought you had a stalker, and you turned to *him* for help. I heard him talking to you in his office at night when I passed by. Then he took off last weekend, and I knew in my gut he was going to see you in California. It wasn't right. You were supposed to be *mine*."

"You sent the flowers to my house in Malibu with Teller's picture."

"I was warning you!" Spit flew from his mouth. "He's not good enough."

So much of it was becoming clear to me. Paul's stupid emails, calling himself Biggest Fan, just distracted us. It didn't seem like Jarod even knew about the fake stalker emails.

"You broke into Piper's house last night, didn't you? Was that to draw Teller away? How did you even know I was in Silver Ridge? We told almost no one."

"It was because of Seth Duncan. He lived next door to me. We were friends. But after you came to town last time and he got to meet you, he acted obsessed with you. Always looking at your social media and going on about your music. Joined one of your fan groups online. It was embarrassing."

Did he even hear how he sounded? Obviously not. If he'd held on to his grip with reality for the last several months, it had to be broken now.

"Seth was good with computer stuff. He managed to set up access to the internal network for Silver Ridge PD at his house. He was able to look up the GPS trackers for department vehicles, and he tracked Chief Landry's. Seth knew the chief had gone to the private airport, and then he saw when the chief's vehicle headed back to Silver Ridge. There's a dashboard cam installed. He caught a glimpse of you yesterday when you walked in front of the SUV. That's how I knew for sure you were back in town."

"You were wearing Officer Duncan's uniform."

Jarod shrugged. His rage had subsided again. "It was time for me to make my move. Seth didn't deserve to know so much about you. He annoyed me too. Always sick all the time. I got rid of him during the night. Went and broke in at Piper's place, so Chief Landry would go there to be with his sister. And I put on Seth's uniform, took his police vehicle, and went to get you. I figured you'd come with me if you thought I was a police officer. If you thought Landry had sent me."

"But Paul was already at my house."

"You mean the record producer guy? I'd seen him in photos with you. Just another creep who wanted to hurt you. I was happy to get rid of him for you. All those other men just want to use you. I'm the only one who really loves you, Ayla. The only one who really knows you."

Jarod stood up from the bench. Started toward me.

"Don't," I said.

"You and I belong together. We'll hide out here, and then we can run away. Like you did before, but the two of us together this time. This is how it was always supposed to be. You and me." He held out the hand that wasn't holding the gun.

"But I don't want this, Jarod." This was my last, desperate hope that somehow he'd listen. "I want to decide my future for myself. Please let me go."

Anger flared in his eyes. He had no intention of ever setting me free.

He took another step toward me.

With a scream, I lunged at him. Grabbed for the wrist holding his gun and pushed it up to aim at the ceiling, while I slammed my knee hard into his groin. The gun went off. Using all my weight, I shoved Jarod back against the stand holding the dumbbells. He flew backward, his head hitting the edge of the washing machine.

My ears were ringing from the gunshot. Jarod had dropped the gun, but I couldn't see where it had gone. He was lying on the ground. Writhing like he was in pain.

I just had to get out of there.

Blood rushed in my ears as my feet pounded on the basement steps. I slammed the door to the basement closed, then grabbed a chair and tried to wedge it beneath the doorknob. No idea if that would hold, but it was the best I could do.

Scanning the kitchen, I looked for the keys to the SUV. But I didn't see them. Shit, they were probably downstairs in his pocket.

Run, my instincts told me. *Just get away.*

I couldn't stay another minute inside this house. But I spotted a knife block on the counter. I grabbed a long black handle. Steel glinted.

I charged through the front door. The gravel stung my bare feet. Holding on to the knife, I sprinted toward a grove of trees.

Then I realized what I was doing. Running and hiding, once again. Like I had done so many times before. I no longer blamed myself. I had done the best I could, and Teller had helped me to see that.

But right now, I had a choice.

It was time to *fight*.

I had to be smart about it, though. Going back inside and confronting Jarod was a bad idea. No, I had to take advantage of the element of surprise. Like he had done when he'd shown up disguised as a policeman earlier.

Instead of the grove of trees, I looked around for a hiding place closer to the house. Where I could watch the front door. I figured Jarod would come that way, since I'd left it open.

There was a small shed to one side of the house. With my breaths loud in my ears, I ran toward it and opened the shed door by just a crack. He would think I'd gone inside.

There was a vibration in the air. Maybe a crash or a yell. Hard to decipher over the ringing in my ears. But it made my heart skip a beat.

He was coming.

My hair tossed as I searched for a place to wait. Where I'd be close enough to strike at the right moment. My gaze caught on a crawl space beneath the porch. It was in shadow.

I hurried to the crawl space and hunched over to get inside, disappearing into the shadows. My fist gripped the handle of the knife.

Jarod stumbled down the porch steps above me. "Ayla, get back here! You can't run from me!" The words were muffled, but I could make them out.

I edged back further as he walked into the yard. A gap between the porch steps gave me a view of him. Jarod had a red mark on his forehead where he'd smashed into the wall. He'd found the gun. It was in his hand again, held out in front of him. Finger on the trigger. His gaze flung left and right, looking for me.

Jarod spotted the shed. I flinched, afraid he'd see me back here, but he went for the door I'd left cracked open. Just as I'd expected. The shed shook as he threw the door wide.

Gripping the knife, I waited, about to dash out of my hiding spot. I planned to attack as soon as he stepped out of the shed.

But then the muffled sound of sirens reached my ears.

A half-dozen police vehicles swerved onto the driveway, coming in fast. They fanned out, stopping in a semi-circle in front of the house. Within seconds, doors had opened and guns emerged.

"Get down on the ground!"

"Put down the weapon!"

My heart raced. I searched for Teller's face and saw him. His vehicle had been the first to roar up the drive. Then his voice rang out, loud enough that I could hear every word.

"Jarod Carpenter. It's over. Where's Ayla?" Teller's words were harsh, each one raw with emotion.

There was a beat of silence, as if time had frozen. I couldn't move, just watching from the shadows beneath the porch.

Jarod put his gun to his head.

"No!" I cried. Dropping the knife in the dirt, I crawled out on my hands and knees. Emerged into the sunlight. "Jarod, don't. You don't have to do this. We can all walk away."

Jarod's gaze jerked toward me. The gun stayed aimed at his temple.

I knew I was being reckless. Teller would probably be furious with me later. But right now, all I saw was the twelve-year-old kid I'd used to babysit. Who'd left a bouquet of birthday flowers on my porch just to make me smile. Who'd comforted me and made me laugh when I was sad.

"It doesn't have to end like this," I said.

He started to lower the gun.

But a split second later, Jarod raised the weapon and aimed it at me.

Multiple gunshots rang out. Jarod's body convulsed. He took several steps back, arms flailing as spots of red appeared on his forehead and chest, and collapsed onto the porch stairs. His finger was still tangled on the trigger guard of his gun. But he hadn't fired.

"Ayla!"

Teller ran toward me. Scooped me into an embrace, tucking my face against his shoulder. There was too much noise. People suddenly surrounding us.

But I focused on the feeling of his heart beating against me. Like it was a beacon showing me the way back home.

FORTY-SEVEN

Teller

MORNING LIGHT CAUGHT in Ayla's hair, turning the strands to silver and pale gold.

I had been awake for a while, just watching her sleep in my bed.

Ayla was home safe. She had survived what happened with Jarod Carpenter. It had only been three days, and I knew from firsthand experience that true healing took longer.

Yet when Ayla stretched and opened her eyes this morning, she had a smile on her lips. "Hey," she whispered, voice hoarse from sleep.

I kissed her temple, running my fingers through her silky hair. "Morning."

Ayla shifted, rolling onto me, so I lay on my back and let her stretch out on top of me. We wrapped our arms around each other and held on tight. "I slept a little better that time," she said. "I actually feel rested."

"That's good."

We'd been up several times during the night. Ayla had been struggling with nightmares. Waking up crying and afraid.

And I'd shared every moment of her agony. Just trying to be here for her every time she reached for me.

"What about you?" she asked. "Did you sleep?"

"A little bit."

She propped her chin on my chest to look at me. "So, not at all."

I laughed softly. "I'm getting what I need."

When I had driven up to that farmhouse and seen Jarod alone with a gun in his hand, I'd thought the worst. That Ayla was gone. Those had been the worst few moments of my life.

And then she had stepped into view, trying to stop Jarod from ending his life. Showing mercy to the man who had terrorized her. Who had murdered two others.

I only wished that Jarod had listened to her. For Ayla's sake. But perhaps Jarod had known exactly what would happen.

By aiming at Ayla, he gave us no choice but to take him down.

I had no idea if the bullet I fired had killed Jarod. River was a sharpshooter, so he was likely responsible for the wound to the center of Jarod's forehead. The coroner's report would detail everything, but I hadn't read it. I wasn't being the chief right now. I'd been taking care of the woman I loved.

In the immediate aftermath of Jarod's death and Ayla's rescue, she had been to the hospital to get checked out. The doctors had said her hearing would return to normal within a week or two. Then she'd been interviewed by multiple officers to detail everything Jarod said and did. The truth about how he'd ended up in Silver Ridge. His motivations. As much as we were able to make sense of them based on what he'd told her.

I wasn't sure I could ever forgive myself for trusting Finn Mackie. Not seeing what was actually in front of me. But he'd managed to do an excellent job of hiding his true self, and I was far from the only person he'd fooled.

One of the brief times I'd been away from Ayla was to give my condolences to Seth Duncan's brother, who arrived the day before yesterday to collect Seth's remains. His brother would hold a funeral and lay Seth to rest in their hometown in the Midwest.

I wished I had gotten to know Seth better. Ayla felt guilty

about his death, though she didn't bear any of the blame, and she had spoken over the phone to Seth's brother as well. She'd made a large donation to a charity for law-enforcement veterans in Seth's honor.

Ayla also had a brief conversation with Paul Ruxton's father, the owner of her record label. Of course, that subject was more complicated. I hadn't wanted her to talk to Ruxton at all, but Ayla had insisted.

When she'd told the official interviewers about her ordeal, she'd been stoic. But alone in my bedroom, she'd given me more details of how it had felt. How afraid she'd been when Jarod locked her in that basement.

And when she'd realized what he wanted from her. *You and I belong together.*

If I could've gone back and killed Jarod again, I'd do it. Unlike Ayla, I didn't have it in me to be merciful toward the man.

But I was awed by her bravery. She'd gotten away from him. Bought enough time for me and my reinforcements to show up. If Ayla had still been down in that basement, we would've had a hostage standoff, and she likely would not have made it out alive.

Fuck. I couldn't breathe around the mass of anger and regret in my chest and throat. My thoughts were going around in circles.

"Teller?" Ayla murmured. "You alright?" She rubbed my sternum.

I blinked, smiling down at her. "Yes. I'm here with you. I love you."

"Love you too." She inched up my body to kiss me.

We were making it through this, together, one moment at a time.

Of course, outside my bedroom, the world had continued to turn. And the future, the big unknown of how we would make this relationship work, kept speeding toward us.

There'd been a lot of more urgent logistics to deal with. Several of the officers in my department, including myself, had been involved in the shooting. Which meant a CIRT investigation. Sheriff Douglas had been involved too. It was a bit of a mess, and we had state authorities crawling all over the place to help untangle it.

Thank goodness Susan Nichols had stayed back at the station. That had been foresight on my part. I'd named her acting chief in my absence.

And you know, Chief Nichols had a pretty nice ring to it.

Since I'd brought Ayla back to my place, the O'Neals had been a constant presence. Emma, Ashford, and Maisie had shown Ayla so much love. Callum had brought guacamole and cracked jokes, while Grace and Dane had brought food from the ski resort's elegant restaurant. Piper and Ollie had come to see us too. They were doing well after the break-in, back home after some repairs to their house.

I'd been conscious about tiring Ayla out with visitors. Maybe I'd been a touch overprotective. I know, *me*? Ha. But having our family and friends around had been making a difference.

Ayla's friends from LA had called a lot too, and Hayleigh had sent a massive box of gourmet chocolates that Maisie and Ollie had loved sampling.

One step at a time.

In my bed that third morning, we kept kissing. "Want you," she whispered.

"Then you'll have me."

My hands wandered beneath the T-shirt Ayla had worn to sleep in, dipping between her legs and finding her wet. We'd actually been having a lot of sex in the past three days. As if getting as close as possible physically could speed along the healing, and it certainly wasn't doing any harm.

I pushed down my pajama pants and kicked them off. My erection sprang up, thick and eager. Spooning her from behind, I slid my cock inside her, rocking our bodies gently together in a slow, sensual rhythm.

After our mutual orgasms, we managed to get out of bed.

Lingered in the shower for more kisses and caresses. After we got out and dressed, Ayla went out to the living room.

I heard her gasp. "Teller!"

I rushed out to follow her. And found her grinning ear to ear.

"It's snowing. It's so beautiful."

A late spring snowstorm. "It is." I circled my arms around her and pecked her cheek.

"Reminds me of getting stuck in the snow with you."

"I *love* being stuck with you."

"Me too." She laughed, a sound full of joy. Light and free for the first time in days. Such a relief to hear.

We still had rocky times ahead. She'd made an appointment with a therapist, probably the first of many. But for right now, we were good.

This storm brought just a couple inches of snow, but we made the most of the chill. I built a fire in the fireplace, while Ayla spread out a blanket so we could have brunch as a picnic in front of the hearth. Toast, scrambled eggs, and coffee. Glasses of fresh-squeezed orange juice, which Dane and Grace had brought yesterday because they were fancy like that.

Then we cuddled, enjoying the warmth, and watched the snow glisten in the sun as the flakes melted outside our window.

"You have some other visitors who'd like to see you today," I said, "if you feel up to it. They arrived yesterday but asked me to let them know when you seemed ready."

Ayla's eyes narrowed. "I can't decide that for myself?"

"I'm asking you to decide right now." I kissed her nose. "Don't be grumpy. That's my job."

"Who wants to see me?"

"Cheryl and Bryan."

Ayla's eyes brightened. "Yeah? I texted with Cheryl. She wanted to see how I was doing. But she didn't say she was heading to Colorado."

"She checked in with me. She'll be here at least a week. She wanted to give you whatever time you need before she came at you with business stuff. It does seem like she cares," I added, only slightly grumbly. "Like you're not just an asset."

Ayla's fingers squeezed my side. "I guess you're not the only one who's protective of me."

"I wouldn't let her near you if I thought otherwise." I'd had my doubts about Cheryl before. I'd warned her about putting Ayla's needs first. She'd listened.

But Cheryl coming here meant another step closer to that unknown future. I just hoped that, in the end, Ayla would still want to share hers with me.

I made a phone call to Cheryl at the ski resort hotel, where she was staying. Bryan was in town as her driver, but I'd made sure he had a nice room at the resort too. Comped by Dane at my request. Geez, those favors were racking up.

Half an hour later, Bryan pulled up my driveway in a rental after passing through our security perimeter. Cheryl sat in the back of the vehicle.

That agency Ayla used had sent some guards to keep an eye on my property since Silver Ridge PD was already overtaxed. A necessary evil given the swell of media attention.

Oh, had I not mentioned that? Yeah. News had broken about Ayla's kidnapping by a crazed stalker who'd murdered an executive from her label. Understandably, the story was getting worldwide attention. Reporters had descended on Silver Ridge yet again.

It was a very good thing I had the woods as a natural barrier around my property, but we'd still needed constant security patrols. The tabloids had even tried flying drones over my house.

But I'd managed to create a tiny bubble of normalcy here for Ayla, and that was what mattered to me.

Ayla was all smiles as she greeted Cheryl and Bryan. "Come in! Have you guys had lunch?"

She led Cheryl inside, while Bryan hung back with me. He grabbed my hand and held it, pulling me into a one-armed hug. "I'd say it's good to see you, Teller, but I've been seeing plenty of you on every screen that I pass."

"Fuck, please don't remind me."

In addition to the story about her stalker, my identity as Ayla's boyfriend was out there too. It had been inevitable. I'd avoided looking at news and social media myself, but we'd had updates from friends and family.

"At least I can say it's good to see *you*." I clapped Bryan on the shoulder. "How's Mikaela and Brody?"

Inside, the four of us chatted, keeping the conversation light at first. Then Ayla shared a little of what the last few days had been like, and there were lots of hugs. It helped when Bryan pulled up his latest pictures of his baby son on his phone. Yes, this was a working trip for him, but he was also here as Ayla's friend. I was beyond grateful for that.

Cheryl was much more formal. I could tell she was antsy to talk business with Ayla. It was her job, after all, to manage the big picture of Ayla's career. And that stood at a crossroads.

"Have you heard back from Ruxton Records about my request to nullify my contract?" Ayla finally asked.

Cheryl glanced from her to me. "I have. That's one of the reasons I'm here. Would you like to discuss alone? Or..."

"We can talk in another room," Ayla said, standing up.

I nodded in acknowledgment. Because she certainly didn't need any permission from me. Ayla's career was her own, and that hadn't changed.

But was I nervous about what this would mean for us? I'd be lying if I said I wasn't.

After she and Cheryl disappeared down the hall toward my home office, Bryan shook his head. "Man, I do not envy you. I'm around famous people all the time, but I'm in the background. I can't imagine being there in the spotlight."

"It's a lot to get used to. And I'm nowhere near used to it yet." The reality of dating a celebrity, of loving a woman like Ayla Maxwell...it was like everything else lately. One step at a time.

But of course, it had been on my mind.

"She clearly loves you. It's obvious. Pretty funny when you consider you almost arrested the both of us a few months ago. It must be one of those opposites attract things. You and Ayla. I never would've seen that coming."

"Neither did I." I laughed along with him. "Sometimes, I feel like a fool to think I can hold on to her," I admitted.

"Can't blame you. But I'm rooting for you. You've got a plan, right?"

"It took me a while to work it out. But yes, I do have a plan."

Before all this, Ayla had worried I would resent the attention our relationship would bring. The *trouble*. But she was worth any bit of trouble and so much more.

She was worth any sacrifice.

And Piper had given me some wise words last week, before I jetted off to LA to be with the woman I loved. Those words had stuck with me. Like a signpost guiding me toward what I was supposed to do.

You don't have to give her the whole entire world. You just have to give her yours.

So, that was what I intended to do.

I just had to hope it would be enough to make Ayla mine forever.

FORTY-EIGHT

Ayla

I SHUT the door to Teller's spare room and turned to Cheryl. "Okay, tell me what Ruxton Records said. I'm ready."

"Shall we sit?" Cheryl pointed at the couch. It was a pull-out, since this room doubled as a space for guests.

"I'd rather you just spit it out. Am I out of my contract?"

During the first couple days after Jarod kidnapped me and I watched him die, I'd been a bit of a mess. Unable to think much further than one minute to the next. But Teller had been there. To listen or talk or hold me. Whatever I had needed.

It would be a while until I was fully over what had happened.

But over the last day or so, my thoughts had turned toward what was next. And that meant knowing what would happen with my contract with Ruxton Records.

A smug smile teased at the corners of Cheryl's mouth. "They tried to fight me on it. They didn't want to let you go. But they saw reason eventually."

"I'm out?"

"You're out."

I heaved an exhale, dropping onto the couch. "Oh, thank God."

"After you made your wishes clear, plus the scolding your

boyfriend gave me, there was no other option." Cheryl sat beside me, placing her hand over mine. "Ayla, I am genuinely sorry I didn't stop Paul from harassing you. I should've realized what was happening. Should have kept a closer eye on the man."

I shook my head. "That's in the past." And I didn't want to speak ill of Paul now that he was dead.

I'd also expressed my sorrow over Paul's death to his father, which had been all the more awkward given his ownership of the record label. The whole thing was an awful, impossible situation.

But that didn't change my decision about my contract. It was time for me to take full control over my career. Over my future. I'd been thinking a lot about that as well over the last day or two.

I finally knew what I wanted and how to make it happen.

Nothing like a brush with death to make it clear what really mattered in life.

"Have you been online at all?" Cheryl asked. "Seen the news?"

"No, I've been avoiding it. But Teller said people are talking about what happened. Reporters are in town." I had no doubt my publicist Beth was working twenty-four-seven to handle all this. Thank goodness she hadn't come along with Cheryl, though. I couldn't have dealt with so many people talking at me.

"That's an understatement," Cheryl said. "There's significant media attention on you. On you *and* Teller, in fact."

I cringed. This was what I'd always known would happen but wished we could avoid.

"The coverage is overwhelmingly positive toward you," Cheryl went on. "Your previous albums are back at the top of the streaming charts right now. We've gotten a flood of mail and social comments expressing your fans' love. Beth's phone has been ringing off the hook with media requests. The world wants to hear from you and know you're doing okay. There's no rush, but we'll send you some possibilities for your first interview when you're ready. Beth is anxious to get started."

"I'll...think about it. I can issue a statement."

I might even share the truth about my father and my childhood. Maybe it could help others, especially other young women who felt the same things I once did. I wanted my experiences to make a difference so others didn't feel so alone.

"Good," Cheryl said. "I'm sure Beth will get you a draft statement right away. As for getting back in the studio, the sooner the better. You've made tremendous progress on your new songs already. Ruxton Records agreed they have no claim on your next album, so long as you start fresh on the recordings. We can record out of your home studio in Malibu. You can be in control of the entire process, but we need to jump on this groundswell of interest while we can."

I sighed. "Cheryl..."

"Just let me know when you'll be back in Los Angeles. Are you thinking next week? I need to make sure we have everything in place."

"*Cheryl*. I don't know when I'll be ready to get back in the studio. But I promise it won't be next week. It might not be this year."

"But what about your upcoming album? You've been so passionate about your new songs." I could tell she also wanted to mention the hard work she and the whole team had done preparing for the album, but she didn't.

"I know." I felt a small twinge of regret, because I loved my music, and that would never change. "I don't even know whether or not I *will* finish it. Teller's more important than an album. I love music, but I love him more. I've decided I'm staying in Silver Ridge. With him."

Her jaw hung open. "You can't stay here forever, though."

"Who says I can't?"

Things were a little tense as Cheryl said goodbye to me and Teller. But she gave me another hug just before she left.

"I'll support you in whatever decision you make, Ayla," she said quietly in my ear. "But have you discussed any of this with Teller?"

"Not yet."

"Well, do that. Then get back to the team on what you'd like us to do."

I promised I would.

Bryan drove Cheryl back to the resort. As Teller shut the door and locked it, I paced across the living room with my arms crossed.

"Didn't she have good news for you?" Teller asked.

"She did. I'm out of my recording contract. My career belongs to me now."

He stepped into my path, hands on my arms. "That's fantastic, sweetheart. But if that's the case, what has you upset?"

"Not upset, exactly. Just anxious. I'm ready to talk about...us. Our future."

"Yeah? I have some things to share about that topic as well."

Crap. Now *he* looked nervous.

I took a deep breath, smiling. "Come on. Let's sit by the fire again."

We took our spots on the blanket, which was still here from our picnic earlier. Teller also grabbed some of the pillows from the sofa.

When we were comfy, snuggled against one another, he asked, "Can I go first?"

"I'd rather do it. Sorry, but I need to get this out." I'd been wanting to tell him since yesterday, maybe even before, but I'd had to hear the final word on Ruxton Records from Cheryl. "I've decided I'm staying here in Silver Ridge."

Teller was quiet for a few long moments. "What do you mean by that?"

Wasn't it obvious? "I mean, I want to be with you. All the time. Nothing can replace what I've found here with you. And to have Maisie close as well, the rest of the O'Neals... It just makes sense."

I had all the money I needed. I could keep making music in Silver Ridge. No matter what, even if I had never signed my first record deal and had my big break, I would still be making music somewhere.

Why not here, with the man I loved?

"Putting out hits doesn't matter to me," I said. "Chasing fame, trying to stay relevant, stay on top. It *doesn't matter*. Not anymore. My house in Malibu is nice, but I was pretty much alone there. And the travel? Most of the time, it sucked. Touring is so exhausting."

"You want to give up your career," he said in a monotone. "For *me*."

"Not give it up. Just take a long break from releasing new albums or touring. A semi-retirement. So I can be with you." My voice cracked. "A few days ago, I looked down the barrel of a gun."

"I know," he murmured.

"I imagined all the things I'd never get to have. The things I cared most about were all here in Silver Ridge. I just want to be with you."

I rested my hand over Teller's heart. Felt it beating fast under my palm. His pale-green gaze looked steadily into mine.

"No," he said.

"*No*?" Panic shot through me. "No to what?"

"No, you are not giving up your career."

"You claimed once that you couldn't say no to me."

"I say no to you all the time."

I huffed a laugh, eyes burning with tears. Happy or sad, I hadn't decided yet. "Teller, I'm serious."

"And I told you, never make yourself small. Especially not for me."

"Then how do we make this work? How—"

"I'm stepping down as chief of police."

My breath left my lungs. "You what?"

"I'm stepping down. There will be a period of transition, but after that, I won't be Chief Landry anymore." He picked up my hand and kissed my fingertips. "I'll just be yours."

"But you can't." I was too shocked to form a more eloquent sentence. "The town needs you."

"I've already done it. I talked it through with Susan Nichols and with Mayor Barker. I've recommended that Susan take my place. She'll be great. It's pretty much a done deal. I'll still be on the force when I'm in town, available to help out, but with a flexible schedule. That way I can travel with you. Assuming you'll have me along for the ride."

"Travel with me?" Was this happening?

"I know what your music means to you. I would never presume to tell you how to run your career, and if you don't want to tour, you don't have to. If you don't want to chase numbers, that's fine. But it has to be your decision. Not something you're giving up for me. You don't have to give up a single thing for me."

"Because you're giving up *everything* for me." A tear broke free from the corner of my eye. "That's not right."

"It is. It's exactly right. It's what I want." He cupped my cheek, smearing my tear with his thumb. "I told you. Nothing and no one will keep us apart."

Speechless. I was speechless.

"What do *you* truly want?" Teller asked. "What do you want our life together to look like, if it could be anything? Because I haven't heard that yet."

Our life together...

"I would have you. Our family." Both the members already in it, and any who might come along. "A big family. And my music."

He nodded, eyes searching mine. "Keep going."

"Well...I would have Silver Ridge and LA. The mountains and the ocean, and all our friends in both places. Time in the quiet, where it's just you and me and I have room to think and breathe. But the excitement too. The rush of finishing a new song and sharing it with the world. Creating and making people smile." After some more thought, I added, "Performing in front of my fans all over the world."

"Because you love that."

"I do," I admitted. "Even when the travel sucks. Even when my career is messy." I had been willing to give it up, but he was right. I loved it.

"Then you're going to have it. *All* of it."

"And always coming home to you. With you. No matter where we are."

He cupped my face, drawing me close. "That is exactly what I want too."

"I can't believe this is happening to me."

Teller grinned. "I'm the one with the Cinderella story. Small-town cop wins the heart of the world-famous pop star."

I could see it. The two of us, living here in Silver Ridge in his house in the woods. Strolling down Main Street to Piper's coffee shop. Days in the park with Maisie and Ollie. Seasonal festivals and shopping at Rosie's market and the downtown boutiques.

Teller would serve his community as a police officer, even if he wasn't their chief. I would find inspiration and write my music every single day.

And then, whenever we were in LA, having Teller there as my plus-one at industry events on the red carpet. My rock when I set out on tour or traveled for promotion. A sounding board for all my most important decisions.

We would dodge tourists, too, since that was my reality, at least at the moment. But Teller would be there at my side. My favorite protector.

"If we do this," I said, "you would be my partner. In everything."

"The man behind Ayla Maxwell. I like the sound of that."

"But would that be enough for you? Really? You have to be sure."

Teller didn't respond right away. Like he was considering

everything he was giving up. Not just his role as police chief and constant member of Silver Ridge PD. But seeing Piper and Ollie during the time we would spend away from Colorado. Giving up his *privacy*.

The anxiety in my stomach grew with every second he was silent.

Then he spoke.

"I've spent decades of my life serving my country and my community. Being your man is a different kind of honor. A different kind of challenge too, if I'm honest. But I'm here for it. I'm ready. There is nothing in this world I want more than to share a life with you."

Trust Teller Landry to make a romantic declaration sound that solemn and serious.

I could not believe how much I loved this man.

"Then you're hired," I said with a teasing smirk.

Growling, Teller pulled me into his lap, wrapping me up in a whirlwind of kisses and exploring hands. Warm, unwavering strength. When his mouth broke from mine, he said, "Just keep in mind, Ms. Maxwell. This is one contract you're not getting out of."

And even though I knew he was teasing back, that sounded like a vow.

"Good. You're not either. It's you and me. From now on."

His eyes glowed like he'd never been happier.

FORTY-NINE
Teller

THREE MONTHS LATER

"STEP RIGHT UP!" Dane shouted. "Who wants to see Police Chief Landry all wet? All proceeds go to charity, but come on, like you need an excuse."

I rolled my eyes at the blue summer sky, fighting back a smile.

There were cheers as the next contestant paid for a chance to dunk me. Nobody had managed it yet. It was early, the mountain air chilly in the morning even in July, but the sun poured warmth onto my head.

Then I saw who was winding up to take a shot.

"I've got this," Ayla said, to a chorus of encouragement. More than one onlooker had their phone up filming, but nobody was filming me. Nope, every eye was on the stunning blond in the baseball cap. She had a tendency to turn heads wherever she went.

Especially mine.

"I'll believe it when I see it, sweetheart," I taunted.

Laughter. Shouts. Ayla's emerald eyes gleamed.

She threw once. Missed. I wasn't a boastful guy, so I just shrugged. All confident in my swim trunks and Silver Ridge PD T-shirt.

Her next ball thunked into the target.

Splash.

The crowd went wild, though I could barely hear them over my own sputtering and laughing.

As I climbed out, Dane met me with a towel and a grin. "We're even now. That was so satisfying to watch."

"Yeah, yeah." I swiped the towel over my wet face.

"The Silver Ridge Children's Center thanks you."

Ayla waved from the side, along with Grace, Emma, Maisie, and Piper. All of them whooping and clapping. A bodyguard stood subtly a few yards away, keeping an eye on everything, but the summer festival attendees were behaving themselves. I waved back at my audience and climbed onto my perch for the next person to take a shot at dunking me again.

And I didn't mind at all.

I'd been adjusting to my new life over the last several months. A life as Ayla Maxwell's other half.

A lot of the time, it felt like a dream. If it was, I never wanted to wake up.

We'd been traveling between Silver Ridge and Los Angeles, spending several weeks at a time in each place. At first, in the spring, I had quite a bit to settle here in town. Cooperating with the state investigators on Finn Mackie's case. Transitioning away from my role as chief of police.

It hadn't been easy to say goodbye to my team. But after the upheaval they'd experienced with Finn/Jarod's betrayal and Seth's murder, it was time for a clean slate anyway. Mayor Barker had officially appointed Susan the new chief, and I made sure she got off to a great start in her role.

Since then, Chief Nichols had been doing a fantastic job. Though she still liked to give me grief. But now I had to listen, since I was just Officer Landry.

In Los Angeles, I'd slowly been getting used to a very different way of doing things. The traffic. The sheer number of people. At least Ayla's home, *our* home, in Malibu was quiet and secluded.

The Mexican food was phenomenal, and I'd taken up running on the beach.

In the mornings, yoga with Ayla on the deck was one of my favorite things. Always put us both in the mood to jump back in bed.

I'd also taken over coordinating Ayla's security detail, and that was a job that suited me.

The couple of red-carpet events I'd attended had *not* been my favorite, but hey, anything for my Troublemaker. At least the media was getting more used to me. I was no longer a top story.

Also, it turned out I looked pretty good in a tuxedo. Who knew?

Ayla and I had sat down for an interview where she explained everything that happened in Silver Ridge with her stalker. And I'd held her hand while she tearfully shared the truth about her childhood. How her father had emotionally abused her. How he'd kicked her out at sixteen, and how the shame of that had made Ayla avoid her sister Lori for so many years.

She'd never spoken about those events publicly before. I knew it had been cathartic for her, and I just hoped having me there made it easier.

During the interview, we'd also officially told the world about our relationship. I'd looked into her eyes and had the privilege of saying how much I loved her for all the world to hear.

That little moment went viral on social media when the interviewer posted it. Or so I'd heard.

Since then, she and I had both declined any further questions about Jarod Carpenter or our romance. We got followed by paparazzi on a regular basis, but Ayla's security detail had never been more airtight. If I said so myself.

I still hated being in the spotlight. But I loved being her man.

And anybody who ever dared to try coming between us would have to deal with a very growly former Green Beret.

That night, I stepped into Hearthstone Brewing and scanned the tables, looking for my friends.

Callum was setting up a few tables in the corner. Looked like he and I were the first to arrive. Ayla was spending time at Ashford and Emma's place, and would head over to meet us later.

I had confidence no street riots would interrupt our plans. Ashford and Emma had already promised to drive Ayla here. No repeats of what happened at the start of their wedding weekend. Even though that weekend had turned out well, all in all.

As a *very* part-time Silver Ridge PD officer, I technically had the power to place people under arrest. If I ever put Ayla in handcuffs again, it might happen in the bedroom, but not on a public street.

Callum grinned when he saw me and clapped me on the back. "Hey, you're actually here for trivia? Let me guess. Ayla made you come tonight."

"No," I grumbled. "It was my idea."

"How about that. Was it your idea to overdo the sun today, too?" He gestured at my nose. "Ouch. Too much time in the dunk tank?"

"Sunblock wears off in water. I blame Dane."

Callum laughed. "At least it was for a good cause."

After my shift in the dunk tank, Ayla and I had strolled through the festival with Ollie and Maisie. Well, more like chased than strolled. Those two kids had been hopped up on cotton candy and ice cream. The bodyguard tailing us today—we had a rotating crew—had to stay on his toes to keep up.

We'd seen Callum at the fire department booth, spreading community cheer with the other firefighters. Ollie had greeted Cal with a big hug.

"Hey, before the others get here, I wanted to thank you for

spending time with Ollie lately," I said. "Especially when I've been away. It means a lot to him."

Callum grabbed an extra chair to add to our tables. "No need to thank me. I like doing it. Ollie's a great kid."

"He is."

Not seeing Ollie had been one of the hardest adjustments to make. When I was out of town, I still spoke to my nephew almost every single day. Piper had all but given up on getting her ex-husband Danny to participate in their son's life. Danny was missing out on a lot, and I would never understand it. Thank goodness for Callum, along with Ashford and Dane, who'd all become fixtures in Ollie's world.

My nephew and I had finished his treehouse, and just a couple of weeks ago, he'd confessed that he liked hanging out with Maisie more than those middle-school boys from down the street. At least that much hadn't changed.

Uncle Tell, they were being mean to Maisie and calling her a baby, he'd said. *So I told them I won't skateboard with them anymore. Not until they're nicer to her.*

I'd ruffled his hair. *I'm proud of you, buddy.*

And I was. So damn proud of my family and our growing circle of friends here and in LA.

Back when I was Chief Landry, it was hard to see past that title. *Chief of Police.* I thought I had to keep myself apart in order to take care of my town. Be the stoic, responsible one.

But falling in love with Ayla made me realize I had room for a lot of love in my heart. And being away from Silver Ridge had just proved how much I valued the people of this town.

I was still gruff, but nobody had accused me of being surly for a while.

"Do we need snacks or anything?" I asked Callum. "I'm buying."

"Then I'm *definitely* glad you came. Yeah. Feel free to order some apps for when everyone gets here." Then he scowled, glancing over at the bar. "Though maybe I would've preferred a change in location tonight if I'd known who would be working."

I followed his gaze to an attractive woman I didn't know. Long black hair, striking features. But there was something familiar about her. "Problems at the office? You still work here, right? I haven't been gone *that* much."

"Yeah, I still work here," Callum snapped. "Unfortunately, now she does too. Not sure there's room for both of us."

The raven-haired beauty caught Callum looking and sent a withering glare right back. *Yikes.*

"I'm guessing there's history between you two?" I asked. "Unless you already did something to make an enemy of the woman. I thought you were the *love doctor*." I added air quotes.

"Love has nothing to do with it. We went to high school together, and she has some kind of grudge against me. Zandra Alvarez."

"Oh, sure. Rosie's niece." The Alvarez family also owned Hearthstone. "Didn't she get a business degree from some top-tier school? Thought she'd settled in a big city. I didn't know she was back home. Or interested in the family brewery."

"Well, she is. I was hoping to get the manager position that opened up, but Zandra will probably take it just because she's the owner's granddaughter. And she hates me."

"Why? There must be a reason."

Color crept up his neck. "I didn't do anything. She's nice enough to everyone else. But not me. She might spit in my beer. Wouldn't put it past her." The poor guy sounded genuinely hurt.

"Then I can order your beer for you when I get the apps. I'm sure you and Zandra will sort out your issues."

"We'll see." Callum's smile returned. "I like the new, friendlier Teller Landry. Seems like being Mr. Maxwell is working out for you."

"It is."

Ayla showed up a little while later with Ashford and Emma. I ordered nachos, potato skins, and soft pretzels, which were Ayla's favorite.

We found our seats around the tables. Dane and Grace joined us, then Piper and Judson. The Lonely Harts club, though everyone had agreed at our last get-together that "lonely" didn't fit anymore. The majority of us were in relationships now, and the others weren't looking to change their single status.

My sister in particular had vowed she'd never couple up again. And Callum seemed happy enough, given the parade of different partners who passed through his bed.

Though this Zandra Alvarez situation did make me wonder.

But we all had each other. Nothing lonely about that.

We played several rounds of bar trivia, laughing with the other tables. We did especially well when it came to the music category. But Grace got the most competitive overall. The woman was known for being sweet, but when it came to trivia, she was so intense it was scary.

After trivia wound down, Ayla slumped against me. Her chair was scooted right up to mine, close enough our sides and legs were pressed together. We'd sat in the corner so the rest of our group could shelter Ayla from any curious tourists. But it hadn't been necessary. Nobody had bothered us.

"This was a great day," she said in my ear. "Especially dunking you."

I laughed and took a sip of my beer. "I just might get you back for that later."

"I hope so." Her gaze was heated. She played with the collar of my T-shirt. Then her expression turned more contemplative. "I know it's been hard for you, being away from Silver Ridge so much."

"Not nearly as hard as I would've imagined."

"No second thoughts?"

"Never, sweetheart."

She'd been working intensely on her new album. Watching

Ayla make her music was awe-inspiring. She had the kind of talent I'd rarely seen in real life.

I never wanted to hold her back. If Ayla chose to quit or change her career, fine. That was her choice. But she had a gift. This world was better for having her voice in it, loud and proud and poetic.

I wouldn't call myself her biggest fan because that phrase was spoiled for us. Besides, it didn't really mean anything. I preferred to show how I felt through my actions. Cheering her on, living for every note and chord and lyric. Standing by her side. Keeping her safe.

It was difficult to believe it had only been six months since we got trapped in that snowstorm. Since she'd turned my world upside down. But I wouldn't change a single thing.

It would get harder once she started touring again. I'd be following her to cities all over the continent. All over the world. But I was old enough that I knew when something felt right. This, *us*, was so right. Making this relationship work wasn't easy, but I'd been fighting battles my entire life. I had no problem fighting for us.

"This is working for *you*, right?" I asked softly, low enough nobody else in our group would hear. "Traveling between here and LA so frequently?"

She'd told me she was fully committed, and I trusted her word. Maybe it was the fact that we had both grown up fast. Ayla knew, as well as I did, how rare this kind of happiness was.

I still worried sometimes, though. She shone so brightly. What if her kind of light was simply impossible for a guy like me to hold on to?

"Are you kidding?" she said. "I love this. Life just feels so... *rich*."

I grinned, knowing exactly what she meant. "Never a dull moment. All because of you, not me. I'm not the fun police anymore, but I'm hardly the life of any party. Much less the red carpet."

"Maybe not. But you're the handsome, quiet guy who whispers jokes in my ear. The man I will always want to go home with. And you're a lot of fun in the bedroom."

I tilted my head back and forth. "That sounds pretty good."

"*Pretty good*," she teased. Ayla snuggled into me again, and we were both quiet for a few minutes before she lifted her head. "Teller, when we have kids, I want us to live here in Silver Ridge full time."

A warm glow radiated from my chest. "Yeah? That would be amazing someday." I'd been hoping we would settle here, but I'd figured we had plenty of time to figure that out.

"But what if it was sooner rather than later?"

Everything stopped.

"What are you trying to tell me?" I asked.

She snickered. "You're so pale under that sunburn. I promise it won't be *that* soon. I don't have any big news."

I exhaled, and my heart started pumping again. "Don't do that to a guy. Of course I would be ecstatic, but...geez, I need some time to mentally prepare."

"Sorry. But I was thinking, why should we wait a long time to start a family? We both know this is what we want. It wouldn't hurt to try."

"That's true." I wasn't getting any younger. Though I never would've pressured her. "But your album is coming out soon. You'll go on tour next year." Cheryl and Ayla's tour manager were already planning it all out and scheduling the venues.

"Yes, but it'll go by fast. We could plan for after, and...see what happens."

I shifted in my seat, glancing around at our friends and family carrying on their own conversations, oblivious to the way Ayla had just blown my mind yet again.

But my Ayla had her own way of doing things. I could always count on her to start up trouble.

I *loved* her kind of trouble.

"Then I guess we should make this official. Change your legal name from Hopkins to Landry."

She stared at me, like I had just stopped *her* world for once. "Did you just propose to me in the middle of trivia night at Hearthstone?"

Uh oh. "That depends. If I did, would you say yes?"

She pressed her lips together, then slowly broke into a brilliant smile. "I would, because this is perfect. I don't need a bunch of fanfare. Just you and me and our friends and family."

Ho-lee hell. I had just proposed to Ayla Maxwell.

And it sounded like she'd said yes.

"So should we tell them?" I asked.

"Nah, not yet. It can be our secret for now." She leaned closer, hypnotizing me with the look in her bewitching, world-famous eyes. "But I do need you to kiss me, Mr. Landry."

"I can make that happen, future Mrs. Landry."

Our lips touched. Slid until they locked together. Then parted as my tongue surged into her mouth, and her fist gripped my T-shirt.

Whoops and whistles suddenly rose around the room, and I knew they were about us. There were probably cameras recording us right now. I didn't care. People could look all they wanted, say what they wanted, but the love I'd found with Ayla would always belong only to us.

In some ways, I had burned down my own world to be with her. Remade it into something new. Ayla had just said it best.

This, right here, was perfect.

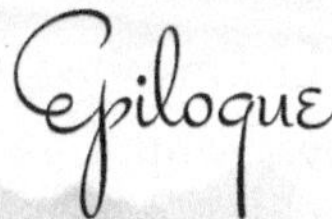

Epilogue

Ayla, One Year Later

"How are you feeling tonight, Denver?"

I looked out at the screaming, cheering crowd. I couldn't make out their faces, but they looked like a sea of lights. The signature crimson stone of Red Rocks Amphitheater bordered the sides of the stage, now faded into dimness.

The air was crisp and cool. An ideal summer night.

"I appreciate you joining me tonight for the final night of my tour. This has been quite a journey. A lot has happened to me in the last few years. You might have heard."

More cheers and laughter. "We love you, Ayla!" someone shouted. "You're amazing!"

I grinned. "Why, thank you. I love you too, Denver. You've all been very good to me. It's fitting that I'm wrapping up my tour here in Colorado. A place I love calling home whenever I'm here."

As I strummed a few familiar chords on my guitar, the screams got even louder as they recognized what song I was about to play.

"But there's one person in particular who has come to feel like home to me. This is a song that I wrote about him."

The crowd just about lost it.

I'd started writing this song in Silver Ridge during Emma and Ashford's wedding weekend. Long before I had any idea what Teller and I could truly become.

This song was also the biggest hit from my new album. My number one.

Just like the man who had inspired it.

Usually, when I was performing, I gave everything to the fans who had come to see me. This was the quieter moment during my show, when I brought out my acoustic guitar and played. An intimate moment between me and the thousands of fans who had joined me on any particular night.

I'd found a new kind of peace in the last year. I liked to think that I had settled into my fame. Both becoming more creative and reaching a new level of independence in the business side of my career. I finally felt like I was the one in charge. I listened to the advice of Cheryl and the rest of my team, but I had the freedom and the confidence to make the final decision that worked for me.

Always after consulting with Teller, of course. Simply because he was my partner. My best friend. The person who understood me the most.

After I'd put the finishing touches on my album, with the help of my most trusted producer and collaborators, I hadn't been sure how my fans would react. I'd been more heartfelt and more honest in these songs than ever before. In a way that Ruxton Records hadn't allowed me to be.

The first single had been this one, the song Teller inspired, and it instantly hit number one. The singles that followed also did well on the charts, and the album went platinum soon after its release.

As soon as my tour was announced, it sold out pretty much instantly. My tour manager had begged me to go with the biggest venues possible. There was nothing like filling a stadium of tens of thousands of people and hearing them scream your name. I loved attending concerts like that too.

But for this album and this tour, I hadn't wanted quite so much spectacle. And I'd known that I had to end the run right here, at Red Rocks. Which had been difficult to book even for me, let me tell you.

Teller had joined me for most of the performances. I adored knowing that he was waiting for me backstage, watching and singing along. My rock. The person who could always make me laugh when I needed it, who steadied me when I felt overwhelmed.

But as our relationship had grown more unshakable, we'd actually been spending a little more time apart. He'd been supervising the building of an addition on our home in Silver Ridge, plus taking more shifts with Silver Ridge PD simply because he loved it.

As for me, I trusted my team more than ever. My band, backup singers, and crew were like another family. Ricky still did my makeup every night, when we got to chat about the latest gossip.

Plus, Hayleigh came to just about every show herself. She'd decided that being a documentary filmmaker was her true calling, and I had agreed to let her film some footage of my tour for her upcoming project on the music industry.

She was backstage tonight. So were several other people I couldn't wait to see. Ashford, Emma, and Maisie.

And Teller. I hadn't seen him for almost *two weeks*, our longest separation in a year, and I was dying to kiss him. Yet I was living for this anticipation.

Maybe that explained why everything seemed to shine brighter tonight. The chords struck against my soul as I sang my heart out. The crowd was absolutely eating up every second of it.

This was not just the final night of my tour, but my final hurrah before taking a long break from my career. I didn't call it a retirement, because I knew I'd be back. But after tonight, I would head home to Silver Ridge for the foreseeable future. Visits to our Malibu house would be occasional and only for fun.

We had *so* much planned.

When the encore was finished and the band and I exited through an underground tunnel, Maisie was one of the first to greet me. The walls of the greenroom looked like they'd been carved directly into the rock.

"That was so cool, Aunt Ayla! Did you see us? We were right near the front, and we got lots of snacks, and I sang all your songs really loud!"

"Good." I beamed as I hugged her. "I loved knowing you were there. I'm glad you liked the show." Maisie was so grown up suddenly. How had that happened? I felt like every time I saw her in person she had changed in the most fascinating ways, even with our regular video calls.

I hugged Emma and Ashford next. "Sorry I'm sweaty."

"I should sell this T-shirt online," Ashford said. "*The* Ayla Maxwell sweated on it."

"Oh, shut it." I spotted Teller behind them. He gave me a smile that had my stomach doing flips.

We walked toward one another, everyone else seeming to disappear.

Then I was in his arms, and he was kissing me. "I missed you so much, Chief Landry," I murmured against his lips. I still called him that, though it wasn't his job title anymore. I knew he liked it.

He growled. "Missed you too. Do you have a dressing room or somewhere I can drag you off to?"

I laughed. "We should probably wait for the hotel. I need a shower."

"And I need you naked."

Teller and I still couldn't keep our hands off each other. Back in February, we'd celebrated the one-year anniversary of getting stuck in that snowstorm. Naturally, we'd gone to Silver Ridge for the occasion. We left the bodyguard back in town and drove out to a secluded spot. Not in Teller's department vehicle, but in the new SUV that I drove whenever I was in Silver Ridge. Teller had been giving me lessons on driving in the snow.

We'd turned off the engine, grabbed the blankets we'd brought, and fogged up all the windows while getting naughty in the backseat.

But alas, no getting naked backstage tonight. There were last hugs and goodbyes with my band and crew. Hayleigh recorded some footage, going on about the Red Rocks backstage and how unique it was.

Finally, Teller and I piled onto the tour bus. I pulled him into the private area at the back, pushing him onto the couch and straddling his lap. I'd wiped off my makeup and changed into a tank top and jeans.

"Hi."

"Hey, Troublemaker. Naked time now?"

"No, we're waiting for the hotel. The tour manager booked us a suite. I plan to make use of it."

He grumbled, but he couldn't stop grinning between kisses. "And tomorrow, I get to take you home."

"I know. I can't wait." I drew back so I could look at him. "You still want to..."

"You think I'd change my mind? Hell no." His grip tightened on my hips. "Have you told the O'Neals yet? I assume not, since they didn't say anything tonight."

I shook my head. "Haven't told anyone. But I asked them to keep their schedules clear tomorrow afternoon after we all meet up for lunch."

"I did the same with Piper."

"Good." I pressed my forehead to his. "I can't believe we're getting married tomorrow."

In less than twenty-four hours, we would head to the Hart County justice of the peace. Our families and very closest friends would be there, and they were going to be *very* surprised. Nobody even knew Teller and I were engaged. We'd picked out rings together in Los Angeles, and they'd been shipped to Teller in Silver Ridge.

"Me neither," he said. "And you...you did the other thing?"

My skin heated. "Yes. I did." A while back, I'd gone to the doctor to discuss going off birth control. Now, that was all taken care of. "So the next time we make love..."

"You mean, *tonight* when we make love."

"Yes, Mr. Impatient, tonight. We might start growing our family."

Teller pulled me in for another slow kiss. "It doesn't have to happen *right* away. But when it does, I'm ready. Our house in Silver Ridge is all ready too. Are you?"

"*So* ready. I can't wait. I love you."

"I love you too, Mrs. Landry."

"Soon," I whispered.

Even though I was taking a break from the music industry, I would always have music in my life. A brand new recording studio was waiting for me at our home in Silver Ridge. Maybe I'd feel like releasing a single or two at some point. There was no pressure unless I put it on myself.

In the meantime, I knew Teller was thrilled to serve his community every day as a Silver Ridge PD officer again. I planned to make frequent visits to the station with lunch for my man.

Someday, I would be back onstage. Touring the world.

But for now, I was thrilled to stay put in Silver Ridge. Live a simpler life. Not simple as in *small*. Because it would be so big. As big as the Rocky Mountains. As big as the horizon across the ocean.

Starting a family with Teller was my next booking, and it was going to be the best of all.

Callum and Zandra's story is next in Sunkissed Colorado...

A small-town, workplace, enemies to lovers romance (as always, with spice and suspense).

A Note from Hannah

When I first imagined Ayla and Teller's story, I knew they'd get stuck in a snowstorm. But I thought the storm would happen at the very beginning of the book. Little did I know, Ayla and Teller would have their own ideas about how their story should unfold.

I love that they both have intense personalities and sometimes tempers. I had no idea Ayla would demand to be arrested until she did it! And then Teller called her bluff. As I wrote, their story got deeper and a bit angstier than I'd expected. Spicier too. They simply would not keep their hands off each other.

Callum's book is next in Sunkissed Colorado. I can't wait to dive into his head, and then watch the fireworks with Zandra Alvarez, who promises to keep this golden-retriever firefighter on his toes.

Piper's story will be the final in the series. Have you guessed who she'll end up with yet?

Many thanks as always to my ARC readers, and to my fans who keep reading and enjoying my stories. It means so much to me to be able to share them with you.

Until next time—
Hannah

More from Hannah Shield

Hart County

Starcrossed Colorado (Ashford & Emma)

Moonlit Colorado (Dane & Grace)

Stormswept Colorado (Teller & Ayla)

Sunkissed Colorado (Callum & Zandra)

Homeward Colorado (Grayden & Piper)

Last Refuge Protectors

Hard Knock Hero (Aiden & Jessi)

Bent Winged Angel (Trace & Scarlett)

Home Town Knight (Owen & Genevieve)

Second Chance Savior (River & Charlotte)

Iron Willed Warrior (Cole & Brynn)

One Last Shot (Dean & Keira)

West Oaks Heroes

The Six Night Truce (Janie & Sean)

The Five Minute Mistake (Madison & Nash)

The Four Day Fakeout (Jake & Harper)

The Three Week Deal (Matteo & Angela)

The Two Last Moments (Danny & Lark)

The One for Forever (Rex & Quinn)

Bennett Security

Hands Off (Aurora & Devon)

Head First (Lana & Max)

Hard Wired (Sylvie & Dominic)

Hold Tight (Faith & Tanner)

Hung Up (Danica & Noah)

Have Mercy (Ruby & Chase)

About the Author

Hannah Shield writes spicy, suspenseful romance with pulse-pounding action, fun & flirty banter, and tons of heart. She lives in the Colorado mountains with her family.

Visit her website at www.hannahshield.com, where you can join her newsletter to receive bonus content and hear about new releases.

www.ingramcontent.com/pod-product-compliance
Lightning Source LLC
LaVergne TN
LVHW041058080826
845145LV00007B/1623